Colección Támesis

SERIE A: MONOGRAFÍAS, 223

THE GOTHIC FICTION OF ADELAIDA GARCÍA MORALES: HAUNTING WORDS

This first in-depth and holistic study of Adelaida García Morales's fiction approaches her works as a contemporary incursion into the Gothic mode. In order to highlight features common to García Morales's texts and the Gothic classics, each of the novels studied is paired with an English-language Gothic text and then read in the light of it. The focus of each chapter ranges from psychological aspects, such as fear of decay or otherness, or the pressures linked to managing secrets, to more concrete elements such as mountains and frightening buildings, and to key figures such as vampires, ghosts, or monsters. The usefulness of such an approach is that new light is shed on how García Morales achieves probably the most distinguishing feature of her novels: their harrowing atmosphere.

ABIGAIL LEE SIX is Professor of Hispanic Studies at Royal Holloway, University of London.

ABIGAIL LEE SIX

THE GOTHIC FICTION OF ADELAIDA GARCÍA MORALES: HAUNTING WORDS

TAMESIS

First published 2006 by Tamesis, Woodbridge

ISBN 1 85566 123 3

Tamesis is an imprint of Boydell & Brewer Ltd
PO Box 9, Woodbridge, Suffolk IP12 3DF, UK
and of Boydell & Brewer Inc.
668 Mt Hope Avenue, Rochester, NY 14620, USA
website: www.boydellandbrewer.com

A CIP catalogue record for this book is available
from the British Library

This publication is printed on acid-free paper

Printed in Great Britain by
Cambridge University Press, England

CONTENTS

ACKNOWLEDGEMENTS

Haunting Words could not have been written without the ongoing support of my College, Royal Holloway, University of London. Equally indispensable was the goodwill of departmental colleagues, who enabled me to take sabbatical leave when I needed it by shouldering my share of administration at a time when we were particularly short-staffed. My students provided a valuable forum for the exchange of ideas on *El Sur* in particular, and Spanish women's writing in general. Finally, a special thank you is due to my husband and children, not only for encouraging me to neglect them in order to write the book, but also for many interesting conversations about the English-language Gothic novels.

ABBREVIATIONS

Texts by Adelaida García Morales

A	*El accidente*
B	*Bene*
B/tr	*Bene* (English translation)
HP	*Una historia perversa*
LV	*La lógica del vampiro*
MH	*Las mujeres de Héctor*
N	*Nasmiya*
SM	*La señorita Medina*
SS	*El silencio de las sirenas*
S	*El Sur*
S/tr	*El Sur* (English translation)
TÁ	*La tía Águeda*

Gothic Novels in English

CO	Horace Walpole, *The Castle of Otranto*
D	Bram Stoker, *Dracula*
F	Mary Shelley, *Frankenstein, or The Modern Prometheus*
JH	Robert Louis Stevenson, *The Strange Case of Dr Jekyll and Mr Hyde*
MU	Ann Radcliffe, *The Mysteries of Udolpho*
PDG	Oscar Wilde, *The Picture of Dorian Gray*
R	Daphne du Maurier, *Rebecca*
TS	Henry James, *The Turn of the Screw*
WW	Wilkie Collins, *The Woman in White*

Other Abbreviations

CUP	Cambridge University Press
MUP	Manchester University Press
OUP	Oxford University Press
UP	University Press

Introduction

This book has twin aims: one is to offer a deepened understanding of Adelaida García Morales's fiction through reading her texts as Gothic,[1] for it is my contention that such a reading can shed new light on how she achieves the extraordinary haunting effect of her narratives. The second aim depends on the success of the first: it is to demonstrate by this example of one writer the usefulness of the Gothic label to Hispanic Studies generally and as such, the present monograph is the first in a larger research project which hopes to put the term *Gothic* on the Hispanic map, beyond its current very occasional or limited uses.[2]

The notion of Gothic is well established in English studies and yet there is no critical consensus on a precise definition of it.[3] Different criteria have been

---

[1] The adjective has been used to refer to single texts, such as Elizabeth J. Ordóñez's reading of *El Sur* (*Voices of Their Own: Contemporary Spanish Narrative by Women* (Lewisburg: Bucknell UP, 1991), pp. 180–81), the article by Kathleen Glenn, 'Gothic Vision in García Morales and Erice's *El sur*' (*Letras peninsulares* (spring 1994), 239–50) or the jacket notes for *La tía Águeda*, and a comparative Ph.D. dissertation by Shoshannah Holdom (Manchester University, 2003 unpublished) uses the term in its title: 'Gothic Theatricality and Performance in the Work of Adelaida García Morales, Cristina Fernández Cubas and Pilar Pedreza'; but the full implications have not yet been explored in the light of García Morales's *oeuvre* as a whole and considered in its own right.

[2] The term is found in Spanish eighteenth-century criticism. See, for example, Guillermo Carnero, *Estudios sobre teatro español del siglo XVIII* (Zaragoza: Prensas Universitarias de Zaragoza, 1997), pp. 144–55, which argues for the recognition of 'elementos góticos' [Gothic elements] in Spanish novels and drama of that century, taking as its example text *La Holandesa* (1787) by Gaspar Zavala y Zamora. On the other hand, Spain is conspicuous by its absence in Neil Cornwell's article on 'European Gothic', which limits itself to discussion of France, Germany, and Russia (in *A Companion to the Gothic* (ed.) David Punter (Oxford: Blackwell, 2000), pp. 27–38. The term makes an occasional appearance in nineteenth-century studies; see, for example, Stephen M. Hart, 'The Gendered Gothic in Pardo Bazán's *Los pazos de Ulloa*', in *Culture and Gender in Nineteenth-Century Spain* (ed.) Lou Charnon-Deutsch & Jo Labanyi (Oxford: Clarendon, 1995), pp. 216–29. On the other hand, an otherwise very informative article on the *folletín*, despite obvious and significant overlap with Gothic concerns, makes no mention of the term (Elisa Martí-López, 'The *folletín*: Spain looks to Europe', in *The Cambridge Companion to the Spanish Novel from 1600 to the Present* (ed.) Harriet Turner and Adelaida López de Martínez (Cambridge: CUP, 2003), pp. 65–80).

[3] Fred Botting opens the Preface to his edited collection of essays with the words: 'These days it seems increasingly difficult to speak of "*the* Gothic" with any assurance.

proposed and different strands of criticism can be discerned, all of them valuable in their way, but none completely reliable or self-sufficient. These include the historical approach, which regards Horace Walpole's *The Castle of Otranto* (1764) as the seminal Gothic work, with a cluster of followers in the late eighteenth century, including works by Ann Radcliffe and Matthew Lewis. In this period, which prided itself on its enlightenment, espousing neoclassical values, but which also was a time of social upheaval and increased class mobility, the concept of Gothic represented medieval barbarism and superstition but also the allure of a nostalgically idealized representation of chivalry and the clear-cut hierarchy of feudalism.[4] Linked to this positively perceived aspect of pre-enlightenment values, there was a new attitude to aesthetic criteria in the eighteenth century, which no longer accorded a monopoly of approval to the classical ideals of proportion, balance and symmetry, but which discovered the sublime in rugged landscapes and huge mountain panoramas as well as rambling medieval architecture.[5]

Then scholars adopting a historical approach recognize a resurgence of the Gothic towards the end of the nineteenth century with a group of texts that include Bram Stoker's *Dracula*, Oscar Wilde's *The Picture of Dorian Gray*, and Robert Louis Stevenson's *The Strange Case of Dr Jekyll and Mr Hyde*, among others. Mary Shelley's *Frankenstein* earlier in the century can be viewed as a late member of the first wave, or a precursor, of the second in this historical approach. Such renewed interest in Gothic themes at the Victorian *fin de siècle* is explained by Glennis Byron: 'the discourse of degeneration [national, social, and human] articulates much the same fears and anxieties as those traditionally found in the Gothic novel.'[6] Twentieth-century Gothic studies in this historical approach tend to emphasize the new life breathed into the Gothic by cinema, often centring on famous film versions of nineteenth-century Gothic novels.[7] The disadvantage with the historical treatment of the

---

[...] The search for *the* Gothic [...] is a vain critical endeavour' (in *The Gothic* (Cambridge: Brewer, 2001), pp. 1–6 (p. 1); Botting's italics). In a similar vein, Punter introduces another recent collection of essays, *A Companion to the Gothic* by warning that 'the notion of what constitutes Gothic writing is a contested site' ('Introduction: The Ghost of a History', in *A Companion to the Gothic*, pp. viii–xiv (p. viii). For information on the original Goths and the meaning of *Gothic* before the eighteenth-century, see Robin Sowerby, 'The Goths in History and Pre-Gothic Gothic', in Punter (ed.), pp. 15–26.

[4] Fred Botting, 'In Gothic Darkly: Heterotopia, History, Culture', in Punter (ed.), pp. 3–14 (pp. 3 and 5). The nostalgic side of this ambivalence is vehemently refuted by Chris Baldick and Robert Mighall, but this is very much a minority view. See 'Gothic Criticism', in Punter (ed.), pp. 209–28 (pp. 213–15).

[5] This is summarized in Botting, 'In Gothic Darkly', in Punter (ed.), pp. 10–12. The sublime will be discussed in greater detail in Chapter 2 below.

[6] 'Gothic in the 1890s', in Punter (ed.), pp. 132–42 (p. 132).

[7] For an example of a historical treatment of the Gothic, see Jerrold E. Hogle, 'The Gothic at Our Turn of the Century: Our Culture of Simulation and the Return of the Body', in Botting (ed.), pp. 153–79, in which the popularity of Gothic works in the 1980s and

Gothic is that it tends to imply a downgrading of the authenticity of post-eighteenth-century works, so that, for example, twentieth-century Gothic classics are overlooked or treated as modern copies, rather like reproduction antiques. It also creates problems for texts that pre-date Walpole and yet have much in common with the Gothic that in this approach he is credited with having created.[8]

This can be partially overcome by balancing the historical approach with parameters based on certain recurrent features of Gothic texts and tracing their evolution over the past three centuries. Thus the semi-ruined medieval castles of Otranto or Radcliffe's Udolpho, for example, evolve into isolated country houses like Wilkie Collins's Blackwater Park in *The Woman in White*, Daphne du Maurier's Manderley in *Rebecca* or Henry James's Bly in *The Turn of the Screw*;[9] wild and foreign mountain scenery in *The Mysteries of Udolpho* or *Frankenstein*, for example, shades into equally frightening dark and/or foggy streets in London's dingier neighbourhoods such as Stevenson's Soho, where Mr Hyde lodges, or Wilde's opium dens in the docklands, frequented by Dorian Gray; indeed, the transition from one to the other is actually part of the narrative of *Dracula*, where the Count travels from the Carpathians to England in the course of the story.[10] The drawback with such catalogues of features is that it remains unclear how many are needed or in what way they need to be used to constitute grounds for considering a text Gothic. Agatha Christie often sets her novels in isolated country houses, but that does not make them Gothic, for example.

Then again, there are those who focus on the characterization of the key figures in a Gothic text, particularly the heroine, who is expected to be unfortunate, rather passive, and often orphaned, set against the Gothic villain,

1990s is related to its earlier highpoints, also at turns of centuries. Twentieth-century film versions of *Frankenstein, Jekyll and Hyde*, and *Dracula* are the subject of Heidi Kaye, 'Gothic Film', in Punter (ed.), pp. 180–92.

[8] Although Walpole himself acknowledges his debt to Shakespeare and so this is recognized by critics, I am surprised as a Hispanist to note the conspicuous absence of parallels with the *Quixote* in Gothic criticism. The story of Bluebeard is another important pre-Walpole text, which is disregarded by this strand of criticism (though not by others).

[9] For example, Susan Wolstenholme states: 'Readers of Gothic novels have long noted the recurrence of the Gothic habitation – the castle or convent or church or abbey, sometimes more than one of these, and often presented in ruined form' (*Gothic (Re)Visions: Writing Women as Readers* (Albany: SUNY Press, 1993), p. 113). Cornwell is one of many who notes the evolution from castle to rural mansion. See 'European Gothic', in Punter (ed.), p. 28.

[10] Allan Lloyd-Smith credits Edgar Allan Poe with the introduction of urban landscapes 'as a version of the incomprehensible castle of early Gothics'. See 'Nineteenth-Century American Gothic', in Punter (ed.), pp. 109–21 (p. 115). Byron convincingly proposes a link between the discourse of degeneration and the move from exotic locations in eighteenth-century Gothic texts to London in nineteenth-century ones ('Gothic in the 1890s', in Punter (ed.), p. 134).

who should be unscrupulous, cruel, and predatory and who evolves from the lord of the afore-mentioned castle or the crazed monk into the mad scientist, taking the Gothic mode into the realms of science fiction.[11] Recurrent extras noted by critics include mother substitutes,[12] loquacious servants, and heroes of a somewhat watery nature,[13] relative to the villain. Some scholars make a distinction between female and male Gothic features (meaning written by and mainly for women, or by and mainly for men), with the emphasis on the heroine's plight being associated with the female and an oedipal pattern of a son's battle against authority tending to be more in the spotlight in the male Gothic.[14] These are useful pointers, but not all Gothic texts utilize all of these characterizations. There is no heroine in *Jekyll and Hyde*, for example, but who would want to impugn its status as a Gothic classic?

Finally, there is the approach that regards these elements as inessential and variable over the centuries, and seeks to uncover the constants of the Gothic mode at a deeper psychological level.[15] Here are found ideas such as nightmare,[16] claustrophobia, entrapment, the surging out of what is repressed in normal life,[17] such as mad or monstrous aspects of the self, often represented by split or doubled characters or, at the level of plot, guilty secrets pertaining to sexuality.[18] Again, these are illuminating, but still cannot serve

---

[11] For Nora Crook, Victor Frankenstein's characterization is a direct transformation of the cloistered monk figure and by the same token, his laboratory descends from 'the mouldering abbey'. See 'Mary Shelley, Author of *Frankenstein*', in Punter (ed.), pp. 58–69 (p. 58).

[12] Tania Modleski, *Loving with a Vengeance: Mass-Produced Fantasies for Women* (New York: Methuen, 1984), pp. 68–70.

[13] For Modleski, the opposition between the villain and the hero in the female Gothic parallels the male tendency to polarize women into whore (evil) and mother (good) (*Loving with a Vengeance*, p. 79). Traces of this pattern can be discerned in *La lógica del vampiro* with Alfonso and Pablo; in *Una historia perversa* with Octavio and Juan; but the issue is problematized in *El accidente*, as we shall see in Chapter 7.

[14] See, for example, Robert Miles, 'Ann Radcliffe and Matthew Lewis', in Punter (ed.), pp. 41–57 (pp. 43–5). Eugenia C. DeLamotte's *Perils of the Night: A Feminist Study of Nineteenth-Century Gothic* (New York & London: OUP, 1990) uses the distinction to structure the book into two clear halves.

[15] For a good survey of the history of psychoanalytical criticism of the Gothic, see Michelle A. Massé, 'Psychoanalysis and the Gothic', in Punter (ed.), pp. 229–41.

[16] Wolstenholme, for example, discusses the relationship between nightmare and woman-authored Gothic in *Gothic (Re)Visions*; see especially, pp. 3–13. Matthew C. Brennan devotes a whole book to a Jungian interpretation of Gothic novels based on dream and nightmare elements. See *The Gothic Psyche: Disintegration and Growth in Nineteenth-Century English Literature* (Columbia, SC: Camden House, 1997).

[17] For claustrophobia and entrapment, see for example Punter, 'Introduction', in Punter (ed.), pp. viii–xiv (p. viii) and for the return of the repressed, p. ix.

[18] Miles calls family secrets 'a theme central to the Gothic' and discusses this, chiefly with reference to Radcliffe, in 'Ann Radcliffe and Matthew Lewis', in Punter (ed.), pp. 45–50.

as defining features, because there are so many other types of fiction that use at least some of them too without seeming Gothic at all.[19] Particularly helpful is the notion of transgression of taboos and boundaries,[20] especially as one such boundary is the very one critics would dearly love to have to circumscribe the Gothic itself. As Cyndy Hendershot puts it: 'The Gothic's disruptive potential is partly predicated upon its lack of respect for generic boundaries.'[21] Like the joke about an elephant, though, much Gothic criticism decides ultimately to take a pragmatic line by relying on the fact that despite the apparent impossibility of a watertight definition we know a Gothic text when we see one.

A concept without a straightforward definition poses a methodological challenge: how to show that García Morales is a Gothic writer when there are no set criteria? The solution adopted here has been to pair each of her novels studied with a text that critics agree is Gothic and to read the Spanish text in the light of it. This is not intended to suggest that García Morales's novels derive from the English-language texts selected; indeed, it would have been possible to choose others that could have worked equally well as comparators or to pair the ones used with different novels by García Morales. The idea is rather to highlight some of the features that her texts and the Gothic classics have in common. As the chapter titles show, the focus of each ranges across the different types of criterion critics have identified as pertaining to – if not sufficient to define what is – Gothic, from psychological concepts such as fear of decay or otherness, or the pressures linked to managing secrets (Chapters 1, 6, 7, and 8), to the more concrete elements such as the use of mountains and frightening buildings as settings (Chapters 2 and 5), to key figures such as vampires, ghosts, or monsters (Chapters 3, 4, and 9). It is hoped that this approach will not only provide a fresh reading of each of García Morales's best known novels for those who are studying a single text by this author, but also, that taken together, the chapters will add up to a new perspective on her as a writer.[22]

---

[19] To name just one example, William Golding's *The Lord of the Flies* deals with children trapped on an island, where what is repressed in normal life surges out leaving certain characters frightened and victimized. Yet it is not a text that anyone would like to label as Gothic.

[20] For example, Fred Botting maintains that 'From its beginnings Gothic writing has [. . .] blurr[ed] sexual boundaries and disturb[ed] aesthetic and moral categories' ('Candygothic' in Botting (ed.), pp. 133–51 (p. 134). Avril Horner and Sue Zlosnik regard this concern 'with boundaries and their instabilities' as one of the only safe claims to make about the Gothic' ('Comic Gothic', in Punter (ed.), pp. 242–54 (p. 243)) and DeLamotte in *Perils of the Night* builds her argument on the concept of boundaries of the self as fundamental to the Gothic.

[21] Cyndy Hendershot, *The Animal Within: Masculinity and the Gothic* (Ann Arbor: University of Michigan Press, 1998), p. 1.

[22] Not all of García Morales's published texts are covered in the following chapters, due to space and time limitations combined with the present unavailability of certain works.

Existing criticism of Adelaida García Morales falls into three categories. She is often (but not often enough)[23] included in lists of, and research on, Spanish contemporary writers – sometimes women writers specifically – considered as a group.[24] It is of course valuable to understand where she fits into the sociocultural framework of post-Franco Spain and she is bound to reflect this in ways which are comparable with others of her literary generation and nationality. She has also been studied illuminatingly as part of a chronological line of Spanish women writers, by Elizabeth J. Ordóñez, where the diachronic and gender-conscious approach places her within an evolutionary process as she adopts and adapts what Ordóñez calls her foremothers' writing practices. Lastly, there have been some articles about single texts, chiefly *El Sur* and *El silencio de las sirenas*, the former often incorporating comparison with, and overshadowed by, criticism of Erice's film version.[25] At their micro-level, such close studies are valuable. However, the present monograph hopes to address a gap in criticism on this writer, as it attempts on the one hand to locate Adelaida García Morales in a larger, trans-national literary sphere and on the other, to articulate what makes her writing a coherent and unique whole. *Haunting Words* will argue that in both cases, this resides in her utilization of the Gothic tradition.

Note

With the exception of the translation of quotations from *El Sur, seguido de Bene*, for which a professional translation is readily available (see Bibliography), all other translations are my own.

---

[23] Here are just three examples of the many overview texts that omit to mention her altogether: Pablo Gil Casado, *La novela deshumanizada española (1955–1988)* (Barcelona: Anthropos, 1990); Christina Henseler, *Contemporary Spanish Women's Narrative and the Publishing Industry* (Urbana & Chicago: University of Illinois Press, 2003); Robert C. Spires, *Post-Totalitarian Spanish Fiction* (Columbia & London: University of Missouri Press, 1996).

[24] For example, she receives a brief descriptive mention in José María Martínez Cachero, *La novela española entre 1936 y el fin de siglo: historia de una aventura* (Madrid: Castalia, 1997) (p. 601). Similarly, in Chris Perriam *et al.*, *A New History of Spanish Writing: 1939 to the 1990s* (Oxford: OUP, 2000), *El silencio de las sirenas* receives half a sentence and the author is included in a list of those published in a series designed 'to promote contemporary Spanish writing' (pp. 176 and 215, respectively).

[25] For example, Glenn, 'Gothic Vision'.

1

El Sur, seguido de Bene (1985) and Oscar Wilde, *The Picture of Dorian Gray* (1890/1891):[1] Physical and Moral Decay

El Sur [*The South*] and *Bene,* two short texts published in one volume, launched Adelaida García Morales on her very successful career. Despite their brevity (*El Sur* is only 52 pages long and *Bene* 58), they already contain much of what would come to be identifiable as this author's hallmarks, many of which this study is arguing can be subsumed under the umbrella term of Gothic features.[2] Whether it was for the convenience of the publishers or in obedience to a desire on the author's part to present the texts as linked, the result is that *El Sur, seguido de Bene* comes to the reader with a built-in suggestion of some kind of twinning of the two stories. Accordingly, this chapter will take their single-volume publication as a signal that they are – figuratively as well as literally – bound up with one another.[3]

---

[1] Oscar Wilde, *The Picture of Dorian Gray* (London: Simpkin, Marshall, Hamilton, Kent, 1913). The first version of the text was published in *Lipincott's Magazine* in July 1890. A revised and expanded version, the one generally known today and used in the present chapter, was published in book form the following year. Future references will relate to the above edition and be given parenthetically in the text. For a discussion of the main differences between the two versions, see Peter Raby, *Oscar Wilde* (Cambridge: CUP, 1988), pp. 67–8.

[2] As we have seen in the Introduction above, Ordóñez and Glenn have observed the Gothic credentials of *El Sur* (see *Voices* (1991), pp. 180–81 and 'Gothic Vision' (1994), respectively). The aspects which they highlight are entirely valid and relevant to the overall reading of Adelaida García Morales posited in the present study.

[3] Robert Saladrigas takes a similar view (if for different reasons) when he refers to *El Sur* and *Bene* as 'un par de historias que en el fondo son una sola' (*La Vanguardia*, 25 July 1985, cited in *La novela española dentro de España* (ed.) Antonio Fernández (Madrid: Heliodoro, 1987), pp. 253–8 (p. 258) [a couple of stories which at bottom are just one]. Ordóñez also treats them as a continuum (*Voices*, pp. 182–3). When the author was questioned on the common ground between *El Sur* and *Bene*, she explained this by saying 'los dos relatos surgen de la misma fuente: son recuerdos de mi infancia. [. . .] No es literalmente mi vida, pero sí tiene que ver.' 'Adelaida García Morales: la soledad gozosa', interview by Milagros Sánchez Arnosi, *Ínsula*, 472 (1986), 4 [the two narratives arise from the same source: they are recollections of my childhood. It is not literally my life, but that does have something to do with it.]

In *El Sur*, the narrator, Adriana, addresses her father, Rafael, beyond the grave and gives him her perspective on the events of her childhood and particularly, her relationship with him. She depicts Rafael as a social outsider: he has rejected the central role of the Church in Franco's Spain, where the story is set and prevents her (at first) from going to school (necessarily entailing religious instruction). Added to this social self-marginalization, his marriage to Adriana's mother is clearly increasingly unhappy and an extramarital relationship with a certain Gloria Valle – which has produced a son, Miguel – is ended by letter from Gloria in the course of the narrative. Finally, Adriana herself seems to meet with her father's growing disapproval as she gradually integrates into society and especially, as she begins to meet boys during adolescence. He takes his own life when she is 15, after which she goes to his home town, Seville, ostensibly to visit his sister Delia, of whom she is very fond. Clearly, however, this is an excuse; what she seems to want to do is to acquire a deeper sense of who her father was and this she achieves, partly through staying in his house and talking to the old family servant, Emilia, partly through meeting Gloria and Miguel.

Bene is narrated by Ángela, who was twelve at the time of the action. In a smooth transition from the end of *El Sur*, it opens as a direct address to her brother, Santiago, another suicide victim, but soon switches into normal first-person narration.[4] The setting is another isolated house in Franco's Spain, where the narrator lives with Santiago; their father, Enrique, who is often absent; and an aunt, Elisa, who is responsible for the children as their mother is dead. Also in the house are an elderly housekeeper, Catalina; Ángela's pious governess, Rosaura; and then there is Bene. This is a 19-year-old maid taken into employment at the beginning of the story. The narrator knows something of her half-sister, a child called Juana, and through her, of the family, so we gradually learn that Bene is also motherless and that her father was a gypsy who took her away to work at the age of fourteen, but is now dead. The plot focuses on the multiple effects of Bene upon Ángela and the rest of the household. These include the brother Santiago's infatuation with her and the consequences of this, culminating in his leaving home with her, only to be brought back by the Civil Guard two weeks later, whereupon he locks himself into the wing of the house they call the 'torre' [tower] and lets himself die. Ángela meanwhile suffers from a terrible ambivalence with respect to Bene. On the one hand she likes her and wants to be her friend; but on the other she is frightened by a strange expression which crosses her face from time to time;

---

[4] Adelaida García Morales, *Bene*, in *El Sur, seguido de Bene*, 22nd edn (Barcelona: Anagrama, 1997), pp. 53–111. Future references will relate to this edition and be given parenthetically in the text. The translations are taken from *The South and Bene* (trans.) Thomas G. Deveny (Lincoln & London: University of Nebraska Press, 1999). The second-person form returns three times subsequently, the last time being the closing section of the text. It is always addressed at Santiago.

Ángela links this to Bene's ongoing relationship with the ghost of the gypsy father who may also be and/or have been her lover. At the end, we learn that Bene has also killed herself. This factual synopsis gives little idea of the power of the story, however, for it derives not from the events themselves, but chiefly from the narrator's incomplete understanding of what is happening around her, so that her anxieties and fantasies melt imperceptibly into the superstitious fears of the aunt and Rosaura (who believe Bene to be an agent of the devil), together with the undecidably proportioned mix of lies and truth coming from the other child, Juana's embroidered and also partial understanding of her sister's life and character.

Oscar Wilde's *The Picture of Dorian Gray* weaves together two key concerns into a haunting narrative. One is true in real life as well as fiction: the inexorability of the ageing process, emblematized in the novel as the terrible transience of the physical beauty of youth. The second is to do with the nature of corruption, which is to say the terrible transience of youthful purity of ideals, but this is represented via an idea that requires a suspension of disbelief on the reader's part. Within the poetic logic of the story, sins committed are physically detectable, or as Basil Hallward puts it: ' "Sin is a thing that writes itself across a man's face" ' (*PDG*, p. 167). The eponymous protagonist personifies the two processes, but by unexplained magic,[5] they are both transferred to a portrait of Dorian painted by Hallward, so that while the years pass for the man and he becomes not only older, but also increasingly depraved, the visible signs of both show only on the picture, while he remains immaculately young and pure in appearance. At the end of the novel, Dorian has reached the point where cohabitation with the picture has become intolerable, but as he attempts to destroy it the act of violence is mysteriously translated to himself, so that the attempted murder of the picture becomes suicide and furthermore, at the same moment the painting returns to its pristine condition, while the dead Dorian takes on the former looks of the picture.

This concept of the transference of the marks which time and one's own life choices brand upon one's self to somewhere else – in this case, the painting – is not only fascinating in the context of Wilde's novel, but has

---

[5] There is an implicit suggestion that Dorian has sold his soul to the devil to have his wish granted, since he declares ' "If it were I who was to be always young, and the picture that was to grow old! For that – for that – I would give everything! Yes, there is nothing in the whole world I would not give! I would give my soul for that!" ' (*PDG*, p. 33). Critics such as Byron take for granted that a pact with the devil is a straightforward fact in the novel ('Gothic in the 1890's', in Punter (ed.), p. 137). However, it is not so clear since the devil makes no appearance to close the deal with Dorian as he does, say, with Ambrosio in Lewis's *The Monk* (1795). Thus, no one is more surprised than Dorian himself when he realizes this wish has come true. See Matthew Lewis, *The Monk* (ed.) Howard Anderson (Oxford: OUP, 1980), pp. 433–8.

richly suggestive implications with regard to García Morales's twin texts. Both *El Sur* and *Bene* have a first-person narrator who has been badly scarred by the events she recounts, but in different ways and for different reasons. As we shall see, Rafael and Adriana of *El Sur* are in a relationship that can be fruitfully paralleled with that of Dorian and the picture, whereas *Bene*'s Ángela stands more at the margins of events (much to her annoyance). There, the Dorian figure has to be Bene and the picture that expresses the corruption of her soul takes the form of the gypsy ghost.

This chapter will argue, first, that the cruelty of the ageing process's inexorability is central to an understanding of *El Sur*. Certainly, the author seemed to concur with this reading of her treatment of time when she was interviewed on the text:

> Creo que el tiempo tiene inevitablemente un lado de destrucción. Es decir, que lo que hay hacia el futuro es más bien muerte, pero también el tiempo tiene ese lado de aprendizaje, de adquirir una experiencia, pero no sé por qué yo veo que es más tremendo lo que tiene de negativo, porque te acerca a la muerte y la destrucción.[6]

However, in a manner not identical to, but resonating with *Dorian Gray*, this is transferred in *El Sur* from Adriana's father to Adriana herself, a sort of portrait of him; in other words, one factor that drives him to despair and eventually suicide, is that he cannot arrest the process of her growing up and concomitantly, the changing nature of their relationship. He tries shutting her away, but this does not succeed because in the end he cannot resist the pressure from his wife to allow her to go to school; then he tries shutting himself away, but this too fails because – like Dorian and his picture – he cannot resist the temptation to look at her from time to time and this will eventually prove fatal to him.[7]

Although the issue of corruption of innocence is relevant to what is meant by growing up, where it really takes centre stage is in *Bene*. As well as drawing on antique motifs of the demonic woman who lures an innocent young man to perdition, itself linked to vampiric notions of the damned soul

---

[6] Sánchez Arnosi interview. [I believe that time inevitably has a destructive side. That is to say, what there is going towards the future is really death, but time also has a side that is about apprenticeship, acquiring experience, but – I don't know why – I see as more terrifying the negative side of time, because it brings you closer to death and destruction.] As we shall see, however, Ángela of *Bene* is trapped by the reverse phenomenon: that of not being old enough.

[7] It is clear that Adriana's growing up is not the only factor that drives Rafael to despair. Nevertheless, her dependence on him seems to have been the key dissuasive factor when she was younger, so his perception of her as no longer needing him can be read as the catalyst. This can be extrapolated from Rafael's bitter advice to Adriana not to marry or have children, if only to have the freedom to die when you want (*S*, p. 28; *S/tr*, p. 27).

sucking the life-blood out of the pure and eventually bringing about the victim's death and recruitment to the ranks of the undead, García Morales's story also addresses the issue of corruption of innocence *per se* and implicitly asks a similar question to that posed by Wilde's text: how does one person's immorality corrupt another? And, how much guilt should we shoulder for the impact of our life choices on those around us? Wilde's text explores – but is careful to provide no easy answers for – these questions in two main ways: one is the effect of Lord Henry Wotton's ideas on Dorian and the other is Dorian's effect on the lives of many others, including Sybil Vane and Alan Campbell, both of whom commit suicide for reasons wholly linked to their relations with him. As we shall see, in *Bene*, a similar domino effect can be discerned as Bene's father seems to have major responsibility for the way she is by the time she appears in the text and then her influence on Santiago leads to the destruction of his life, which in turn scars his sister, the narrator of the text.

The Gothic effects of Wilde's novel include some superficial ones, analogous to lighting techniques in a film. Thus, there are murky London streets, an opium den, and the sound of blood dripping onto the threadbare carpet of the disused nursery in the attic where Dorian hides the picture, for example. In like fashion, Gothic devices can be found in García Morales's texts: the silent, isolated, and semi-ruined house of *El Sur* and the Udolpho-like tower in which Santiago immures himself to await death in *Bene*.[8] However, this chapter will argue that these effects, although atmospheric, are not so crucial to the texts' Gothic credentials as the ideas underlying all three, namely, that we can become trapped claustrophobically in a self whose relationships destroy us. As with Jonathan Harker and Dracula's castle, we appear to walk into them of our own free will, but a complex network of ambivalence interwoven with social pressures then bar our exit on this side of the grave.[9]

First, it is important to establish the extent to which it can be argued that Adriana is in some sense like a picture of her father and then to assess the implications of considering their relationship in the light of that of Dorian with his picture. As with the painting in Wilde's text, the physical resemblance is striking: 'Heredé de ti [. . .] tu rostro, teñido con los colores de mamá' (*S*, p. 6) ['I inherited [. . .] your face, shaded with Mama's coloring', *S/tr* p. 4]. This painterly self-description by Adriana as she speaks to her dead father, reminds the reader that as in Wilde's construct, there is a

---

[8] Raby mentions the blood dripping in a list of Gothic effects in Wilde's text (*Oscar Wilde*, p. 76). Glenn notes the Gothic effects of Erice's gloomy lighting in the film adaptation of *El Sur* (see 'Gothic Vision', 247).

[9] *Dracula* and the implications of Stoker's treatment of free will among the vampire's victims, will be discussed in Chapter 3.

triangular relationship here, not just a dyadic one. As well as Dorian and the painting, there is the person who put the colours on the canvas, Basil Hallward, who feels so deeply implicated in his masterpiece, that he cannot bear to exhibit it: ' "I have put too much of myself into it", ' he explains to Lord Henry, elaborating a little later: ' "Every portrait that is painted with feeling is a portrait of the artist, not of the sitter. [. . .] The reason I will not exhibit this picture is that I am afraid that I have shown in it the secret of my own soul" ' (*PDG*, pp. 9 and 12, respectively). If the analogy is followed to its logical conclusion, Adriana's mother is the Hallward figure in *El Sur* and what the events of the story do to her will be explored presently. For the moment, however, let us note Adriana's striking physical resemblance to her father.

The picture of Dorian is not only a masterpiece for the 'wonderful likeness' that it captures (*PDG*, p. 32); long before its magical properties are revealed to him, Basil threatens to destroy it, whereupon Dorian declares that to do so would be murder, adding ' "I am in love with it. It is part of myself. I feel that" ' (*PDG*, p. 35). At this early stage of the novel, Dorian's words appear merely to chime with a recent description of him as a Narcissus (*PDG*, p. 9), but when one re-reads the text with the benefit of hindsight, the prefiguring of the suicide and the depth of the identification between Dorian and the picture are far more chilling.[10] Adriana too is more than a remarkable physical likeness of her father; the above quotation continues that she inherited not only her father's looks 'sino también tu enorme capacidad para la desesperación y, sobre todo, para el aislamiento' (*S*, p. 6) ['but also your enorme capacity for despair and, above all, for isolation', *S/tr* p. 4]. Perhaps most significant of all, though, is that Adriana possesses the same gift as her father for water-divining with a pendulum and much is made of her excitement and pride on discovering this. Less emphasized – because of the perspective being Adriana's throughout[11] – is how Rafael felt on realizing that his daughter shared this special talent with him, but the strength of his feelings can be deduced from the patience he shows and the time he takes to develop Adriana's skill, as well as from his enthusiasm (*S*, p. 16; *S/tr*, p. 14) to exhibit his little daughter's inheritance from him when he takes her to replace him on a water-divining job (*S*, pp. 17–19; *S/tr*, pp. 16–18). Thus, it would seem legitimate to read Adriana as having – like the picture of

[10] The moment when Basil takes up a knife to destroy the picture also anticipates in reverse fashion the terrible scene when Dorian will murder him, since, as we have just seen, Basil has posited the idea that the painting is in some sense his own soul.

[11] The perspective being Adriana's also leads to a different connection with the Gothic, beyond the scope of this chapter, but worth noting nevertheless. Fred Botting (2001) asserts: 'The paternal figure [. . .] with all its superegoic and symbolic power, becomes a crucial feature of all Gothic fiction, central to its desires and transgressions' ('Candygothic', in Botting (ed.), p. 135).

Dorian – something of her father's soul and not just his face. Furthermore, there appears to be sufficient evidence to assert that as with Dorian's attachment to the painting, Rafael's love for Adriana has a narcissistic component.

It is, doubtless, significant that the idyllic relationship between father and daughter reaches almost exactly to Adriana's seventh birthday, the age of reason, according to Catholic tradition, when an individual must begin to take responsibility for his or her own actions and hence start going to confession and taking communion.[12] This is the point, in other words, when a child stops being merely an extension of the parents and acquires spiritual autonomy. Thus, it could be argued that the period prior to this moment is analogous to the first stage of Dorian's relationship with his picture: when he and it have not yet parted company and he can be proud of it simply as a beautiful copy of himself as he still is. He says, ' "I must admit that I delight in it" ' (*PDG*, p. 65) and we learn that it is hanging in the library of his London residence (*PDG*, pp. 101–2) where 'once, in boyish mockery of Narcissus, he had kissed, or feigned to kiss, those painted lips [. . .]. Morning after morning he had sat before the portrait, wondering at its beauty, almost enamoured of it' (*PDG*, pp. 118–19).

It is only after he has cruelly broken off his engagement to Sybil Vane that he first notices a change in the picture's expression and thereupon places a screen in front of it (*PDG*, p. 104). The equivalent in *El Sur* of this first divergence would be Adriana's First Communion. The physical changes wrought on her for the occasion cry out for a symbolic interpretation: 'Mientras me rizaban el pelo con unas tenazas me quemaron la frente en un descuido' (*S*, p. 22) ['While they curled my hair with a curling iron, they accidentally burned my forehead', *S/tr*, p. 20]. Not only are the women changing her hairstyle and in the process, perhaps diminishing the resemblance to her father, but they manage (albeit accidentally) to brand her forehead like Cain's in Genesis 4:15. God, represented by Josefa and Adriana's mother, has laid claim to the child, as surely as a farmer brands his cattle to prove his ownership. Even though the reader knows that Adriana is more than somewhat ambivalent about the First Communion, hating the religious instruction beforehand and being attracted to the event itself less than working the pendulum and only because of the pretty dress (*S*, p. 19; *S/tr*, p. 18), there is no evidence that she conveyed these feelings to her father.[13] From his perspective, then, this could well have seemed a rejection

---

[12] *The Oxford Companion to Christian Thought* (ed.) Adrian Hastings *et al.* (Oxford: OUP, 2000), p. 110.

[13] Not only is there an absence of any mention of this, but there is also some positive evidence that Adriana has not discussed the First Communion event with her father beforehand, since she wrongly assumes he will not attend (*S*, p. 22; *S/tr*, pp. 20–21).

of the anti-Church position he had championed, a choice on Adriana's part to distance herself from him and his values, preferring her mother's. Even though the text narrates no tangible distancing between father and daughter hinging upon this event, it is clear that the idyll of the previous era is now over: 'Empezó un tiempo largo y monótono' (S, p. 24) ['a long and monotonous period of time began', S/tr, p. 23]. The picture of Dorian Gray is still in the library, but a screen now stands between him and it; in analogous fashion, the closeness of the relationship between the father in *El Sur* and his image-daughter has started to crumble too.

In Wilde's novel, the next significant development is when Dorian has the picture moved upstairs to the disused schoolroom to which he will henceforth keep the key. He does this supposedly to ensure that nobody should chance to see it on calling at his house (*PDG*, p. 132) but it is clear to the reader that he is equally keen to remove it from his own sight. Indeed, the story goes on to enumerate the many ways in which he tries to distract his own attention from the picture, taking up extravagant hobbies, spending time abroad and calling these 'means of forgetfulness, modes by which he could escape' (*PDG*, p. 157) and yet, every so often he cannot resist the dual temptation of indulging his vices and looking at the reflection of them in the picture. When Basil Hallward comes to warn him of his wrecked reputation (*PDG*, pp. 166–70), we begin to have a sense of how low he has sunk over the past eighteen years and in particular, of the havoc he has wreaked on the lives of those – male and female – with whom he has associated. At this point too, we are allowed to see how the portrait has changed, showing both the marks of ageing and those of sin: 'There was still some gold in the thinning hair and some scarlet in the sensual mouth. The sodden eyes had kept something of the loveliness of their blue, the noble curves had not yet completely passed away from chiselled nostrils and plastic throat' (*PDG*, p. 173).

In *El Sur*, Adriana also describes both the external signs of the years passing for her and the internal development which accompanied these:

> Poco a poco, sin que tú lo advirtieras, fui conectando, aunque tímidamente con el exterior. [. . .]
> Yo crecía soñando esperanzas, llena de vagos deseos. [. . .] A los catorce años era ya una mujer. Recuerdo mis primeros tacones como los más altos y difíciles que he llevado nunca. A tus espaldas nacía una vida diferente y advertí que me amaban por las calles.   (S, pp. 31–2)[14]

She seems to be making a mistake here, though, in believing that her father was not noticing these changes, because she also chronicles the steep decline

---

[14] 'Little by little, without you noticing, I began making contact, albeit timidly, with the outside world. [. . .] I grew up dreaming, hopeful, full of vague desires [. . .]. At fourteen, I was already a woman. I remember my first high heels as the highest and most difficult ones I have ever worn. Behind your back I began a different life' (*S/tr*, p. 31).

in their relationship at this point due to his ambivalent attitude to her growing up. On the one hand, he tries to arrest the process: 'Un día me invitaban a una fiesta. Tú no me dejabas ir, así que tampoco al cine con amigas o de excursión en bicicleta' ['One day they invited me to a party. You wouldn't let me go, just as you wouldn't let me go to the movies with girlfriends, or on bike trips']; on the other, he bitterly encourages this connection with society: 'Me empujabas casi con desprecio hacia los demás' (both *S*, p. 31) ['You pushed me toward others almost with disdain', both *S/tr*, p. 31]. Worth noting here is that the father's resistance to Adriana's social life is not a simple matter of trying to stop her meeting boys (although this is obviously an important part of it). As with Dorian's adoption of New Hedonism, all pleasures are encompassed – indulged in Dorian's case, denied in Adriana's –, not only boys, but also cinema and cycling for Adriana; also music, perfumery, and more for Dorian. And even though Adriana feels that as far as their former intimacy is concerned, her father has ended it – 'Me vaciabas de todo y abrías un hueco desolador en mi alma. Me dejabas sola' (*S*, p. 32) ['You emptied me of everything, and you opened a desolate cavity in my soul', *S/tr*, p. 31] – she also notes that like Dorian's inability to stop looking at the picture, he cannot help looking at the daughter who he feels no longer resembles him, whose existence perhaps symbolizes for him the anxieties he suffers about the choices he has made in life and whose growing independence is perhaps resisted precisely because it emblematizes for him a loss of control over the direction his life is taking: 'Cuando regresaba por la carretera, ya anocheciendo, te adivinaba impaciente ante la cancela, esperándome. Aunque tú siempre me mentías, balbuciendo con poco humor que habías salido a dar un paseo, yo sabía que me espiabas' (*S*, pp. 32–3) ['When I returned home on the road with dusk already falling, I sensed that you would be waiting impatiently for me at the gate. Although you always lied to me, mumbling in a bad mood that you had gone out to take a stroll, I knew that you were spying on me' *S/tr*, p. 32].

Finally, the evening before he commits suicide, Adriana and her father try to communicate as they used to be able to do. Ostensibly, the attempt fails, since there are no explicit revelations and Adriana's rejoinders to her father's description of his depression seem banal: ' "El sufrimiento peor es el que no tiene un motivo determinado. Viene de todas partes y de nada en particular. Es como si no tuviera rostro" [says the father]. "¿Por qué? Yo creo que siempre hay motivos y que se puede hablar de ellos," te dije sin convencimiento alguno y desalentada' (*S*, p. 37) [' "The worst suffering is the kind that doesn't have any particular reason. It comes from everywhere and from nothing in particular. It's as if it didn't have a face". "Why? I think that there are always reasons and that you can talk about them," I said without any conviction, discouraged' *S/tr*, p. 37]. The haunting poignancy of this last conversation between father and daughter resides in the juxtaposition of the facile remarks spoken out loud by Adriana with the depth of her understanding of her father, a depth which she does not convey to him and which might have made him feel that despite the passing of time and the changes in her looks and lifestyle, the special bond between them had not been irredeemably severed. The reader can see this enduring link precisely and ironically in the sixth sense that Adriana has inherited from him: she detects the 'aliento de muerte' ['breath of death', *S/tr*, p. 36] in the garden, which the reader feels goes well beyond the moribund plant life and dried-up fountain, although this is all that is mentioned explicitly; but most clairvoyantly of all perhaps, Adriana feels the significance of the ravages time has wrought on her father, even though it has been stated that she can hardly see him in the crepuscular light:

> Te miraba fijamente, tratando de adivinar lo que no me decías. A través de aquel velo de penumbra vi años enteros pasando por tu rostro envejecido. Aquella noche sentí que el tiempo era siempre destrucción. [. . .] El jardín, la casa, las personas que la habitábamos, incluso yo con mis quince años, estábamos envueltos en aquel mismo destino de muerte que parecía arrastrarnos contigo.   (*S*, p. 37)[15]

Thus, when the father commits suicide that same night, it is easy not to notice that his access to Adriana's feelings had been far more limited than our own. He does not know about the dream she had of his rescuing her and in which she wanted to marry him (*S*, pp. 33–4; *S/tr*, p. 33). He has been told nothing of the 'congoja insoportable' ['unbearable distress', *S/tr*, p. 36] that Adriana had felt when he reminded her of their shared past, because she did not even answer his question: ' "¿Te acuerdas?" Claro que me acordaba, pero no te respondí' (*S*, p. 36) [' "Do you remember?" Of course I remembered, but I didn't answer you' *S/tr*, p. 36]. From his point of view only Adriana's attempts to put ever greater distance between them are visible, a distance which ultimately becomes intolerable to him: like Dorian, who can neither walk away from the picture, nor live under the same roof with it, a constant reminder of how far he has travelled from youth and innocence, the father cannot walk out on Adriana and the world she represents because the other doors have been closed on him: his mother has died, precluding going home to her and Gloria has ended their relationship, so starting a new life with her and Miguel is not viable either. He evidently cannot endure staying to watch Adriana lose more and more of what they once shared either, though.

If the analogy with *The Picture of Dorian Gray* were neat, tidy, and facile, we should expect him to have murdered the mother earlier in the story (the Basil

---

[15] ['I stared at you, trying to guess what you were not telling me. Through that veil of shadow, I saw entire years passing across your aged face. That night, I felt that time always meant destruction. [. . .] The garden, the house, the people that inhabited it, even me at fifteen, we were all entangled in that same destiny of death that seemed to drag us along with you,'] (*S/tr*, p. 37).

Hallward figure), then to murder Adriana, the 'picture', and then turn the gun on himself. However, the parallel is a subtler one. We shall return to the mother in the conclusion to the present chapter. For the rest, it should be remembered that although Dorian plunges a knife into the picture, the servants will find it intact and the knife in the heart of a man 'withered, wrinkled, and loathsome of visage', only identifiable as Dorian by the rings on his fingers. Meanwhile, the picture now shows him 'in all the wonder of his exquisite youth and beauty' (both *PDG*, p. 248). In other words, it is the old, jaded, and corrupted man concealed inside Dorian who has committed suicide, while the beautiful picture is destined to outlive him, now cleansed of the scars it bore on his behalf during his lifetime. So it is with Adriana, for although her recovery is not instantaneous or miraculous, the remainder of *El Sur* does narrate the beginning of the healing process, one which seems precisely to hinge upon her acquiring some sense of the young man her father once had been, both via his childhood home and the servant Emilia's memories and through meeting Miguel, his son by Gloria: 'descubrí [en Miguel] un gesto insignificante, una sonrisa fugaz, un ademán descuidado que, estaba segura, ya había conocido en ti' (*S*, p. 46) ['I discovered an insignificant expression, a fleeting smile, a careless gesture that I was sure I had seen in you', *S/tr*, p. 47]. This healing may be what the author was referring to when she spoke about Adriana's trip to Seville being about something more visceral than merely understanding her father:

> Ir al Sur es una manera de seguir teniendo presente al padre, más que desve-lar un misterio. El padre se hace presente cuando la protagonista encuentra los lugares en que vivió de niño y las personas que se relacionaron con él. Pero la comprensión no es lo más importante. Hay un lado en este relato más visceral. No hay propósitos explícitos de ir al sur para comprender.[16]

If *El Sur* thus dramatizes the same anxieties surrounding the inexorable passage of time as Wilde portrayed in his novel, *Bene* picks up the other key aspect of Dorian's downfall: moral corruption. This second text in the volume introduces an arresting image of frightening sexual energy right at the

---

[16] Sánchez Arnosi interview. [Going to the South is a way of keeping the father present, more than unveiling a mystery. The father makes himself present when the protagonist finds places where he lived as a child and people who had relations with him. But comprehension is not the most important thing. There is a more visceral side to this narrative. There is no explicit intention to go to the south to understand.] Claire Nimmo's interpretation of the significance of the trip to Seville diverges significantly both from the author's and the one presented in this chapter: 'It permits her [Adriana] to assert her own sense of identity, independent of paternal authority.' Despite this, Nimmo still seems to regard the trip as instrumental in allowing Adriana to move forward in her life: 'When she returns to the North she has stepped over the boundary of adolescence, entering the adult world.' (see 'García Morales's and Erice's *El Sur*: Viewpoint and Closure', *Romance Studies*, 26 (autumn 1995), 41–9 (both quotations from 47).

beginning, before Bene's arrival, when Ángela, enclosed and lonely in the isolated house, spends much time looking through the barred, prison-like gate to the road for entertainment:

> Allí fuera empezaba el mundo, donde yo imaginaba que podrían ocurrir las cosas más extraordinarias. Claro que sólo conseguía ver las manadas de toros que pasaban con frecuencia, levantando una nube de polvo que los envolvía, y haciendo temblar la tierra bajo los golpes poderosos de sus pisadas. Siempre iban corriendo, y cuando los tenía muy cerca, salía disparada a refugiarme tras una columna de la marquesina.   (B, p. 55)[17]

Dorian Gray too acknowledges fear at the power of his own nascent sexuality, when Lord Henry boldly asserts at their first meeting:

> 'You, Mr Gray, you yourself, with your rose-red youth and your rose-white boyhood, you have had passions that have made you afraid, thoughts that have filled you with terror, day-dreams and sleeping dreams whose mere memory might stain your cheek with shame-'
> 'Stop!' faltered Dorian Gray, 'stop! You bewilder me.'   (PDG, p. 26)

Like both of these, the sexual images in *Bene* and *The Picture of Dorian Gray* are invariably implicit, but all the more effective for that: exactly what Bene does with, and to, Santiago and Enrique, let alone the gypsy ghost, is never spelt out, any more so than what form Dorian's depravity takes. Wilde explained that this way 'Each man sees his own sin in Dorian Gray'[18] and similarly, active participation from the reader is demanded by García Morales on reading the non-specific sexual innuendo in *Bene*. The result of such a strategy is not just to stimulate the reader to construct meaning rather than passively receive it, it is also to unsettle him or her, for there is always an uncertainty surrounding how much it is justified to read into the text. For example, when on learning that Bene's father took her away by force when she turned fourteen 'para que empezase a trabajar' (B, p. 56) ['so she could begin to work', B/tr, p. 60], one wonders at first how safe it is to assume that this is

---

[17] ['Outside was where the world began, where I imagined that the most extraordinary things could occur. Of course the only thing I could ever see was the herds of bulls that frequently passed by, raising up a cloud of dust that covered them and making the ground tremble beneath the power of their hooves. They were always running, and when they came very near I would dash off and take refuge behind a column of the porch' (B/tr pp. 58–9).] Ordóñez links the passing of the bulls to the passing of gypsy caravans as inscribing the gender and class parameters of the protagonist (*Voices*, p. 183). Without disagreeing with this, it should be pointed out, however, that Ángela is not frightened when the gypsies pass.

[18] *The Letters of Oscar Wilde* (ed.) Rupert Hart-Davis (London, 1962), p. 266, cited in Raby, *Oscar Wilde* (1988), p. 68.

a reference to prostitution. Circumstantial evidence will come to light: is the 'gracia enorme de sus ademanes y de los movimientos de su cuerpo al caminar' ['the enormous grace of her gestures and the movement of her body'] sexually provocative because it betrays a precocious grasp of carnal knowledge, as Elisa seems to imply by telling her to 'andar [. . .] sin moverte tanto' [' "walk [. . .] without moving around so much" ']? Or is it just the reverse: sexual naiveté of the type immortalized by Nabokov's Lolita, betrayed by the inappropriate flaunting of her sexual charms? Does the 'vaga tristeza' ['vague sadness'] of her facial expression merely speak of a generally hard life or one of sexual exploitation and is Elisa right to jump to conclusions about how she could have come to be the owner of one smart dress: '–¡Sabrá Dios quién se lo habrá regalado y lo que la desgraciada habrá tenido que dar a cambio!' (all B, p. 58) [' "God only knows who must have given it to her and what the poor woman must have had to give in exchange!" ', all B/tr, p. 62]?[19] For the next thirty-six pages we are to remain unsure about this key point in the characterization of Bene; only on page 94 [B/tr, p. 99] will the balance of probability tip towards the prostitution hypothesis, based on Juana's information: after the father took her away she made a great deal of money, she had many boyfriends (disbelieved by Juana) and the man she was living with had no need to work. Nevertheless, it is possible to propose other ways of understanding all of the above, neither more nor less verifiable than the sexual reading and this awareness in one's mind throughout Bene leads to a powerful – because irresolvable – tension as one continues to try to maintain at least two interpretations of all the events, one which construes Bene as sexually knowing and therefore in a position to pass on that knowledge to those around her, including Santiago; the other, that it is the sexual knowledge of the older women, Elisa and Rosaura, which they project neurotically onto Bene, with disastrous self-fulfilling prophecy results.[20]

However, even Ángela, who is favourably disposed towards Bene from the outset, also reports a frightening aspect of her, the strange look which crosses her face from time to time and which to the child is suggestive of death, a frozen mask: 'Había [. . .] algo turbio, brumoso [. . .] que sentía como si fuera una morbosa emanación de la muchacha. [. . .] Aquella expresión de muerte [. . .] no parecía pertenecerle, como si fuera una espantosa careta [. . .]. En

---

[19] One could add more to this list. For example, Bene admits to having frequent bad dreams (B, pp. 61–2; B/tr, p. 66); again, one could read these as nightmares relating to her sexual exploitation, or simply as a reflection of a poor and miserable existence to date.

[20] Ordóñez draws a convincing parallel in this regard between Elisa and the governess in Henry James's The Turn of the Screw (though I would argue that Rosaura offers a closer analogy) (see Voices, p. 187). The undecidability of the extent to which both characters are projecting their own sexual anxieties onto others is obviously as central to an understanding of Bene as it is to James's narrative. However, this question will be considered fully in Chapter 4, with respect to Las mujeres de Héctor.

aquellos momentos su mirada helada adquiría el poder de convocar a nuestro
alrededor un espacio otro, terriblemente vacío y amenazador' (B, p. 70)
['There was [. . .] something turbid and nebulous that [. . .] felt like it was a
morbid emanation from the girl. [. . .] That expression of death [. . .] didn't
seem to belong to her, as if it were a dreadful mask [. . .]. In those moments,
her frozen gaze acquired power, summoning a different, terribly empty and
threatening space around us' B/tr, p. 74.] Ángela will explain that at that age
she considered being in love as something 'diabólico' (B, p. 73) ['diabolical',
B/tr, p. 78]; hence it is plausible that as with the bulls charging past the house,
she could be frightened by a sexual aura surrounding Bene and so perhaps
label it deathlike. As she also states that she saw being in love as something
beyond the control of the individuals involved (B, p. 73; B/tr, p. 78), chiming
with the idea that the look 'no parecía pertenecerle' ['didn't seem to belong to
her'], it also remains possible that this belief could enable her to continue to
like and admire Bene in spite of quite acute anxieties in this regard. Ángela
links this frightening aspect of Bene to the ghostly figure of a gypsy and she
is further convinced that this is Bene's father/lover. According to the unreliable
Juana, this man had committed suicide before Bene came to work in the house
and Ángela believes that Bene continues to commune with him secretly.

A consideration of this strange figure in the light of Wilde's text enables us
to make some sense of him, as the player of two recognizable parts: as Bene's
father, the gypsy is playing a role analogous to that of Lord Henry in *The
Picture of Dorian Gray*; thus, he is the one who has deliberately and quite
unscrupulously exposed her to the moral depravity of the world and drawn her
into participation in it. As Bene's lover, on the other hand, he corresponds to the
painting of Dorian. In other words, Ángela offloads the evil of the sexual
corruption that she semi-consciously fears lies within Bene onto this ghostly
other, leaving Bene herself to be the innocent friend that she wants and needs
in her loneliness. As with Wilde's premise, Ángela believes that Bene's physical
appearance would betray any evil within her and so is reassured and willing to
dismiss her nocturnal suspicions on the basis of how she looks in the morning:

> Sentía la necesidad de mirar a Bene, como si su imagen fuera un espejo que
> pudiera reflejar, iluminándolas, todas aquellas oscuridades que la acom-
> pañaban. Pero la encontré en el lavadero con las mangas remangadas y las
> manos enrojecidas por el frío del agua y la cáustica del jabón. Era, en aquel
> trance, una mujer terrenal, sin secretos, entregada de lleno a un quehacer
> cualquiera.   (B, p. 77)[21]

---

[21] ['I felt the need to look at Bene, as if her image were a mirror that could reflect all
the darkness that accompanied her, illuminating it. But I found her in the washroom with
her sleeves rolled up and her hands all red from the coldness of the water and the caustic
of the soap. She was, in that difficult moment, an earthly woman, without secrets, fully
devoted to her chores'] (B/tr, pp. 81–2).

The ending of the novel, when with both Bene and Santiago dead, Ángela now encounters the gypsy ghost alone, could be read in many different ways, but following the logic of the interpretation proposed in this chapter, the scene would represent the moment when the child can no longer hide behind either other people or – to remember the opening image of the charging bulls and the locked door of Dorian's nursery – a physical barrier to keep herself separate from the frightening sexuality represented by the gypsy. Now she admits to having reached out towards it – 'acerqué mi mano a su hombro' – and in a transparently erotic image 'me entregué voluntariamente a aquella manera de muerte' whereupon the fear melts: 'todo se fundió en una negrura perfecta, y le sentí a él envolviéndome con dulzura' (all *B*, p. 111) ['I moved my hand toward his shoulder [. . .]. I voluntarily surrendered to that way of death [. . .]. Everything faded away to a perfect blackness, and I felt him surrounding me with sweetness', *B/tr*, p. 117].

If the eponymous character is the analogue to Wilde's Dorian Gray, then Santiago would correspond to Sybil Vane, the actress who commits suicide when Dorian breaks off their engagement. Indeed, his level of adoration of Bene does seem as excessive as Sybil's for Dorian. It is in one of the second-person meditative sections that this emerges most clearly. Here is where Ángela refers to her perception of her brother as 'un cuerpo con el alma ausente' ['a body with an absent soul']; and in case we might have attributed this description to her imagination, it is immediately followed by visible symptoms just as melodramatic as the portrayal of Sybil Vane's attachment to Dorian: 'ojos hundidos en el llanto [. . .] lágrimas [. . .] silencio' (both *B*, p. 98) ['eyes, sunken in tears [. . .] silence', both *B/tr*, p. 103]. Glossing these, she concludes: 'tu amor por Bene era como una posesión sobrehumana y parecía venir de la misma muerte' (*B*, p. 99) ['your love for Bene was like a superhuman possession and it seemed to come from death itself', *B/tr*, p. 104]. Thus, once again, from Ángela's perspective, sexual desire is linked with the devil and death, joining up with the gypsy ghost as its personification in her imagination.

A strikingly symmetrical pattern of gender and class difference also appears in the comparison between Dorian and Sybil with Bene and Santiago. In both cases the woman is not only from the opposite end of the social spectrum to the man, but also from the same end: the gutter. Yet the character who is wielding the power so great that it leads to the other's suicide in Wilde's case, is the aristocratic man, whereas in García Morales's, it is the low-born woman. Thus, there is a striking gender reversal of the demon-lover motif, as this has been elucidated, for example, by Toni Reed (1988). A few brief quotations from her work on the subject juxtaposed with extracts from *Bene*, will suffice to illustrate the closeness of the figure to Bene's characterization:

> The mythological figure on which the demon-lover is based is clearly Satan.
> Aquella figura suya y tenebrosa, recortada sobre el negro de la noche, en la
> que se había transfigurado durante breves instantes, allí arriba, en la torre,

se convirtió para mí en el testimonio de que aquel espanto que se le atribuía existía realmente. (*B*, p. 68)[22]

Stories about demons who seduce women are about power and powerlessness.

Me miró [Bene] clavando sus ojos en mí con desprecio, mientras rodeaba con su brazo el cuello de mi hermano igual que lo haría una serpiente. [. . .] La descubrí como mi enemiga. Pero [. . .] me tuve que retirar sin decir nada. Una vez más me había vencido. (*B*, p. 102)[23]

Critical to the medieval concept of demonology [is the idea that] Satan [. . .] takes whatever form necessary to seduce [. . .] people.

– El Diablo ronda esta casa [. . .] Puede tomar cualquier forma para engañarnos: un perro manso, un mendigo desgraciado, una niña indefensa, un sacerdote, un hombre justo, una mujer honesta. (Rosaura to Ángela, *B*, p. 99)[24]

The demon-lover seeks to destroy another's will, another's spirit.[25]

Tus ojos [. . .] ya sólo miraban hacia dentro, hacia aquella pena extraña que te consumía. [. . .] No puedo creer que fuera sólo el amor lo que te derrotó de aquella manera. (*B*, pp. 98–9)[26]

---

[22] ['That tenebrous form of hers, outlined against the black of night, in which she had become transfigured during a few brief instants up there in the tower became testimony for me that the terror they attributed to her really existed'] (*B/tr*, pp. 72–3).

[23] ['She [Bene] [. . .] looked at me, disdainfully stabbing me with her eyes, while she wrapped her arm around my brother's neck like a serpent. [. . .] I saw that she was my enemy. But [. . .] I had to withdraw without saying anything. Once again, she had defeated me'] (*B/tr*, pp. 107–8).

[24] ['"The devil is stalking this house [. . .]. He can take any form to trick us: a tame dog, an unfortunate beggar, a defenceless girl, a priest, an honourable man, an honest woman"'] (*B/tr*, p. 105, adapted).

[25] Toni Reed, *Demon-Lovers and Their Victims in British Fiction* (Lexington: University of Kentucky Press, 1988), pp. 8, 20, 26, and 105, respectively. Dorian's aristocratic class status ties in with that of the character Reed calls 'the most famous demon-lover of all time' (p. 17), namely, Count Dracula, but Heathcliff, another one she discusses, is more like Bene in this respect, being of gypsy stock and unknown parentage and picked up off the streets by the philanthropic Mr Earnshaw, who little suspects the havoc his action will wreak in the future. Likewise, Enrique's motives are claimed to be charitable, even though Elisa takes a cynical view of them. For Heathcliff's origins see Emily Brontë, *Wuthering Heights*, 2 vols (London: Dent, 1912), chap. 4, pp. 38–9. Another echo of *Wuthering Heights* is to be found in *Bene*, with the branch of a tree frighteningly scratching Ángela's bedroom window (*B*, p. 71; *B/tr*, p. 75), rather like Lockwood's dream of Cathy's ghost scratching at the window, which he attributes to the branch and cones of a fir-tree (*Wuthering Heights*, chap. 3, vol. I, pp. 25–6). Thus the class issue seems not to be decisive to the demon-lover type as understood by Reed, whereas his masculinity is.

[26] ['Your eyes [. . .] now only looked inward, toward that strange sorrow that consumed you. [. . .] I can't believe it was just love that defeated you in that way'] (*B/tr*, pp. 103–4).

Satanic women are of course plentiful in literature and legend, with Eve-like temptresses, predatory vampiresses, and witches only some of their manifestations. In Spanish literature alone, one could mention predecessors such as Unamuno's Raquel in 'Dos madres' or Pardo Bazán's Sabel (through Julián's eyes) in *Los pazos de Ulloa*. Nevertheless, Bene's portrayal still resonates strikingly with the male demon-lovers charted by Reed. Most of all, perhaps, the depiction of her relationship with Santiago would seem reminiscent of the gender-reversed pattern in Wilde's novel: Dorian Gray with his short-lived interest in Sybil Vane, does not set out deliberately to break her heart, but simply loses interest in her on the basis of one theatrical performance and cares too little for anyone's feelings apart from his own to fret about the effect on her of his suddenly breaking off their engagement. This seems rather like Bene's attitude to Santiago. On the first picnic, she appears to enjoy flirting with him: 'sus ojos centelleaban al mirar a Santiago' (*B*, p. 69) ['her eyes sparkled as she looked at Santiago', *B/tr*, p. 74] and her voice is altered too (*B*, p. 70; *B/tr*, p. 75). Santiago metamorphoses both visibly and audibly as well: 'junto a ella, parecía ya un hombre, con su nueva voz y su nuevo aspecto' (*B*, p. 70) ['he, next to her, already seemed like a man, with a new voice and a new appearance,' *B/tr*, p. 75]. However, she rapidly moves on to Enrique, wearing high heels (*B*, p. 73; *B/tr*, p. 77) and red lipstick for his benefit and making a special effort to set the table prettily when he is at home (*B*, p. 74; *B/tr*, p. 79). On a subsequent picnic, Ángela now describes Bene's behaviour towards Santiago very differently, referring to 'la indiferencia con que la muchacha respondía a sus gestos y palabras de admiración, a pesar de exhibir ante él una coquetería mecánica' (*B*, p. 83) ['the indifference with which the girl responded to his gestures and words of admiration, in spite of exhibiting a mechanical flirtation with him' *B/tr*, p. 88]. Finally, after Enrique's departure, Bene seems to decide to pick up where she had left off with Santiago, but even then it is he who runs after her when she is finally sacked. No information is provided as to the circumstances in which Santiago and Bene were finally separated nor the timescale of this relative to her suicide, with the effect that once again we are destabilized with respect to our understanding of her, deprived of knowing whether she played an assertive role at this point or was manipulated by others. In this way, the author sets the seal on her characterization as beyond our understanding, just as she was for Ángela and as with Wilde's characters, one factor which makes her so opaque is the class gulf separating the two of them.

In conclusion, it is worth turning to a consideration of the two characters who ought to be central to *El Sur* and *Bene*, respectively, yet who remain forlornly on the sidelines, helpless to alter the inexorable downward spiral of the plot yet deeply affected by it. Do they have a counterpart in *The Picture of Dorian Gray* and what does that reveal about how to read them? These characters are the mother in *El Sur* and Ángela herself in *Bene*. Despite her ostensibly negative portrayal by Adriana, it is possible to discern in the mother a woman who does not seem to deserve such a cruel depiction. Her worst sin appears to be a desire for social conformity and integration. She worries about Adriana's isolation from other children, enjoys educating her, and helps a woman (Josefa), whose alcoholic husband has maltreated her. The fact that Rafael may regret marrying her does not make her guilty of anything except being who she is, with her more northern temperament and religious faith (both, surely, things he must have known well enough from the outset). Yet, it would definitely be to read against the grain of the text to decide she is a sympathetic character; Adriana's resentment of her is almost tangible and as she is the storyteller, that attitude is the one that gives the text the grain it has. The resentment has at its core the fact that Adriana sees her as offering an opposing world view to that of her father and feels obliged to take one side or the other. Choosing her father's automatically sets up an antagonism towards everything her mother represents. A similar triangular structure dominates Wilde's text, since Dorian also feels constrained to choose between Lord Henry and Basil Hallward and having gravitated instinctively towards the former, automatically finds it necessary to reject the latter. Both Dorian and Adriana choose their allegiance only semi-consciously, since the empathy they feel for their mentor comes from far deeper within them than any cerebral decision-making process and the resulting rejection of the third character is a mere bi-product of the magnetic pull of the second. In *El Sur*, this irresistibility of the father is emblematized by the phallic pendulum; in *Dorian Gray* by the poison book, perhaps, symbolizing the power of words (Lord Henry seduces Dorian with his voice as well as the present of the book); but the result for the non-chosen character is the same: despite the undeniable fact that both Basil and Adriana's mother are logically central, they are pushed pitilessly to the margins not only of the life of someone they love deeply – Dorian and Adriana, respectively – but also of the narrative itself, never depicted with the care and completeness they logically deserve.

Ángela's case is comparable but different. As the narrator of *Bene*, she is bound to be central to an understanding of the text. However, she is pathetic in her marginality to the events she records.[27] For example, even though she knows rather more about Bene than the others (with the possible exception of Enrique) due to her friendship with Juana, nobody is interested in finding out what she thinks of her. Again, when Santiago stops going to school, he does not confide his feelings to Ángela, even though she believes them to have had a close relationship in the past. When he is brought back home by the Civil Guard, neither Elisa, nor Santiago involve her in the terrible final events. Indeed, the image of her sitting endlessly outside the locked door of the 'torre' [tower] with Santiago dying on the other side of it is a powerful image

---

[27] Ordóñez discusses the issue of gender, age, and class marginality in Bene with reference collectively to Bene, Juana, and Ángela (*Voices*, p. 187).

of her exclusion and helplessness in the plot as a whole. The reason for this is clear enough: in an ironic reversal of Wilde's treatment of youth as all too short-lived, here it is shown cruelly stigmatizing Ángela: '¡Qué edad más difícil tenía yo entonces! Doce años. Conoces el dolor y, sin embargo, aún no llegas a comprenderlo y, mucho menos, a remediarlo' (B, p. 98). ['What a difficult age I was at then! Twelve years old. You know pain, but you still don't manage to understand it, much less relieve it,' B/tr, p. 103].

'Darkness, passion, superstition, [. . .] violence, [. . .] prohibition and taboos, [. . .] hidden natural instincts and wishes' are listed by Fred Botting as classic elements of the Gothic[28] and all are as prominent in El Sur and Bene as they are in The Picture of Dorian Gray. However, this chapter has argued that at the core of the haunting effect of the three texts are the specific narrative patterns they share: a character – Dorian, Rafael, Bene – whose downward spiral we follow, watching with horror not only what is happening to that individual, but its repercussions on those whom we are watching watching: the picture and Basil Hallward; Adriana and her mother; Ángela and Santiago. Heightening the poignancy and the power of the three stories and ensuring that they cannot be reduced to a facile good-versus-evil reading, the authors are careful to make the issue of culpability undecidable: Wilde shows aspects of the human condition, of Dorian's family background and upbringing as well as the impact on him of others' attitudes and ideas (not only Lord Henry's but also Basil Hallward's), that do not exonerate but do help to explain the peculiar confluence of circumstances that led him to make the doomed life-choices he did. García Morales also lays before the reader a panoply of contributory factors: the socio-political situation of Spain in the 1950s, including the stigmatization of ex-Republicans, inadequate welfare support for the poorest, the power of the Church and the most benighted interpretations of its doctrines, prejudice against gypsies, traditions concerning how to bring up children, and more. But ultimately, to seek to decide whom to blame for the misery the storylines recount is to miss the point; as in a nightmare, once we are trapped in any one of the three narratives, they gather their own momentum which sweeps the characters to their doomed fate and we, horrified voyeurs on the margins – replicating eerily the position of internal characters Basil, Adriana's mother, and Ángela – are condemned to watch.[29]

---

[28] 'Preface' in Botting (ed.), pp. 2–3.
[29] The inspiration for this concluding paragraph linking nightmare, voyeurism, and the Gothic comes from Wolstenholme (1993), pp. 3–7.

2

El silencio de las sirenas (1985) and Ann Radcliffe, *The Mysteries of Udolpho* (1794): The Sublime

El silencio de las sirenas [The Silence of the Sirens] is set in an isolated village in the Alpujarra mountains of southern Spain. The two principal characters, Elsa and the narrator, María, are outsiders to the community and the mountains and are portrayed as relating to their geographical setting with the wonder and appreciation of its beauty and majesty that locals – for whom it is nothing more nor less than normality – do not share. The main storyline contains many elements familiar to readers of Gothic fiction: the doubling of characters – Elsa, the protagonist and Agustín Valdés, the man she loves, re-appear in the former's dreams and hypnotic trances as nineteenth-century figures in Germany called Otilia and Eduardo, linked with characters in Goethe's *Elective Affinities* – , the use of supernatural elements – hypnotism, Moorish magic, and the evil eye – and the encounter with them by modern characters who wonder (as we do too) whether to dismiss them as ignorant superstition or quaintly picturesque folk-beliefs, on the one hand, or to respect them as expressions of ancient wisdom lost in the hurly-burly of the contemporary world, on the other.[1] There is also a different type of Gothic echo in *Silencio*, this time a structural, rather than a thematic one: García Morales's narrative repeatedly intercalates stories that seem tangential to the reader's main centres of interest, namely, the relationships between Elsa and María and between Elsa and Agustín.[2] The novel ends with Elsa's rapid

---

[1] For Biruté Ciplijauskaité, there is no doubt over this: the villagers live in a 'mundo de la superstición' [world of superstition] which conflicts with both Elsa's and María's respective perceptions of reality. Yet if it were as clear-cut as this, why would Elsa and María participate in the evil eye rituals more than once? Their attitude to these seems more than somewhat ambivalent. See 'Intertextualidad y subversión en *El silencio de las sirenas*,' *Revista Hispánica Moderna*, 41 (1988), 167–74 (170). The incorporation of folklore into Gothic fiction is acknowledged as widespread. For more on this, see Jacqueline Howard, *Reading Gothic Fiction: A Bakhtinian Approach* (Oxford: Clarendon, 1994), pp. 239–42.

[2] Maggie Kilgour discusses Radcliffe's use of intercalations as delaying tactics in *The Rise of the Gothic Novel* (London & New York: Routledge, 1995), pp. 122–4. She also notes similarities between these and Horace Walpole's rambling servants in *The Castle of*

decline following Agustín's abrupt termination of all contact. Finally, María discovers her dead and frozen body in the mountain snows beyond the confines of the village, a death that is portrayed lyrically as a chosen fusion with the landscape.

The use of mountain landscapes in Gothic fiction has been noted by many scholars and linked to Edmund Burke's notion of the sublime, expressed in *A Philosophical Enquiry into the Origin of Our Ideas of the Sublime and the Beautiful* (1757).[3] E. J. Clery glosses the sublime as 'an apprehension of danger in nature or art without the immediate risk of destruction'[4] and Jerrold E. Hogle explains, 'Sublimity is thus aroused for Burke [. . .] by linguistic or artistic expansions into "Vastness" or "Infinity" [. . .] because they terrifyingly threaten the annihilation of the self.'[5] Botting comments on the link between this and mountainous scenery: 'a sense of the sublime occurs in an encounter with an immensity the mind cannot comprehend, a natural and divine power found in the sovereign shape of rugged, mountainous landscapes.' He even goes so far as to assert that 'mountains were the foremost objects of the natural sublime'.[6]

Ann Radcliffe makes the most of this connection between sublimity and mountains in *The Mysteries of Udolpho*, where the heroine, Emily, whose home in southern France is suggestively called La Vallée, experiences first, a pleasurable journey accompanied by her beloved father through the Pyrenees, which provides the location for her first encounter with Valancourt, her future husband. Once the nightmare which the bulk of the novel narrates gets underway, she is first taken over the Alps to Italy and then, after a brief period in Venice, is conducted through the Apennines to be imprisoned in Castle Udolpho there, from where she eventually escapes to the coast and a boat back to France. Her appreciation of each of these settings is developed in depth in the novel and serves as a telling index of her character and sensibility, as well as that of others.

This chapter will consider how to read García Morales's use of the Alpujarras in *El silencio de las sirenas* and compare this with Radcliffe's use

---

Otranto. Most resonant with *Silencio*, though, is her assertion that 'the subplot is [. . .] a means of displacement that allows the author to work through metaphorically the problems of the heroine in another location' (p. 155). See Miles, 'Ann Radcliffe and Matthew Lewis' in Punter (ed.), p. 46, for a discussion of Emily's poetic digressions in *The Mysteries of Udolpho*.

[3] Ed., Adam Phillips (Oxford: OUP, 1990). See Fred Botting, *Gothic*, (London & New York: Routledge, 1997) pp. 38–43 for a clear summary of the notion of the sublime and how it relates to the Gothic. Burke was not, of course, the only eighteenth-century commentator on the sublime. Others discussed by Botting include John Baillie in 1747 and Hugh Blair in 1783.

[4] 'The Genesis of "Gothic" Fiction', in *The Cambridge Companion to Gothic Fiction* (ed.) Jerrold E. Hogle (Cambridge: CUP, 2002), pp. 21–39 (p. 28).

[5] 'Introduction: the Gothic in Western Culture', in Hogle (ed.), pp. 1–20 (p. 14).

[6] 'Aftergothic [*sic*]: Consumption, Machines, and Black Holes', in Hogle (ed.) (pp. 277–300), p. 278 and *Gothic* (p. 38) respectively.

of the three mountain ranges included in her text.[7] Does García Morales, for
example, display her characters' response to these settings as a measure of
their sensibility, as Radcliffe does?[8] What, in particular, is one to make of
Elsa's choice of death in the mountain snows?[9] As well as acknowledging
critical work that has fruitfully explored the connections between the Spanish
novel and various intertexts including Kafka's short story of the same title,[10]
together with the Ulysses episode which it in turn connotes, the present
chapter will approach *Silencio*'s strange, oneiric narrative by juxtaposing the
Gothic sublime element with a consideration of Hans Christian Andersen's
tale, 'The Little Mermaid'. This story also employs the notion of silence:
losing her voice is the price Andersen's mermaid is forced to pay a witch to
exchange her tail for legs.[11] Furthermore, it has a denouement which also
presents the protagonist's death as chosen and although deeply poignant,[12]
somehow poetically satisfying and consolatory. The little mermaid expects to
merge with foam on the sea, also white and undulating, of course, but in fact

---

[7] Interestingly, both Radcliffe and García Morales use Venice as a location to contrast
with the mountains (liquidity versus solidity, society versus seclusion, civilization versus
nature) and also in both texts, the romantic hero is associated with an urban setting: Paris
corrupts Valancourt in *Udolpho* and Barcelona is where Elsa cannot bear to go and visit
Agustín in *Silencio*. This chapter will focus on the mountain landscape side of the
equation, but it is worth noting that both writers include counterbalancing locations in
similar fashion.

[8] As Kilgour notes, 'Radcliffe's characters are measured by their responsiveness to
nature, suggesting the interdependence of virtue and taste' (p. 119).

[9] Currie K. Thompson's interpretation of this as a return to the womb/Great Mother
would seem problematic because of the coldness and whiteness of the snow. ('*El silencio
de las sirenas*: Adelaida García Morales' Revision of the Feminine « Seescape »', *Revista
Hispánica Moderna*, 45 (1992), 298–309 (305)). Ciplijauskaité (172) notes an interesting
echo of the Tristan and Isolde story and the same article demonstrates parallels with
courtly love traditions, a relevant consideration in the present study, since classic Gothic
texts frequently hark back to the medieval period.

[10] This title (along with many others first published after Kafka's death), was not
chosen by the author, but by the first editor, Max Brod (see *The Complete Short Stories of
Franz Kafka* (ed.) Nahum N. Glatzer (London: Vintage, 1999), p. 459.

[11] Interestingly, Kafka misrepresents the episode of Ulysses's encounter with the sirens
(Ciplijauskaité calls this a transformation ('Intertextualidad', 173)), since he refers to
Ulysses having plugged his ears with wax to deafen him to their song. Kafka's text rests
on that misrepresentation since it revolves around the idea that perhaps the sirens were
in fact silent and Ulysses only imagined and assumed them to be singing. According to
Homer's account, however, Ulysses plugs the ears of his crew and has himself chained up
so he cannot react to the sirens' song, but he does listen to it himself. I am grateful to Henry
Lee Six and James Renshaw for drawing this to my attention. Thus, the notion of a silent
siren seems more evocative of Andersen's tale than the classical text, though of course it
too rests on the assumption that a mermaid's voice is particularly beautiful and so to take
it away is an inordinately cruel price for the witch to exact and a supreme sacrifice on the
little mermaid's part.

[12] Having lost the prince to another, she is offered – but does not take – the chance to
recover her mermaid's tail and marine existence if she murders him before sunrise.

becomes an invisible child of the air who can win herself an immortal soul after three hundred years of performing good deeds.[13] Finally, it is worth mentioning, by way of introduction, that García Morales characterized *Silencio* as 'una historia de amor no correspondido que sucede en una aldea medio abandonada de la Alpujarra' [a story of unreciprocated love which takes place in a semi-abandoned hamlet in the Alpujarras];[14] thus, for her at least, the two defining features of her text were the one-sidedness of Elsa's love for Agustín and the mountain setting, the latter being its point of contact with Radcliffe and the former its echo of Andersen; these two will thus constitute the twin structuring principles of the present chapter.

First, it is worth surveying the features of the mountain scenery and its effects on the two main characters in García Morales's text. There are the visual panoramas: majestic 'cumbres nevadas', 'picos helados e inhumanos' [snow-covered summits, inhuman, frozen peaks][15] and 'pueblecitos blancos [. . .] apretados como líquenes, en la ladera y en la cumbre de una montaña inmensa' (*SS*, pp. 14–15) [little white villages, clinging like lichens to the slope and on the summit of an immense mountain]; there is the sense of height and plunging drop provided by the view of the sea, fifteen hundred metres below (*SS*, p. 14): 'el triángulo invertido que el mar formaba en el horizonte, allí donde dos montañas se cruzaban' (*SS*, p. 19) [the inverted triangle made by the sea on the horizon where two mountains crossed over one another]. Auditory features are mentioned too: silence, described by María, for example, as 'quietud intemporal', 'silencio perfecto' (*SS*, pp. 14, 17) [timeless quietude, perfect silence], but also the sound of the wind. For instance, Elsa's diary records how when she climbs up into the mountains above the village, she listens to ' "el sonido del viento o el silencio de las montañas" ' (*SS*, p. 117) [the sound of the wind or the silence of the mountains]. María, for her part, mentions the wind in the village as having originated in the snowy peaks: 'el viento seguía silbando desde las cumbres nevadas' (*SS*, p. 38) [the wind went on whistling down from the snow-covered summits]; there are references to the strange effects when the clouds

[13] The incorporation of fairy-tale elements into Gothic narrative is discussed in Howard (1994), *Reading Gothic Fiction*, pp. 241–2. For her, the most important aspect of this is that these are combined with other types of discourse to create a 'dialogic interplay of ideas which evoke doubt and fear' (p. 242). Chapter 9 will discuss the importance of another fairy-tale, Perrault's 'La Barbe bleue' with reference to *Una historia perversa*.

[14] This comes from an interview given before *Silencio* was published, when the author is asked about what she is currently writing. Thus the comment relates to her conception of the text at the time of creating it, rather than a subsequent interpretation or re-interpretation of it (see Sánchez Arnosi interview). Ordóñez reports that García Morales began writing *Silencio* before *El Sur* and *Bene* (*Voices*, p. 192), but by the comments in the interview it appears that she considered it work in progress in 1986.

[15] Adelaida García Morales, *El silencio de las sirenas*, 21st edn (Barcelona: 1993), pp. 164, 165. Future references will relate to this edition and be given parenthetically in the text.

descend (*SS*, p. 15), to cold (*SS*, p. 38, for example), and to the sensation of wind on the skin, 'un viento enérgico [. . .] azotaba mi cuerpo' (*SS*, p. 165) [a lively wind whipped my body]. As for the positively weighted characters' reactions, we note that these are firmly grounded in traditional notions of appreciation of the sublime: their surroundings give them an impression of having left the everyday world behind and make their souls soar heavenward, even when the circumstances of the plot give them every reason for misery. María feels she has crossed 'una frontera precisa' [a clear frontier] and entered 'un mundo extraño' [a strange world] when she arrives at the Alpujarras (*SS*, p. 14) and she refers to 'la exaltación que en un principio provocan estas montañas' (*SS*, p. 45) [the overexcited state which these mountains provoke at first]. Elsa, for her part, will find solace when she climbs to the snow-covered heights above the village: 'Me aseguró que en aquella intemporal blancura había encontrado, al fin, algo parecido a la paz' (*SS*, p. 164) [She assured me that in that timeless whiteness she had finally found something resembling peace].

The Mysteries of Udolpho is a far longer novel than *El silencio de las sirenas*: 632 pages compared with 168. It is not surprising, therefore, that Radcliffe has space to dwell on the description of landscapes in leisured detail which García Morales chooses to deny herself. Nevertheless, leaving aside the quantity of the description, the quality is very similar. Here too, 'the deep silence of these solitudes' is emphasized;[16] Emily also describes the 'eternal snow [which] whitened the summits of the mountains' (*MU*, p. 43)[17] and the sound of the wind punctuating the silence (*MU*, p. 157 in the Alps, p. 214 in the Apennines). When she enters the Alps, she too feels she is in 'another world' (*MU*, p. 157) and like María, she also wonders at the strange effects of being 'among the clouds' (*MU*, p. 159).[18] As we shall now see, however, the

---

[16] *The Mysteries of Udolpho* (ed.) Bonamy Dobrée, with introduction and notes by Terry Castle (Oxford & New York: OUP, 1998), p. 44. Future references will relate to this edition and be given parenthetically in the text. This quotation refers to the Pyrenees, but see p. 157 for the solitude of the Alps and p. 214, for the 'solitary silence' of the Apennines.

[17] Again, this refers to the Pyrenees, but see *MU*, p. 157 for a 'snow-topt mountain' in the Alps. The tops of the peaks in the Apennines are not described as snow-covered, but as 'fad[ing] from the eye in misty hues' (*MU*, p. 229), recalling the descriptions of low cloud in *Silencio*.

[18] The effect of the clouds in the Pyrenees is dramatized further in one of the intercalated stories when a character called St Foix 'viewed, with emotions of awful sublimity, the long volumes of sulphureous clouds, that floated, along the upper and middle regions of the air, and the lightnings that flashed from them, sometimes silently, and, at others, followed by sullen peals of thunder, which the mountains feebly prolonged, while the whole horizon, and the abyss, on which he stood, were discovered in momentary light' (*MU*, p. 566). While the visual effects of a storm do not appear in García Morales's text, extreme weather conditions are present: as well as recurrent mentions of great cold (*SS*, pp. 71 and 75, for example), María's house is flooded by heavy rain while she sleeps, leading her to muse that 'vivir aquí era como viajar en un barco que navegara a la deriva, perdido en el mar, lejos de

similarity of detail of the mountain scenery and climate between the two texts is less significant than their evocation in those characters of each who are portrayed as possessing taste and sensibility of sublime emotions – 'wonder, awe, horror and joy' – believed 'to expand or elevate the soul and the imagination with a sense of power and infinity'.[19]

In *Silencio*, Elsa's character is established from the outset as one delicate enough to experience and appreciate the subtleties of the sublime. Presented in flashback, the reader's first encounter with her depiction comes with the opening of the novel, via the items she leaves for María to find after her suicide. Displayed 'sobre una mesita de madera, cubierta con un paño de terciopelo ocre', these include 'una postal que reproducía un cuadro de Paolo Ucello [. . .]; una flor seca y azul que, según decía, se llamaba "Love in a Mist"; una vieja caja china [. . .]; un retrato de Goethe [. . .]; una sortija de platino con incrustaciones de diamantes [. . .]; la reproducción de una litografía de Goya' (*SS*, p. 13) [on a small wooden table, covered with a mustard velvet cloth [. . .] a postcard with a reproduction of a painting by Paolo Ucello [. . .]; a blue dried flower which, so she used to say, was called 'Love in a Mist'; an old Chinese box [. . .]; a portrait of Goethe [. . .]; a diamond-encrusted platinum ring [. . .]; a reproduction of a Goya lithograph]. Later in the novel, the specific significance of each of these items will emerge, but on first reading, the impression created is one of refined tastes and sensibility. It is no surprise, therefore, when we come to know more about Elsa, to discover that she had studied music, and to find her imposing silence on María to listen to a Handel sonata (*SS*, p. 41). In fact, it transpires that music and the mountains both give rise to sublime emotions for Elsa. As for María herself, she is certainly a more down-to-earth individual; the contrast between the two is brought out when she dares to suggest to Elsa that normality might be desirable in her relationship with Agustín. '–¡Dale con lo normal! [. . .] ¡Qué prosaica eres!' Elsa retorts (*SS*, p. 135) ['You and your normal! [. . .] You're so prosaic!']. Nevertheless, María is also sensitive to the effect of the mountains and perceptive enough to understand Elsa better than one might expect.

In both cases – although to a more extreme extent in Elsa's – the effects of the sublime seem to revolve around reactions to two key interconnected notions: limitlessness and monstrosity. The link between these lies in the fact that monstrosity is definable as a transgression of boundaries, such as human and animal, alive and dead, masculine and feminine. Thus, limits are effaced or at least challenged in the figure of the monster.[20]

---

todas las costas' (*SS*, p. 45) [to live here was like sailing in a boat adrift, lost at sea, far from all coastlines], highlighting the appropriateness of mermaid imagery.

[19] Botting, *Gothic*, p. 38 (both quotations).

[20] Byron (2000) discusses this link in her analysis of the relationship between discourses of degeneration in the 1890s and the Gothic fiction produced at that time. She demonstrates that the discourse of degeneration places 'its emphasis on the breaking down

The descriptions of both Elsa's and María's feelings fit convincingly with an understanding of the sublime grounded in these concepts. A few examples will suffice to illustrate the point: María describes herself as 'anonadada' [overwhelmed] by the beauty of the view when she first arrives in the Alpujarras, but she has also commented just before on the silence and the timelessness there (*SS*, p. 14). Thus, it can be argued that the sense of unbounded temporality and soundlessness on the immense scale of the panorama before her combine to overwhelm her, the sublime reaction here. Then, to take an example from Elsa's experience of sublime emotions, one could look at her description of her inner life and obsession with Agustín: '–Cierro los ojos y percibo en mi interior algo sin fondo, sin límites' (*SS*, p. 66) ['I close my eyes and inside myself I perceive something bottomless, limitless']. This helps one to understand the attraction the mountains have for her, since clearly they provide her with an external counterpart to chime with her inner life:

> Ella misma me había dicho que solía subir andando hasta lugares muy alejados [. . .], por donde las montañas permanecían nevadas durante casi todo el año. Decía que allí arriba el silencio de la nieve era más intenso que cualquier pensamiento o sentimiento. Y sumergirse en aquella inmovilidad era como salirse de los límites del cuerpo.   (*SS*, pp. 163–4)[21]

Thus, the impression of both spatial and temporal boundlessness is portrayed in classic fashion as triggering sublime emotions.

The other side of the same coin, though, is the frightening, monstrous aspect of an effacing of limits. Indeed, Elsa is haunted by the idea that she could be perceived as monstrous. Notwithstanding the above-quoted scorn she pours on María for advocating normality in her relationship with Agustín, at one point and with no obvious provocation, she shouts tearfully down the telephone at Agustín: '–¡Yo soy normal! [. . .] ¡No soy un monstruo! ¡No soy un monstruo!' commenting subsequently that she perceived herself at that point as 'algo informe, repugnante, era un pozo repleto de horrores y amenazas contra mí. Era la monstruosidad

---

of boundaries, the dissolution of certainties' and in that respect, she argues, it 'articulates much the same fears and anxieties as those traditionally found in the Gothic novel [. . .] so Gothic monstrosity reemerged with a force that had not been matched since the publication of the original Gothic at the previous *fin de siècle*.' Her article culminates in the analysis of Richard Marsh's *The Beetle* (1897), which contains a character who equals 'Count Dracula in the number of boundaries she manages to transgress [for she] is both human and animal, animal and insect, male and female, and [. . .] heterosexual and homosexual' ('Gothic in the 1890s', in Punter (ed.), pp. 132, 140, respectively.

[21] [She had told me herself that she used to walk up to very remote spots where the mountain snows remained almost all the year round. She used to say that the silence of the snow up there was more intense than any thought or feeling. And to submerge oneself in that stillness was like coming out of bodily limitations.]

misma' (*SS*, pp. 62–3) ['I'm normal! [. . .] I'm not a monster! I'm not a
monster!' [. . .] something formless, repugnant, I was a well, brimming over
with horrors and threats to myself. I was monstrosity itself]. Since form is
determined by having an outline, the link between lack of boundaries,
formlessness, and monstrosity is clearly seen here. The monster theme is
continued via the postcard she sends to Agustín of Paolo Ucello's painting of
St George and the dragon, in which a woman is depicted as leading the
dragon on a rope while St George attacks it with his lance. On the back of
the card, Elsa sarcastically if masochistically invites Agustín to identify with
dragon-slayer by asking ' "¿No te gustaría ser tan valiente como san
Jorge?" ' (*SS*, p. 64) ['Wouldn't you like to be as brave as St George?'].[22] The
link between monstrosity and the mermaid figure emerges specifically a
little later, in a dream recorded in Elsa's Venice journal. There she describes
an eagle forcibly separating her from Agustín's arms as they embrace with
sublime intensity in a boundless sea:

> Al dolor de perderte se unió entonces el miedo a que descubrieras mi mons-
> truosidad: yo no era en realidad una mujer, sino una sirena. Cuánto tiempo
> duró aquel angustioso vuelo hacia el vacío de lo alto, exhibiendo ante tus
> ojos mi cuerpo monstruoso, signo, quizá, de una fatal prohibición de nues-
> tra unión.   (*SS*, p. 81)[23]

Before proceeding to consider what can be drawn from this cluster of
images around sublimity, mountains, and monstrosity in Elsa's case, it is
useful to return to *The Mysteries of Udolpho* and 'The Little Mermaid' to see
what parallels are available there. In the first place, one cannot fail to notice
Radcliffe's explicit use of the sublime to describe the emotions evoked by the
mountains, but these take on different associations according to Emily's state
of mind. At first, Emily loves 'the mountain's stupendous recesses, where the
silence and grandeur of solitude impressed a sacred awe upon her heart, and
lifted her thoughts to the GOD OF HEAVEN AND EARTH' (*MU*, pp. 9–10). Once
she has met Valancourt, the sublime chimes with her experience of love for

---

[22] Ordóñez convincingly identifies Agustín with Kafka's Ulysses (*Voices*, p. 190). This
reading is entirely compatible with the dragon-slayer image, as both figures represent the
man who emerges victorious from the challenge of the monstrous.

[23] [To the pain of losing you then was added the fear lest you discover my monstrosity:
I was not in reality a woman, but a mermaid. How long that anxiety-ridden flight lasted up
into the empty heights, exhibiting before your eyes my monstrous body, a sign, perhaps, of
a fateful prohibition of our union.] María also links Elsa with a mermaid, when she wonders
why Agustín 'no estuviera ya fascinado, que las cartas, la voz, el amor de Elsa, no hubieran
sido para él como un canto de sirena a cuyo hechizo ya tenía que haber sucumbido',
concluding that [he] 'se había tapado los oídos con cera, igual que Ulises (*SS*, p. 143) [why
Agustín was not fascinated by now, why Elsa's letters, voice, love, hadn't been like a siren's
bewitching song to which he should have succumbed by now. [. . .] he had blocked his ears
with wax, like Ulysses], thus following Kafka's misrepresentation of Homer.

him. Thus, the latter part of her trip through the Pyrenees, now with him and her journey through the Alps when she has just been taken away from him, but is still trying to remain optimistic about their future, emphasize how the spectacular immensity of the vistas echoes the boundless excess of feeling she has for her suitor. Before she has admitted her feelings to herself, the link remains implicit:

> Around, on every side, far as the eye could penetrate, were seen only forms of grandeur – the long perspective of mountain-tops, tinged with ethereal blue, or white with snow; vallies [sic] of ice, and forests of gloomy fir. The serenity and clearness of the air in these high regions were particularly delightful to the travellers; it seemed to inspire them with a finer spirit, and diffused an indescribable complacency over their minds. They [Emily, Emily's father, and Valancourt] had no words to express the sublime emotions they felt. (MU, p. 44)

As she first discovers the Alps, Emily's response to the scenery is inextricably bound up with her now acknowledged feelings for Valancourt:

> Here such scenes of sublimity opened upon them [Emily, her aunt, Montoni and their entourage] as no colours of language must dare to paint! Emily's mind was even so much engaged with new and wonderful images, that they sometimes banished the idea of Valancourt, though they more frequently revived it. These brought to her recollection the prospects among the Pyrenées, which they had admired together, and had believed nothing could excel in grandeur. How often did she wish to express to him the new emotions which this astonishing scenery awakened and that he could partake of them! [. . .] She seemed to have arisen into another world, and to have left every trifling thought, every trifling sentiment, in that below; those only of grandeur and sublimity now dilated her mind, and elevated the affections of her heart. (MU, p. 157)[24]

Finally, when Emily is taken into the Apennines to go to Castle Udolpho, where she fears she will be forced to marry a man of Montoni's choosing (Count Morano), the sublime emotions emerge in their negative aspect. Now boundless awe evokes boundless fear and anxiety: 'the gloom of these shades, their solitary silence, except when the breeze swept over their summits, the tremendous precipices of the mountains [. . .], each assisted to raise the solemnity of Emily's feelings into awe; she saw only images of gloomy grandeur, or of dreadful sublimity, around her' (MU, p. 214). Whilst monstrosity is not explicitly mentioned in regard to this negatively weighted sublime, it could be argued that it appears implicitly in the frightening and personified character of the castle in the mountains: 'the gothic greatness of its features, and its mouldering walls of dark grey stone, rendered it a gloomy

---

[24] We should note in passing the identical idea here to that of María in *Silencio*, whereby climbing into the mountains is likened to entering another world (SS, p. 14).

and sublime object. [. . .] Silent, lonely and sublime, it seemed to stand the sovereign of the scene, and to frown defiance on all, who dared to invade its solitary reign' (*MU*, p. 216).[25] The fear engendered by the castle itself is intensified by the apparently supernatural phenomena experienced there, suggesting that it houses beings who challenge the boundary between life and death, this world and the next, just as disturbingly as the mermaid does for the boundary between human and fish, between the underwater world and that of dry land.

In 'The Little Mermaid', Hans Christian Andersen handles the distinctions between the world under the sea, on the one hand and the world of dry land, on the other, together with their respective inhabitants, by carefully balancing similarity and difference, so that aspects of life familiar to his readers have their analogues on the sea floor, but these are charmingly adapted to the different element. Thus, for example, there are marine gardens and buildings with windows but these are made of different materials, fishes replace birds, and there are social rules and rituals too, so that the eponymous character and her sisters, all princesses, have to wait until the age of fifteen before they are allowed to visit the surface of the sea and look out upon the human world. It is in this context that we read a comparison of waves in a storm with mountains.[26]

Whereas for Kafka in his short story, the silence of the mermaids in the Ulysses story is 'a still more fatal weapon than their song',[27] in Andersen, the mermaid's muteness handicaps her in her attempts to win the prince's love because it not only deprives her of her beautiful singing voice, which could

---

[25] Emily's maid perhaps senses this monstrous aspect when she comments that the castle would seem a fitting abode for a giant (*MU*, p. 220). See Kilgour, *The Rise of the Gothic Novel* (p. 120), for a discussion of the ambiguous gender identity of the castle, which indirectly contributes to this personification.

[26] Andersen, Hans Christian, 'The Little Mermaid' (1837), in *Hans Andersen's Fairy Tales* (trans.) L. W. Kingsland (Oxford: OUP, 1985), pp. 60–84. See pp. 60–1 for the comparison between the undersea world and our own; p. 62 for the rule about being fifteen before going to the surface of the sea. On p. 67 there is the night-time storm in which the 'wild sea' resembles the sublime of the mountains: 'the waves rose like great black mountains' and the ship is 'like a swan' among them. This imagery is echoed on the next page when the mermaid brings the unconscious prince ashore: 'she saw dry land in front of her, high blue mountains with snow shining white upon their summits as if it were swans that lay there' (p. 68).

[27] Kafka, Franz, 'The Silence of the Sirens' (trans.) Willa & Edwin Muir, in *The Complete Short Stories of Franz Kafka* (ed.) Nahum N. Glatzer (London: Vintage, 1999), pp. 430–32 (p. 431). Ciplijauskaité interprets Kafka's meaning as 'no hay defensa contra lo no formulado, contra lo que sólo existe en la imaginación' ('Intertextualidad', 170) [there is no defence against what is not formulated, against what exists only in one's imagination], yet Agustín does defend himself quite effectively against Elsa's imagination and Elsa herself does not show any inclination to defend herself against her own imagination; on the contrary, it is that which gives her her *raison d'être*, so much so that when Agustín, by terminating contact, succeeds in depriving her of the springboard upon which it depends, she chooses to end her life.

have increased her charms for him, but also and most importantly, it prevents her from telling him her story, their story (how, unbenknownst to him, she had saved him from drowning, followed by the terrible sacrifices she has made to be with him). Thus, it is arguably the loss of narrative ability that leads to the unhappy ending of this tale.

Elsa, for her part, apparently fears that Agustín may discover what might be termed a mermaid aspect to her; this much can easily be surmised from both her bad dream in which she is trying to conceal it from him and her uncalled-for protestations that she is not a monster, but normal. However, what is more problematic is to establish what she understands by this: that she is dangerous, like the sirens of classical antiquity and may lure him to his death if he listens to her voice; that she is only a beautiful woman from the waist up and that her true sexual identity is as cold-blooded and inhuman as a fish's tail? Such a fear of abnormality is difficult to sustain because at the same time, she seems to be trying to establish herself in Agustín's mind as someone who transcends normality. For example, when she nearly goes to Barcelona to see him she tries in vain to achieve a particularly unnatural look:

> Pasaba las horas frente a un espejo [. . .]. Ensayaba diferentes combinaciones de vestidos, peinados y maquillajes. Y no es que pretendiera impresionar con su belleza a Agustín Valdés. Lo que buscaba en su rostro, en toda su figura, era aquel aliento sobrenatural que había quedado grabado en la única fotografía suya que le había enviado.   (SS, p. 134)[28]

Perhaps it is not in the specificity of mermaid lore that the key to Elsa's psyche lies. In the light of Andersen's tale, a more fruitful approach may be to see her identification with the mermaid figure as a symptom of an – albeit ambivalent – longing to be part of a magical world set apart from humdrum relationships, where a voice (such as Elsa's on the telephone from the Alpujarras to Agustín in Barcelona?) and a deceptive appearance – the mermaid looks like a human woman as she sits on a rock with her lower half under the water and the photograph Elsa sends Agustín of herself makes her look more ethereal and less human than she really is – is enough to drive a mortal man demented with love, where love can be powerful enough to justify any sacrifice, including life itself, and where the enormity of the sacrifice willingly undertaken wins demonstrable divine approval.[29] Certainly, there

---

[28] [She would spend hours in front of a mirror. [. . .] She would try on different combinations of dresses, hairstyles, make-up. And it was not because she wanted to impress her beauty upon Agustín Valdés. What she was seeking in her face, in her whole look, was that breath of the supernatural which had been stamped onto the single photograph of herself that she had sent him.]

[29] In 'The Little Mermaid', God rewards the mermaid with the chance of obtaining an immortal soul in three hundred years' time, rather than letting the witch's spell run its course, which would have left her without any hope of immortality.

is ample evidence in *El silencio de las sirenas* for arguing that Elsa is more interested in savouring and nurturing the sublime emotions engendered by her love, than in trying to bring a real-life relationship into being, with all the risks of disappointment, mediocrity, and failure that that entails. María, at least, seems to take this view of Elsa's mind-set:

> Siento un profundo respeto por sus palabras, su esperanza, su dolor, su melancolía, su inapetencia, su abandono. . . . Todo ello se engarzaba en el hilo de un sentimiento que quizá no fuera sino amor al Amor. Pues ahora estoy convencida de que era el amor [. . .] lo que le hacía resplandecer de aquella manera.   (*SS*, p. 50)[30]

In this respect, Elsa's love can be likened to that of Emily in *The Mysteries of Udolpho*. As with Emily, she is separated from the man who represents for her the sublime emotions produced by true love and as for Emily, the actual experience of being with the man in question – Valancourt, Agustín – is quite flimsy relative to the enormity of the emotions produced and sustained for the best part of the novel. However, Radcliffe eventually takes Emily through a process of discovering the fallibility of the actual man in contrast to the idealized image of him that has been her lifeline through adversity, thus bringing the couple to a more mature relationship at the end of the novel.[31] By contrast, Elsa resists María's attempts to push her story in a similar direction, preferring to create for herself an Andersen-like ending of a chosen death following Agustín's casual dismissal of her monumental devotion. For all her attempts to do so (on paper and by telephone), she has failed to tell him her story as assuredly as the little mermaid whose tongue had been cut out by the witch. But in all her wordy communications with him, she has also failed to ensnare him by the power of silence noted by Kafka and, ironically, by herself, since, as we have seen, it is the silence of the mountains and the wordlessness of classical music that both she and María recognize as generators of the sublime.

Kilgour writes of *The Mysteries of Udolpho*:

> Mountains play an ambiguous part in the text: at the opening they offer protection and shelter; during Emily and her father's journey they come to represent the sublime; afterwards, through association, they represent for Emily both her father and Valancourt [. . .]. Mountains thus suggest a male power which, originally protective and unifying, associated with her

---

[30] [I feel a profound respect for her words, her hope, her pain, her melancholy, her loss of appetite, her sense of abandonment. . . . All of it was strung together by a sentiment which was perhaps none other than love for Love. For I am now convinced that it was love [. . .] that made her glow in that way.]

[31] Valancourt's fallibility consists of his having let himself be tempted by the vices of parties and gambling in Paris, which led him into debt and a spell in prison (*MU*, pp. 612–13).

father and her fatherlike lover, becomes divisive and threatening as Emily
develops. [. . .] Montoni is the human version of the sublimity of the
mountains, whose impenetrability reveals to Emily her lack of power over
her own fate and keeps her in the dark.[32]

For Elsa, unlike Emily, there is no Montoni-like Gothic villain; it can be
argued, however, that that role is played by the mermaid anxiety. The mermaid
which Elsa fears she may in some sense be is as impenetrable sexually (the
tail replacing female human genitals) as it is psychologically: her attempts to
reach a deeper understanding of herself through hypnotism only serve to
complicate matters further with the introduction of different characters,
temporal and spatial settings, and stories, posing a whole series of new
questions for every old one they partially elucidate. The mermaid anxiety also
emblematizes Elsa's lack of power over her own fate; she has no conscious
control over her dreams, trances, nor, surely, over her 'no soy un monstruo'
outburst to Agustín; she claims and seems to believe genuinely that the whole
direction her life is taking is beyond her control too and is bewildered by the
many ways in which fate seems to keep intervening, 'dejándose sorprender
por las huellas de un destino que parecía dedicado a ella. Eran signos cargados
de significado que la asaltaban inesperadamente y que ella iba guardando' (SS,
p. 139) [letting herself be surprised by destiny's footprints, a destiny that
seemed dedicated to her. They were signs laden with meaning that would
assail her without warning and which she would store up].[33]

In Andersen's tale, the little mermaid tries to take control of her life and
transcend the limitations of her condition as a mermaid, but her success is
partial at best: she fails to win the love of the prince and will have to work for
three hundred years to acquire the immortal soul she also wanted;
nevertheless, she does enjoy the prince's company for a limited period on
earth and in the devout frame of reference in which the story situates itself,
the hope of eventual immortality has to be read positively. Elsa too has made
some attempt to take control: she has arranged to be able to take up residence
in the Alpujarras and has established a line of communication with Agustín
which is enough to nurture her love for him during a limited period. When
that period comes to an end – as surely as it does when day dawns following
the prince's wedding in 'The Little Mermaid' – she chooses a death which is
consonant with her sensibility. Andersen's protagonist returns to the sea,
identified with her father's undersea kingdom (the mother is long dead)
before her posthumous elevation to the air by a benevolent father-God, thus
thwarting the evil mother-figure of the witch. Elsa, having been let down by
Agustín as decisively as the mermaid by the prince, also chooses a death

---

[32] *The Rise of the Gothic Novel*, p. 119.
[33] María dismisses Elsa's convictions (SS, pp. 144–5) and the reader is likely to be
equally unconvinced, but the point is that Elsa really believes fate is directing her life.

which can be read as an enfolding in a paternal embrace, since her suicide in the mountain snows has a gendered significance, according to Kilgour's above-quoted reading of Radcliffe in the light of Burke. Elsa too is posthumously relocated as God intervenes via the well-meant offices of Matilde, a far more ambiguous witch and mother-figure than Andersen's.[34] As Matilde donates her niche in the cemetery, she enables Elsa to have a Christian burial and thus the hope of eternal life in heaven and yet, like María, the reader is likely to feel she has been cheated of the final resting-place she chose: 'Me arrepentí de no haberla dejado allá arriba, en las cumbres nevadas, en aquella hermosa tumba que ella misma había elegido' (SS, p. 167) [I regretted not having left her up there, on the snow-covered summits, in that beautiful tomb that she had chosen herself]. This can be compared with the ending of Andersen's story, which feels frustrating too, almost as though one were being told to be pleased about something that actually does not satisfy as much as the marine resting-place would have and where the mermaid herself thought she belonged. The reason in Silencio is not only attributable to the tradition of respecting the last wishes of the dead, but there is also an element of claustrophobia in the closed niche relative to the openness of the snowy peaks. María experiences 'angustia irresistible' [intolerable anguish] when she thinks about 'Elsa encerrada en aquel aseado agujero' (both SS, p. 167) [Elsa shut into that clean hole], even though by normal social standards her body has been treated entirely decently, indeed generously.

This brings us back to the ending of The Mysteries of Udolpho, when Emily is due to live happily ever after with Valancourt in the paternal home of La Vallée. Kilgour argues that Gothic novels often have unsatisfactory endings and also that they 'enable [. . .] us to see that the home is a prison, in which the helpless female is at the mercy of ominous patriarchal authorities.'[35] Thus, the endings of 'The Little Mermaid' and El silencio de

---

[34] According to Modleski (1984), 'Real mothers are often conspicuously absent in [. . . Gothic] literature by women [. . .] but [. . .] one encounters no lack of mother substitutes. [. . .] This substitution, one might speculate, provides a means by which ambivalence towards the mother can be worked through while it simultaneously prevents the mother/daughter relationship from being confronted too openly' (Loving, p. 68). Indeed, Emily's mother dies in the opening pages of Udolpho and her insensitive aunt takes over her care after the father's death. In Silencio, Elsa's parents are both dead too. The little mermaid chooses to turn to the evil witch, having rejected the advice of her grandmother and elder sisters. In García Morales generally, it is true that mother–daughter relationships are a rarity, with that between Laura and her daughter in Las mujeres de Héctor barely developed and that of Adriana in El Sur and the two sisters in La señorita Medina providing definitely negative portrayals. Thompson uses the Great Mother archetype in Silencio as a central plank of her argument, but this is quite problematic in places, as we have seen.

[35] The Rise of the Gothic Novel, p. 8 (unsatisfactory endings); p. 9 (quotation; Kilgour's italics). DeLamotte (1990) makes similar points; see Perils of the Night, pp. 132 (disappointing endings); pp. 157 and 178 (Gothic fiction presenting escape from imprisonment as a metaphor for women's domestic entrapment).

las sirenas broadcast the same message as Radcliffe's, albeit in different guises: swaddled in the paternal home by a paternal husband, Emily finds happiness; but is the little mermaid's sentence to three hundred years' hard labour under a paternal God's surveillance or Elsa's fate, wrapped in a winding-sheet in that 'aseado agujero' [clean hole] presided over by an institution as patriarchal as the Roman Catholic Church, so very far removed in essence? In all three, patriarchal control of the female protagonist emerges victorious, claustrophobic enclosure – psychological, physical, or both – is shown to be a woman's lot, and the sublime expanses of mountain scenery give her no more than a tantalizing and short-lived taste for a boundlessness that is incompatible with attractive – which is to say, non-monstrous – femininity.

3

La lógica del vampiro (1990) and Bram Stoker, *Dracula* (1897): Vampirism

This chapter will propose a reading of *La lógica del vampiro* [The Logic of the Vampire] predicated upon an exploration of the vampire motif which the author's choice of title spotlights. In keeping with some – but not all – of her fiction,[1] this title highlights a disjunction between the main storyline and the underlying subject matter of the text, the former being ostensibly about the first-person narrator, Elvira's search for her missing brother, Diego, culminating in the confirmation of her worst fears, that he is dead, having probably committed suicide. The setting is in and near Seville, the protagonist's home town, to which she has returned from her present base in Madrid, having received a telegram from Diego's friend, Pablo, reporting her brother's death. On arrival, however, she meets others from his social circle who allege Pablo's unreliability and melodramatic character and seem to be unconcerned for Diego's safety; they assume he is fine and staying in the country house of one of them, Alfonso. The plotting carefully makes plausible the protagonist's inability to confirm either version of events for the bulk of the novel, by adopting a slow pace and detailing all the circumstances (the house is off the beaten track, impossible for a taxi driver to find, for example, making Elvira dependent on Alfonso to give her lifts there only when he is available) that thwart the protagonist's attempts to track her brother down. It also adds to these a characterization of Diego and his relationship with his sister that allow the reader to accept both that he might disappear for some time without contacting anyone and that his sister would not necessarily know if he had been going through problems serious enough to make him suicidal. When Diego is finally found dead, his ex-girlfriend, Mara and Alfonso are with the protagonist and behave completely credibly, seeming shocked and horrified themselves and trying to offer moral support to his sister.

However, this plot summary does not convey what the novel is really about. In fact, as the title seems to corroborate, the apparent mystery of the disappearance of Diego is little more than a premise enabling the author to

---

[1] *El Sur* and *El silencio de las sirenas* are examples of the author's use of oblique titles, whereas *Bene* and *Nasmiya* are straightforward, referring as they do to the key character of each text.

pursue a different and far more Gothic agenda: the possibility that Alfonso is in some sense a vampire and preying on those around him, including his wife, Teresa, the afore-mentioned Mara, who rooms in the same boarding house as Diego, where his sister is now staying too, a younger woman called Sonia who has actually moved in with Alfonso and Teresa, and Elvira herself is also at risk of being drawn in. Pablo, the friend who sent the telegram to Madrid, has managed to escape from Alfonso's clutches, but at some considerable personal cost it seems, and Diego's suicide, it is implied, may have been motivated by desperation to emancipate himself from Alfonso.

The Gothic motif of the vampire can be considered from many angles, three of which will shed light on how García Morales's novel might be understood: first, antique folk legends, beliefs, and superstitions (mainly originating in eastern Europe, but with analogues and migrations worldwide); second, literary and cinematic representations of the vampire which are dominated by Bram Stoker's *Dracula*;[2] and third, present-day self-confessed vampires of different types ranging from those who feel they need to drink human blood for their health and strength (and do so), via those who draw and drink blood for sexual pleasure, to the so-called psi-vamps, who claim to need to draw energy and life-force from others.[3] These three facets of vampirism are tightly enmeshed of course: (i) vampire narratives in literature and film draw on the legends and the folklore; (ii) modern-day vampires draw on both, such that it can be difficult to distinguish cause from effect. It is impossible to be sure, for example, of the extent to which a modern-day blood-drinking vampire who finds daylight painful is modelling him- or herself on portrayals of vampires in fiction or, on the other hand, the legends from which these fictions have arisen reflect a rare but pre-existing human type of which such a person is a contemporary example; (iii) or perhaps a third possibility is that a complex two-way process is at work here.[4]

At first sight this might appear to be of only peripheral interest to the reader of *La lógica del vampiro* as Alfonso is never associated with biting or drinking blood; he does not seem able to shape-shift and appears quite at ease

---

[2] A critique of this domination is to be found in William Hughes, 'Fictional Vampires in the Nineteenth and Twentieth Centuries', in Punter (ed.), pp. 143–54 (see especially pp. 143–4).

[3] Much bibliography could be cited here, but on East European folklore vampires, see for example, Felix Oinas, 'East European Vampires', in *The Vampire: A Casebook* (ed.) Alan Dundes (London & Madison: University of Wisconsin Press, 1998), pp. 47–56. On vampire fiction, including Stoker's novel, see Markman Ellis, *The History of Gothic Fiction* (Edinburgh: Edinburgh University Press, 2000), pp. 183 &ff. On vampire films, see Gabriel Ronay, *The Dracula Myth* (London: W. H. Allen, 1972), pp. 164 &ff. For modern-day real-life vampires, see Tony Thorne, *Children of the Night: of Vampires and Vampirism* (London: Indigo, 1999), pp. 160 &ff.

[4] Alan Dundes, 'Introduction', in *The Vampire: A Casebook* (London & Madison: University of Wisconsin Press, 1998), p. viii.

in daylight; nor are any of the other familiar accoutrements of the vampire story present: no mentions of garlic, no graveyards, no bats, no stakes, no Communion wafers. What then is left? Pablo is the first internal character to make the vampire connection explicit: 'se alimenta. [. . .] Es su único fin. [. . .] Desde luego no es uno de esos vampiros que beben sangre. Él bebe de la raíz misma de la vida, absorbe de ella hasta secarte por completo' ['He feeds. [. . .] It is his only objective. [. . .] He's not, of course, one of those vampires that drink blood. He drinks from the very root of life, absorbs from it until he has drained you dry].[5]

The central allegation, then, is that he feeds off others' life-force, sapping them of their energy, but there are other features that strike chords with vampires of folklore, literature, and celluloid at least: vampires are generally thought of as revenants[6] and even though this idea is not highlighted, a point is made of Alfonso's unwillingness to talk about his past or his family background, leaving this possibility tantalizingly open. Mara tells the narrator that 'apenas sabía nada de su pasado, pues Alfonso no acostumbraba hablar de sí mismo. Si alguien le dirigía alguna pregunta que pudiera resultarle personal, él la eludía abiertamente' (*LV*, p. 35) [she knew hardly anything of his past, since Alfonso was not in the habit of talking about himself. If someone asked him a question which could be taken as personal, he openly evaded it].[7] Other suggestive remarks are unobtrusively slipped in too. For example, when he turns off his 'power', the narrator describes his changed way of looking at her as 'la mirada paradójicamente viva de un muerto' (*LV*, p. 34) [the paradoxically living gaze of a dead man].

---

[5] Adelaida García Morales, *La lógica del vampiro*, 3rd edn (Barcelona: Anagrama, 2002), p. 71. Future references will relate to this edition and be given parenthetically in the text.

[6] Eastern European legend distinguishes between living and dead vampires, but the former are more like what a lay-person would tend to call witches and I would argue that in the popular imagination, away from expert folklorists and dominated instead by Stoker's novel and film versions thereof, the vampire exists more or less exclusively as someone who has risen from the grave.

[7] Jo Labanyi interprets the fact that vampires have no mirror image or shadow as implying that they have no memory ('History and Hauntology: or, What Does One Do with the Ghosts of the Past? Reflections on Spanish Film and Fiction of the Post-Franco Period', in *Disremembering the Dictatorship: The Politics of Memory in the Spanish Transition to Democracy* (ed.) Joan Ramón Resina (Amsterdam: Rodopi, 2000), pp. 65–82 (p. 75)). This fits well enough with Alfonso's portrayal here but is problematic with regard to vampires generally. Count Dracula keeps Harker up all night talking about Transylvanian history in vivid detail (*D*, pp. 38–41), for example. Therefore, it would seem safer to regard Alfonso's reticence as an unwillingness to disclose his own past, not an inability to recollect it (as an archivist, his job is, after all, to be skilled at preserving the past in good order). The lack of a shadow or reflection seems to have more to do with the vampire's lack of a soul than of a memory.

Another traditional feature emerges when Pablo refers to Alfonso's cruelty
(*LV*, p. 69)[8] and particularly suggestive, he alludes to the way in which he
subjugates his victims thus: 'Siempre consigue retirarte el mismísimo suelo
que estás pisando. Te deja suspendido en el vacío, encerrado en un hueco
insoportable que, de alguna manera, le pertenece. Te detiene en el tiempo. Te
archiva para él' (*LV*, p. 70) ['He always manages to pull the very ground out
from under your feet. He leaves you hanging in the void, imprisoned in an
unbearable hollow space which, somehow or other, belongs to him. He files
you away for himself.'] In other words, Alfonso seeks power and control over
others to the extent that they are reduced to resembling the inanimate
documents he orders for a living (he is an archivist). Cruelty and the desire to
control and dominate others are complemented by another cornerstone of
vampire theory, that is, its sexual connotations: 'by forcing the woman to
submit to his will, Dracula symbolically rapes her'.[9] Indeed, García Morales's
narrator experiences Alfonso's treatment of her as seductive and there is
perceptible jealousy of a type at least similar to the sexual variety coming
from other female acolytes – chiefly Mara – when he turns his attention
to her.[10]

First, it is worth considering how well founded these accusations and
suggestions are, so as to be able then to focus on the key questions of power
and sexuality in connection with the portrayal of Alfonso and his social circle.
From there it will be possible to reach a conclusion as to what the vampire
concept contributes to the meaning of the novel as a whole. Does the text,
then, provide evidence of Pablo's claim that Alfonso feeds off others' life-
force? Here is an extract from the narrator's first meeting with Alfonso, when
he looks at her twice, as they shake hands initially and then when they say
goodbye. The first look gives a feeling of euphoria:

> Su mirada me sobrecogió. [. . .] Me sentí admirada y amada, me percibí a
> mí misma, a través de sus ojos inmóviles y fijos en los míos, como un ser
> maravilloso, como nunca había sospechado que yo pudiera parecer ante
> alguien. No me extrañó ni el ligero temblor de mi pulso, ni la brusquedad
> de los latidos de mi corazón, ni tampoco aquella leve asfixia que me

---

[8] Reed asserts that Stoker's Dracula stands out from other demon-lovers because he
'destroys women randomly without any discernible motivation behind his cruelty
whatsoever, aside from his need for blood' (*The Demon-Lover*, p. 108).

[9] Reed, *The Demon-Lover*, p. 62.

[10] Mara displays 'una actitud de indiferencia y desapego' [an attitude of indifference
and detachment] towards the narrator (*LV*, p. 52), but her motivation for doing so is unclear
to the latter. We are unsure too whether to attribute it simply to her character, or to some
sense of guilt for having ended the relationship with Diego and perhaps in so doing, driven
him to despair, or else to jealousy over Alfonso's interest in the narrator. As the novel
progresses, however, the last hypothesis gains in credibility, even though the others
probably remain co-existent with it.

sobrevino, como si mi pecho se encontrara ligeramente oprimido en el interior de una coraza invisible.   (*LV*, pp. 32–3)[11]

The second look, although icy, remains predatory: 'su concentración en mis ojos era absoluta y supe que hacía algo más que mirarme. Sentí, de súbito, la necesidad de defenderme' (*LV*, p. 34) [His concentration on my eyes was total and I realised that he was doing more than looking at me. Suddenly, I felt the need to defend myself]. That night, she is haunted by the memory of the two looks, the second of which she now characterizes as inhuman (*LV*, p. 36). Later in the novel, Alfonso's gaze is experienced as equally threatening: 'Hundió su mirada en la mía [. . .]. Fue como si un tigre me descubriera en mi escondite' (*LV*, p. 61) [He sank his gaze into mine. . . . It was as if a tiger had discovered me in my hiding-place], the tiger image alluding to the predatory element in the look and the choice of the verb implying that his gaze is a lethal (and phallic) weapon like a dagger or indeed, a sharp pair of canines.

The next time the narrator is on the receiving end of one of Alfonso's looks, she is even more explicit about what seems to be happening:

> Fijó sus ojos en los míos y su mirada despertó en mí una euforia repentina, era como un alumbramiento interior, como una suerte de amor tal vez, pero que inmediatamente desaparecía, haciéndome sentir que era absorbido por él al ritmo de su respiración. Era como si respirara de mí, como si me arrebatara lo que él mismo me había provocado.   (*LV*, pp. 92–3)[12]

It seems unnecessary to labour the point further: García Morales is clearly portraying what has been called a psychic Vampire, defined as those who 'practise deliberately or unwittingly a parasitism on the energy or will of others'.[13]

Secondly, does the novel provide evidence that this predatory behaviour saps the strength and drains the will of Alfonso's victims? The answer is that it certainly does and, indeed, emphasizes the point. Sonia is described thus: 'Unas profundas ojeras señalaban en su rostro [. . .] un cansancio y un sufrimiento impropios de su edad' (*LV*, p. 39) [Deep bags under her eyes marked her face [. . .] with fatigue and suffering inappropriate to her age].

---

[11] [His gaze overwhelmed me. [. . .] I felt admired and loved, I perceived myself through his eyes, motionless and staring into mine, as a wonderful being, as I had never suspected I could seem to anyone. I was not surprised by my somewhat shaky hands, nor the sudden pounding of my heart, nor even the slight breathlessness which overtook me, as if my chest were slightly compressed inside an invisible breastplate.]

[12] [He stared into my eyes and his gaze awakened a sudden euphoria in me, it was like being lit up from within, like a sort of love maybe, but one which immediately started disappearing, making me feel that I was absorbed by him in tempo with his breathing. It was as if he was breathing out of me, as if he had snatched back what he himself had provoked in me.]

[13] Thorne, *Children of the Night*, p. 216.

Diego was apparently 'siempre cansado' (LV, p. 54) [always tired]; the three
as yet unidentified youngsters socializing with Alfonso are described as 'sin
miradas, como si estuvieran aquejados de algún pesado sufrimiento' (LV,
p. 60) [without any gaze, as if they were laid low by some grave suffering]
and Teresa, Alfonso's wife, repeats the by now familiar pattern: 'Su aspecto
sugería sobre todo sus carencias: una vitalidad perdida [. . .]. Sus
movimientos eran lánguidos y, cuando hablaba, parecía hacerlo como si
hubiera tomado la deliberación de economizar palabras' (LV, p. 61) [Her look
suggested above all what it lacked: lost vitality [. . .]. Her movements were
languid and, when she spoke, she seemed to do so as if she had resolved to be
economical with her words].

Thirdly and notwithstanding the idea contained in the quotation from
Thorne above that a psychic vampire may drain others unwittingly, it is worth
noting that in Alfonso's case, he seems to be aware and in complete control
of his power. This in turn contributes to the cruelty feature of the vampire
type, so that when the narrator pleads with him to leave her alone, he is able
to switch it off just like that: 'supe que me había abandonado' (LV, p. 178) [I
realized that he had deserted me]. The narrator's choice of abandonar here
underlines well her ambivalence: even more explicitly perhaps than in a
traditional vampire narrative, the sexual attraction for the vampire felt by his
victims at the same time as fear and revulsion, is emphasized by García
Morales from the outset.[14]

Underpinning and framing the vampiric plot motifs in this novel are its
Gothic setting and atmosphere. Even though the clichéd locations –
graveyards, crypts, Transylvania and so on – are not introduced, the author
cleverly renders the more mundane cityscape of modern-day Seville equally
eerie and claustrophobic. Shadows and penumbra are utilized effectively:[15]
darkened indoor rooms, from the 'salón umbrío' [shadowy sitting-room] of
the boarding-house, for example (LV, p. 24), to the spine-chilling scene in
Alfonso's flat where 'había una sola lámpara encendida' [just one lamp was
lit] and the objects in the room 'se diluían en la penumbra' [were blurry in the
penumbra], leaving the narrator, sitting next to Alfonso 'visualiz[ando]

---

[14] An even clearer expression of this appears earlier in the novel when Elvira describes
herself as 'imbuida por una fuerte atracción hacia él y a la vez por una inexorable
repulsión' (LV, p. 80) [imbued with a strong attraction towards him and at the same time
by inexorable repulsion]. Likewize, on p. 159 we find: 'tal vez, pese al temor que me
infundía, una inconfesable fascinación me retuviera a su lado' [perhaps, despite the fear he
instilled in me, an unconfessable fascination kept me at his side.]

[15] Botting reads shadows in Gothic works as more than merely atmospheric: 'They
marked the limits necessary to the constitution of an enlightened world and delineated the
limitations of neoclassical perceptions. Darkness, metaphorically, threatened the light of
reason [. . .]. Gloom cast perceptions of formal order and unified design into obscurity; its
uncertainty generated both a sense of mystery and passions and emotions alien to reason'
(Gothic, p. 32).

involuntariamente su mirada excepcional' (*LV*, pp. 129–30) [involuntarily visualizing his exceptional gaze]; to the streets – 'calles angostas, irregulares y umbrías' (*LV*, p. 100) [narrow, winding, and shadowy streets] – and the shivery sensations experienced by the narrator, explained away rationally by her to herself, as ever: 'yo sentía que un frío húmedo me penetraba, tal vez estuviera destemplada después del viaje nocturno' (*LV*, p. 29) [I could feel damp cold penetrating me, perhaps I was under the weather after the overnight journey]. Nightmares and intuition complete the Gothic picture. The narrator dreams of a sense of being 'inmersa en una negrura sin forma precisa' filled with 'fragmentos de ranas, de sapos, de lagartijos' [immersed in a blackness devoid of any clear shape [filled with] bits of frogs, toads, lizards] and displays the classic symptom of pressure on the body associated with incubus/succubus phenomena as she wakens, her 'cuerpo casi paralizado por un peso insoportable' (all *LV*, pp. 87–8) [body almost paralysed by an unbearable weight].[16]

Taken together, the vampire motifs in the plot and the other Gothic elements in the style and setting – both geographical and psychological – of the novel could have provided the raw material for an escapist, popular fiction fantasy, but García Morales ensures that this is not the result in *La lógica del vampiro*. One of the ways in which she avoids this is via a classic Gothic device: balancing the fantastic against an equal weight of plausibility, chiefly by means of dwelling on the narrator's own reluctance to accept a supernatural interpretation of what is happening around her and to her. Each time Elvira is tempted towards a paranormal interpretation of her experiences, she searches for a common-sense explanation instead. As we saw above, when she felt inexplicably shivery, she told herself it was the long journey that had lowered her resistance; when a presentiment later predicts that going back to look for Diego at Alfonso's country house will not bear fruit, she puts it down to plain pessimism (*LV*, p. 113). And near the end of the novel, when she boldly confronts Alfonso as explicitly as she can, saying, 'Creo que tienes una necesidad única y montruosa, sí, monstruosa' ['I believe you have a unique and monstrous need, monstrous, yes'], she is thinking as she says it, '¿Y si Alfonso fuera tan normal como trataba de aparentar?' (*LV*, p. 160) [And what if Alfonso were just as normal as he was trying to seem?]. Indeed, it would be possible to construct a textually defensible reading whereby Alfonso had no supernatural powers and the whole vampire theme would become a projection by the suggestible narrator of her own anxieties about her missing brother onto an ordinary man whose worst sin is his imperfect fidelity to his wife. Diego's apparent suicide also admits a social realist reading at the same time as the supernatural one. In his study of suicide in real life, Mark Williams (2001) observes that 'Predictors of suicide will all be elements that

---

[16] See for example, Wolstenholme, *Gothic (Re)Visions*, pp. 39–43 for a discussion of the relationship between nightmares and incubus/succubus phenomena.

decrease a person's sense of control over external and internal events.'[17] Such perceived loss of control could be understood here as arising from a clinical condition such as depression sparked by job and girlfriend loss (both the case for Diego) just as much as it could be the outcome of any sinister controlling powers of a paranormal kind attributable to Alfonso. However, the anti-supernatural reading would go against the grain of the text, a grain carved deeply into it first by the title and then by the array of Gothic features that make the vampiric proposition poetically convincing and all the more so because the narrative persists in trying to explain them away.[18]

How does this compare with the treatment of credulity in classic examples of Gothic fiction? Like Matthew Lewis's *The Monk* from the first wave of Gothic novels, Stoker's *Dracula* can be placed at one end of a spectrum, whereby the main characters are at first more than sceptical about the existence of the supernatural but they – and we – are forced to accept it when incontrovertible proof is laid before them. Other Gothic novels exploit their characters' waverings between credulity and incredulity at greater length and with more or less open endings; at the opposite extreme from Stoker's clear demand from his readers that disbelief be suspended and the supernatural accepted, Ann Radcliffe's *The Mysteries of Udolpho*, for example, dismantles each of the ghostly events recounted at a later point in the narrative.[19] García Morales opts for a middle and slippery position of undecidability in this novel, which has been acknowledged as a common Gothic strategy too: 'Gothic fictions generally play with and oscillate between the earthly laws of conventional reality and the possibilities of the supernatural [. . .] raising the possibility that the boundaries between these *may* have been crossed, at least psychologically, but also physically or both.'[20]

---

[17] *Suicide and Attempted Suicide: Understanding the Cry of Pain* (London: Penguin, 2001), p. 60.

[18] Gonzalo Navajas describes this as the 'unreliability of human reason and the impossibility of replacing that reason with legitimate alternatives', arguing that it is a feature that this novel has in common with Soledad Puértolas's *Queda la noche* and he concludes that 'the ontological uncertainty of many characters in contemporary fiction is still unresolved, but it is viewed from a more confident perspective in the fiction of the contemporary women writers in Spain.' See 'Intertextuality and the Reappropriation of History in Contemporary Spanish Fiction and Film', in *Intertextual Pursuits: Literary Mediations in Modern Spanish Narrative* (ed.) Jeanne P. Brownlow & John W. Kronik (Lewisburg: Bucknell UP, 1998), pp. 143–60 (p. 154).

[19] For example, Du Pont eventually explains why he pretended to be a ghost, convincing all in the castle that it was haunted and confirming pre-existing superstitions to this effect. See *MU*, p. 457–60. For a discussion of this device, known as the explained supernatural, see Kilgour, *The Rise of the Gothic Novel*, pp. 121–2.

[20] Jerrold E. Hogle, 'Introduction', in Hogle (ed.), pp. 2–3 (my italics). Scott Brewster convincingly links this hesitation over whether to accept the supernatural with the fear of madness, not only on the internal character's part, but especially on the reader's too: 'Reading Gothic, we compulsively interpret random signs, haunted by the

Once the vampiric elements of García Morales's third novel are established in their Gothic setting, what they contribute to the overall meaning of the novel then needs to be considered. Here it is necessary to return to two key features of scholarship on the subject – power and sexuality – since it is to be argued that they are the categories where the vampire construct can contribute most materially to an understanding of the dynamics of the relationships portrayed.

A brief survey of writings on the connections between power and vampirism yields the following results. Tony Thorne, writing about real-life vampires today reports that 'their crimes seem to be motivated by uncontrollable fantasies of dominance and a desire for power.'[21] Reed, subsuming Count Dracula into a larger category of demon-lovers convincingly argues that 'stories about demons who seduce women are about power and powerlessness.' She goes on to point out the way in which 'the demon-lover typically crushes his victim's will.' Elsewhere in her book, she elaborates further, highlighting the gender aspect of her argument: 'The demon-lover has recurred through the ages because it demonstrates the power of men as well as the powerlessness of women and serves as a warning to women who would assert themselves and exhibit their capacity for rational action.'[22] Of course, this categorization emphasizes only one aspect of the Dracula/male vampire figure – the heterosexual side, played out in Bram Stoker's novel via his attacks on Lucy Westenra and Mina Harker and (by implication) on the vampiresses residing in his castle – but as he is not averse to Jonathan Harker's blood either, the question is more complex and will be revisited below, when we turn to consider the sexual facet of the figure.

Power over others, men and women, is indeed central to Alfonso's portrayal too. Reduced at the explicit level to merely giving advice and offering support, the narrative invites an interpretation that sees this as the tip of an iceberg whose lethal potential lies in the far greater mass lurking out of sight. For example, consider how the dialogue in which he advises the narrator to move to Seville works. All the exchange actually contains is this:

> – Me temo que tu vida es extremadamente solitaria –dijo Alfonso.
> – No lo creas. Tengo amigos.
> – Pero eso no es suficiente.
> – ¿Suficiente? ¿Suficiente para qué?

possibility that we may be deluded, that we have not seen enough or have seen too much' ('Seeing Things: Gothic and the Madness of Interpretation', in Punter (ed.), pp. 281–92 (p. 291)). Modleski makes a similar point with reference to *The Mysteries of Udolpho*: 'One's own paranoid tendencies are somewhat intensified [. . .] since we are left with a strong sense that [. . .] everything is always a great deal more or a great deal less than it seems' (*Loving*, p. 63).

[21] *Children of the Night*, p. 160.

[22] *Demon-Lovers*, pp. 20, 104, and 98, respectively.

> – Para que no estés como estás.
> – Lo que dices es muy vago.
> – No, en absoluto. – Y, después de una pausa, añadió– : ¿Por qué no
>   te vienes a Sevilla? Seguro que aquí vivirías mejor.
> – No es nada fácil.
> – Si lo intentas puede que sí lo sea.
> – No sé . . . de momento no tengo intención de abandonar Madrid.
>   En realidad, ninguna otra ciudad me atrae especialmente.
> – Pues a mí sí me atrae la idea de que te vinieras a Sevilla.
> Sus palabras me [. . .] parecieron amenazantes y halagadoras a un
> tiempo. (*LV*, pp. 128–9)[23]

Nothing in Alfonso's actual words here seems threatening out of context. At
worst they are mildly flirtatious, at best, the genuine concern of a friend for
another's welfare, displaying the quaintly provincial belief that life is better
away from the metropolis. So what is the source of their ominous character?
The answer is twofold: first there is the setting: the room in semi-darkness, a
clock's single chime in the silence. Just as Count Dracula's words of welcome
to Jonathan Harker are friendly at face-value, but terrifying in their setting
of the castle in the wilderness, so Alfonso's words have an effect which
transcends their explicit meaning here.[24] Secondly, there is the narrator's fear
of Alfonso's effect on her by this stage, which causes her to receive his words
with the utmost mistrust. Just as Harker narrates his first meeting with the
Count after his fears have already been aroused by the attitudes of the
Transylvanians he has met on the way there, so García Morales places this
conversation at a point in the novel by when the narrator is already terrified
of the power Alfonso seems to have over her, so that the seemingly anodyne
suggestion that she should come and live in Seville seems like an imperative

---

[23] ['I'm afraid your life is extremely lonely', said Alfonso.
      'Don't you believe it. I've got friends.'
      'But that's not enough.'
      'Enough? Enough for what?'
      'Enough for you not to be in the state you're in.'
      'That's very vague, what you're saying.'
      'No, absolutely not.' And then, after a pause, he added: 'Why don't you
      move to Seville? You'd be sure to have a better life here.'
      'That's not so easy.'
      'If you try, it may be.'
      'I don't know . . . right now I have no intention of leaving Madrid. No
      other city really attracts me much.'
      'Well, the idea of you moving to Seville attracts me.'
      His words [. . .] struck me as both threatening and flattering at the same
      time.]

[24] 'Welcome to my house! Enter freely and of your own will!' Bram Stoker, *Dracula*,
Puffin Classics (London: Penguin, 1994), p. 21. Future references will relate to this edition
and be given parenthetically in the text.

she fears she may not be at liberty to resist.[25] Thus, the first-person mode of narration operates here in analogous fashion to the diary and epistolary form used by Stoker: it filters the reader's perception of the vampire through the fears of the narrator. However, the key difference between the two is that whereas Stoker ensures that the events of his novel corroborate his narrators' suspicions unequivocally and force the sceptics one after the other to jettison their attempts at rational explanation, García Morales denies her readers such satisfying closure. The novel ends without any conclusive proof of any paranormal elements: Alfonso may be a psi-vamp who has preyed on Teresa, Sonia, and Mara, driven Diego to suicide, and terrorized the minor characters (such as the women running the boarding-house) into silence; but equally, he may be nothing more than a philanderer who likes to dole out advice to others and whose generosity attracts no-hopers, including the depressive Diego and the neurotic Pablo. Most intriguing of all is the possibility that these two readings can and do co-exist, paradoxically seeming compatible.[26]

Thorne asserts that vampire beliefs 'have served to focus their societies' most profound anxieties'. These anxieties are inextricably bound up with sexuality, as he later explains: 'the sex of the victim and the mechanics of the sexual performance do not matter, only the Vampire's irresistibility and the act of consumption count.'[27] Juxtaposing these two ideas with the identification of the Vampire with evil,[28] it becomes apparent that the figure can be read as a personification of anxieties over an irresistible attraction to transgressive sex, that which occurs outside the safe confines of Christian marriage, that which is not primarily for the sanctified purposes of procreation, but driven by the physical and psychological needs and desires

---

[25] Among the factors that create the climate of apprehension prior to Harker's first encounter with Dracula, one might mention the innkeeper's wife begging him not to go to Castle Dracula and when he insists he must, her hanging a crucifix round his neck '"For your mother's sake"' (*D*, p. 7). Then his fellow stage-coach travellers intensify the suspense and the horses 'neigh and snort and plunge wildly' as Dracula's coach arrives to meet Harker (*D*, p. 13).

[26] It is worth noting that leaving aside the modern-sounding term *psi-vamp*, Jan L. Perkowski defined the classic vampire of Slav folklore as 'a being which derives sustenance from a victim, who is weakened by the experience', adding that 'the sustenance may be physical or emotional in nature' *Vampires of the Slavs* (Cambridge, MA: Slavica, 1976, p. 136) cited by Oinas in Dundes (ed.), p. 47 Punter also calls one of the 'oldest senses' of vampirism 'the power of the dead to draw off force from the living.' *Gothic Pathologies: the Text, the Body and the Law* (Basingstoke & London: Macmillan, 1998), p. 136.

[27] Thorne, *Children of the Night*, pp. 129 and 260, respectively.

[28] For the vampire as personification of evil, see for example Botting, *Gothic*, p. 149; Thorne, *Children of the Night*, p. 266; also Ronay: 'Vampires were believed to be endowed by the Devil with supernatural powers [and this . . .] justified the Church's crusade against them. Man was universally considered the battle ground between good and evil, and vampirism was conceived of as a clear-cut victory for evil.' (*The Dracula Myth*, p. 32).

of the adult individuals involved: the pleasures of domination and submission, thirst-quenching, the irreversible merging of two selves, and so on.[29]

In this context it is not surprising that the hold Alfonso is portrayed as having over those around him is articulated as sexual in essence, nor that this remains figuratively represented: we never see him engaging in sex with any of his 'victims', just as in the nineteenth century, 'vampire fiction permitted strait-laced Victorians a lightly disguised depiction of sex [. . .]; only the site of penetration is displaced above the waist.'[30] Furthermore, as with Stoker's novel, the homoerotic connotations are there but faint.[31] When Harker cuts himself shaving and Dracula's eyes blaze with desire, only the crucifix round Harker's neck protects him and the Count warns him about the dangers of the country (*D*, p. 35), which one later realizes is as much a reference to the vampiresses whom Harker will encounter in the castle as to his own desire for the man's blood. However, in England, with the whole population to choose from, Dracula selects two attractive women (Lucy and Mina) and seems to reject the advances of the madman Renfield. In analogous fashion, Alfonso's choice victims are principally female, it seems: Teresa, Mara, Sonia, and the narrator. But the possibility of male victims also remains tantalizing in the background: was Diego's desperation only due to losing Mara to Alfonso; is Felix's only about the same thing except with Sonia; and what led Pedro to reach the conclusion he did about Alfonso? Was it only through observation of his effect on women?

In conclusion, *La lógica del vampiro* taps strategically into vampire lore: not only does it utilize the atmospheric effects in a clever translation of them to modern-day Seville, it serves as a kind of shorthand for the reader to grasp a depth of understanding of the dynamics of the relationships in the novel that spares the author lengthy psychological analysis of her characters and enables her to use a sparse, almost laconic style. Indeed, she has said that this is what her use of language aims to achieve: 'Me gusta que el lenguaje sea muy preciso y que se manifieste ocultando, es decir, que tenga poder de convocar una realidad, pero que no esté en primer plano' [I like language to

---

[29] Botting alludes to the way in which 'fluid exchanges [that is, drinking or transfusing blood] present a perverse sexuality, unnatural in the way it exceeds fixed gender roles and heterosexual distinctions' (*Gothic*, p. 150). Hughes adds to this the way in which the vampire's indiscriminateness between male and female victims thus 'evad[es] the taboos that polarize heterosexuality and homosexuality' ('Fictional Vampires' in Punter (ed.), p. 145).

[30] Thorne, *Children of the Night*, p. 254.

[31] Hendershot points out that 'Jonathan's feminized position in Castle Dracula is further underlined through the Bluebeard intertext', whereby he is identified with Bluebeard's new wife, via the prohibition that he breaks to visit certain parts of the castle (*The Animal Within*, p. 27). This topos of the forbidden room will be analyzed further in Chapter 9 with respect to *Una historia perversa*. Glenn notes a link between the same story and *El Sur*; see 'Gothic Vision', p. 242.

be very precise and to reveal its meaning obliquely, that is to say, for it to have the power to conjure up a reality, but not one that is in the foreground.] Going on to express her appreciation of Lezama Lima's baroque language, she concludes that for herself, 'lo prefiero austero.'[32] [I prefer it to be austere.]

The vampire concept also raises questions about power and powerlessness inflected by gender. If Alfonso is in some sense a vampire, does that make the women affected by him – including Elvira – pure victims? Or should Stoker's disturbing caveat that a vampire only enters by invitation (and Harker only enters his castle of his own free will) be taken into account?[33] *Dracula* seems on the surface to be suggesting that the vampire's victims are impelled towards their fate by the Count's trickery and supernatural powers, making the women open windows to him in a trance that he has placed upon them and luring Harker into his lair by having created professional business for him to conduct there. On the other hand, the more disturbing idea that Dracula taps into his female victims' deepest drives and that the trance only frees them from the constraints of their Victorian values remains present.[34] The same ambivalence runs through the implications of the vampire motif for García Morales's novel. On the one hand, Elvira paints herself as powerless to resist Alfonso's advances and paralyzed by him into inaction in the search for her brother, an analogue to the trances placed upon Lucy and Mina. On the other hand, like them, the possibility that she is a willing participant at a less conscious level remains unsettlingly present in the reader's mind.[35] Widening the focus to a consideration of heterosexual relations generally, could the author be suggesting that women may prefer consciously to believe themselves the helpless victims of men, when they are actually collaborating

---

[32] Sánchez Arnosi interview.

[33] Van Helsing explains: '"He may not enter anywhere at the first, unless there be someone of the household who bid him to come"' (*D*, p. 328).

[34] In this reading, Stoker is working with ideas that were a central preoccupation of his time and another key Gothic theme, most famously explored in Stevenson's *The Strange Case of Dr Jekyll and Mr Hyde*, which will be analyzed in Chapter 7, with respect to *El accidente*. See Botting, *Gothic*, pp. 138–43 for a discussion of Stevenson's text and pp. 150–51 for his comparison with Stoker's novel.

[35] Ana Bundgård sees as a feature common to this author's first three published texts (*El Sur/Bene, El silencio de las sirenas,* and this one) the centrality of 'personajes misteriosos [. . .] dotados de un poder de seducción que raya en lo mágico [. . . que] transforman en víctimas [. . .] quienes se dejan arrastrar por el hechizo' [mysterious characters [. . .] endowed with a power of seduction that borders on the magical [. . . who] turn into victims [. . .] those who allow themselves to be dragged into the sorcery.] ('Adelaida García Morales: El silencio de las sirenas (1985)', in *La dulce mentira de la ficción: ensayos sobre narrativa española actual* (Bonn: Romanistischer Verlag, 1995), pp. 15–30 (pp. 18–19)). The use of *dejarse* here [allow themselves] suggests some questioning of how complicit the 'victims' are, but this is not explored in the article.

in maintaining the status quo of gendered power relations, if only
unconsciously? Hendershot thinks so:

> The female subject's belief in the masterful male subject is perhaps more
> powerful than the male subject's belief. [. . .] Thus, paradoxically, feminine
> [authored] Gothic texts [. . .] find it *more* difficult to reveal a fragile mas-
> culinity than masculine [authored] Gothic texts [. . .] do. [. . .] Thus, from
> this perspective feminine desire may not be the subversive force many fem-
> inist critics have outlined it to be but may in fact work to reinforce views of
> masculinity as dominant.[36]

Furthermore, by not spelling out the implications of the vampire allegation
levelled at Alfonso, the reader fleshes them out independently and this
mirrors effectively what the narrator herself is doing: just as she wonders if
she is reading too much into her own feelings, we wonder how much credence
to give to the supernatural reading of the novel. Thus, the issues explored in
La lógica del vampiro – self-doubt, emotional predation, power,
powerlessness, insecurity, dependency, and the relationship between these
and sexual attraction – are vividly reflected in the reading experience itself,
explaining – at least in part – the potent effect of a deceptively light novel.

---

[36] *The Animal Within*, p. 204 (Hendershot's italics). For an opposing view, which sees
women as genuinely helpless victims, see Reed: 'The demon-lover typically crushes his
victim's will, annihilates her sense of self-preservation, and ultimately oppresses her
somehow' (*Demon-Lovers*, p. 104). Even she concedes, however, that among the recurrent
features found in the victims of demon-lovers is their 'willingness' to become one (p. 92).

4

Las mujeres de Héctor (1994) and Henry James, *The Turn of the Screw* (1898): Ghosts

Adelaida García Morales already had ghosts in mind when she wrote *El Sur, seguido de Bene*. In addition to the gypsy ghost of *Bene*, the author referred to the dead addressees as ghosts and went on to explain that 'de esta manera se hace presente, es algo que va más allá del recuerdo, es hacer que el personaje muerto casi vuelva a aparecer' [in this way the dead character makes himself or herself present, it's something that goes beyond recollection, it's making him or her almost re-appear.][1] However, that *casi* [almost] is significant and the removal of it marks a significant change in approach to be found in *Las mujeres de Héctor* [Héctor's Women]. Now she moves onto a different type of Gothic terrain, away from the treatment of the supernatural used hitherto whereby the reader was allowed a relatively free choice of whether to accept it at face value and suspend disbelief or to prefer a common-sense interpretation of events.[2] In this text the paranormal is not ultimately going to be rationally explicable. By reversing the Radcliffean approach of making the supernatural seemingly irrefutable in the first instance, and then eventually explaining it away in this novel, the author appears to be leaving open – indeed, encouraging – the possibility of a realist explanation for most of the novel and then she snatches that option away from the reader at the very end. In this respect, the novel conforms to Julia Briggs's definition of a ghost story (as opposed to a story that merely happens to contain one or more ghosts): 'The ghost story's "explanations" do not operate to rationalize or demystify the supernatural events, but rather to set them inside a kind of imaginative logic.' She goes on to observe that this logic is often based on revenge, glossed as 'the instinct to inflict upon others the pain we have received', which seems to fit the implied reasons for the central haunting of this narrative.[3]

---

[1] Sánchez Arnosi interview.

[2] Ordóñez describes this freedom of choice for the reader from a different perspective, as 'rhetorical ambiguity [whereby ghosts] evad[e] attempts to grasp at them and confine them as the either/or of reality or fantasy' (*Voices*, p. 175). She relates this illuminatingly to Todorov's notion of the fantastic, which obviously intersects with but is not co-extensive with, the Gothic.

[3] 'The Ghost Story', in Punter (ed.), pp. 122–31 (pp. 123 and 128, respectively).

The novel uses third-person omniscient narration to recount how Laura, ex-wife of the eponymous Héctor, accidentally kills a certain Delia, friend of his mistress, Margarita, when on the first page of the novel she hits out at her in a temper and repeatedly bangs her head against a wall. The rest of the text deals with the aftermath of this death as far as plot is concerned: the awkwardness of Delia's handbag inadvertently left in view, getting rid of the body, and then the police investigation, complicated by deliberate lies told by an immature admirer of Héctor called Irina. However, running under the surface of this *novela negra*, quasi-police-procedural feel are the developments in the personal relationships of the main characters as these are inflected by events and their Gothic presentation. From the point of view of this study, the most important aspects of these relate to haunting: Laura's increasing anxiety and sense of being haunted by the ghost of Delia, her possible protection by the benign ghost of Andrés, her former lover and Margarita's late husband, a normal variety of haunting of Margarita by memories of her dead husband, and also, what one could call haunting by the living: chiefly, Irina by her fantasies of Héctor. Until the last page of the novel it is possible to read all of this, including Delia's recurrent visitations, as both a symptom of, and a metaphor for, the haunted character's mental state. In the case of Laura, for example, she is wracked with guilt, traumatized by what she has done, and frightened of ending in prison, separated from her daughter. Similarly, psychologically plausible explanations can easily be found for Laura's dreams of Andrés, Margarita's haunting by the memory of him, and Irina's by fantasies of Héctor. However, on that last page of the novel, the hitherto reliable narrator gives Delia's ghost an unequivocal appearance at Laura's window late at night.

This forces us to question how we have understood the novel up to this point. As we shall see, if we have read with the grain of the text, we are likely to have understood Laura's fearful sensing of Delia's presence (and relief at Andrés's) as a mere device – albeit a most effective one – to evoke her (understandably) obsessive anxiety, nerves, and other post-traumatic stress reactions to the accidental killing, but having accepted the ghosts as residing purely inside Laura's imagination (though no less frightening for that), we are confronted nine lines from the end of the novel with a description that closes the door on such a reading. This is no longer a description of how she felt or what she believed she heard or saw; now we face the words: 'abrió los ojos y entonces la vio, vio a Delia'[4] [She opened her eyes and then she saw her, she saw Delia].

A similar paradox pervades Henry James's narrative, *The Turn of the Screw*, in which the reader is torn between one fact which makes a rational

---

[4] *Las mujeres de Héctor* (Barcelona: Anagrama, 1994), p. 153. Future references will relate to this edition and be given parenthetically in the text.

explanation based on the psychological disturbance of the narrator-protagonist impossible, on the one hand, and others which strongly suggest that she is giving a ghostly form to her own anxieties. The inassimilable element for a rational reading, whereby the ghosts are entirely the governess's hallucinations, is that never having seen Peter Quint, nor even knowing of his existence, she is able to describe his ghost in sufficient detail for the housekeeper, Mrs Grose, to identify him easily.[5] Her description is unusual, including, for example, red hair; but her employer had only referred vaguely to having parted with 'his own servants' for the sake of the children's welfare (*TS*, p. 120), without specifying how many or even whether they were male or female, let alone giving a physical description. The fact that his valet, the infamous Quint, was one of these servants only comes out later, following the governess's disclosure to Mrs Grose of what she has seen. At the time of the vision itself, she is not only ignorant of the fact that the master had left his valet at the house, but also that the man is now dead. Hence, she does not even know that what she has seen is a ghost when she tells Mrs Grose about it, believing instead that it is perhaps a sinister but living intruder. This is highlighted by the fact that she 'almost shriek[s]' when, having identified the apparition as Quint, Mrs Grose tells her that he is dead (*TS*, p. 147).[6]

Notwithstanding the enormous volume of criticism that has sought to give an unequivocal resolution, perhaps what makes James's text so disturbing is the fact that whichever end of the spectrum the reader prefers to tend towards – hallucinatory at one extreme, paranormal at the other – neither satisfies fully; indeed, it might be argued that it is the interpenetration of the two readings that produces a dynamic tension to which one can attribute a large part of the harrowing effect of the story. And be that as it may, whatever proportion of it may be wholly inside the narrator's head, this fluidity between self and other is at least as terrifying for the reader and as dangerous – for the governess and those around her – as any clear-cut reading of either an external ghoul or a psychiatric condition.[7]

---

[5] Henry James, *The Turn of the Screw and Other Stories* (ed., intro. and notes) T. J. Lustig (Oxford: OUP, 1998), pp. 113–236 (pp. 146–7). Future references will relate to this edition and be given parenthetically in the text.

[6] Lustig's Introduction to *TS* alludes to the popularity of a reading that sees the ghosts as the governess's hallucinations, but does not address the problem of this inassimilable element (p. xv). Edmund Wilson is one of the most famous champions of what Martha Banta calls 'the anti-ghost, pro-Freudian position', with Robert Heilman a good example of the 'pro-ghost' camp. Banta herself is closer to my own reading in emphasizing the effects of 'the story's duality of interpretations consciously imposed by its well-placed ambiguities,' but she still does not pick up on the implications of Quint's detailed description. See Martha Banta, *Henry James & the Occult: The Great Extension* (Bloomington & London: Indiana UP, 1972), p. 115.

[7] Ordóñez discusses James's text with reference to *Bene*. Her observations are that there 'as in *The Turn of the Screw*, unnamed sexual desire apparently transforms into fantasmal

Thus, the present chapter will explore this interplay between inside and outside: how does Adelaida García Morales balance the haunting by one's own memories, anxieties, and imagination against the presentation of the ghostly appearances of Delia (and maybe Andrés) as paranormal phenomena? What do the undecidable elements contribute to the effect? To what extent are we manipulated into preferring the realist reading right up to the denouement, thus maximizing the shock value of the ending? Finally, the fact that Delia's ghost, when it does finally appear on the last page of the novel is outside the window looking in at Laura, suggests that the contrast between interiority and exteriority is indeed material to an understanding of *Las mujeres de Héctor* just as much as it is in *The Turn of the Screw*, where the same image of a ghost (Peter Quint's) looking in at a window serves to raise the same questions in the reader's mind.

To begin, it is worth sketching in the backcloth of other hauntings upon which the central figure of Delia's haunting of Laura is projected. Margarita, who started her affair with Héctor only two months after being widowed (*MH*, p. 22) and first made love with him while Andrés was lying on his deathbed in the next room (*MH*, p. 58), is haunted by her husband in a non-supernatural fashion, to the point where she feels the need to get drunk:

> Margarita alcanzaba todas las tardes un perfecto estado de embriaguez gracias a las cervezas que bebía. De esa forma podía esconder ante sí misma una herida abierta, la herida que le había dejado la muerte de Andrés [. . .]. Se sentía observada por él desde todas sus fotografías distribuidas por la casa [. . .]. Entonces disipaba su aflicción bebiendo cerveza y esperando a Héctor [. . .]. Ante él todas las fotografías de su difunto esposo parecían cerrar los ojos.' (*MH*, p. 92)[8]

Despite the lack of a paranormal element here, the effect is serious enough for it to be a major factor leading her to end her relationship with Héctor: '– [. . .] Creo que estoy cansada de nuestra relación. Es algo sin futuro, distante. Yo sigo sintiéndome sola y, además, echo de menos a Andrés, cada vez más.

---

signs visible only to those for whom sexuality is still repressed in ignorance or irresolution (Angela, the governess)' (*Voices*, p. 185). She goes on to draw a parallel between the role of Elisa and that of the governess: 'Aunt Elisa attempts to grasp at meaning; her suspicions demand interpretation, a posture that can result only in suffocating, stifling, and killing the ambivalence before her' (p. 187). These most convincing points suggest that García Morales has picked up and developed ideas in *Las mujeres de Héctor* with which she was already experimenting earlier in her career, contributing to the cohesive character of her work.

[8] [Margarita reached a state of perfect inebriation every evening thanks to the beer she drank. In this way she could hide from herself the wound that Andrés's death had left [. . .]. She felt watched by him from all the photographs spread around the house [. . .]. Then she would dissipate her affliction drinking beer and waiting for Héctor [. . .]. In his presence all the photographs of her deceased husband seemed to close their eyes.]

Nunca podré olvidarle' (*MH*, p. 139) ['I think I am tired of our relationship. It has no future, it is too distant. I still feel lonely and moreover, I miss Andrés, more and more. I'll never be able to forget him.]

As well as this non-supernatural haunting by the dead, there is another non-supernatural variety in Irina's obsession with Héctor. This is the twenty-four-year-old daughter of his landlady, herself an old friend, but too busy to manage the letting. So it is that the lonely and bored young woman comes into contact with Héctor, is flattered by his kindness to her and from there, develops an obsession with him, which has the side-effect of tremendous resentment towards Margarita, leading to Irina's making a false statement to the police to try to incriminate her for Delia's death. Most significant for our purposes, however, is how Irina's obsession is portrayed as increasingly uncontrollable as it fills the void she considers her life to be:

> Irina pasaba la tarde intentando leer sin conseguirlo plenamente. De cuando en cuando cerraba los ojos impulsada por una imagen apremiante de Héc- tor que se le aparecía con insistencia. Todo cuanto no había podido suceder había entrado de lleno en sus fantasías eróticas, de tal modo que ahora se convertían en memoria en virtud de un extraño mecanismo, tejiendo así un pasado que sólo su imaginación había pergeñado y con el que le resultaba doloroso en extremo romper. (*MH*, p. 126)[9]

It is worth noting that even in this case where there is no suggestion of a supernatural element in Irina's experiences, the issue of interiority versus exteriority plays an important role since her obsessive fantasies invade her thoughts as if from the outside: the image 'se le aparecía' [appeared to her]. Thus, we can conclude these observations concerning the hauntings that provide the backcloth to the central, supernatural ones, that it is not the paranormal that poses the troubling question about where inside melts imperceptibly into outside, but is perhaps a feature of how the human psyche itself works, defending itself from what is problematic by disowning it as coming from without.[10]

[9] [Irina used to spend the afternoon trying to read without really succeeding. Every so often she would close her eyes driven by an overwhelming image of Héctor that would insistently appear to her. Everything that had not been able to happen had entered fully into her erotic fantasies, so that now they were turning into memories by virtue of a strange mechanism, thus weaving a past which only her imagination had fabricated and with which she found it extremely difficult to break.]

[10] We are reminded here of observations made by Williams on the subject of real-life suicidal depression, explaining that the external force of satanic possession was blamed historically for the condition and even in modern-day therapy it can apparently be helpful to consider depression as an external enemy of the individual suffering from it (see *Suicide*, p. 17). Julia Kristeva's notion of abjection is of course an important contribution to our understanding of this phenomenon.

It is in this context that we should consider the moments in *Las mujeres de Héctor* when we seem to have a choice of whether to interpret what we are reading as an internal psychological experience or an external paranormal incident. Then we shall explore how the author has made the psychological haunting the reading that goes with the grain of the text prior to the closing page.

The first occurrence that could conceivably be read as beyond normality takes place when Laura is about to dump Delia's body beside a road inside the Casa de Campo in the middle of the night:

> Estaba convencida de que en aquel lugar donde se había parado no había nadie, sin embargo se sentía vigilada y acusada. Incluso los árboles inmóviles y sumergidos en la oscuridad de la noche derramaban sobre ella un aliento amenazador, parecían dotados de ojos humanos y acusadores. Sus ramas inanimadas la atemorizaban, como si lentamente, en un movimiento imperceptible, se le fueran aproximando para atraparla y retenerla allí para siempre, junto a su víctima.   (*MH*, pp. 18–19)[11]

Here we recognize the familiar image of the malevolent, enchanted wood, animated in cinema classics such as Walt Disney's *Snow White and the Seven Dwarfs* (1937), where the frightening trees whose branches seem to have become fingers snatching at Snow White's clothes could just be sharp twigs moved by the wind as she blunders, panicking, into them and whose fierce eyes turn out to be those of friendly woodland animals when dawn breaks. The strategy of this scene, in other words, is the Radcliffean one known as the explained supernatural (although this is obviously not the case for the film's treatment of the rest of the magic in the story). In the enchanted forest though, as here in the Casa de Campo, the suggestion is that the character's understandable distress, heightened by darkness and bad weather, makes rationally explicable and harmless phenomena seem evil and supernatural. At the opposite end of the same spectrum, one could cite the modern Gothic classic, Stephen King's *The Shining* (1977), where the hedges in the haunted hotel garden, clipped into the shapes of animals, are represented as really coming to life when they creep malevolently up on three of the characters (Jack, the father; the young psychic child, Doc; and fellow-psychic adult, Hallorann), actually attacking Doc and Hallorann. Ironically, however, Jack tries to dismiss the evidence of his eyes and that of his son, by putting it down, first to his own state of nerves and then to what he feels more comfortable

---

[11] [She was convinced that there was nobody else in the place where she had stopped. Nevertheless, she felt under surveillance and accused. Even the motionless trees, submerged in the darkness of the night, spread over her a threatening breath; they seemed endowed with human eyes, accusing ones. Their inanimate branches frightened her, as if slowly, with imperceptible movements, they were coming closer to her, to trap her and hold her there forever, next to her victim.]

labelling as his son's trances and hallucinations. For his part, Doc fears he may be insane and in danger of being taken away to an asylum.[12] However, the internal characters' attempts to explain away the supernatural paradoxically confirm the reader's belief in it, bolstered by the authority of the narrative voice. Where to locate the scene in *Las mujeres de Héctor*, therefore, may only appear to be a matter of choice, for the fact that Laura does not dismiss her feelings, but instead 'sintió pánico' (*MH*, p. 19) [she panicked], tends to encourage the reader towards the Radcliffean/*Snow White* direction of putting it down to her own extreme nervousness at the time. This in turn gives us the satisfaction of a sense of superiority over the character: we can see this for what it is – a product of imagination – unlike her.

Immediately after this incident, Laura comes home to find mysterious, faint muddy footprints on the bedroom floor. Since she had initially hidden Delia's body under her bed and since mud has already become a source of anxiety for her as she tried to avoid any tell-tale signs of her trip to the Casa de Campo in the November rain, this appears inexplicable and eerie on first reading. However, 44 pages later (*MH*, p. 63), García Morales dismantles this in the Radcliffean manner; it is revealed that having let himself in on the rainy day of the killing while Laura was out, Héctor had seen Delia's handbag in the sitting-room and gone round all the rooms of the house looking for her. This type of device lends weight to a general feeling that is quietly gaining ground in the reader's mind, namely, that whatever seemingly uncanny incidents are described in the novel, there will come a rational explanation sooner or later.

The next contender for a supernatural reading appears at first sight to receive the same Radcliffean treatment. Laura sees a harrowing apparition of Delia as she sits up in bed unable to sleep in the small hours of the morning:

> Se fijó de súbito en el rostro de Delia, que parecía suspendido en el aire e iluminado por un rayo de intensa luz lunar. Veía con claridad su tez cetrina y sus ojos negros mirándola fijamente pero sin expresión, como si estuviera abstraída en algún secreto pensamiento. El cabello mojado enmarcaba su frente y sus mejillas. (*MH*, p. 38)[13]

---

[12] Stephen King, *The Shining*, New English Library (London: Hodder & Stoughton, 1978). References to the supernatural phenomena connected to the topiary animals are as follows: pp. 94–5 (Halloran warns Doc); pp. 226–30 (Jack experiences the topiary's threatening behaviour); p. 272 (Jack denies having seen anything untoward); pp. 316–23 (Doc is threatened, pursued, and attacked by the topiary animals but Jack tries to convince him it was a hallucination leading to injury from a fall); pp. 450–51, 458–60 (Halloran is attacked by the topiary lion until he manages to set it alight).

[13] [She suddenly noticed Delia's face, which seemed to hang in mid-air, illuminated by an intense moonbeam. She could clearly see her sallow complexion and her black eyes staring at her but expressionless, as if she were preoccupied by some secret thought. Her wet hair framed her forehead and cheeks.]

The next sentence reveals, however, that a moment later 'supo que soñaba que estaba despierta' [she realized that she was dreaming she was awake]. This proffers the attractive option of reading the event as a nightmare produced by the traumatized state of the dreamer, even though it also remains theoretically possible to regard it as a visitation by the spectre of Delia, her hair wet from the rain in the Casa de Campo, to Laura in her dreams. Since it is so plausible that in Laura's situation, anyone could be expected to suffer nightmares of this type, a supernatural interpretation carries little weight, on first reading of the novel, at least.

Haunting via dreams becomes an increasingly important motif as the novel progresses. Not only is Laura troubled by recurrent nightmares featuring Delia in revenant mode (*MH*, pp. 70, 100, 104), but she also dreams of Andrés, Margarita's late husband, with whom she had had a fleeting affair. He appears to serve a reassuring purpose as one dream is set in a now benign wood where he and Laura make love and in another he actually saves her from Delia's ghost (*MH*, pp. 64, 70). Laura's own reaction to these dreams is to think 'con tristeza que los muertos sólo volvían en los sueños' (*MH*, pp. 64–5) [sadly that the dead only return in dreams] and it is tempting to read them simply as a wholly believable defensive reaction of a woman who feels friendless and frightened. A further dream appears to give even more weight to the privileging of a psychological reading of Laura's experiences, as there are no possible ghosts in it and it cries out for a psychoanalytical interpretation. In this one, Laura is a tearful eight year-old and Delia appears in the guise of a broken doll she holds as she stands in an arid landscape (*MH*, p. 108).

As well as the recurrent dreams, Laura feels haunted in her waking moments too:

Le parecía que alguien la vigilaba desde dentro y desde fuera de la casa. [. . .] Una presencia invisible la acompañaba.   (*MH*, p. 80)

A veces le parecía que seguía viéndola [a Delia] al despertarse de madrugada, percibía su gélida presencia y tenía que encender la luz para disipar todas sus figuraciones. Una noche antes de retirarse a dormir, notó un movimiento casi imperceptible frente a ella [. . .]. ¿Habría algo real en la casa, sería verdadera la presencia invisible que ella intuía?   (*MH*, p. 100)

Por las noches, antes de irse a dormir, escuchaba sonidos que no podía identificar. [. . .] Sonaban en el aire, a su lado, en el espacio vacío del salón. (*MH*, p. 145)[14]

---

[14] [It seemed to her that someone was watching her from inside and outside the house. [. . .] An invisible presence was staying with her.] [. . .] [Sometimes it seemed to her that she could still see her [Delia] when she awoke in the early hours of the morning, she could perceive her chilly presence and she had to switch on the light to dissipate all her imaginings. One night, before she retired to bed, she noticed an almost imperceptible movement opposite her [. . .]. Might there be something real in the house, might the

By page 149, Laura appears to have come to believe in Delia's presence as a supernatural phenomenon, since she includes this in a list of her fears, the rest of which are perfectly rational: 'Laura se sabía presa del miedo, atenazada por el miedo a la cárcel, miedo a la presencia de Delia en su propia casa, miedo a lo que pudiera suceder a su hija si se separaban durante unos años' [Laura knew she was held prisoner by fear, held in the vice-like grip of fear of prison, fear of Delia's presence in her own house, fear of what might happen to her daughter if they were separated for some years]. However, the question remains as to whether the reader will follow Laura, or whether, on the contrary, we are more inclined to see her growing panic as a likely cause for losing her grip on reality and transforming an internal psychological haunting by Delia into an unfounded belief in the paranormal, perhaps influenced in this suggestible state by her friend Elisa.

The textual grounds for preferring to read some or all of these incidents – both dreaming and waking ones – as paranormal seem somewhat flimsy by the side of the psychological arguments outlined above, but are nevertheless important. Their presence becomes all the more so on re-reading the novel, when the shock of the rationally inexplicable apparition on the final page is defused because it is foreknown. They can be reduced to two. First there are Aurora's reactions, for she calls her mother and says she is frightened on two occasions (*MH*, pp. 100, 152), the first of which is just at the precise moment when Laura is experiencing the ghostly presence. Of course, it is possible on first reading to dismiss this as the child's sensitivity only to her mother's state of nerves. Indeed, Laura herself considers this possibility: '¿Estaría ella transmitiéndole su propia ansiedad?' (*MH*, p. 152) [Might she be transmitting her own anxiety to her?]. Furthermore, traditionally it is quite common in ghost stories for apparitions only to be visible to those who are the targets of the haunting, so one might say that the innocent child's ability or inability to perceive Delia's presence is immaterial anyway.[15] It remains true, though, that there is a possible corroboration of the ghostly presence in Aurora's fears.

---

invisible presence that she could sense be truly there?] [. . .] [At night, before going to bed, she would hear sounds that she could not identify. They were ringing in the air, next to her, in the empty space of the sitting-room.]

[15] Examples of narratives where a ghost is visible only to those it wishes to haunt include Henry James, 'Sir Edmund Orme' (1900), in *The Turn of the Screw & Other Stories*, pp. 1–35. On the other hand, M. R. James's classic ghost stories tend in the opposite direction, with ghosts afflicting unfortunate bystanders of one sort or another, who happen to waken them by unwittingly or rashly disturbing the past somehow. Just one example will suffice: in ' "Oh, Whistle, and I'll Come to You, My Lad" ' Professor Parkins wakens a ghost by trying out an ancient whistle he has found, the implication being that anyone who had blown on it would have suffered the same fate. See *The Ghost Stories of M. R. James* (London: Edward Arnold, 1931), pp. 120–50. García Morales has used both of these approaches in different texts: in *La tía Águeda*, only the eponymous character sees the ghost, whereas in *El secreto de Elisa*, a whole village can hear the moans and sighs of the ghosts in Elisa's house. Thus, we cannot posit one or the other position as habitually preferred by the author.

Secondly and more powerfully, there is the characterization of Elisa, Laura's confidante. This woman seems to have adopted an amalgam of eastern beliefs: she fasts and meditates in the oriental manner (*MH*, p. 41), for example. Despite her interest in the occult, though, she is not portrayed as a daft, if sympathetic friend; on the contrary, García Morales paints her in eminently sensible colours. She, for instance, thinks that Laura should simply tell the police the truth (*MH*, p. 77). Adding to the positive weighting of Elisa's portrayal is a striking humility. She leaves Laura after hearing her confession 'cabizbaja, sin saber qué añadir a sus palabras y convencida de que tendría que haber dicho algo más certero' (*MH*, p. 78) [her head bowed, not knowing what more she could have said and convinced that she should have said something more to the point]. As well as being kind and supportive, beautiful and happy, she is cultured and intelligent; she reacts with admirable common sense to Laura's growing panic and yet, she is the one who does not reject the supernatural out of hand. Elisa is a believer in it; she reads Laura's cards, for example, and it is she who raises the explicit possibility that the dreams may be visitations: '–Los muertos visitan a sus amigos en sueños [. . .]. Creo que es posible que Andrés quiera ayudarte' (*MH*, p. 76) ['The dead visit their friends in dreams. I think it's possible that Andrés wants to help you']. She goes on to suggest that Laura should try to say sorry to Delia when next she encounters her in her dreams (*MH*, p. 77), but this idea could be a wise piece of advice to calm and help bring peace of mind to her friend, just as much as an admission that she definitely believes Delia's ghost is visiting Laura in her dreams and could be placated by an apology. Either or both could be her intended meaning when she follows up this advice with '–Eso es algo que puede ayudarte' (*MH*, p. 77) ['That's something that may help you']. In general, her approach seems to come steeped in the wisdom of the east: 'Le decía a Laura que tenía que contemplar los acontecimientos de su vida con la distancia y la indiferencia de una espectadora. Para Elisa existía el destino, un destino que cada uno se había labrado en una vida anterior. Todo cuanto tenía que suceder, sucedería' (*MH*, p. 75) [She used to tell Laura that she must contemplate the events of her life with the detachment and indifference of a spectator. For Elisa, destiny existed, a destiny that each person had forged in a previous life. Everything that had to happen would happen]. Thus, she comes across as someone who is humble enough to be open-minded, unlike Laura who at first is a rather silly mixture of total scepticism as far as ghosts and Elisa's eastern beliefs are concerned (*MH*, p. 75), but total credulity for the Tarot cards: 'Laura creía firmemente en las cartas, aunque, después, la realidad fuera siempre diferente' (*MH*, pp. 41–2) [Laura firmly believed in the cards even though afterwards reality was always different]. The strongly favourable depiction of Elisa is surely the loudest signal in the novel that the text is inviting us not to dismiss the supernatural reading out of hand and reduce the ghosts of Delia and Andrés to the confines of Laura's tortured consciousness. Yet Elisa's refusal to reject this either suggests that an either/or approach is itself unwise.[16] Indeed, if we are to heed Elisa, as her portrayal seems to be encouraging us to do, perhaps we should not be scouring the text as if it were the detective novel that it sometimes resembles, in search of clues which will reveal a single truth about what is 'really' happening. On the contrary, maybe we should be opening our mind to the more disturbing idea that the boundary between interior and exterior is false: the spectral Delia and Andrés are not *either* inside *or* outside Laura's head, but in some different, nameless – unnameable? – space between, or perhaps astride, the two.

Here is where it becomes useful to compare García Morales's text with Henry James's and the critical response to it. *The Turn of the Screw* is narrated for the most part by a young governess[17] who takes a position looking after two orphans, Miles, aged ten and Flora, aged eight, in an isolated country house. Her only adult company is provided by Mrs Grose, the housekeeper, and her brief is not to consult her London-based employer, an uncle of the children who is prepared to pay for them, but does not care to be troubled by news of them (*TS*, p. 122). As with *Las mujeres de Héctor*, almost all of the ghostly apparitions can be read as symptoms of the psychological state of the governess, who is only twenty, impressionable, and overwhelmed by the magnitude of her responsibilities, by the celestial beauty of the children, by the spotless innocence she at first believes matches it and she has a duty to preserve, and by two puzzling and worrying facts: the unexplained expulsion of Miles from boarding-school and the untimely death of her predecessor, Miss Jessel.

It is easy, for example, to read her first encounter with the ghost of Miss Jessel, when she is convinced that Flora saw her too, but hid the fact from her, as the product of her overworked imagination. The tremendous weight of meaning she attaches to the quite possibly insignificant fact that Flora had fallen silent, turned her back on the apparition and seemed suddenly too absorbed in play (*TS*, p. 155), seems to demonstrate just how unreliable an interpreter of events she is; that Miss Jessel was seen to be dressed in black and very beautiful, but infamous-looking, is vague enough to chime with Mrs Grose's memories of her, seemingly corroborating the external truth of the

---

[16] Ordóñez reads 'the ambiguity of the phantasmal' as García Morales's 'strategy for textual and cultural transgression' in her earlier fiction (up to and including *El silencio de las sirenas*), arguing that this is her way of resisting the patriarchal (*Voices*, p. 174). This over-arching interpretation coordinates well with the reading proposed here, which, however, is considering her texts at a more micro-level as she exploits the effects of representing ghosts in the different ways familiar to readers of Gothic fiction.

[17] Her narrative is presented at two removes; an authorial voice tells of a friend called Douglas recounting the tale. Its authenticity rests on Douglas's personal acquaintance with the woman later in her life and the authorial voice's subsequent inheritance of her manuscript (see *TS*, pp. 115–19).

vision.[18] The further fact that Mrs Grose is a simple, illiterate woman, makes it perfectly plausible that she could be swept along by, and unwittingly fuel, the governess's convictions. Almost all of the supernatural phenomena and – to the governess – the suspicious behaviour of the children contained in *The Turn of the Screw* are susceptible to such an hallucinatory reading, though none the less harrowing for that, of course.

James puts his inassimilable element near the beginning of the story, though, in sharp contrast to García Morales's strategy of saving it until the end. What is the impact on the overall effect of the one or the other choice? One could venture that in both novels there is a strategic necessity for the protagonist to be unsettled, even traumatized at the beginning of the story, if the possibility of a hallucinatory reading is to stand up. For García Morales, this is accomplished by the accidental killing, whereas in James's case perhaps the natural apprehension at starting a new job, coupled with the letter from Miles's headmaster does not suffice as grounds to argue for the governess's extreme psychological vulnerability. Even when we add to this her young age and sheltered life to date, plus the emotional upheaval of having been swept off her feet by her employer's charm and panache, these factors alone might not have sufficed to render plausible the onset of ghostly hallucinations, particularly as the frame story alludes to her having been an excellent governess later in life. In other words, prima facie, she is not to be dismissed as a lifelong sufferer from mental illness.[19] There is all the more necessity, therefore, to subject her to a terrible shock at the outset. James also uses a shock ending – the death of Miles, seemingly from fright, either caused by Quint's ghost, successfully carrying the satanic child off to damnation at last, or from the totally innocent child's reaction to being imprisoned with – or maybe crushed to death by – a madwoman, or any number of combinations lying between these extremes. Thus, the ending sets the seal climactically on the undecidability of the narrative, for even if the recognition of Quint has led us to exclude a wholly hallucinatory reading of the governess's visions, the implications of this for the children – how good or evil, how knowing or innocent they might be – remains a separate and even more troubling aspect of the ambiguity of the plot.[20]

---

[18] Ned Lukacher points out that what the governess takes to be Mrs Grose's recognition of Miss Jessel as dressed in mourning could in fact be her registering surprise at a detail which does *not* fit with her memory of her. See ' "Hanging Fire": The Primal Scene of *The Turn of the Screw*', in *Henry James's Daisy Miller, The Turn of the Screw, and Other Tales* (ed.) Harold Bloom (New York, New Haven, & Philadelphia: Chelsea House, 1987), pp. 117–32 (p. 124).

[19] Muriel G. Shine presents a strong argument for reading the governess as 'a notable, if heightened, portrait of an adolescent'. See *The Fictional Children of Henry James* (Chapel Hill: University of North Carolina Press, 1969), p. 132.

[20] Shine is surely right to separate the issue of the children's character from that of how deluded or sane the governess is. In other words, even if we read the governess as right to believe in her ghostly visions as external to herself, that does not mean she is right to

Las mujeres de Héctor places the shock death at the beginning and the inassimilable ghostly apparition at the end – an exact reversal of James, but an equally effective one, indeed a mirror image of it. This observation leads to the question of reflections, the utilization of glass in both texts, and how these emblematize the issue of whether the protagonist of each is looking outside herself at the ghosts, as if her eyes were a transparent medium such as plate glass, or whether, instead, the glass is metaphorically silvered, and what she is seeing is a reflection from within.[21] Critics of *The Turn of the Screw* such as Lustig have noted the importance of the 'proliferation of references to windows and glass' in connection with the governess's 'attempts to control the frontier between the inside and the outside' in that text.[22] Banta, for her part, notes the doubling and mirroring effects in the cast-list of James's story. She is worth quoting at some length:

> In 'The Turn of the Screw' the wholeness of relationship pivots around the governess's duplication of her inner fears by the outer figures she confronts. Unadmitted to herself, the governess's infatuation for the absent uncle repeats itself symbolically before her eyes in the persons of Quint and Miles, Miss Jessel and Flora. The living children and the dead servants are, all four, *Doppelgänger* ghosts mirroring her own desires. [. . .]
>
> The absent uncle and the present Quint are the same 'type' (with little Miles in training to duplicate the master-mold), while the governess and Miss Jessel (and Flora in the just opening bud) have too much in common for comfort.[23]

These observations lead to similar questions for *Las mujeres de Héctor*: is there any sense in which Delia or Andrés could be read as *Doppelgänger* ghosts mirroring Laura's own desires? To answer this, we must first look at what information the text provides as to these characters. Delia is single and unattached (*MH*, pp. 17–18). She has many friends and a free and easy lifestyle which involves much going out and sometimes not coming home all night, with

---

believe that the children are implicated. As Shine points out: 'Whether Flora and Miles are evil or not, whether they actually see the ghosts and have formed an unholy alliance with them or not, depends entirely on the habit of mind and emotional make-up of the individual reader.' (*Fictional Children*, p. 138.)

[21] In James's turn-of-the century English, a glass was more commonly used to mean a mirror than in present-day usage; hence the resonance is louder than it might seem to a twenty-first-century reader. As far as Spanish is concerned, it is notable that the word used in the final climactic scene to describe the window-panes through which Laura sees Delia is *cristales*, which also has a possible meaning of 'mirror' (albeit archaic). However, Spanish also has the term *luna* for 'mirror' and it is therefore noticeable that the earlier apparition of Delia in Laura's bedroom when she discovers she was only dreaming she was awake is 'iluminado por un rayo de intensa luz lunar' (*MH*, p. 38) [illuminated by a bright moonbeam].

[22] *Henry James and the Ghostly* (Cambridge: CUP, 1994), pp. 133 and 131, respectively.

[23] Martha Banta *Henry James & the Occult* (1972), pp. 122–3.

the implication that she may be sexually promiscuous (*MH*, pp. 31 and 35–6).
This could hardly contrast more with the picture we receive of Laura:

> Era una mujer de cuarenta y cinco años, delgada y tímida. Caminaba por las
> calles con paso inseguro y por lo general, mirando al suelo, como si quisiera
> contar sus propios pasos. Desaparecía en las reuniones de amigos y conoci-
> dos en un silencio tenso y, a veces, parecía pedir perdón por su mera exis-
> tencia, como si ningún lugar de este mundo le perteneciera.   (*MH*, p. 24)[24]

One could almost assert that Delia, with her suggestively impersonal name
(it sounds like *de ella* [of her]) emblematizes what Laura at this stage of her
life is aspiring to achieve, so far with only limited success. This is
contentment with being single and general peace of mind, since following the
breakdown of her marriage she suffers from insomnia, a 'dolor y una opresión
en el pecho que la asfixiaban'; in short, 'una angustia y una ansiedad
imparables' peopled by a 'vorágine de pensamientos morbosos y amargos'
(*MH*, all p. 23) [pain and oppression in the chest that choked her, the worst
possible anxiety and anguish, peopled by a whirlwind of morbid, bitter
thoughts], from which she is only beginning to recover by the time of the
action of the novel. What a far cry from the 'persona tranquila, afable y
pacífica' [calm, affable, and peaceable person] that Delia apparently was
(*MH*, p. 36).

Moving on to consider what Andrés might represent for Laura, we can start
by noting a similar generic quality to his name, as it evokes *andros*, the Greek
for 'man, male'. He was an architect by training, like Héctor, but made more
money than he did (*MH*, p. 29). Héctor, by contrast, is notable for nagging his
ex-wife not to waste money by leaving lights on or overheating the house, and
is paying her insufficient alimony for her to employ a cleaner (*MH*, pp. 14,
15, and 37). Together with being a better breadwinner, Andrés's hobby,
collecting motor-cycles, has sexual overtones that further contribute to a
certain cliché of manliness.[25] There seems to be some regret on Laura's part
that she and Andrés stopped their affair after only twice making love,
probably arising from the bitter irony that they stopped seeing each other out

---

[24] [She was a shy, slim woman of forty-five. In the streets, she walked hesitantly and
usually looking at the ground, as if she wanted to count her own steps. At meetings of
friends and acquaintances she would disappear into a tense silence and sometimes she
seemed to be apologising for her own existence, as if she belonged nowhere in this world.]

[25] For more on the relationship between breadwinning and masculinity in Spain, see
Perriam *et al.*, *New History* (2000), p. 72. For a more general discussion of the issue, see
Drucilla Cornell, 'Fatherhood and its Discontents: Men, Patriarchy, and Freedom', in *Lost
Fathers: The Politics of Fatherlessness in America* (ed.) Cynthia R. Daniels (Basingstoke:
Macmillan, 1998), 183–202 (p. 190). Glenn refers to riding a motor-cycle as 'a vivid
representation of sexuality' with reference to the film adaptation of *El Sur* in which the father
of the narrator uses one (in the written text, he rides a bicycle). See 'Gothic Vision', 245.

of a sense of loyalty to their respective spouses, Héctor and Margarita. With Andrés now dead, moreover, the opportunity to resume their relationship has been cruelly precluded by fate, apart from the dream-visitations of course. Although the reader learns of the problems in Andrés's marriage to Margarita and her reasons for being dissatisfied with him as a husband,[26] it remains true that from Laura's perspective, he may have seemed to represent what she thought she wanted in a man; at all events, now that he is dead, we are clearly told that Laura 'necesitaba a Andrés' (*MH*, p. 65) [needed Andrés].

In the light of these observations, it would appear that Laura's experience of haunting does reflect her inner needs, fears, and desires. While Andrés's ghost serves the benign purpose of providing comfort to her in her dreams, this only intensifies her awareness that, once awake, she is alone; this ghost, in other words, perhaps personifies a fear that she is doomed never to find a man to replace and improve on Héctor. By contrast, Delia's frightening appearances, as we have seen, are not confined to Laura's dreams as she senses her presence even when awake, possibly representing her fear that any hope of being an independent, well-balanced woman is quite dead.

Before turning to analyse the final climactic scene of Delia's appearance, it is worth first considering the possible parallels in *The Turn of the Screw*, when Quint appears to the governess looking through a window at her. In James's narrative as in García Morales's, the scene behind the window occurs after the ghost has already been seen in a location that blurs the boundary between inside and outside; the governess's first sighting of Quint was when she was outside in the garden and he was standing on a tower of the house (*TS*, p. 136). Thus, he was *in* the open air, but *on* the building looking down at her from behind battlements, as if he commanded the inside and she were the interloper. This ambiguous space between interior and exterior could perhaps be considered analogous to the dream visitations of Delia to Laura's bedroom and the mysterious sounds and atmosphere that she senses inside her house prior to the climactic window scene. When Quint appears to the governess for the second time, he is looking through the dining-room window with 'his face [. . .] close to the glass'; however, she hastens to remove the separation, not, as we shall see, like Laura, by opening the window, but by rushing outdoors to meet him. However, by the time she gets there he has vanished (*TS*, p. 142) and her reaction is relief even if her initial motivation for running outdoors was presumably to challenge him.[27] Her next action is described as instinctive: 'I applied my face to the pane and looked, as he had looked, into the room'

---

[26] Clearly, the omniscient narrative voice knows more than Laura as far as Andrés is concerned, most notably that his hobby led him to neglect his wife and also that he was financially successful thanks to Margarita (*MH*, p. 29).

[27] At this point in the narrative she has not yet talked to Mrs Grose, so is unaware of who Quint is or that he is a ghost. Nevertheless, she had already noted at the first appearance that 'the scene had been stricken with death' (*TS*, p. 136) and on this second one he makes her 'turn cold' (*TS*, p. 142), so it is clear that she perceives him as some kind

(*TS*, p. 143). Now Mrs Grose comes in and is startled by the governess who is apparently 'as white as a sheet', which is to say ghostly-looking herself.

Turning now to the final apparition of Delia, she looks, as she has done in all earlier visitations, as she did when her body was found, muddy and with wet hair. This may seem to call attention only to the sensationalist effects of a ghost-story well told, but significantly, she pushes this hair off her face now, drawing attention to what is behind it: the enigmatic smile she wore in the first dream (*MH*, p. 70) has now turned into a malevolent one. This surely signals that her revenge is about to be played out, for when Laura opens the window, expecting that this will make her disappear, she does not, suggesting that Laura can no longer keep the ghost separate from her self, safely behind glass and bars to be observed like a specimen in a zoo, even if a terrifying one. In other words, a very similar play with inside and outside is to be found in both texts: a ghost behind glass which is undecidably transparent or mirrored, the haunted woman's attempt to remove it in a spirit of defiance, but the backfiring of this reaction as the ghost thus seems to be able to penetrate the self of the victim of the haunting all the more effectively. Indeed, Quint's next appearance in *The Turn of the Screw* will be inside the house, still next to a window, but now, more ominously, on the inside of the glass (*TS*, pp. 170–71).

And now, correspondingly, there is nothing to stop Delia from invading Laura's house – a commonplace symbol for the self [28] – for in seeking to put the ghost to flight, she has in fact given it free access and most haunting, most Gothic of all, the boundary between inside and outside, between self and other is obliterated with the closing words of the novel:

> Abrió los ojos y entonces la vio, vio a Delia por detrás de los cristales de la ventana, detrás de las rejas de hierro. Se levantó furiosa y aterrorizada a un tiempo y abrió la ventana para hacer desaparecer aquella alucinación. Pero al abrirla Delia le sonreía malignamente y se retiraba, con una mano muy pálida, el cabello mojado de su rostro. Laura, paralizada por el pánico, permaneció frente a ella, muy cerca. De haberlo intentado, pensó, habría podido tocarla.   (*MH*, p. 153)[29]

---

of indeterminate threat. Indeed, it is this second fright which prompts her to tell Mrs Grose of her experiences, leading to the identification discussed above.

[28] This notion of the house as self will be discussed further in Chapter 7, with reference to *El accidente*. The opening of the window to the ghost also strikes a chord with Stoker's *Dracula*, discussed in Chapter 3, when he gains access to his victims in this way. Thus, the imminent entry of Delia is strongly coloured as threatening by association.

[29] [She opened her eyes and then she saw her, she saw Delia on the other side of the window-panes, behind the iron bars. She stood up both furious and terrified and opened the window to make that hallucination disappear. But when she opened it, Delia smiled malevolently at her and pushed her wet hair off her face with a very pale hand. Laura, paralyzed with panic, stood there opposite her, very close. Had she tried to, she thought, she could have touched her.]

5

La tía Águeda (1995) and Horace Walpole, *The Castle of Otranto* (1764): Frightening Buildings

In this novel, Marta, a young girl who has recently lost her mother, is entrusted by her father to the care of the eponymous aunt (his elder sister) and in this unfamiliar small-town environment and disciplinary regime, the ten-year-old feels lost, trapped, orphaned and exiled from her home in Seville. As if the situation were not frightening enough, a ghost also appears in the house, that of Martín, Águeda's husband who dies in the course of the narrative, haunting his widow thereafter. Having discussed the representation of ghosts in Chapter 4, this one will not place the focus on the haunting, but rather on the fears generated by the house itself, limiting discussion of Martín's ghost to how it impacts on the representation of the house as a frightening space.

Horace Walpole's seminal Gothic work, *The Castle of Otranto*, is set mainly in a large castle complete with trapdoors, secret underground passages leading to a church and adjoining convents, courtyards, and at least one tower. There is an abundance of supernatural phenomena here, revolving around the figure of Alfonso the Good, the ancestor who reacts from beyond the grave to the usurpation of the principality of Otranto by the villain of the piece, a certain Manfred. The central storyline – which is extremely fast-moving and itself as labyrinthine as its setting – involves one of the main characters, Isabella, needing to escape from the castle, to distance herself from Manfred's sexually predatory intentions; this and several other twists and turns of the plot give the author a reason to use description of the buildings to intensify the frightening atmosphere.

Noticeable features of Walpole's text and ones that will serve as useful comparators for those of García Morales, are the sense of claustrophobia, of being trapped inside a building (a sensation not limited to the hapless Isabella) and the ingenious establishment of an almost seamless relationship between the hostile architecture and the unwelcome and unlawful authority of its owner. In Walpole's medieval setting, this is nothing short of tyranny, whereas *La tía Águeda* [Aunt Águeda] deals in subtler power games, but at bottom the dynamics are similar, even to the final humbling of the villain at the end of the story.[1]

---

[1] For Botting, the Gothic is 'a genre enmeshed in representations of tyranny' (Botting (ed.), p. 4).

The cast-list of minor characters in both texts and how they relate to the architectural space and power structure of each offers incidental resemblances too, worth mentioning by way of introduction, since they contribute to the overall 'retablo provinciano y gótico' [provincial Gothic tableau], as the jacket notes characterize the Spanish novel. There is Pedro, the teenaged son of Martín from a former marriage. He becomes the object of Marta's dawning sexual awareness and could be compared with Theodore in *The Castle of Otranto*, a young man who at the outset believes himself an orphaned peasant, but is eventually identified as the true heir of the principality of Otranto, marrying Isabella in the final paragraph of the text. Of particular note too is García Morales's hunchbacked maid Catalina, a far cry from the coquettish Bianca in Walpole's text, which is no surprise since her function is also very different. Catalina's deformity seems at first sight to be a rather crude and superficial injection of ugliness into the household, to intensify its nightmare atmosphere for Marta, yet by the time the end of the novel is reached it has become clear that this character's contribution is more complex, for she is the person on whom the undecidability of the supernatural phenomena hinges. If she is read as innocent, then the haunting by Martín is being presented as paranormal; if she is staging the otherwise inexplicable happenings, then she becomes a cruel and vengeful person herself, instead of the pitiable victim not only of Águeda's long-standing tyranny but now also of groundless suspicion. Conclusive evidence to sway us in the direction of one reading or the other for Catalina is carefully avoided by the author, thus adding this text to the list of those where a supernatural reading and a common-sense one are forced into uneasy cohabitation. In this way, Catalina is a multi-purpose character for García Morales: she contributes to the gloomy atmosphere with her ugliness and the hunchback in particular almost makes of her a stock Gothic figure (especially from the cinema branch of the genre); but more importantly, she sets the seal on the undecidability of the supernatural element of the text. Far from the early Gothic tradition of letting servants provide mere comic relief as in Walpole, or stand for ignorant superstition in contrast to the main characters' more enlightened attitudes, as we find in texts by Ann Radcliffe or Matthew Lewis, for example, here we have a servant who just may be – but is not necessarily – as sinister as Mrs Danvers of *Rebecca*.[2]

In the first place, it is worth considering the ways in which both authors convey a sense of the building ruled by the anti-hero being an extension of the latter: how do Walpole and García Morales imbue the setting of their text with

---

[2] Catalina's final position and significance, after the death of her mistress, is also important and will be discussed at the end of the present chapter. *Rebecca* will be discussed in Chapter 6 in comparison with *Nasmiya*, but as we shall see in Chapter 9, García Morales will only return to the figure of the sinister maid with the creation of Sila in *Una historia perversa*.

the character who rules it? How do they stamp it so indelibly that it emblematizes the tyranny of its inhabitant? Secondly, what is achieved by so doing?

Clery asserts that 'the castle [of Otranto] is central to the fable and seems to have a life of its own. It traps and conceals; its walls frame almost all the main events. [. . .] Its alien modes of ingress and egress give rise to the prototypical scene of Isabella's desperate flight from the villain through an underground tunnel.'[3] Following from this, it should be noted that in both texts, the building is not merely the location of the action, but a key driver of the plot in partnership with the tyrant in charge of it. In *The Castle of Otranto*, the storyline springs from Manfred's attempts to circumvent an ancient curse which he knows hangs over him for usurping the principality of Otranto along with its castle. At the opening of the novel, he has arranged a marriage between his son, Conrad, and Isabella, daughter of the rightful heir (as he believes), in hopes that uniting the two families will safeguard his own blood-line's attachment to the title and property entailed, thwarting the curse '*That the castle and lordship of Otranto should pass from the present family [. . .]*'.[4] *La tía Águeda* also introduces the house and its significance at the very beginning of the narrative (the second paragraph, compared with the first in Walpole). If the castle is to be frightening for the ways in which it will dramatize the realization of the curse, so Águeda's house also enters the narrative with a strong foretaste of how Marta is to be intimidated there. It is 'muy grande' [very big], with a doorknocker in the shape of 'una mano de hierro' [iron hand].[5] It has 'un patio de suelo empedrado' [a cobbled courtyard] which is 'en penumbra, iluminado sólo por un farol de una luz muy débil' [in penumbra, lit only by one lamp casting a very weak light] and Marta reports that 'me sentí inmersa en una atmósfera mortecina y triste' [I felt plunged into a sad, deadly dismal atmosphere].[6] Thus, from the outset the house is associated with darkness, sadness, and death, all of which will prove prophetic as the novel develops.

Secondly, in both texts, the architecture is imbued with the tyranny of the character who rules it, to such an extent that the building and the human

---

[3] 'The Genesis of "Gothic" Fiction', in Hogle (ed.), p. 26. While the present argument endorses the centrality of the castle proposed in this reading, it will disagree with the idea of the castle having a life of its own, asserting instead that its life is drawn from, and dependent on, Manfred.

[4] Horace Walpole, *The Castle of Otranto* (ed.) Michael Gamer (London: Penguin, 2001), p. 17 (italics in the original). Future references will relate to this edition and be given parenthetically in the text.

[5] Perhaps noteworthy is that this disembodied iron hand not only contributes to the generally Gothic atmosphere of the house, but also specifically recalls the various body parts – including a gauntleted hand – that haunt Manfred in the Castle of Otranto (*CO*, p. 90).

[6] *La tía Águeda* (Barcelona: Anagrama, 1995), all p. 10. Future references will relate to this edition and be given parenthetically in the text.

almost melt into one another. For example, Águeda's house is characterized by its dismal lighting; the courtyard is not the only part that is inadequately and depressingly lit: 'La penumbra parecía ser la iluminación de toda la casa' (*TÁ*, p. 11) [Penumbra seemed to be the lighting of the whole house] and indeed, Marta's bedroom is typical for its feeble light, 'una luz débil, la misma iluminación que brillaba por toda la casa' (*TÁ*, p. 12) [a weak light, the same as illuminated the whole house]. Águeda is not only associated with this lighting by Marta's logical inference that her aunt must have decided on low wattage throughout (*TÁ*, p. 33), she becomes specifically linked with actively depriving Marta of light when she removes even this wan light-bulb in her bedroom as a punishment to teach her she should not be frightened of the dark (*TÁ*, p. 26). Perhaps surprisingly, however, the complete darkness into which she plunges the child is found to be preferable by Marta to the flickering half light of a lantern which Catalina smuggles to her a few minutes later (*TÁ*, pp. 26–7).[7] Later in the novel, after the death of Martín, when Águeda begins to suffer from nightmares and ghostly visitations, Marta comments that 'me pareció que el infierno mismo se había instalado en la oscuridad de la casa' (*TÁ*, p. 105) [it seemed to me that hell itself had moved into the darkness of the house], thus making the traditional link between darkness and hell. This is followed up by the association of darkness with a ghostly atmosphere which spills over from the aunt's experiences of being haunted to affect Marta too:

> Yo percibía ya, en cuanto oscurecía, una presencia maligna e invisible que invadía la casa. No importaba que a ella se le hiciera real o no, para mí se presentaba cada noche. [. . .] La atmósfera que creaba la tía Águeda con sus apariciones se me hacía irrespirable. Era una atmósfera densa y poblada de amenazas desconocidas.   (*TÁ*, p. 117)[8]

Thus, the (semi-)darkness of the house is linked to Águeda: she has decided to have such poor lighting and to deprive Marta even of that if she tries to leave her light on when she goes to sleep; and her ghostly experiences too (the ones that frighten Marta, at least) are limited to the hours of darkness.

---

[7] Later on, however, Marta mentions that she prefers the dim light to the complete darkness left if her aunt removes the bulb (*TÁ*, p. 33). On the other hand, at another point in the narrative, Marta declares that 'no me atrevía a atravesar la casa a oscuras y, menos aún encendiendo las luces que envolvían todo con su penumbra' (*TÁ*, p. 87) [I didn't dare walk through the house in darkness and still less if I switched on the lights that enveloped everything in their penumbra]. These apparent contradictions could be read as expressing the impossibility of discriminating consistently between two frightening experiences.

[8] [I could already sense, as soon as it grew dark, a malign, invisible presence invading the house. It did not matter whether or not it was real to her, for me it appeared every night. [. . .] The atmosphere that Aunt Águeda created with her apparitions was becoming stifling. It was a dense atmosphere, peopled with unknown threats.]

Walpole uses similar descriptors for the eponymous castle of his text. It is also poorly lit (more understandable in the pre-electricity medieval period of the chronological setting, but no less depressing for that); at twilight inside the castle, for example, Manfred cannot distinguish the face of his own daughter, Matilda (*CO*, p. 22). This is partly because of the poor light but it is described as 'concurring with the disorder of his mind' at the time, thus establishing a link between his own benighted mentality and the darkness of the castle environment. Soon after, when Isabella is fleeing in terror from his sexual advances and finds her way into the lower part of the castle, it is described as a 'long labyrinth of darkness' (*CO*, p. 26). Also in common with Águeda, Manfred is personally responsible for the loss of light; when a torch-bearing servant brings Isabella to him, 'he started and said hastily, Take away that light, and begone' (*CO*, p. 23).[9] Moreover, Isabella, like Marta, will suffer the terror of being plunged into complete darkness when she is at her most frightened. As she flees from Manfred through the 'subterraneous regions' of the castle (*CO*, p. 26), 'a sudden gust of wind that met her at the door extinguished her lamp, and left her in total darkness', whereupon she is described as being in 'an agony of despair' (both *CO*, p. 27), which would be just as appropriate a description for Marta's state when Águeda takes away the light bulb. Thus, the castle (in this instance, its draughtiness) appears to be a confederate of its tyrant, Manfred, cruelly removing light when Isabella needs it most.

Darkness has been noted by scholars of the Gothic as an emblematic characteristic of the mode, since it counters the light images associated with the eighteenth century as the age of reason and enlightenment. As Botting puts it, for example, ' "Gothic" functions as the mirror of eighteenth-century mores and values: a reconstruction of the past as the inverted, mirror image of the present, its darkness allows the reason and virtue of the present a brighter reflection.'[10] Thus, for Clery, by espousing the pre-enlightenment, dark past, Walpole was issuing an 'outright challenge' to the prevailing view that in a narrative 'there could be no appeal to the imagination that went beyond rational causes', which is to say, enlightened ones.[11]

As well as the visual effects of *La tía Águeda*, however, there are the auditory qualities of the house, which are equally inextricably connected with the aunt. Predominating here is silence, punctuated by very few other sounds mentioned inside the house, all of which serve to accentuate the silence they disturb more than neutralizing it: creaking hinges (*TÁ*, p. 16), the sound in the night of Marta's own heartbeat and 'multitud de ruidos casi imperceptibles, de origen desconocido, que me resultaban amenazadores' (*TÁ*, p. 26) [a multitude of

---

[9] The archaic lack of inverted commas for direct speech is as in the edition used.
[10] 'In Gothic Darkly: Heterotopia, History, Culture', in Punter (ed.), p. 5.
[11] 'The Genesis of "Gothic" Fiction', in Hogle (ed.), p. 23.

almost imperceptible noises, of origin unknown, which I found menacing];
arguing between Águeda and Martín, followed by sobbing (*TÁ*, pp. 33–4); the
somewhat comforting sound of a quiet recitation of the rosary (*TÁ*, p. 82);
Águeda's shuffling slippers in the corridor (*TÁ*, p. 86, for example); the
different and cheerful sound of Pedro's footsteps (*TÁ*, p. 103), the absence of
which, once he leaves, makes living there all the more unbearable: 'la casa
adquirió una quietud mortal y un silencio desolador' (*TÁ*, p. 142) [the house
acquired a deadly quietude and a desolate silence]. That the almost complete
silence is attributable to Águeda comes out most clearly when her younger
sister, Clara, who briefly visits, counter-attacks her, following Águeda's
accusation that she has been flirting with Martín: '–¿Es que no se puede hablar
en esta casa, hay que estar siempre en silencio?' (*TÁ*, p. 46) ['Is there to be no
talking in this house, have we always to be silent?'].

The auditory qualities of Walpole's castle are equally similar to those of
García Morales and equally linked to the tyrant: 'an awful silence reigned
throughout these subterranean regions' and like Marta, frightened by every
little sound in the night, Isabella listens in panic to creaking hinges, possible
breathing and footsteps that could be Manfred's:

> Every murmur struck her with new terror; – yet more she dreaded to hear
> the wrathful voice of Manfred [. . .]. Frequently she stopped and listened to
> hear if she was followed. In one of those moments she thought she heard a
> sigh. She shuddered, and recoiled a few paces. In a moment she thought she
> heard the step of some person. Her blood curdled; she concluded it was
> Manfred.   (*CO*, p. 26)

The other features mentioned to describe the atmosphere of the Spanish
house are less tangible but just as powerfully fused with Águeda's
characterization as these visual and auditory qualities:

> siempre terminaba la tía Águeda imponiendo aquella amargura que ema-
> naba de su persona y que impregnaba todo cuanto la rodeaba;
> En la casa de la tía Águeda nunca llegué a encontrarme realmente bien. Su
> sombra me perseguía por todos los rincones;
> Desde el fallecimiento del tío Martín un aliento de muerte invadía la casa.
> [. . .] Su fantasma se paseaba por el dormitorio de la tía Águeda casi cada
> noche;
> En aquella casa, junto a Catalina y a la tía Águeda, se respiraba un aire
> viciado, una atmósfera densa y pesada se había extendido por todas partes.
> (*TÁ*, pp. 47, 63, 89, 90)[12]

---

[12] [Aunt Águeda always ended up imposing that bitterness that emanated from her and
impregnated everything around her.] [. . .] [I never really managed to feel good in Aunt
Águeda's house. Her shadow pursued me into every nook and cranny.] [. . .] [Since Uncle

While these do not echo *The Castle of Otranto* in a literal way, it is nevertheless true that the ghostly phenomena in Walpole's story are wholly related to Manfred's usurpation of the principality; thus, the spectre that comes out of a portrait of Manfred's grandfather and the outsized body parts and accoutrements that keep appearing so spectacularly in accomplishment of the curse,[13] greatly intensify the frightening quality of the castle, in a manner analogous in its effects if not in its details, to the above-quoted descriptions of bitterness, shadows, death, and the stifling atmosphere in Águeda's house.

In *La tía Águeda*, part of what makes living with her aunt such a nightmarish experience for Marta are the restrictions on her freedom to come and go as she pleases. While she is not physically imprisoned there (she goes to school, for example), Marta feels as if she were because she has to seek her aunt's permission for any absences and obtaining it is far from a foregone conclusion. For example, when she wants to go to the park with Pedro, she decides not even to ask as she knows the answer will be no. This is borne out by Águeda's reaction when the children return:

> –¿Con qué permiso has salido, Marta?
> –He ido con Pedro, no iba sola.
> –¡Vaya compañía! Sabes que no quiero que salgas sin una persona
>   mayor por el pueblo.
> –Pues todas mis amigas salen cuando quieren.
> –Que salga quien quiera. Tú no te vas por ahí sola. Y si vas con Pedro
>   tienes que pedirme permiso.   (*TÁ*, p. 67)[14]

This is not an isolated incident. She is also sent to bed without supper for going to her friend Florita's house after school without permission (*TÁ*, pp. 53–4) and a bitter row ensues when she decides not to come home for lunch one day (*TÁ*, p. 61). All of this contributes to a sense of entrapment; Marta has failed to persuade her father to allow her to come home – hence her initial

---

Martín had passed away, a breath of death had invaded the house.] [. . .] [His ghost paced Aunt Águeda's bedroom almost every night.] [. . .] [In that house, alongside Catalina and Aunt Águeda, the air was stagnant, a dense, heavy atmosphere pervaded it all.]

[13] References are as follows: the spectre comes out of the portrait on pp. 24–5; the helmet appears on p. 18; an armour-clad leg and foot on p. 32; a hand in armour on p. 91. A sword on the same giant scale has been brought by Isabella's father, Frederic (p. 58); once inside the castle gates its magical qualities are such that it becomes immovable (p. 59).

[14] ['Whose permission did you have to go out, Marta?'
  'I went with Pedro. I wasn't on my own.'
  'Fine company! You know very well that I don't want you going around the town
    without an adult.'
  'But all my friends go out when they want.'
  'They can do as they please. You are not wandering off on your own. And if you
    go with Pedro you have to ask my permission.']

condemnation to the 'care' of her aunt – and that aunt curtails her movements claustrophobically, as we have seen. Thus, Marta's description of life there as 'aquella pesadilla que me envolvía junto a la tía Águeda' (*TÁ*, p. 81) [that nightmare which enveloped me at Aunt Águeda's side] comes as no surprise, showing that it is not just any kind of nightmare, but one with straitjacket qualities. More explicitly still and underlining that seamlessness between the aunt and her house, she elaborates one page later: 'La casa entera se me antojaba una prisión' (*TÁ*, p. 82) [The whole house felt like a prison to me] and clarifies why when she comments that adding to the lack of freedom to go out at will, is the fact that 'dentro de la casa me sentía bajo la inexorable vigilancia de la tía Águeda' (*TÁ*, p. 116) [inside the house I felt I was under Aunt Águeda's inexorable surveillance]. She will accumulate images to convey these feelings of restriction, containment, claustrophobia, always eliding the house with her aunt's character: 'me sentía agobiada con mi encierro [. . .]. [A] la tía Águeda [. . .] la percibía como una pesada losa sobre mi cabeza que yo no podía levantar. [. . .] En el interior de su casa, ella dominaba todos mis movimientos' (*TÁ*, pp. 125–7) [I felt weighed down by my imprisonment [. . .]. I felt as though Aunt Águeda were a heavy slab on my head that I couldn't lift off it. [. . .] Inside the house, she dominated all my movements]. She will also twice (and in identical words) allude to 'aquella asfixia a la que me tenía sometida mi tía' (*TÁ*, pp. 128–9 and 134) [that suffocation to which my aunt had me subjected].

These sensations of enclosure, entrapment and claustrophobia are not only common to many protagonists of Adelaida García Morales's fiction, they are also recurrent features of classic Gothic narrative, as has been observed by many scholars,[15] and in this respect, *The Castle of Otranto* is no exception. Conrad dies, 'dashed to pieces and almost buried' (*CO*, p. 18) beneath the weight of a supernatural gigantic helmet, recalling Marta's image of the 'pesada losa' [heavy slab]. Physical imprisonment is inflicted on Theodore repeatedly by Manfred (*CO*, p. 21 under the giant helmet; p. 29 in an underground vault beneath it which the weight of the helmet has cracked

---

[15] See, for example, Cornwell, who discusses the association between 'images of tyranny or incarceration' and particular buildings ('European Gothic', in Punter (ed.), p. 28). Howard mentions 'confining crypts' as one of the conventional settings for Gothic texts (*Reading Gothic Fiction*, p. 13). Hogle observes that from *The Castle of Otranto* onward, 'women are the figures most fearfully trapped' and goes on to discuss how Radcliffe picked up and developed 'the primal scene of a woman confined' ('Introduction', in Hogle (ed.), pp. 9–10). Modleski, writing about modern-day pulp Gothics, understands this leitmotif by saying they are 'concerned with [. . .] driving home to women the importance of coping with enforced confinement and the paranoid fears it generates' (*Loving* (1984), p. 20). Kilgour makes a similar point with relation to the classic Gothic texts: 'Reading [Gothic texts] is [. . .] a dangerously conservative substitute for political and social action, offering [women] an illusory transformation to impede real change by making women content with their lot, and keeping them at home – reading' (*The Rise of the Gothic Novel*, p. 8).

open; p. 35 in a locked chamber to which he keeps the key himself; p. 65 in 'the black tower'); Isabella encloses herself first in the church (*CO*, p. 44) and then in caves (*CO*, p. 67) to protect herself from Manfred, 'determined, if no other means of deliverance offered, to shut herself up for ever among the holy virgins' (*CO*, p. 25); Matilda promises to 'smother' her own anguish at the death of her brother so as not to upset her father (*CO*, p. 23), a kind of self-inflicted emotional claustrophobia that is echoed by Marta's *agobio* [sense of being weighed down] and figurative use of 'asfixia' [suffocation]; finally, more than once in the course of Walpole's narrative Manfred has the castle locked and guards posted, collectively imprisoning his family, Isabella, and Theodore, plus the servants (*CO*, pp. 21, 35).

In both texts too, a church is presented as a mere adjunct of the enclosing space of the castle/house. In Walpole's architecture, the two are actually joined by an underground passage and in García Morales's, the same could almost be argued, by recourse to the collapsing of Águeda with the house, for she is always at Marta's side when they go to mass. Perhaps for this reason, in neither case does the church offer appreciable sanctuary; although Isabella takes refuge there briefly, she feels the need to put herself further beyond Manfred's reach when she escapes to the caves. The unfortunate Matilda, mistaken for her, will eventually be fatally wounded by her father in the church (*CO*, p. 95), bearing out Isabella's distrust of the space as supposedly safe. Likewise, the weekly outing to mass for Marta, becomes as much of a nightmare as staying at home with her aunt, since it is automatically followed by an obligatory visit to the cemetery, which terrifies her (*TÁ*, pp. 22–3). In this way, it could be posited that even though three locations are negatively weighted in the novel – house, church, cemetery – they all bleed into one another via the aunt's association with them: all become associated with confinement, fear, death, tyranny. There is little difference, for example, between the ways in which Águeda imposes her will on Marta inside the house and how she does so at church (forcing her to go to confession, for example) or at the cemetery (first making her enter and then kneel and pray at her grandparents' tomb). Reinforcing this blurring, Marta's fear of the cemetery is barely distinguishable from what makes her want to keep her light on at home: terror of ghosts, particularly her mother's:

> Sentía [. . .] una suerte de miedo por un lugar [el cementerio] que se me antojaba habitado por seres muertos que, no obstante, conservaban de alguna manera la suficiente vida como para observer a sus visitantes. [. . .] Pensé que mi madre se hallaba en un lugar semejante.   (*TÁ*, p. 23)
>
> Sentí un miedo que iba aumentando a medida que luchaba contra él. [. . .] En aquella penumbra [del dormitorio] adivinaba el fantasma de mi madre vigilándome.   (*TÁ*, pp. 25–6)[16]

---

[16] [I felt [. . .] a kind of fear for a place [the cemetery] which seemed to me to be inhabited by dead beings, who nevertheless somehow retained enough life in them to

If Águeda is effectively indistinguishable from her house in their combined emblematic significance of tyranny and confinement; if too, Manfred and his castle operate in a similar fashion, how does this affect the turn in the story that both texts use, whereby supernatural phenomena eventually intimidate and humble the tyrant figure? Both tyrants know they are guilty of wrongdoing: Águeda had refused to call the doctor who might have been able to save her husband's life or at least to alleviate his suffering in his last moments; Manfred is aware that he is not the rightful heir to Otranto (even though he is mistaken in believing it to be Frederic) (*CO*, pp. 55–6). It is therefore logical that both should interpret the extraordinary events that ensue as a punishment or revenge for their moral crime. García Morales leaves the reader with a choice as to whether to read the haunting of Águeda by Martín as paranormal or staged by the maid, Catalina, to play upon Águeda's nerves, whereas Walpole leaves no room for a non-supernatural interpretation in his presentation of events, but this difference matters little from the point of view of the character's own experience of them; meanwhile, from the reader's perspective, the tyrants are so antipathetic that what comes to the fore is a primitive sense of just desserts. Thus, we are relatively uninterested in the credibility of the phenomena themselves and more so in gleefully spectating on the psychological downfall of the villain, which we predict will be balanced by the triumph of the sympathetic characters. In both works, these expectations are only partially met: Marta does escape from the house and go home to Seville at the end of *La tía Águeda*; Theodore does marry Isabella and successfully claim his right to Otranto. However, the dawning romance between Marta and Pedro comes to nothing as they lose touch at the end of the Spanish novel and the resolution of *The Castle of Otranto* involves the untimely death of a character at least as sympathetic as Isabella, namely, Matilda. These frustrations for the reader are offset, however, by the satisfaction derived from the pages leading up to the denouement, when the gathering momentum of the villain's come-uppance can be observed.

It is useful to compare the implications of the downfall of the respective tyrants across the two works relative to the architectural setting. In both it is spread over quite an extended proportion of the text. In *La tía Águeda*, it dates from the beginning of the haunting by Martín, at roughly the halfway point in the book (page 77 in a book of 147 pages) and it is matched exactly by a proportional loss of power over Marta. After the first account of the haunting, Águeda is too upset to notice that Marta is leaving her light on (*TÁ*, p. 78), a habit which she now indulges regularly without punishment (see, for example, *TÁ*, p. 92); a few pages later, Águeda tries to re-assert her authority over Marta

observe their visitors. [. . .] The thought came to me that my mother was to be found in just such a place. [. . .] A fear came over me which grew and grew the more I fought against it. [. . .] In that penumbra [of the bedroom] I guessed my mother's ghost was watching me.]

by forcing her to finish her lunch, but Marta manages to win the battle over the food and over going back to school in the afternoon: 'Le dije a la tía Águeda que me dolía el estómago. Ella, al principio, creyó que era una excusa para no comer, pero ante mi insistencia y mis lágrimas cedió. [. . .] Me quedé en casa' (TÁ, p. 81) [I told Aunt Águeda I had a stomach-ache. At first, she took this as an excuse not to eat, but in the face of my insistence and my tears, she gave in [. . .] I stayed at home]. Once Pedro comes to live in the house, the scale of Marta's disobedience to her aunt escalates. Now she secretly visits Pedro in his room when she has been ordered to bed (TÁ, p. 96) and increasingly boldly defies her aunt's ever weaker authority: 'La tía Águeda se estaba transformando en una mujer cada vez más frágil. [. . .] Apenas hablaba, ni siquiera para dar órdenes a Catalina o a mí' (TÁ, p. 113) [Aunt Águeda was turning into an ever more frail woman. [. . .] She barely spoke, not even to issue orders to Catalina or me]. By page 129, Marta has even overcome her aunt's resistance to her wearing her hair loose and so it comes as no surprise to read soon after: 'Aunque aún ejercía sobre mí una gran influencia y su presencia me provocaba siempre vagos temores, a medida que la iba viendo desmoronarse crecía mi seguridad y entereza. Estaba dejando de ser una niña amilanada ante la autoridad de la tía Águeda' (TÁ, p. 131) [Even though she still exerted a strong influence over me and her presence always made me feel vaguely fearful, as I watched her crumbling my own security and solidity grew in equal measure. I was leaving behind the little girl intimidated by Aunt Águeda's authority]. Particularly suggestive here is the choice of the verb *desmoronarse* [to crumble] used for Águeda's increasing frailty, since it spotlights once more the elision of the woman with her house. The network of architectural imagery is continued on the next page, when Marta turns the tables on her aunt, forcing her to go to Martín's tomb in the cemetery (which she has stopped visiting since the haunting began). As Marta lays flowers on 'la losa de mármol' [marble slab] there, one is powerfully reminded of her earlier description of feeling her aunt's authority to be like a slab on her head: thanks to her uncle's posthumous intervention (or at least Águeda's belief in it), that stone is now back where it belongs.

Walpole chose a spectacular special-effect ending for his eponymous castle: not only is Alfonso to be seen 'dilated to an immense magnitude' pronouncing Theodore the true heir and then ascending to Saint Nicholas in the sky, but also, 'a clap of thunder at that instant shook the castle to its foundations [. . .]. The moment Theodore appeared, the walls of the castle behind Manfred were thrown down with a mighty force' (CO, p. 98). Thus, as Manfred abdicates, his authority in ruins, from his usurped principality and dominion over the castle, the latter dramatizes this as it is violently demolished, confirming itself as a cipher for his tyranny.

La tía Águeda concludes in a less sensationalist manner, but is nevertheless interesting in how it handles the connection between the tyrant and the house at this point. Even though the house does not literally fall down at the end of the novel, when Águeda dies, three points are perhaps worth making. Two are about the implications of the 'impulso irracional' (*TÁ*, p. 146) [irrational impulse] which leads Marta to try to find solace in Pedro's former bedroom just after her aunt's death. Ostensibly, this action would seem to be an attempt to find in his bedroom the antidote to the misery inflicted by the aunt that Pedro used to provide in person for Marta when he was staying there. However, the plan fails: 'Nada quedaba de él, ninguna huella de su paso por aquel dormitorio. Parecía pertenecer a una casa abandonada. El vacío se agrandaba ante mi mirada, que buscaba alguna señal que indicara el paso de Pedro por allí. Pero no quedaba nada' (*TÁ*, p. 146) [Nothing of him remained, his stay in that bedroom had left no mark. It seemed like part of an abandoned house. The emptiness grew as I gazed upon it, looking for some sign that would point to Pedro's having passed through there. But nothing remained]. What this shows is that firstly, people do not normally fuse with the space they inhabit; thus, Águeda is thrown into relief as an abnormal being, aligning her with the strong Gothic tradition of monstrosity, which is to say the fascination with creatures that, as we saw in the discussion of *El silencio de las sirenas* in Chapter 2, transgress the boundaries of what we would prefer to feel safe in assuming is a coherent and clear-cut outline of a self.[17] Secondly, it confirms that very fusion by referring to the house (and not merely that room) as 'abandonada' [abandoned]. Like a body without a soul, Marta is acutely aware of the empty shell – 'el vacío' [the emptiness] – which the hitherto living and breathing, if evil house has become.

Finally, it is worth noting that in the closing paragraph of the novel, it emerges that Catalina is to remain in the house 'guardándola y cuidándola, para no tener que cerrarla' (*TÁ*, p. 147) [keeping it and looking after it, so as not to have to close it]. In other words it is to be preserved, embalmed as it were. The question which hangs uneasily in the air, though, is whether this sets the seal on Catalina's ultimate victory over Águeda's tyranny: is she at last to be effectively the mistress of the house, a triumph towards which the narrative may seem to have been moving as with Águeda's increasing weakness, she had begun asserting herself more and more? Or, has Águeda managed to regain her authority from beyond the grave via the house that emblematizes her, consigning Catalina for the remainder of her life to continued servitude to her/its needs?

There is one space in Águeda's house which seems largely to escape the atmosphere created by its tyrannical owner: the attic, where Marta enjoys dressing up in old clothes stored there and discovers a hobby – lace-making – that provides some much-needed entertainment. On one level, this is a credible and realistic detail: the attic is a space which a bored and lonely ten-year-old could love to make her own, but if that were the only function of

---

[17] Monstrosity will be discussed further in Chapter 9.

the attic in the text, it could be seen as strange that Marta should abruptly stop
liking it as soon as the dead Martín's effects are put up there, even though he
was her ally in the house during his lifetime. Granted, we know that she is
frightened of ghosts and might fear that his possessions being put in the attic
would draw his spectral presence there, but this is not all there is to how she
describes the loss of attraction for the attic at that point. 'Con aquellos objetos
dentro, el desván se convertiría de pronto en un lugar inquietante' (*TÁ*, p. 81)
[With those objects inside it, the attic would soon turn into a disquieting
place] does suggest that Marta's fear of ghosts might be the whole
explanation, but one page later, she expands thus: 'Yo ya no me atrevía a subir
al desván. Algo fundamental había cambiado en él desde que la tía Águeda
guardara allí las pertenencias del tío Martín. Incluso me desinteresé por
el encaje de bolillo que tanto me había distraído hasta entonces' (*TÁ*, p. 82)
[I no longer dared to go up to the attic. Something fundamental had changed
there since Aunt Águeda had put away Uncle Martín's effects there. I even
lost interest in the lace bobbin which had entertained me so much until then].
A subtler reading would seem to be called for here, to account for Marta's
losing interest in the lace-making as well as the space where she discovered
it first and had enjoyed practising it. It appears that what the attic had
represented for Marta hitherto was not just a spatial escape from the main part
of the house, but also an escape from the present time, for here were the
clothes and accessories of previous generations, here too a hobby from the
past with which Marta could connect and so escape the nightmare of her
present predicament: 'Había varios [baúles] y todos contenían vestidos que a
mí me parecían de otra época y muy lujosos. Tal vez habían pertenecido a mi
abuela' (*TÁ*, p. 35) [There were several [trunks] and they all contained dresses
which seemed very luxurious to me and to date from another era. Perhaps
they had belonged to my grandmother]. This past world with its gorgeous
clothes and fancy hats, including one 'confeccionado con una paja brillante y
negra y [. . .] un tul que yo suponía iba sobre el rostro' (*TÁ*, p. 36) [made out
of gleaming black straw and [. . .] a piece of gauze that I assumed went over
the face], offers Marta the same attraction which has always formed part of
what the Gothic genre has offered its readers, namely the allure of a bygone
era.[18] Indeed, rummaging in dusty old trunks and pulling out some beautiful
antiquated garments to try on is an arresting image for reading a Gothic novel,
particularly as Marta specifies that there was no mirror in the attic, but this

---

[18] For example: 'The gothic is symptomatic of a nostalgia for the past' (Kilgour, *The
Rise of the Gothic Novel*, p. 11). 'Gothic novels seem to sustain a nostalgic relish for a lost
era of romance and adventure' (Botting, *Gothic*, p. 5). Hogle refers to both characters and
readers of early gothic texts being drawn by the 'enticing call of aristocratic wealth and
Catholic splendour, beckoning back toward the Middle Ages and the Renaissance'
('Introduction', in Hogle (ed.), p. 4). Black veils are often to be found in Gothic texts,
shrouding mysterious and/or ghostly bodies.

did not spoil the fun because 'yo me imaginaba ataviada con [los vestidos]' (*TÁ*, p. 36) [I used to imagine myself all dressed up]. In other words, the attic affords Marta the opportunity to imagine herself living in another time, one of luxurious clothes and delicate ladylike pastimes such as lace-making, to indulge that nostalgic rose-tinted view of the past that has always been half of the attraction of the Gothic. The other half – the horrors of a benighted pre-enlightenment world, which can be comfortably consigned to another era, thus relieving anxiety about their lurking all too closely to ourselves in the present – are precisely what Marta is experiencing in her everyday life and when they intrude into her attic via the suitcases of Martín's belongings, we suddenly notice the echo in the names of these two characters and realize that Marta's rejection of the attic at this point is her rejection of all those fears and anxieties within herself, projected onto the external ghost with a name too much like hers. No wonder that this is the point where the house is described as a prison: with this development, the one escape route Marta had had – into her own imagination – clangs shut; thus, she is forced to attempt to break out by the only other possible way, which is open rebellion and defiance against her aunt's tyranny.

This play between a nostalgic view of the past in a nightmare present for an internal character is present in *The Castle of Otranto* while at the same time, the reader's perspective has an analogous distance from the present of the novel, enabling the other half of the Gothic formula to work, whereby we can be relieved to project onto a bygone era the benighted values and frighten-ingly irrational world of which we are reading.[19] Like Marta, Walpole's Matilda looks back longingly, in her case to the period and person of Alfonso the Good, adoring the portrait of him that hangs in the castle more than can be accepted as normal aesthetic appreciation of a work of art. Indeed, it is principally Theodore's remarkable resemblance to the portrait (*CO*, p. 78) that makes her fall in love with him instantly (*CO*, p. 49) as she seems to find the past in him miraculously able to rescue her from her present nightmare existence; indeed, Matilda is living a nightmare, hated by her father, Manfred, all her life and now, in the course of the novel, betrothed to Isabella's father (*CO*, p. 79), when she is in love with Theodore.

---

[19] In this respect, according to Botting's approach to the mode, *La tía Águeda* fits specifically with the eighteenth-century Gothic tradition, when 'the emphasis was placed on expelling and objectifying threatening figures of darkness and evil' (*Gothic*, p. 10). Hogle draws on Kristeva's notion of abjection to discuss the idea, concluding that 'the process of abjection [. . .] encourages middle-class people in the west [. . .] to deal with the tangled contradictions fundamental to their existence by throwing them off onto ghostly or monstrous counterparts that [. . .] convey [. . .] overtones of the archaic and the alien in their grotesque mixture of elements viewed as incompatible by established standards of normality' ('Introduction', in Hogle (ed.), p. 7; Hogle's italics).

We can be relieved on reading *La tía Águeda* to convince ourselves that the values espoused by the aunt are those of provincial 1950s Spain and thus a far cry, thankfully, from the world we live in today. In like fashion, readers of Walpole's novel, when it was first published and up to the present, can enjoy the same reassuring feelings of distance and superiority over the benighted world presented there, thus confronting – but at a safe distance – fears and anxieties that they know at a deeper level are actually far from extinct. These revolve around power and powerlessness, tyranny and victimization, and how these resist containment in specific bilateral relations between named individuals; on the contrary, both *The Castle of Otranto* and *La tía Águeda* vividly depict the far more harrowing idea of tyranny seeping into the very building – its gloom, its silence, its hauntedness – in which its victims are entrapped.

6

Nasmiya (1996) and Daphne du Maurier, *Rebecca* (1938): Fear of the Other (Woman)

Nasmiya is about one family in a community of Spanish converts to Islam living in Madrid. It focuses on the emotional fall-out occasioned by Khaled, the husband of Nadra, the narrator, who precipitates the central storyline by deciding to take a second wife. Nadra is his first wife and the mother of three children of this still supposedly happy union. The new wife, Nasmiya, unlike Khaled or Nadra, is a second-generation Spanish Muslim; she is young, beautiful, and appears to have no difficulty with the idea of sharing her husband, just as her own mother shared her father with another wife. Nadra, on the other hand, is tortured by jealousy and self-doubt, which eventually drive her to such a state of anguish that she moves out, taking the children with her. Her absence, however, leads to problems between Khaled and Nasmiya, who plead with her to come home and eventually win her over. The novel ends with a new harmony in the family: the children are back in their old beds and the three adults share an embrace during which, however, Nadra's thoughts recognize that there will still be difficult times ahead.

One of the most striking features of this extraordinary novel, as it comes to the reader, filtered through the consciousness of Nadra, is the characterization of Nasmiya, a fact to which attention is drawn from the outset by the choice of naming the book after her and not, say, the narrator or the triangular family structure. Nadra tries to understand what she finds to be the entirely alien character of this other woman and to measure herself against it. How, she wonders, does Khaled feel about the two of them relative to one another?[1] Why does Nasmiya seem not to have these thoughts?[2] At 421 pages, the novel

---

[1] For example: 'Me preguntaba desolada si todavía [. . .] existiría en él ese amor que aseguraba sentir por mí. Sospechaba que en su interior sólo había espacio para ella' (Adelaida García Morales, *Nasmiya* (Barcelona: Plaza & Janés, 1996), p. 13) [I despairingly wondered if that love that he claimed to feel for me might still exist. I suspected that there was only room for her inside him]. Future references will relate to this edition and be given parenthetically in the text.

[2] For example: 'Yo estaba convencida de su intenso amor por Khaled y no atinaba a encontrar una explicación sobre su forma, tan desenfadada, de aceptar compartirlo conmigo' (*N*, p. 40) [I was convinced as to the intensity of her love for Khaled and I could not come up with an explanation for her calm acceptance of the need to share him with me].

is longer than any other that García Morales has produced to date, giving her the space to delve deep into the evolving feelings and developing relationships of Nadra herself and those she imputes to others, but ultimately this narrative can be reduced to a profound insight into the insecurities of a woman as she discovers more and more about herself, her husband, and the other woman whom, she greatly fears, he is perhaps right to love more than her.

Daphne du Maurier's *Rebecca* – 'the epitome of the feminine Gothic romance' for at least one critic[3] – is also named after the other woman relative to the narrator, although in this case the latter is the second wife, following the death of Rebecca, the first. Even though this novel therefore does not need to go into the anguish produced by the husband's choice of bed each night,[4] in most other respects, du Maurier's protagonist is living with a struggle for the bulk of *Rebecca* similar to that of Nadra in most of *Nasmiya*, namely a sense of her own inferiority relative to the other wife, a fear that de Winter, the husband, loves her less, and perhaps most hauntingly of all, a fruitless quest to understand this radically other kind of woman and the relationship she had with the husband they have in common.[5] In *Rebecca*, a ghastly secret is eventually revealed – that de Winter murdered Rebecca (*R*, p. 313) – but it could be argued that the power of the novel does not lie there so much as in the suffering that Rebecca's legacy inflicts on the narrator who is in effect sharing the house with her.[6]

[3] Hogle, 'Introduction', in Hogle (ed.), p. 11. Clive Bloom cites the novel as an example of 'Gothic tales that are not horror fiction'. See 'Horror Fiction: In Search of a Definition' in Punter (ed.), pp. 155–66 (p. 155). Avril Horner and Sue Zlosnik take for granted the Gothic status of the work, using the adjective in passing several times. See *Daphne du Maurier: Writing, Identity and the Gothic Imagination* (Basingstoke, Hants: Macmillan, 1988), especially Chapter 4 (pp. 99–127).

[4] Nevertheless, the bedroom that Maxim, the husband, had shared with Rebecca has been left intact and the narrator does wonder anxiously whether he visits it in secret from her, to touch Rebecca's belongings, still imbued with her distinctive perfume (Daphne du Maurier, *Rebecca* (London: Virago, 2003), p. 220). Future references will relate to this edition and be given parenthetically in the text.

[5] The quest is fruitless because de Winter and others who knew Rebecca are reserved out of tact and the narrator herself is too shy and tactful herself to ask the right questions; so the questing remains inside her own imagination and based on a false premise, namely that it had been a successful marriage. She meditates on these mistakes after she discovers the truth (*R*, p. 309).

[6] Even after her death this omnipresence of Rebecca in the house (reminding us of Águeda's similar effect on her house, discussed in Chapter 5 above) arises without the author having recourse to supernatural effects; the narrator is psychologically haunted because, for example, all the servants work to the routine that she established and the second Mrs de Winter even finds herself writing at Rebecca's desk with its every pigeon-hole labelled in her hand in a room furnished and decorated by her. Many more examples of how this haunting effect is produced could be cited. Horner & Zlosnik also point out that the living Mrs Danvers is not only described in a ghostly fashion, but also can be read as 'a grotesquely reductive version of Rebecca' (*Daphne du Maurier*, p. 119).

Woven into both texts are criss-crossing threads of sexual jealousy and possessiveness, coming from the two narrator-wives as we have just seen, but also from the husband in each novel. Mistakenly, as it transpires, De Winter believes Rebecca to be pregnant with another man's child when he murders her and her infidelity had tortured him during their marriage (*R*, pp. 313 and 307–10, respectively); Nasmiya also arouses Khaled's jealousy for her friendship with a man closer to her own age and she is also pregnant at the end of the novel, although there is no reason to suppose the father is anyone other than Khaled. The latter's suspiciousness, however, leads Nasmiya to keep meetings with her younger man-friend secret, giving them a complexion of guilt and she is also willing to cover for Nadra when she has a male admirer, though in this case too the acquaintance leads nowhere. It is useful to contrast the implications of these presentations of male jealousy in the two novels because they highlight the differences in the sources of tension within the two novels' triangles, despite their structural similarities. In *Nasmiya*, Khaled's jealousy has two main effects: it serves to accentuate Nasmiya's otherness as she alone stands above these anxieties felt by both Khaled and Nadra, and it contributes to the unsympathetic portrayal of Khaled, who regards it as quite respectable for him to have two women and as unreasonable for Nadra to find this difficult to bear, but for whom it is not acceptable for either of them to have two men. In *Rebecca*, on the other hand, de Winter is a sympathetic character even though a murderer; his jealousy serves two different purposes: it is the passion which enables the reader and his second wife to take a more indulgent view of his crime, particularly as Rebecca – strongly antipathetic at this point of the narrative – taunts him cruelly over her infidelity to him; and it is a mark of his presentation as a decent and respectable English gentleman, who has a right to want his beloved estate, Manderley, to pass to a true son and not the child of his wife's lover, a child who is 'other', rather than an extension of self.

This chapter will thus consider the Gothic topos of what is felt to be threatening because of its otherness. At one level – a sociohistorical one – this plays itself out in *Nasmiya* as the Catholics in the text struggle to come to terms with the other religion that is Islam and the changes that it has wrought on Ana/Nadra and Lucas/Khaled, who have assumed new names to reflect the changed persons their conversion has made them, names that their old friends and relations have difficulty in accepting precisely because of this emblematic significance of the change.[7] However, from the perspective of a study of the novel's Gothic elements, the focus needs to be on the

---

[7] Nadra's mother, for example, insists on using her original name and Ángela, her Christian friend, refuses to call Khaled anything but Lucas (*N*, pp. 114–15 and 48, respectively).

relationship between otherness and possession since these are the twin
sources of Nadra's sense of entrapment, a staple of the Gothic.[8] She feels
trapped, firstly, by the invasion of her life and of her marriage by a woman
who is radically other precisely because her attitude towards possession and
possessiveness is so alien to Nadra. Not only that, but secondly, Nasmiya's
influence on Khaled is to change him, to make him other, relative to how
Nadra had understood him hitherto and, thirdly, the strangeness of the
situation in which she finds herself is to change Nadra herself, for she too
seems to become an alien figure in her reactions: 'Me surgían renovados
deseos de escapar de aquella tortuosa situación. Pero ¿adónde huir? No
imaginaba ningún lugar en este mundo que pudiera acogerme, pues el mal se
hallaba en mí misma y me acompañaría allá donde fuese' (N, p. 94) [Renewed
desires to escape from that tortured situation surged up in me. But where to
run to? I could imagine nowhere in this world that could afford me shelter,
since the problem was inside myself and would go with me wherever I went].
In all of these cases, as will be discussed below, possession is inextricably
bound up with otherness.

The novel invites a feminist reading which also needs to be related to the
Gothic nightmare which Nadra lives through: there are many signs of
solidarity between women in the text that interrogate a facile reading of
bigamy as an institution which is necessarily worse for women than
monogamy, however phallocratic it may be in essence. Indeed, if Khaled is
undoubtedly to blame for inflicting the nightmare on Nadra in the first place,
her (somewhat qualified) escape from it is arguably attributable to Nasmiya
more than to anyone or anything else. Thus, the chapter will also address the
question of where supportive relationships versus rivalry between women fit
into the Gothic scheme.

The conclusion will attempt to decide the extent to which García Morales
endorses or, conversely, subverts the Radcliffean sanctification of 'woman's
continuing incarceration in the home that is always the man's castle' and
consider the extent to which her answer to the question is analogous to
Daphne du Maurier's in *Rebecca*.[9]

First, it is important to establish what makes Nasmiya so alien in Nadra's
eyes. She is different in a whole variety of ways that Nadra may not
particularly like, but which are not mysterious to her. For example, she is only
nineteen, while Nadra is in her forties; she is not only beautiful, but makes an

---

[8] For Kilgour, this is especially true of female-authored Gothic fiction: 'The domestic
realm appears in nightmare forms in the images of the prison, the castle, in which men
imprison helpless passive females' (*The Rise of the Gothic Novel*, p. 38). Nevertheless,
women are also imprisoned in male-authored texts, including Walpole's *The Castle of
Otranto*, Matthew Lewis's *The Monk*, and Wilkie Collins's *The Woman in White*, to name
but three particularly famous examples.

[9] Kilgour, *The Rise of the Gothic Novel*, p. 38.

effort to look her best at all times (something Nadra only admits to doing on one occasion in the whole novel). She is openly very affectionate to Khaled, throwing him loving looks, holding his hand, giving him kisses, and generally clinging to him, habits that Nadra does not share.[10] However, the single feature that makes Nasmiya an alien being to Nadra, radically other from her perspective, is her complete lack of jealousy and possessiveness with respect to Khaled.

> Tenía la certeza de que los celos eran un mecanismo esencial e inseparable del amor. Sin embargo, Nasmiya aparentaba [. . .] hallarse libre de ellos por completo. Nunca había advertido en ella ni el más leve signo que indicara o mostrase, de alguna manera, un atisbo de celos ante mi relación amorosa con Khaled.   (*N*, pp. 189–90)[11]

Nasmiya herself explains this as follows: 'En realidad no tengo ningún sentimiento de posesión sobre él, creo que sólo nos pertenecemos a nosotros mismos, o ni siquiera eso' (*N*, p. 45) ['I really have no possessive feelings over him; I believe that we only belong to ourselves, if that'].

Secondly, what does the presence of this alien being do to effect change on Khaled, from the familiar man Nadra thought she had married, to the sequence of other Khaleds she watches now take possession of him? The first change comes to Nadra's notice on return of Khaled and Nasmiya from their honeymoon. So far, so realist, but the imagery Nadra uses to describe the change evokes the frightening transformations and revelations of horror Gothic,[12] reflecting her own state of mind at the time: 'me parecía que la expresión de su rostro y todo su cuerpo estaban impregnados por la figura de

---

[10] 'Las gozosas miradas que ambos se dirigían, las caricias de sus manos entrelazadas,' here quoted from *N*, p. 32, are often mentioned [The adoring looks that they exchanged, the stroking of their entwined hands]; see, for example, p. 156, when Nasmiya's 'manifestaciones amorosas de costumbre' [usual amorous display] win Khaled over following a row.

[11] [I was certain that jealousy was a mechanism essential to and inseparable from love. However, Nasmiya appeared [. . .] to be entirely free of it. I had never noticed even the slightest sign to indicate or somehow show a twinge of jealousy relating to my amorous relations with Khaled.] Further quotations containing similar sentiments are to be found as follows: *N*, pp. 193, 198–9, 208, 229–30, 273, 309, 360, 395–6, and 400.

[12] One could cite Jack Finney's *The Invasion of the Body Snatchers* (1956) as just one example of this Gothic motif, whereby a familiar person becomes frighteningly other, taken over by an alien being. This text and the films based on it are discussed by Hendershot (*The Animal Within*, pp. 29–40). Hogle discusses the concept with reference to the television series *The X Files*, which he shows is 'consistently and quite traditionally Gothic', in a section entitled 'The Alien Within' of his article, 'The Gothic at our Turn of the Century: Our Culture of Simulation and the Return of the Body', in *The Gothic*, Botting (ed.), pp. 153–79 (pp. 168–72). Hogle shows how the key characters of Mulder and Scully are 'invaded by the paranormal or alien in ways that threaten the supposed boundaries of their once-assumed identities' (p. 168).

Nasmiya, como si ésta se le hubiera adherido a la piel de alguna extraña manera' (*N*, p. 18) [it seemed to me that the expression on his face and his whole body were impregnated with Nasmiya's form, as though she had been glued onto his skin in some strange way]. This image is deepened and developed later in the novel when she asserts that 'Khaled la llevaba [a Nasmiya] incrustada en su interior' (*N*, p. 153) [Khaled had her [Nasmiya] incrusted into his insides]. When he becomes jealous on account of Nasmiya's friendships at art school, Nadra finds this to be 'una faceta nueva' which 'me hacían sentirme expulsada de su vida de manera definitiva' (both *N*, p. 94) [a new facet which made me feel definitively expelled from his life]. Furthermore, he handles the problem in a manner that does not fit with Nadra's expectations, a 'postura nueva, ajena a sus costumbres, rara para mí' (*N*, p. 98) [a new attitude, alien to his habits, strange to me]. As she sums this up later on: 'Nasmiya había descubierto una faceta del carácter de Khaled que ni siquiera había intuido con anterioridad' (*N*, p. 153) [Nasmiya had exposed a facet of Khaled's character that I had never even suspected was there beforehand]. García Morales maintains plausibility by showing that the changes wrought on him are consistent with a part of him which Nadra knew about, but due to Nasmiya they have become so accentuated that he is now split into 'esos dos hombres que se manifestaban en él, aquél con el que yo había convivido y este otro que amaba a Nasmiya con una pasión descontrolada y mostraba su lado más sombrío' (*N*, p. 155) [those two men who were manifesting themselves in him, the one I had lived with and this other one who loved Nasmiya with an unbridled passion and showed his darker side]. These examples demonstrate that in the characterization of Khaled the author expresses an entirely realist proposition – that having a new love affair can bring out new aspects of a man's personality – but does so in a Gothic idiom: the changes are a frightening takeover of his inner and outer self by Nasmiya, or they make of him that recurrent Gothic figure, the split or doubled personality.[13]

How these changes affect Nadra, making her a stranger to herself, sets the seal on the Gothic mode in which this novel is written. Her unhappiness is painfully realistic to read and the Gothic has no monopoly on unhappy personal relationships, of course. Nevertheless, it is once again the expression of her psychological state which strikes the Gothic note. On one level there is

---

[13] The split or doubled personality in Gothic fiction will be analyzed in Chapter 7, with reference to probably its most famous version, Dr Jekyll and Mr Hyde. Nevertheless, examples of the motif are as plentiful in García Morales's fiction as in Gothic narrative generally. We have already noted examples of it in *El Sur* (father/daughter), *Bene* (Bene/gypsy ghost), *El silencio de las sirenas* (Elsa/Otilia; Agustín/Eduardo), and *Las mujeres de Héctor* (Laura/Delia). A particularly interesting and complex version of splitting and doubling will be examined in *Una historia perversa* in Chapter 9 below.

a nervous digestive complaint, which causes her to lose much weight, changing her outer appearance from that of the contented, middle-aged mother of three to the gaunt and fragile Gothic heroine:

> Desde la boda de Khaled con Nasmiya, yo había perdido nueve kilos de peso. [. . .] Los rasgos de mi rostro se habían afilado, mis pómulos, más prominentes ahora, marcaban una línea ovalada en mis mejillas, y mis ojos se habían agrandado de forma considerable. También resaltaban con mayor nitidez las arrugas que el paso de los años había ido formando en mi rostro, mis ojeras aparecían más hundidas.   (*N*, pp. 187–8)[14]

The same inability to eat is also a transparent metaphor for her visceral (*N*, p. 123) inability to 'swallow' the situation, even if consciously she wishes she could take it all in her stride like her friend Laila, also the first wife in a bigamous marriage. Indeed, the eating disorder expresses vividly the way in which Nadra loses control, via this dichotomy between what she thinks she would like – to be able to eat normally, to be able to accept the situation calmly – and what she seems unable to avoid feeling – gnawing, stomach-churning jealousy – leading to a self-alienation which is perhaps the most harrowing part of the nightmare:

> Me había convertido en espectadora de mis rápidas transformaciones y no atinaba a detenerlas. Añoraba a aquella mujer que había sido yo en un pasado reciente [. . .]. Ante mis propios ojos yo era otra persona. [. . .] El paso del tiempo me resultó abrumador, y sentí una dolorosa nostalgia por unos años y por unas personas, Khaled y yo, que ya no éramos los mismos. (*N*, p. 138)[15]

It is perhaps significant that Nadra's eating problems wear off during the month of Ramadan, when fasting seems to help her develop greater spiritual strength and make peace with herself. At the end of the novel, when she transcends her own feelings sufficiently to be able to agree to move back home, it is interesting in this regard that she expresses her reservations with a related image: she is no longer unable to swallow food, but feels she has trained herself not to let anything into or out of her mouth in the first place: 'me sentía retraída e

---

[14] [Since Khaled's wedding with Nasmiya, I had lost nine kilos in weight. [. . .] My facial features had sharpened, my cheekbones, more prominent now, marked an oval line on my cheeks and my eyes had enlarged considerably. The wrinkles which the passage of the years had gradually left on my face now also stood out more clearly and the circles under my eyes looked more sunken.]

[15] [I had become a spectator on my rapid transformations and I could not find a way to arrest them. I yearned after that woman that I had been in the recent past [. . .]. In my own eyes I was another person. [. . .] The passage of time overwhelmed me and I felt a painful nostalgia for those years and those people, Khaled and me, who were no longer the same.]

inexpresiva, *como si yo misma me hubiera amordazado* para no enturbiar su regocijo [de Nasmiya] con mis dudas y temores, con mi desconfianza ante ese futuro inmediato que ambas íbamos a compartir' (*N*, p. 400; my italics) [I felt withdrawn and expressionless, *as if I had gagged myself* so as not to cloud her joy [Nasmiya's] with my doubts and fears, with my lack of confidence in that immediate future that we were both going to share].

The issue of possession is central to a consideration of *Nasmiya* as Gothic, a narrative mode which uses this motif in a range of different but connected ways. As Hendershot observes, a character often appears in Gothic narratives who is frighteningly 'other' due to his or her possession by an alien being, from Satan to extra-terrestrial body-snatchers.[16] Then, in a different sense, Gothic villains, whether or not possessed themselves, generally want to possess their hapless victims, body, soul, and often inheritance, hence the recurrent motif of imprisonment.[17] Thirdly, the traditional heroine of a Gothic romance wants to give herself to – which is to say, be possessed by – the hero who rescues her from the clutches of the villain.[18] Thus, it is important to ask where this novel locates itself relative to these notions of possession. Nasmiya, as we have seen, rejects it outright; Nadra, on the other hand, has difficulty relinquishing exclusive rights to Khaled, a form of possession perhaps, or to put it more conventionally, she wants him to want only one wifely possession – her – and points out in the very first paragraph of the novel that her Muslim name was chosen by Khaled 'porque significa "única"' (*N*, p. 9) [because it means 'the only one']. Thus, Khaled plays an oddly double role in the novel, considered from a Gothic perspective: he is the villain, possessed by his obsessive passion for Nasmiya, for betraying Nadra and for imprisoning her in a psychological torture-chamber, but he is simultaneously the hero whom she loves, needs, and desires. On the other hand, he demands total and exclusive possession of his two wives, the only real source of conflict between him and Nasmiya, who will not accept this attitude.

[16] 'A Gothic body is frequently a possessed body, a body inhabited by an alien other' (*The Animal Within*, p. 43). Hendershot reads Finney's *The Invasion of the Body Snatchers* and the two films based on it as 'science fiction [. . .] invaded by the Gothic mode' (p. 31). Reed, on the other hand, clarifies that the traditional demon-lover of medieval ballads is not so much a man possessed by Satan as Satan himself in disguise (*Demon-Lovers*, p. 26). Nevertheless, in her discussion of the portrayal of similar characters in more modern narratives, ranging from Heathcliff to Dracula, Reed refers to them as 'demonic' rather than as Satan himself (p. 92).

[17] Examples include Radcliffe's Montoni who imprisons both his wife and the heroine, Emily, in the eponymous castle in *The Mysteries of Udolpho*, principally to wrest their estates from them. In *The Monk*, Matthew Lewis's Ambrosio, on the other hand, has no monetary motive, but in his case imprisons Antonia so as to be able to enjoy her sexually without tarnishing his reputation as a virtuous and chaste monk. Innumerable further examples could be adduced.

[18] To follow through with the example texts cited in the previous note, one could mention Valancourt for Emily, or Lorenzo for Antonia.

If one is to believe Mrs Danvers, the housekeeper who adored her and remains in post, intimidating the second Mrs de Winter, Rebecca resembles Nasmiya, in the sense that she refused to let herself be possessed by any one person, including her husband: 'Of course he [de Winter] was jealous. So was I. So was everyone who knew her. She didn't care. She only laughed. "I shall live as I please, Danny [her pet-name for Mrs Danvers]," she told me, "and the whole world won't stop me"' (*R*, p. 275). For de Winter, indeed – and only perhaps half metaphorically – Rebecca was herself demonic: 'It doesn't make for sanity, does it, living with the devil,' as he puts it (*R*, p. 305). The second Mrs de Winter is imprisoned just as unequivocally by her sense of inadequacy relative to Rebecca, as any Gothic heroine in a dungeon. She is just as truly freed too, as if physically unchained when she finally discovers that de Winter never loved his first wife: 'My heart [. . .] was light and free. [. . .] Rebecca's power had dissolved [. . .]. I was free of her forever.' (*R*, pp. 319–20). Like Khaled too, de Winter plays the paradoxical role of both villain and hero: by not telling his second wife about the failure of his first marriage, he effectively consigns her to the same sort of mental prison-house as that suffered by Nadra and when he finally does open up to her and reveals that his marriage to Rebecca had been disastrous, he is her liberator.[19]

Nadra's mental incarceration does not derive from a total misconstruction of Nasmiya's relationship with their husband; on the contrary, it is because she understands only too well how much she and Khaled love each other that she feels trapped in an intolerable situation. She cannot hope, therefore to be freed in a manner reminiscent of the narrator of *Rebecca*. The escape route that she finds is a different one, as she decides to throw off her preconceptions about what constitutes normality in a relationship and how much this matters: 'De súbito e inesperadamente se me impuso un cierto sentido común desde el que nuestra situación, nuestra relación amorosa y bígama, se me apareció como un absoluto disparate. [. . .] Pero al instante rechacé estos efímeros pensamientos que sólo podían aparentar sensatez en la distancia, desde una mirada que desconociera a Nasmiya' (*N*, p. 400) [All of a sudden and quite unexpectedly, a kind of common sense imposed itself on me, from which perspective our situation, our amorous and bigamous situation, struck me as completely crazy. [. . .] But the next moment I threw off these ephemeral thoughts that could only appear sensible from the distance, from a point of view unacquainted with Nasmiya].

---

[19] Commenting on the ways in which Edgar Allan Poe advanced the Gothic mode, Clive Bloom accentuates the importance from this stage onwards of the variety of psychological solitary confinement that he calls 'the horror of the mind isolated with itself'. This could be regarded as one way to characterize the main body of both *Nasmiya* and *Rebecca*. See 'Introduction: Death's Own Backyard: The Nature of Modern Gothic and Horror Fiction', in *Gothic Horror: A Reader's Guide from Poe to King and Beyond* (ed.) Clive Bloom (Basingstoke: Macmillan, 1998), pp. 1–22 (p. 3).

As with *Rebecca*, though, and as in Gothic novels generally, even though the denouement brings some degree of closure, the narrative grips the reader for the portrayal of the imprisonment, not the release.[20] And despite the many differences in the specifics of the two plots, in the characterization of the three central figures and that of the minor players, the second Mrs de Winter's and Nadra's respective nightmares are the same in essence: they both are in love with a man who they believe finds them inferior to another woman who is so strange and different from them that they can never hope to compete with her. For Horner and Zlosnik, Rebecca 'seems to embody all that the narrator is not' for the body of the novel,[21] but by the time of narration, the gap has narrowed, since with Maxim's confession, his second wife grows up by her own admission, acquiring some of the self-confidence – and maybe sexual maturity if not promiscuity – she had admired in her predecessor. In analogous fashion, though Nasmiya's otherness is at the very heart of García Morales's novel, by the end, Nadra has also gone some way towards bridging the gulf between them, having decided wilfully to espouse some of her attitudes.

This leads to a consideration of how friendships, closeness and distance between women are depicted in *Nasmiya*, for the purposes of proposing a feminist reading of the novel. Strangely, perhaps, the otherness that separates Nadra from Nasmiya as far as their personalities and attitudes are concerned, does not prevent them from growing more and more fond of each other as the novel progresses, so that in the end, Nadra's return with the children is at least as much agreed for Nasmiya's sake as it is for Khaled's: 'yo deseaba reanimarla, verla de nuevo recuperada, evitarle tanto desaliento. Así pues, tratando de ignorar mis persistentes temores [. . .] opté por dar yo ese paso que Nasmiya me reclamaba, y [. . .] la informé [. . .] que ya había adoptado la determinación de reanudar mi vida con Khaled y con ella' (*N*, pp. 397–8) [I wanted to cheer her up, to see her recovered again, to spare her so much downheartedness. So, trying to ignore my persistent fears [. . .] I chose to take that step which Nasmiya was asking of me and I informed her [. . .] that I had made up my mind to take my life with Khaled and her back up again].

Nadra's other friends are also very unlike her: Laila takes a completely different view of her situation, downgrading the importance of any man in a

---

[20] Kilgour finds that in Gothic novels generally 'the endings are often [. . .] unsatisfactory' (*The Rise of the Gothic Novel*, p. 8) and DeLamotte makes a related point that resonates particularly with these two texts, even though her book is devoted to the nineteenth century: 'the sense of disappointment, even of being cheated, that most readers experience at the end of many Gothic works is shared by the characters themselves and is actually a subject of many Gothic narratives' (*Perils of the Night*, p. 132).

[21] *Daphne du Maurier*, p. 108.

woman's life, which is very far removed from Nadra's attitude. Ángela, at the opposite end of the spectrum – and an equally close friend to Nadra – attributes tremendous importance to having a man and being in love but does not seem to mind quite a rapid succession of relationships, which Nadra is not at all interested in having. Finally, Fardós, the wife in a childless couple with whom Nadra moves in temporarily, leads a more ascetic life, working long hours alongside her husband, again a very different type of lifestyle from Nadra's, for whom her children are absolutely central and having or not having a job of no importance. Despite these significant differences, García Morales portrays the relationships between Nadra and each of these women as warm, close friendships providing real support at a time of great need. 'Desde que Khaled contrajera matrimonio con Nasmiya, casi todas las mujeres del grupo me manifestaban un apoyo silencioso y discreto. De alguna manera, me sentía con frecuencia arropada por ellas' (*N*, p. 129) [Ever since Khaled had married Nasmiya, almost all the women in our group had shown me silent, discreet support. I often felt somehow swaddled by them]. In this context it does not seem implausible that she is able to develop genuine fondness for the alien being that her husband has seen fit to marry, without downplaying the magnitude of their differences. It is striking, for example, that very close to the end of the novel, when the two women's friendship and solidarity are at their peak, Nasmiya shows Nadra some of her art-work and the latter is surprised by the 'ostensible y enorme desolación' [ostensible and enormous desolation] contained in her pictures, concluding that 'existía algo en ella que me desbordaba, algo, o tal vez mucho, que se me escapaba todavía' (*N*, p. 412) [there was something in her which passed me by, something or maybe a great deal, which still escaped me]. And even if she comes to appreciate Nasmiya by the end of the novel, it remains true that she still finds her to be like a creature from another world: 'no pertenecía a este mundo' (*N*, p. 309) [she did not belong to this world].

A similarly positive portrayal of friendship and mutual support between women, even very different ones, is less in evidence in *Rebecca* since the narrator has been quite removed from her territory and so, unlike Nadra, has no network of pre-existing friends to whom to turn. Mrs Danvers, almost the only woman with whom she has daily contact, hates and resents her. On the other hand, with her personal maid, Clarice, a new appointment, there are signs of genuine solidarity, within the limitations that such a relationship is bound to have.[22] More importantly, perhaps, with de Winter's sister, Beatrice, an entirely different type of woman again, 'the sort of person who would nurse dogs through distemper, know about horses, shoot well' (*R*, p. 104), there is a sense of warmth, albeit quite mutually incomprehending. Indeed,

---

[22] See, for example, their shared secret over the fancy dress costume (*R*, p. 220).

the narrator's conclusion after the first meeting (and not undermined by later contact) is that she 'liked her very much', simply because she was 'kind' and 'sincere' (*R*, p. 110).[23]

Further examples of warmth between Gothic heroines and other women with whom they have little in common are not hard to find: Emily in Radcliffe's *Mysteries of Udolpho*, who shows tremendous loyalty to her hateful aunt, is as close as can be allowed across the class boundary with her personal maid, Annette, and with Theresa and Dorothée, two elderly servants.[24] The otherwise friendless Antonia in *The Monk* would willingly cling to her own foolish aunt, as well as her astute maid, Flora, and is grateful for the support received from the otherwise tedious landlady Donna Jacintha. Thus, the pattern drawn by Gothic novelists seems clear: in adversity, women cling together and are able to draw comfort from one another, even if they would not have a reason to be friendly otherwise. The relationship between Nadra and Nasmiya can therefore be read through this prism: they are both good – if radically different – women who, thanks to Khaled, find themselves in a terrible predicament, but a subtly different one for each. For Nadra, she wants the continuation of her monogamous relationship, but Khaled has destroyed all hope of this by bringing Nasmiya into the household and soon after, making her pregnant; for Nasmiya, she wants a harmonious relationship, whether monogamous or bigamous, but she cannot achieve this after Nadra leaves because Khaled misses her and the children too much and she cannot achieve it beforehand because it is making Nadra too unhappy.

These are extreme situations, but it is also possible to argue that García Morales posits a more everyday version of the phenomenon through her portrayal of the daily grind of housework, cooking, and childcare.[25] Laila is at pains to show how a significant factor in the harmonious relationship of herself and Ekram, her husband's second wife, is that the latter willingly does much of this household labour: 'Ekram me ayuda mucho en los quehaceres

---

[23] Inhibiting the formation of other friendships with women and to some extent this one too, however, is the narrator's perception of its predecessor having been a friendship with Rebecca, a friendship she keeps imagining to have been far superior to anything she can offer. In this respect, the fact that *Rebecca* is told from the second wife's point of view and *Nasmiya* from that of the first makes for a significant if logical divergence, even though it remains possible in both texts to glimpse something that might be termed a kind of gender solidarity that transcends the typical prerequisites of friendship, namely similarity of background, interests and attitudes.

[24] She finds comfort too in her friendship with a nun and with a certain Blanche, but with these she has more in common. This reading is at odds with Kilgour's. She asserts that 'what links the convent, Udolpho, and the Chateau together is that they are all private spheres associated with women turning against each other' (*The Rise of the Gothic Novel*, p. 128).

[25] DeLamotte discusses this issue with relation to *Jane Eyre*. See *Perils of the Night*, p. 201.

de la casa, y atiende a mis hijos igual que al suyo' (*N*, p. 30) [Ekram helps me a great deal around the house and she cares for my children just as she does for her own child]. Nasmiya also lightens Nadra's housework and childcare burden increasingly as their cohabitation develops, something portrayed as a form of drudgery that is imposed by the ultra-traditional division of labour demanded by Khaled (and presumably by Laila and Ekram's husband, too):

> Consideraba que su ocupación consistía en atender la tienda, administrarla y enfrentarse a todos los problemas que surgían en ella con frecuencia. Para Khaled la casa era un lugar de descanso y de ocio. En cualquier caso, yo ya había aceptado, desde hacía años, que mi trabajo consistía en cumplir con mi papel de ama de casa.   (*N*, p. 55)[26]

Only at the very beginning of their cohabitation does Nadra mention that she is left to do the housework (*N*, p. 21, for example). From page 33 onwards, when Nasmiya offers to help prepare the evening meal, the latter willingly takes on more and more of the domestic labour. The sharing of it partially liberates the two pairs of bigamous wives in the novel and their mutual gratitude contributes positively to the relationship between them: 'Me alentó el comprobar que podría contar con su colaboración en las tareas domésticas,' [I found it heartening when I realized that I could count on her help with the housework] comments Nadra at this first gesture of willingness to help (*N*, p. 33). By page 81, Nadra is to be found making Nasmiya coffee as a thank-you gesture for her having done all the housework unbidden, while Nadra was out. In other words, *Nasmiya* indicts the traditional imposition of endless, thankless domestic labour on women while simultaneously portraying the positive and practical way in which cohabiting women can partially relieve and thus liberate one another. As Laila describes it: 'Yo vivía [prior to Ekram's arrival] encerrada en casa, con los niños, y casi nunca salía. [After her arrival] empecé a ir al cine, a visitar exposiciones, a asistir a conciertos, o simplemente a dar un paseo o a tomar algo con alguna amiga' (*N*, p. 30) [I used to live shut up in the house with the children and I hardly ever went out. [After Ekram's arrival] I began to go to the cinema, to visit exhibitions, to attend concerts, or simply have a walk or a drink with a girlfriend.]

These observations on domesticity and the restrictions it places upon women lead us to Kilgour's observations defining the Gothic, which pinpoint precisely the elements on which *Nasmiya*'s haunting qualities hinge: 'the female gothic [. . .] by cloaking familiar images of domesticity in gothic forms [. . .] enables us to see that the home *is* a prison, in which the helpless

---

[26] [He considered it his occupation to serve in the shop, to manage it and deal with all the many problems which arose there. For Khaled, the house was a place for rest and leisure. In any case, I had accepted years back, that my work consisted of fulfilling my role as a housewife.]

female is at the mercy of ominous patriarchal authorities' (Kilgour, p. 9; her italics). Adelaida García Morales has built her prison without recourse to medieval architecture or an exotic location: an ordinary flat in present-day Madrid confines Nadra, not even because she is locked in, but simply because she has the housework to do, meals to prepare, children to supervise and no real excuse to go out for any length of time. Even when she defies Khaled by going out with Ángela, she knows she has to go back in the end and since she finds her husband waiting up for her, it is clear that such outings do not give her any real sense of freedom at all. Yet the prison is bigger than the flat, for even though she derives considerable relief from moving out, she now has to live with the guilt of how many others are being hurt by this – her children, Khaled, and Nasmiya – a kind of psychological entrapment.[27] However, the novel may be very quietly and tentatively suggesting that the way out of Nadra's prison is not through the front door, but by throwing off the shackles of sexual possessiveness as Nasmiya has done. In fact, Nasmiya's willingness to share the domestic labour (including childcare), mirrored by a similar situation in the other bigamous household of the novel, implicitly suggests that if rivalry and jealousy can be set aside, this may actually be a way of relieving women's sense of domestic imprisonment. It remains true too, though, that Nadra's ambivalent return home, chiefly for the sake of everyone else,[28] underlines – and tacitly indicts – the old expectation that women should be self-sacrificing.

Be that as it may, Kilgour comments: 'most commonly, gothic novels revolve around a battle between antithetical sexes, in which an aggressive sexual male, who wants to indulge his own will, is set against a passive spiritual female, who is identified with the restrictions of social norms.'[29] This highlights how inextricably bound up with social norms is the Gothic heroine's predicament generally. However, in the specific case of *Nasmiya*, the social norms themselves are uncertain: Nadra's situation is exacerbated by the fact that she is unsure how to negotiate the clash between Islamic and Spanish values. These are conflictual because of the issue of differing perceptions of bigamy in Islamic cultures versus Western European countries

---

[27] Khaled and Nasmiya are quite explicit about this, with Nasmiya eventually leaving Khaled herself and only willing to return if Nadra will move back too. With the children it is unspoken but equally obvious: Said, the teenaged son, becomes apathetic and falls behind in his schoolwork while they are living with Fardós and Ahmad; the younger girls only show their feelings by the euphoria they display on returning home (see *N*, pp. 312 (Said's unwonted apathy)); 326 (Khaled's unhappiness at Nadra's departure); 363 (Nasmiya leaves Khaled); 378 (Nasmiya's ultimatum to Nadra); 407 (children's euphoria and relief).

[28] She has made it clear that her first choice, if no-one else needed to be taken into account, would be to go on living away from home, but to have Khaled to stay at weekends (*N*, p. 403).

[29] *The Rise of the Gothic Novel*, p. 12.

such as Spain, exacerbated by Spain's especially bloody historical relationship with Islam.[30] This clash between two sets of contradictory social norms – Islamic and Spanish – places Nadra in an impossible situation: if she refuses to accept Khaled's marriage to Nasmiya, some at least will interpret this as a rejection of Islam, to which she is portrayed as being truly devoted; if she accepts it once and for all, her family and friends like Ángela will see it as proof of the barbarity of Islam, of her weakness and perhaps culpable passivity as a woman and as a wife. This problem remains unresolved but not unacknowledged at the end of the novel:

> Pensé en mis amigas, Ángela y Laila; quizá debería informarlas de mi regreso a casa con Khaled. Durante algunos minutos me mantuve en una duda inquieta e inexplicable sobre si llamarlas o no. Al fin me abstuve de telefonearlas, y ni siquiera le communiqué a mi madre que volvía de nuevo a mi casa. No sé por qué, deseaba, de momento, guardar en secreto mi decisión.   (N, p. 408)[31]

In similar fashion, but for different reasons, the second Mrs de Winter is in an impossible situation as regards social norms. The sense of inadequacy that tortures her through the majority of the novel is portrayed as being wholly bound up with these. On her own with her husband, all is ostensibly well; the worries she voices in the novel are that he is embarrassed by her failure to be the impeccable hostess and household manager that she imagines (rightly, in fact) that Rebecca was.[32] Yet to be so – and especially to bring Mrs Danvers to heel – would require an authoritative style that conflicts with the attributes of the social construction of virtuous femininity: passivity, diffidence, humility, modesty, and so on.[33]

---

[30] See Andrew Wheatcroft, *Infidels: The Conflict between Christendom and Islam 638–2002* (London: Viking, 2003), for an account of the folklore *vs* the historical events in Spain, to which the whole of Part II of his book is devoted (pp. 63–161).

[31] [I thought of my friends, Ángela and Laila; maybe I should inform them of my return home to Khaled. For a few minutes I was inexplicably in doubt and worried over whether to ring them or not. In the end I did not phone, and I did not even let my mother know that I was returning home. I do not know why, but for the moment I wanted to keep my decision secret.]

[32] Critics have also detected an implicit anxiety on the narrator's part relating to sexual immaturity relative to Rebecca. Horner and Zlosnik assert that Rebecca 'is clearly symptomatic of a cultural anxiety concerning adult female sexuality' (*Daphne du Maurier*, p. 112) and Alison Light argues that the narrator is 'haunted and paralyzed by the idea of a female sexuality more confident than her own' (*Forever England: Femininity, Literature and Conservatism Between the Wars* (London & New York: Routledge, 1991), p. 166).

[33] Marina Warner discusses the problems that these ideals pose for women in the context of the exemplary status of the Virgin Mary who successfully combines being Queen of Heaven (an authoritative figure who can intercede with God) and the personification of meek obedience. See *Alone of All Her Sex: The Myth and Cult of the Virgin Mary* (London: Vintage, 2000), pp. 81–117 and 186. Claire Colebrook discusses the issues around

Ultimately, one can read *Nasmiya* as Beauman reads *Rebecca*: 'rais[ing] questions about women's acquiescence to male values'.[34] García Morales is careful to differentiate these from Muslim values, since it is made clear that having more than one wife is not an option taken by the majority of the born Muslims, but is liked by Spanish (and other Western) converts to the religion (*N*, p. 41).[35] One can argue, therefore, that the author is commenting more on Spanish *machismo* than Islam here and showing how this religion offers Spanish men an opportunity to be more authoritarian and selfish than they could have got away with otherwise. In other words, the adoption of the eastern religion of Islam offers to western men the promise of realizing some of their orientalist fantasies. As Cyndy Hendershot remarks, paraphrasing Edward Said: 'Pointing to the East as despotic or pointing to it as a source of pleasure and wisdom are two sides of a coin that represents the East as the Other against which the West defines itself.'[36]

By choosing to convert to Islam, Nadra had decided on one level to embrace identification with the other, even though she did so with some reservations concerning Muslim attitudes to women (*N*, p. 11) and in part to secure the affections of Khaled (*N*, p. 10). Yet her espousal of otherness in the spiritual and sociocultural domains and the sacrifices she has willingly made accordingly, do not extend to an acceptance of bigamy, which might be termed conjugal otherness. That is where she both consciously and viscerally cannot follow Khaled. When she finally decides to override her reservations and accept a triangular marriage, the closing pages of the novel make it abundantly clear that if her fears of this ultimate espousal of otherness are to be successfully kept in check, it will be chiefly thanks to the solidarity and closeness that has grown up between her and Nasmiya, Khaled having become something of a pathetic (if still lovable) figure towards whom Nadra now feels protective in a semi-maternal way; when she refuses him her sexual favours towards the end of the separation, for example, his downcast reaction makes her wonder whether to 'ofrecerle mi protección como a un niño que

expectations placed upon wives in *Gender* (Basingstoke, Hants & New York: Palgrave Macmillan: 2004), pp. 142–4.

[34] Sally Beauman, 'Introduction' to Daphne du Maurier, *Rebecca* (London: Virago, 2003), pp. v-xvii (p. xvii).

[35] While the most central monogamous converts, Fardós and Ahmad, do not express a view on the subject, Nadra does find one outspoken ally among her Muslim acquaintances, a certain Samira, who makes a point of telling Nadra that she and her husband, Nizar, 'consideraban que se trataba de una costumbre implantada en una cultura que no era la nuestra, y afirmaban que no tenía ninguna relación con la práctica del Islam' (*N*, p. 213) [considered it a custom established in a culture that was not our own and asserted that it bore no relation to the practice of Islam].

[36] *The Animal Within*, pp. 169–70. See also Edward Said, *Orientalism* (New York: Pantheon, 1978), p. 172. The particular association of the Muslim East with 'ravening lust, raw sex and brutal passions' comes to the fore in the early nineteenth century, according to Wheatcroft, p. 283.

llora asustado a media noche' (*N*, p. 376) [offer him my protection as one would to a child who was crying and frightened in the middle of the night]. Domestic imprisonment promises to be alleviated by sharing not only the labour, but also the psychological burdens of marriage and motherhood and perhaps most important of all, the failure of Khaled's marriage to Nasmiya once they were left on their own together serves to reassure Nadra that she is wanted and needed by Khaled, an approximate psychological equivalent to the narrator's realization in *Rebecca* that Maxim did not love Rebecca.

Thus, the future looks like being a tolerable compromise at the end of *Nasmiya*, thanks principally to the eponymous character and despite the selfish and inconsiderate behaviour of the main male figure, Khaled. In conclusion, it is worth noting that there is a similar air of tolerability hanging over the final state of affairs in *Rebecca*, although this is described at the start of the novel, due to its flashback structure. In both novels there is a sense of relief that the acute pain and torment are over, that a storm has been weathered and that calmer waters are therefore to be welcomed even if that comes at the price of sacrificing stronger passions, pleasures, and principles. In both novels too, a key factor in the achievement of this relief is the narrator's restored sense of self-worth relative to her husband's feelings for the other woman. But in both novels too, the veneer is palpably thin: *Rebecca* opens with a disturbing and possibly recurrent dream evoking past anxieties,[37] while *Nasmiya* closes with a similarly troubling image of 'múltiples amenazas, invisibles todavía, pero agazapadas por todos los rincones de la casa' (*N*, p. 421) [multiple threats, invisible as yet, but lurking in every corner of the house]. The Gothic threat of the other has grown subtler, but still crouches just out of sight and may yet pounce again.

[37] 'Last night I dreamt I went to Manderley again' (*R*, p. 1), the unforgettable opening words of the novel, contain the ambiguity that the word *again* could refer to returning to Manderley or, equally – and part of the power of the sentence comes from this, no doubt – it could mean that the dream is a recurrent one.

7

El accidente (1997) and Robert Louis Stevenson,
The Strange Case of Dr Jekyll and Mr Hyde (1886):
Keeping Guilty Secrets

As far as its premise is concerned, *El accidente* [The Accident] resembles the author's earlier work, *Las mujeres de Héctor*, since the main driver of the plot is once again an accidental murder, this time of an old man called Emilio. However, in this later narrative, the haunting that follows is not of the paranormal variety, but a combination of guilt, fear, and indecision on the psychological level, plus a flesh-and-blood haunting of the culprit, named Fernando, by the victim's sons, who intimidate him with their repetition of the proverb 'Quien a hierro mata, a hierro muere'[1] [Live by the sword, die by the sword]. Fernando is the friend and would-be suitor of Berta, the main focus of the narrative and narrator of alternate chapters and the deed takes place at a New Year's Eve house party, when in a somewhat inebriated state, he punches the elderly street musician who had entered the courtyard of the house uninvited and been reluctant to leave as soon as he was asked. Emilio suffers a fatal blow to his head as he falls against a stone bench. The aftermath of this death (as in *Las mujeres de Héctor*) dominates the rest of the plot: what to do with the body, to whom to tell or not to tell the true story – the police, the defence lawyer, the man's relations, others in the village – fears of the consequences, tensions created and changes in the social dynamics within the group of friends due to differences in reaction and opinion over how to handle the affair. The end of the short novel (117 pages) appears to bring closure: Fernando and the whole group are acquitted, thanks to a brilliant lawyer engaged by Berta (*A*, p. 109); the same group of friends celebrate the following New Year's Eve in the same country house together; Berta and the friend she has been attracted to all along, Alberto, consolidate their relationship; Emilio's sons are persuaded by Berta to stop intimidating him.

However, the semblance of neat and simple plotting that this summary suggests is misleading. Despite its brevity, *El accidente*, is complex both in

---

[1] Adelaida García Morales, *El accidente* (Madrid: Anaya, 1997), pp. 87, 88, 115, for example. Future references will be to this edition and will be given parenthetically in the text.

its narrative forms and in its use of sub-plotting and narrative blind alleys. Briefly, these can be enumerated as follows. The mode of narration alternates with each new chapter between first-person narration by Berta, and a third-person, omniscient narrator; additionally, there are two short excursions into written journal-type, oneiric sequences by Berta (*A*, pp. 80–83 and 93–4). These semi-stream-of-consciousness interludes explore a new dimension of Berta's psyche, thus deepening and adding complexity to our understanding of her. Thus, the reader is provided with a plural perspective on the events and characters of the novel: internal and limited – Berta's accounts – as well as extradiegetic, in the sections narrated in the third person. The sub-plot of the novel concerns Berta's adolescent love-life, as her feelings for Alberto and Fernando fluctuate, and Alberto also swings between wanting Berta and dallying with the shallow but prettier Sonia. The most important blind alley down which García Morales leads us concerns the application of the novel's title. Although the author's tendency to choose titles that appear at first sight to be tangential to their novel's plot has already been noted, this one misleads in a different way: the opening pages deal with a car accident that kills both of Berta's parents, inviting the reader to assume that this is the event to which the title alludes and that the rest of the text will concern the aftermath of that tragedy. Not expecting any further accidents, one is more shocked, therefore, when Emilio is killed, than one would have been without the first car accident, when one would have been looking and waiting for the accident of the title on every page of the novel.

What makes *El accidente* an interesting novel and not just an expanded version of a story similar to one that might be found on the inside pages of a newspaper any day of the week is the powerful evocation of the psychological effects on those involved, collective possessors of a guilty secret – the accidental murder – whose reactions differ across a wide spectrum from wanting not only not to disclose it but even to try to forget it, to wanting to go to considerable lengths to track down the man's next of kin. With his fate resting most of all on the others' handling of the affair, Fernando in particular is not content to differ from them on how to react, but also seeks to influence them, specifically by threatening Alberto with further violence if he seeks out the dead man's sons (*A*, pp. 28–9). This range of reactions serves as an index of the different characters' moral conscience and self-image, opening a Pandora's box inside the psyche of Fernando most of all, but to a significant extent as well, for Berta and Alberto, leading to the relationship between these two finally developing into a love affair as the main plot and sub-plot converge at the end of the novel. Both positive and negative reasons are portrayed as bringing the couple together, but both are directly related to the accidental death: Alberto loses interest in Sonia and Berta in Fernando partly because of their respective ways of dealing with the issue and it is this discarding of rivals that finally unites Berta and Alberto, alongside their shared feelings on the matter.

Robert Louis Stevenson's even shorter narrative (70 pages), *The Strange Case of Dr Jekyll and Mr Hyde* also begins with an accident and is followed by a murder. The story opens with Richard Enfield, a minor character, telling the chronicler figure, Mr Utterson, a lawyer friend of Dr Jekyll, about his encounter with Mr Hyde in the small hours of the morning when he witnessed the latter colliding with, and then heartlessly trampling, a small girl.[2] However, this accident, like the car crash at the beginning of *El accidente*, is incidental to the main thrust of the tale, which turns on a far more sinister accident, as Henry Jekyll himself explains in his 'full statement of the case' (*JH*, pp. 81–97):

> Had I approached my discovery in a more noble spirit, had I risked the experiment while under the empire of generous or pious aspirations, all must have been otherwise, and [. . .] I had come forth an angel instead of a fiend. The drug had no discriminating action; it was neither diabolical nor divine. [. . .] At that time my virtue slumbered; my evil, kept awake by ambition, was alert and swift to seize the occasion.   (*JH*, p. 85)

The outcome of this accident, coupled with another one, relating to a chance impurity in the first batch of chemical salt Jekyll uses to make the metamorphosing draught, brings about the advent of Mr Hyde, who will gratuitously murder Sir Danvers Carew using a walking-stick belonging to Jekyll.

The accident at the beginning of García Morales's text sensitizes the protagonist to death and helps to shape attitudes which will be brought to the surface when the second accident takes place and be articulated by her in a speech to Emilio's sons at the end of the novel:

> Hace algún tiempo, no mucho, murieron mis padres [. . .]. Todavía sufro por su pérdida. Y hace un año murió aquí, en este patio, vuestro padre, también a causa de un accidente. [. . .] Ahora pretendéis vengar a vuestro padre asesinando a Fernando. Eso ya no sería un accidente sino un crimen. [. . .] Nunca os reconciliaréis con vosotros mismos si quitáis la vida a un ser humano, pues la vida es sagrada e intocable.   (*A*, pp. 115–16)[3]

---

[2] In Robert Louis Stevenson, *The Strange Case of Dr Jekyll and Mr Hyde and Other Stories* (ed.) and (intro.) Jenni Calder (Harmondsworth: Penguin, 1979), pp. 27–97 (p. 31). Future references will be to this edition and will be given parenthetically in the text.

[3] [Some time ago, not much, my parents died. [. . .] Their loss is still a source of suffering for me. And one year ago, in this courtyard, a death occurred here – your father's – also due to an accident. Now you plan to avenge your father by murdering Fernando. That would not be an accident, but a crime. [. . .] You will never be reconciled with yourselves if you take the life of a human being, because life is sacred and untouchable.]

In analogous fashion, the beginning of Stevenson's narrative sensitizes Utterson to the 'strange case', awakening his dormant curiosity to find out who Hyde is.[4]

However, these details of the narrative are easily forgotten: the power of *El accidente* lies in the murder of Emilio and its aftermath of secret-keeping and sharing; that of *The Strange Case* lies in the horrible secret that Jekyll jealously guards in his lifetime, preferring suicide to the ignominy of surviving revelation at the end of the text. It is true that two other factors could be read as at least part of the protagonist's motivation for taking his own life before Utterson succeeds in breaking down the door: the fact that Hyde (in whose body Jekyll is now trapped, partly due to the unavailability of a key ingredient of the draught, but also because he can no longer fully control its effects) is wanted for murder and possibly the fact that Jekyll now shuns his evil self (a repugnance that appears to date from the murder of Carew by Hyde) and therefore cannot endure being forced to inhabit that body any longer. However, if the latter point were the decisive one, he would not have waited until discovery was imminent to commit suicide. For the majority of the story, Jekyll has been at pains not to reveal his amazing scientific discovery to anyone, not to trusted and long-standing friend Utterson, nor to schoolfriend and fellow-doctor Lanyon, nor even to his faithful and devoted butler, Poole. Lanyon only discovers the truth when Jekyll is forced to seek his help as a last resort to rescue him from entrapment in his Hyde self and then, like a poisoned gift, the secret knowledge which Lanyon too feels obliged to continue guarding appears to be largely responsible for killing him. Indeed, the only person who survives knowing the secret – Utterson – is the one who strips it of its secret status by publishing it, suggesting a possible reading whereby the psychological pressure of keeping the guilty secret seems as lethal as the fateful drug itself.

The dreadful secret is a staple of the Gothic mode, according to many scholars, such as Punter: 'The colouring of guilt is automatically applied to certain classes of secret; and these are particularly the ones in which the Gothic deals.'[5] Indeed, a long list of classic Gothic texts could be listed which use one or more secrets as a major plot device, including, for example, *The Castle of Otranto, The Mysteries of Udolpho, The Woman in White, Rebecca* and so on, to name only some of the texts used in the present study. Critics including Punter have explored the nature of the secrets and guilt involved, spotlighting their sexual connotations (incestuous/oedipal, homosexual, adulterous . . .) and considering the implications thrown up, overtly or merely suggested in the texts under consideration. These analyses are obviously

---

[4] As Jekyll's lawyer, Utterson knows the name of Hyde because he holds Jekyll's will which intriguingly bequeaths all to him (*JH*, p. 35).

[5] *Gothic Pathologies*, p. 207.

valuable in their own right.[6] However, the present chapter will take a different line, which aims to shed light on the way in which García Morales utilizes the motif of the guilty secret: rather than dwelling on what the secret is, it will concentrate on the psychological impact of keeping it and how the narrative presents this, in comparison with Stevenson's analogous treatment.

Both *Jekyll and Hyde* and *El accidente* focus on what had been a close-knit group of friends, but pay special attention to three of their number. Stevenson acquaints us with a clique of professional men including Jekyll, Utterson, and Lanyon, but alluding to others – 'five or six old cronies' – who also form part of the group and who regularly dine together (*JH*, p. 43). García Morales has a similar sized group of teenagers[7] destined for the same types of prestigious profession[8] with a similar focus on three of them, Berta, Fernando, and Alberto. In both texts, the solidarity of the group is disturbed by the events of the plot, more dramatically and fatally in the case of *Jekyll and Hyde*, of course, since Utterson is the sole survivor of the central triad, whereas García Morales opts for apparent re-unification as they repeat their New Year's celebrations in the final chapter. However, in both texts, the psychological pressures of the secret-keeping related to the cornerstone of the plot – Jekyll's shape-shifting, Emilio's murder by Fernando – are shown to be indicative of a more radical emotional isolation that no amount of shared gaiety can do more than lightly camouflage.

Both authors actually address the discomfiting gulf between social jollity and the radical aloneness of the individual that it is so powerless to remedy. In *El accidente*, there is a discussion between the friends at the lunch prior to the first New Year's Eve dinner-party:

> Alberto, sentado frente a Berta y mirándola con insistencia, comentó que a él todas las fiestas le resultaban agradables, pero creía que las más alegres eran aquellas que surgían de manera espontánea, sin que ninguna celebración oficial las impusiera. Enseguida respondió Fernando que para él no

[6] For discussion of secrets as a cornerstone of the Gothic mode, see, for example, Hogle, who narrows the notion of the secret to one from the past returning to haunt characters (in Hogle (ed.), p. 2). A clever irony of *Jekyll and Hyde* is of course that Utterson erroneously assumes Hyde's hold over Jekyll to relate to such a past misdeed when in fact the secret is a present one. Ellis discusses secrets in *The Castle of Otranto*, Ann Radcliffe's life and works, and *Frankenstein* (see *The History of Gothic Fiction*, pp. 33, 50, and 144, respectively). Botting discusses secrets in the context of the portrayal of the family and what is concealed at home in the Gothic. See *Gothic*, pp. 70 and 114–15.

[7] Punter sees adolescence as 'integral to Gothic' because it is 'a time when there is a fantasized inversion of boundaries'; this is later linked to his notion of the 'dark imagination [. . .], born of the absence of boundaries.' *Gothic Pathologies*, pp. 6 and 178, respectively.

[8] Alberto and Pedro start a law degree in the course of the novel; Ana, Teresa, and Miguel choose English; Berta History, and Fernando Philosophy, all gateway degrees to prestigious careers (*A*, p. 112).

contaba el carácter oficial de la Nochevieja. Podía ser un día cualquiera, le
parecía indiferente el motivo de la celebración. A él le entusiasmaba
cualquier fiesta que celebrara con amigos.   (*A*, p. 20)[9]

Superficially, this appears to be a rather trite exchange of adolescent
banalities, although the mention of eye contact between Alberto and Berta
highlights its thinly disguised purpose: the locking of horns between the two
rivals for Berta's affections. Such a reading is partly encouraged by the
following sentence, which notes that it is at this point that Berta suddenly falls
out of love with Fernando, apparently steering the narrative quickly away
from the uncomfortable question of the value or otherwise of conventional
socializing. In fact, the change of tack subtly makes a related but different
point: it reveals how a light-hearted social event like this is less about
teenagers simply enjoying one another's company over lunch and more about
individuals absorbed by their own thoughts and feelings, since while this
conversation is going on, Berta is actually watching Alberto and Fernando
and privately changing her feelings on the latter.

    Stevenson deals with similar issues when he notes that after 'pleasant
dinners', 'hosts loved to detain the dry lawyer [Utterson] [. . .]; they liked to
sit awhile in his unobtrusive company, practising for solitude, sobering their
minds in the man's rich silence, after the expense and strain of gaiety' (*JH*,
both quotations p. 43). Scholars have posited that the wording here implies a
homosexual connotation to these evenings attended by 'reputable men' (*JH*,
p. 43) in each others' homes instead of at their clubs, the normal venue for
convivial evenings between men-friends of a non-sexual nature.[10] Thus, in
both texts, we find sexual tensions thinly veiled by self-deceptively jovial
wining and dining and in both cases we could read this as a secret of social
hypocrisy shared – consciously or unconsciously – by the participants.

    Later in the novel, reflecting on the suddenness of her falling in love with
Alberto, Berta at first imagines there to be two Albertos, the one she has
known since childhood and this new alluring one, but 'concluyó que era
imposible conocer por completo a una persona, era como si se pretendiera

---

    [9] [Alberto, sitting opposite Berta and staring hard at her, commented that as far as he
was concerned all parties were pleasant, but he thought the merriest ones were those which
happened spontaneously, without the imposition of an official celebration. Fernando
answered straight back that from his point of view the official character of New Year's Eve
was of no importance. It could be any day, the reason for the celebration did not matter to
him. Any party celebrated with friends was fun for him.]
    [10] For more on this see Alan Sandison, *Robert Louis Stevenson and the Appearance of
Modernism: A Future Feeling* (Basingstoke & London: Macmillan, 1996), pp. 252–3.
Botting limits himself to noting the suggestion of a homosexual relationship between
Jekyll and Hyde as a misinterpretation by others within the narrative (*Gothic*, p. 142).
Stephen Heath discusses the sexual meaning of *expense* in Victorian English. See *The
Sexual Fix* (Basingstoke: Macmillan, 1982), p. 14.

coger con los dedos una bola de mercurio: se escapaba y se dividía en numerosos fragmentos' (*A*, p. 73) [she concluded that it was impossible to know a person completely, it was like trying to pick up a ball of mercury; it slipped out of one's grasp, dividing into numerous fragments]. How strikingly close these sentiments are to Dr Jekyll's theory: 'Man is not truly one, but truly two. I say two because the state of my own knowledge does not pass beyond that point [. . .] and I hazard the guess that man will ultimately be known for a mere polity of multifarious, incongruous and independent citizens' (*JH*, p. 82).

In both texts too, the implications of these disturbing ideas about the human condition are dramatized after a sociable evening gives way to a turning-point in the dynamics of the group, the effect of which is to overlay the tacit agreement to share the secret of social hypocrisy with a need for a new type of collective secret-keeping. In *El accidente*, the death of Emilio follows the New Year's Eve dinner-party; in *Jekyll and Hyde*, Utterson tries (in vain) to persuade Jekyll to share the secret of Hyde's identity with him. From that point on, García Morales's Berta discovers new facets to the personalities of both Fernando and Alberto, while Stevenson's Utterson comes to see Jekyll's secret as blacker and more impenetrable than he had supposed. Let us now track the evolution in the dynamics of friendship in each novel from this point on as the pressures of secret-keeping inflect it.

Berta's feelings for Fernando had begun to turn to repulsion even before Emilio's death (*A*, p. 21) as noted above, but he seals his fate by his flippancy just afterwards: 'no era sino un desconocido y un desgraciado pordiosero que, quizá, se hallara mejor muerto que vivo. En aquellos instantes, Fernando caía derrotado, para mí, por sus propias palabras' (*A*, p. 24) [he was merely a stranger and an unfortunate beggar who might even be better off dead than alive]. Some slight show of remorse partially rehabilitates him subsequently (*A*, p. 26), but the damage is irrevocable, since Berta believes that the affair has revealed 'ciertas facetas de su personalidad' [certain facets of his personality] and consequently 'le contemplaba como a una persona diferente de ese otro Fernando del que se había enamorado' (*A*, both p. 31) [she looked upon him as a different person from that other Fernando with whom she had fallen in love]. Now she develops pity for him (*A*, p. 33) which leads to a new type of solidarity between them, whereby Berta is willing to help him keep the secret of his fear of Emilio's sons from their mutual friends and discreetly lets him sleep at her flat, even pretending not to have noticed that he has been working his way through the drinks cabinet in the night. Nevertheless, the depth and extent of his fears and self-doubt are secrets he will not share even with Berta, despite her attempts – like Utterson's with Jekyll – to persuade him to confide in her:

> [Berta] pensó que tendría que hablar con él e intentar que se confiara a ella, que no se encontrase tan solo con su sufrimiento y su miedo. Mantuvo una

> larga conversación con él aquella misma tarde [. . .] y advirtió que Fernando
> cerraba las puertas de un mundo interior y de una sensibilidad que nadie le
> atribuía y que, sin embargo, Berta pudo intuir. Supo entonces que vivía
> encerrado en una enorme soledad y que ninguno de sus amigos, ni siquiera
> ella, le conocía realmente.   (A, p. 99)[11]

Berta's intuitions about Fernando's vulnerability have already been confirmed
by the omniscient narrator's revelation of his secret feelings: his 'auténtico
pánico' (A, p. 97) [genuine panic] at the threatening behaviour of Emilio's
sons and his feeling that he is 'desprotegido' [unprotected] because he cannot
run to his mother for help any more (A, p. 98). These are the guilty secrets
surrounding his doubts about his own masculinity that even the closest friend
or the cleverest lawyer cannot prevent him from being punished for, since the
punishment is self-inflicted, if arising from the socially constructed notion of
masculinity that he has assimilated. As the author herself put it (albeit in
another context): 'La norma social se interioriza aunque sea a nivel
subconsciente y de alguna forma se sufre el castigo'[12] [Social norms are
interiorized if only at the subconscious level and one way or another one
suffers the punishment]. According to Hendershot, 'masculinity as a
masquerade may be articulated through Gothic texts, which frequently reveal
the fragility of traditional manhood. [. . .] The Gothic continually reveals the
gulf between the actual male subject and the myth of masculinity.'[13] What
remains tantalizingly undecidable in García Morales's portrayal of Berta's
loss of attraction for Fernando, however, is the extent to which she is a 'new
woman'[14] put off precisely by the traditional markers of raw masculinity

---

[11] [[Berta] decided that she would have to talk to him and try to make him confide in
her, so that he should not be so alone in his suffering and fear. She held a long conversation
with him that same evening [. . .] and she noticed that Fernando shut the doors on an inner
world and sensitivity that no-one attributed to him and which Berta had nevertheless been
able to sense. She learnt then that he was living enclosed in enormous loneliness and that
none of their friends, not even her, really knew him.]

[12] Sánchez Arnosi interview. García Morales was referring to the incestuous
implications in El Sur, seguido de Bene.

[13] The Animal Within, p. 4. Peter Middleton emphasizes the link between traditional
masculinity and emotional invulnerability. See The Inward Gaze: Masculinity and
Subjectivity in Modern Culture (London: Routledge, 1992), p. 179. Byron addresses these
points from the perspective of the discourse of degeneration rather than gender, but reaches
a similar position to that of Hendershot and one as true of El accidente as it is of the text
she is discussing, Jekyll and Hyde: 'the text suggests that the repressive forces of society
are [partly . . .] responsible. [. . .] Gothic novels of the Victorian fin de siècle often suggest
that the evil is sinuously curled around the very heart of the respectable middle-class norm'
('Gothic in the 1890s', in Punter (ed.), p. 137).

[14] Hendershot discusses the anxieties generated in fin-de-siècle Britain and postwar
America because she sees the Gothic as addressing 'the threat of the New Woman [which]
was largely perceived as one in which sexual difference was breaking down' (The Animal
Within, p. 22).

expressed through Fernando's shows of violence and anger, and preferring Alberto's subtler variety of masculinity (reading Conrad, facing up to his responsibilities . . .); or, on the other hand, whether she is more conformist, taking the traditional view that masculine attractiveness needs to demonstrate bravery and the kind of controlled violence which would never unleash it on a defenceless old man and then try to run away from the consequences.

In *Jekyll and Hyde*, the close friend and the clever lawyer are represented by a single character, Utterson. Like Berta's, his efforts to gain the full confidence of his friend, though appreciated by the guilty party – Jekyll – are rebuffed:

> 'My good Utterson [. . .] this is very good of you, this is downright good of you, and I cannot find words to thank you in. [. . .] This is a private matter and I beg of you to let it sleep. [. . .] If I am taken away, Utterson, I wish you to promise me that you will bear with him [Hyde] and get his rights for him.' (*JH*, p. 44)

Just as Berta's lawyer can protect Fernando (and the other friends) only from the superficial punishment of a prison term, but not from the self-inflicted life-sentence of guilt and self-loathing, so Utterson can deal with the formalities of Jekyll's will efficiently, but can do nothing to help him with the complex love–hate relationship he has with his Hyde self. Clearly (and in common with Fernando), an important part of Jekyll's ambivalence relates to his understanding of the concept of masculinity. On the one hand, his status as a man of science, 'self-possessed, objective, rational', bestows upon him the 'ideal male subject' label for society at large.[15] Counterbalancing this, Hendershot argues for a reading of Hyde that feminizes him, both from a Darwinian perspective (as raw nature versus the civilized male Jekyll) and a religious one (as evil in the traditional equation of man with good and woman with evil),[16] but her own argument could be interpreted differently. Thus, the 'leap of welcome' Jekyll reports on first seeing the reflection of Hyde in a mirror, because 'this, too, was myself' (*JH*, p. 84) might relate to a recognition of a more primitive, predatory masculinity than he can be sure of in his Jekyll self. If there are any question marks over the doctor's heterosexual virility – and as we have seen, there do seem to be some coded clues to this effect in the text – this newly discovered self may both revolt and delight him because its very animality affirms his masculinity, assuring him that it can co-exist with the all-male evenings of 'expense and gaiety' that he enjoys as Jekyll.

The domino effect of a murder leading to the revelation of a host of private insecurities jealously guarded as secrets by the central male character in both

---

[15] Hendershot, *The Animal Within*, p. 69.
[16] Ibid., pp. 105–14.

texts spills over into self-examination by the bewildered and deeply shaken close-friend figure, Berta, in *El accidente*; Utterson, in *Jekyll and Hyde*. Taking Berta first, she is assailed by a potent mix of practical fears – will she go to prison for being an accessory after the fact? – and psychological anxieties – how can her love be so fickle that it can just switch off, as it did in the case of Fernando, over a chance remark and the way he was eating a chicken drumstick? So an outside view from a sensible person who holds her dear is an attractive option to provide an outlet for her concerns and some sound advice. This role in *El accidente* is played by Adora, the long-standing family maid and the nearest the recently orphaned protagonist has to a mother.[17] Reinforcing her position of trust and love is the revelation, relatively late in the text (*A*, pp. 100–102), that even during the parents' lifetime, Berta used to turn to Adora for a sympathetic ear, as her mother had little time for her childish worries. However, what makes Adora a good person to turn to also makes her someone to whom Berta feels she cannot at first tell the whole truth: 'Dada su mentalidad conservadora y su vida ordenada, me sentía impotente para confiarme a ella, no podía contarle cómo había muerto el viejo Emilio' (*A*, pp. 34–5) [In view of her conservative mentality and her well-ordered life, I felt powerless to confide in her, I could not tell her how old Emilio had died].

Utterson feels similarly burdened by his albeit limited access to Jekyll's secret; he knows enough, though, to be extremely worried about Jekyll's relationship with Hyde following the murder by the latter of the eminent Sir Danvers Carew. Thus, he also turns to a sensible outsider, in this case his head clerk. Again, however, the man's very appropriateness – because he is outside the coterie of friends – is what prevents Utterson telling him all he knows: 'he [Utterson] began to cherish a longing for advice. It was not to be had directly; but perhaps, he thought, it might be fished for' (*JH*, p. 53).

A further echo of Stevenson in the handling of the self-doubting domino effect on Berta in *El accidente* is the way in which the trouble that Fernando has brought upon himself causes her to ask herself questions about her own guilt: 'era incluso más culpable que Fernando, ya que él se encontraba obnubilado por el alcohol y yo, en cambio, me hallaba consciente y lúcida' (*A*, p. 44) [I was even more guilty than Fernando, since his judgement was clouded by alcohol and I, on the other hand, was conscious and lucid]. Utterson too anxiously searches his conscience when he supposes that the

---

[17] Kilgour notes the 'important and distinctive role' of servants in Gothic texts from Walpole on, adding, 'The gothic's idealization of the devoted servant is part of its nostalgia for the good old days.' *The Rise of the Gothic Novel*, pp. 180 and 181, respectively. The dark side of this, explored by García Morales in *Una historia perversa*, will be discussed in Chapter 9. Adora's role also chimes with Modleski's comments mentioned in Chapter 2, when she asserts that Gothic fiction provides few mothers but many mother substitutes (*Loving*, p. 68).

hold Hyde has over Jekyll must be one of blackmail resting upon a youthful indiscretion of some kind (*JH*, p. 42).

Thus, both texts narrate a secret-keeping web in which characters collectively cover for each other's social hypocrisy, in which lawyers see their role as protecting their clients from official justice rather than rendering them up to it[18] and in which the secret selves that hide behind this social façade half want but cannot quite bring themselves to expose their vulnerabilities to each other, particularly as these are inextricably bound up with their sexual attractiveness and social acceptability.

The image of the façade raises the ingenious utilization of architectural metaphor in *Jekyll and Hyde*; indeed, critics have expounded on the significance of the different doors, windows, keys, back and front of Jekyll's house, and how they reflect the dichotomies between inner and outer lives and selves that the main plot dramatizes.[19] Thus, it is worth considering whether García Morales has used the buildings in *El accidente* to similar effect.

The accident that opens the Spanish narrative – the car-crash that kills Berta's parents – is one that takes place on the public highway, just as it is in Stevenson's text – the collision between Hyde and the little girl – but the central secret of both novels originates within the confines of private property. However, in both cases, the location is not wholly within but in a liminal space that is neither truly inside nor outside: Jekyll secretly drinks his special draught inducing his metamorphoses in the room above the former dissection laboratory, an outbuilding reached from his house by crossing a yard; Fernando lets the violence within himself escape after drinking alcohol inside his family's country house, but he throws the lethal punch in its private courtyard, which Emilio had entered from the street via the 'portal' that had been inadvertently left unfastened (*A*, p. 23). It is fitting in both cases that the emergence of the evil self takes place where it does, beyond the 'prison-house' (*JH*, p. 85) of the respectable home that demands social conformity, but still inside its protective outer boundary.[20]

---

[18] For example, Jekyll entrusts a potentially incriminating letter to Utterson, leaving with him the decision of whether to show it to the police and Utterson is not ambivalent because of a sense of duty to the law, but because he is unsure whether to disclose it or to conceal it will be more beneficial to his client, Jekyll (*JH*, pp. 52–3). Leslie J. Moran observes that 'lawyers, solicitors, barristers and judges, appear as characters in Gothic texts embodying a certain ambivalence between good and evil, between law as order and right reason and law as corruption' ('Law and the Gothic Imagination', in Botting (ed.), pp. 87–109 (p. 88)).

[19] See Sandison, pp. 215–48 and Irving S. Saposnik, *Robert Louis Stevenson* (New York: Twayne, 1974), pp. 96–7. Punter also notes that houses and castles in Gothic works generally represent 'the dream-house, which is also the house of the body', *Gothic Pathologies*, p. 216.

[20] In this play of interiority and exteriority we find an echo of *Las mujeres de Héctor* and *The Turn of the Screw*, discussed in Chapter 4.

Fernando's parents' house in Chinchón where the friends have gone for New Year's Eve is described thus: 'una casa que sus padres habían restaurado'; 'era enorme y estaba muy cuidada. Sus muebles habían sido elegidos en los mejores anticuarios de Madrid: eran de gran valor y belleza' (*A*, both p. 19) [a house which his parents had restored [. . .]. It was enormous and very well looked after. The furniture had been chosen from the best antique dealers in Madrid; it was very valuable and beautiful]. As a cipher for Fernando himself it could hardly be more suggestive. It has already been made clear how dependent he still feels on his parents (especially but not only on his mother) to look after him even though he knows he is too grown-up to turn to them without jeopardizing his masculinity. Indeed, they appear to have raised him with the same care and attention that they used to choose the furnishings for the house and the description of this upbringing, much later on in the book, even sounds like a solid edifice built around Fernando: 'su madre había sido siempre, durante su infancia, el más *seguro refugio*, la protección contra todo mal que le aconteciera, y su padre aparecía en su memoria como un hombre *de hierro*, poderoso, para el que nada era imposible' (*A*, p. 98; my italics) [during his childhood, his mother had always been the *safest refuge*, protection against anything bad that might happen to him, and his father appeared in his memory as a man *of iron*, powerful, for whom nothing was impossible]. Nevertheless, at the time of the New Year's Eve party and in the all-important verbal exchange between Fernando and Emilio, preceding the punch that will kill the latter, Fernando refers to the house not as his parents' but his own: 'Fernando se acercó a él y puso sus manos sobre el acordeón, amenazándole con arrebatárselo si no se marchaba de *su* casa enseguida' (*A*, p. 23; my italics) [Fernando went over to him and put his hands on the accordion, threatening to seize it from him if he did not leave *his* house at once]. In other words, he experiences the uninvited Emilio's entry as an invasion of his property (read self), not his parents', suggesting the sort of psychological blurring and poor separation from them that fits well with the immature characterization of the character as a whole.[21]

The different bedrooms chosen by each of the friends when they arrive at the house also reflect and underpin the relationships that the narrative is starting to develop: Fernando puts Berta in his parents' bedroom and she will, indeed come to act as a substitute or adjunct for them when she has the money to buy him out of trouble via the services of a top lawyer, as well as offering him the refuge of her own home to escape the daily intimidation by Emilio's sons. Fernando himself takes a bedroom next to Berta's, prefiguring the revelation later in the text that he used to run to his mother when he had night terrors (*A*, pp. 97–8). Alberto chooses 'un dormitorio que formaba una

---

[21] Adding to his immature image is the fact that Fernando is 19, older than the other friends, but in their class at school because he has had to repeat a year twice (*A*, p. 16). Berta gives her age as 16 at the time of her parents' death (*A*, p. 8).

especie de pequeña torre, ya que era el único que se hallaba en una tercera planta' [a bedroom which constituted a kind of small tower, since it was the only one on the third floor] and he will stand alone and isolated on the moral high ground after the death of Emilio, 'towering' above the others in his unflinching adherence to what he believes to be right. Ana and Teresa voluntarily share a bedroom just as they will be indistinguishable in their shared alibi and reactions to the tragedy; Miguel, a character who lets himself be intimidated by Fernando into helping dispose of the body, takes the easiest option by laying claim to the first empty bedroom he happens upon and Pedro, who plays a very small role in the narrative, picks one which is small and austere (all A, p. 20). These choices of bedrooms, however, are thought by them to be academic, because the friends intend to stay up all night together. In the event, they do not do so, following Alberto's lead and running away to their respective temporary 'home' territory after the horror of Emilio's death and in spite of Fernando's protestations that 'ahora había que olvidarse de lo ocurrido y continuar con la fiesta' (A, p. 24) [now they should forget about what had happened and go on with the party].

Another noticeable house in *El accidente* appears when Berta persuades Alberto to spend a week with her and Adora in an isolated and primitive property in Ibiza. This house decidedly does not belong to any of the characters in the story. Indeed, the author goes to some lengths to distance it from Berta's heritage.[22] Thus, the three are staying in an equally alien property for them all, cut off from mains electricity and running water, the comforts of which they are deprived echoing well the uncomfortable emotional conditions of their trip. It is here that Berta falls in love with Alberto (A, p. 57), quite as suddenly and without warning as she had fallen out of love with Fernando at Chinchón; just as seeing the latter framed by the parental over-indulgence that had shaped his personality appeared to kill the feelings she had had for Fernando, so seeing Alberto removed from home, washing at the well in the pouring rain proves to be indeed a watershed in her feelings for him. A clue to the undecidability mentioned above with respect to which criteria of masculinity attract Berta and which repel her, could be suggested in this scene, where superficially Alberto's naked torso looks beautiful to her, but more important perhaps is the positive value she places on that age-old relationship of Spartan habits going hand in hand with masculinity, judging by the overstated language she chooses to describe merely stripping to the waist and washing in cold water: 'aquello era un acto heroico, imposible para la mayoría de los seres humanos' (A, p. 57) [that was a heroic act, impossible for the majority of human beings]. But even here, right away, one might have thought, from the hypocrisies of social convention, the relationship is unable to develop, since Berta finds she cannot

---

[22] It actually belongs to the boyfriend of a cousin of Berta's (A, p. 52).

emancipate herself from normal etiquette enough to reveal the secret of her changed feelings for him and he is too absorbed in his obsessive worrying about Emilio's death to notice any subtler hints. The escape from home, then, does not provide relief for Alberto's un-secret but guilty feelings concerning Emilio, nor for Berta's unguilty but secret feelings for Alberto. The house in Ibiza, if anything, shows that even if one's home can personify the self in some sense, it does not follow that getting away from it will automatically provide a way of escaping from that 'prison-house' (*JH*, p. 85).

Does this 'non-home' have an analogue in *Jekyll and Hyde*? If it did, one would expect it to be a neutral territory in which Utterson and Lanyon could come together, but in Stevenson's narrative, this encounter takes place at Lanyon's house in Cavendish Square. Despite the precision of the address, though, this abode retains a fairly neutral – because undescribed – value. All that is revealed about it is that the square in general is a 'citadel of medicine' (*JH*, p. 36); the dining-room into which Utterson is conducted the first time he goes there is given not one whit of description and on the second, crucial visit about to be discussed, one is not even told in which room he is received. Thus, it is possible to argue that even in Lanyon's home, there is something of the same neutrality as was noted in the Ibiza house of *El accidente*. Be that as it may, there is certainly the same type of awkwardness that pervades the atmosphere in García Morales's Ibiza. Utterson tries to re-establish the strength of the friendship between the three men, only to have his gesture rejected:

'Can't I do anything? [. . .] We are three very old friends, Lanyon [. . .]'
'Nothing can be done' returned Lanyon.   (*JH*, p. 57)

Rather as Berta and Alberto return to Madrid early because they cannot get on in Ibiza, needing as they do each to talk about different things – Berta about her feelings for him, Alberto about Emilio's death – so Utterson cuts his visit to Lanyon short because the only thing he wants to talk about is what is wrong with Jekyll, whereas for Lanyon that topic is quite unbearable: 'If you can sit and talk with me of other things, for God's sake stay and do so; but if you cannot keep clear of this accursed topic, then, in God's name, go, for I cannot bear it' (*JH*, p. 57).

The third significant location of *El accidente* is Berta's own flat, where she has left her parents' bedroom and bathroom untouched since their death, 'inducida quizá por la esperanza de que así sentiría que su ausencia no era definitiva' (*A*, p. 44) [perhaps driven by the hope that this way she would feel their absence was not definitive] and where she has a spacious study of her own, furnished comfortably in neutral style and colour (*A*, p. 35). Does this space reflect her self in any way analogous to the obvious correspondence between Fernando and the house in Chinchón? The large size and smart, central location of the flat ('en una calle perpendicular a la de Alfonso XII, muy cerca del Retiro' *A*, p. 34 [in a street running at right-angles to Alfonso XII Street, very close to the Retiro Park]) help to confirm Berta's well-to-do background but tell us little more about her. It would seem, therefore, that if anything, they present her as a relatively blank canvas to be turned into what she is by what happens to her rather than what she spontaneously does herself. In this respect, the contrast between Fernando's house/self and Berta's fits with a classic type of Gothic pattern, as this is characterized by Kilgour: 'Most commonly, gothic novels revolve around a battle between antithetical sexes, in which an aggressive sexual male, who wants to indulge his own will, is set against a passive spiritual female, who is identified with the restrictions of social norms.'[23]

Further, does Utterson's house in *Jekyll and Hyde* function in a manner similar to Berta's? In spite of his maleness and the lack of (overt) sexual dynamics in Stevenson's text, what the two characters do have in common is their role as close friend and confidant of the central man in the story and partial chronicler of his tale. Like Berta's, Utterson's house is described sparingly, providing enough for the reader to be assured of his respectability but little more.[24] Taken together, what can be noted in both texts is the sharp contrast between the obviously over-determined house of the man at the centre of the action on the one hand and the other relatively neutral descriptions of houses.

In conclusion, *El accidente* and *The Strange Case of Dr Jekyll and Mr Hyde* dwell on the nature of the human condition and in particular, that part of it which we usually keep well secreted behind the closed doors of our houses or our selves. Both take as their premise what will happen if such a secret self gets out or is let out. Both tacitly ask the question whether this primitive self affirms or undermines the masculinity of the subject and both seem to reach the conclusion that the animal within is best kept there. More importantly, though, in both novels, the owner of that violent, evil self is drawn not as himself a villain, but a pathetic figure, taken over by the ruthless being within. Perhaps here is where the Gothic mode takes its power, because it resonates with notions of demonic possession, body-snatchers, and aliens lurking within us: 'This was the shocking thing: that the slime of the pit seemed to utter cries and voices [. . .] and [. . .] that that insurgent horror [. . .] lay caged in his flesh, where he heard it mutter and felt it struggle to be born' (*JH*, p. 95). If Berta has learnt anything at the end of *El accidente*, it is that pathos of the human condition. *El accidente*, despite the apparently happy ending, actually closes without confirming that Emilio's sons never

---

[23] *The Rise of the Gothic Novel*, p. 12.
[24] All we can glean is that it is in Gaunt Street (*JH*, p. 39), a 'bachelor house', convenient for church, containing a business room as well as his living quarters and his bed is 'great' and 'dark' in a 'curtained room' (*JH*, pp. 35–7).

will haunt Fernando again; indeed, the final two sentences refuse to allow us the satisfaction of assuming this to be the case: 'Todos me felicitaron por el éxito de mi improvisado discurso. Y yo me preguntaba si volvería a ser válido en el caso de que los hijos del anciano músico intentaran de nuevo vengarse de Fernando' (A, p. 117) [They all congratulated me for the success of my improvised speech. And I wondered whether it would be valid a second time if the old musician's sons tried to take their revenge on Fernando again]. That haunting by the sons is a most powerful metaphor for the lifelong haunting of which Fernando – and all the characters – will never rid themselves: the knowledge of what the accident revealed about what was living caged in their flesh.

8

La señorita Medina (1997) and Wilkie Collins, *The Woman in White* (1859–60): Discovering Guilty Secrets

Published in the same year as *El accidente*, *La señorita Medina* [Miss Medina] also revolves around a secret, but unlike it, this is one that the original possessor has taken with her to the grave. The novel opens in a manner reminiscent of the author's first narratives, *El Sur* and *Bene*, since a first-person narrator is talking directly to her dead sister, Nieves, and indeed, as one learns more about her in the course of the novel, this Nieves turns out to be another social misfit, like the father in *El sur*, quite alien to the rest of the family's and the community's idea of normality. Like him too, she ended her own life and the narrator, called Silvia and just sixteen herself at the time, has only memories from thirty years earlier at the start of the novel, with which to try to piece together why. In search of a better understanding of her sister and their shared past, she develops a friendship with the eponymous character, a former nun and teacher from the school both girls had attended, but with whom Nieves had formed a special bond of friendship. Later in the novel, Silvia will also re-establish contact with Julio, Nieves's boyfriend, and start a love affair with him herself. Gradually, Silvia's two relationships – with Srta Medina and Julio – begin to link together as the secret of the suicide motive is slowly revealed to be one of multiple sexual jealousy. Srta Medina, it transpires, is a lesbian who was in love with Nieves and, whether she admitted it to herself at the time or not, she was jealous of her pupil's relationship with Julio.[1] Julio, on his side, was secretly having an affair with a man, Ginés, while simultaneously seeing Nieves and it is Srta Medina's revelation of this infidelity *in flagrante delicto* that drives the already emotionally fragile Nieves to despair and death.

Thus, a search to find out a single secret – why Nieves committed suicide – turns out to be just one piece in a complex mosaic of interlinked secrets, only a few of which have been mentioned in the brief plot summary just given.[2]

---

[1] *La señorita Medina* (Barcelona: Plaza & Janés, 1997), p. 26. Future references will be to this edition and will be given parenthetically in the text.

[2] The image of a mosaic comes from a review of Wilkie Collins, *The Woman in White*, published in *The Times* and cited in Walter M. Kendrick, 'The Sensationalism of *The Woman in White*', in *Wilkie Collins* (ed.) Lyn Pykett (New York: St Martin's Press, 1998), pp. 70–87 (p. 77).

The final twist is that the revelation of the secret thirty years on by Srta Medina to Julio and Silvia leads Julio to his own death in a car crash. Thus, the novel closes not with resolution, but with two new secrets, which are destined to remain so: did Julio consciously seek death in his car[3] and if not, was this Nieves's revenge from beyond the grave, Srta Medina's malevolent wish granted, or just a terrible accident? In choosing such a denouement, was the author simply avoiding a trite 'happily ever after' ending; was she wreaking her own revenge on Silvia and/or Julio for daring to seek happiness together; was she aiming to condemn and highlight Srta Medina's spitefulness, or according the last victory to Nieves and endorsing the power – supernatural or otherwise – of the dead to haunt, damage, even destroy the lives of those they leave behind?

Wilkie Collins's novel, *The Woman in White* also centres on two women and one man, two of whom are determined to find the key to one secret about a fourth person – what the connection of Anne Catherick (the eponymous character) is to them – but as in the Spanish novel, it soon becomes clear that it is not the revelation of one, but a web of interlinked secrets that will lead them to the solution of the mystery. Also as in the Spanish novel, there is a strong sexual current – both homo- and heterosexual – flowing between the three central characters, Walter, Marian, and Laura; and the principal secret eventually revealed is a sexual one here too, albeit at one remove from the protagonists because it relates to an affair between Laura's late father and the eponymous character's mother, making Anne (who dies in the course of the novel) and Laura half-sisters by their father, just as Laura and Marian are by their mother (also long dead).[4] In this respect, the novel fits with classic conceptions of the Gothic discussed in Chapter 7 as dealing with raking up guilty family secrets from the past.[5] Although in Collins's case, the past can

---

[3] This echoes the fate of Don Juan in Miguel de Unamuno's short story 'Dos madres', whose death in his car also remains open as to whether it was consciously sought. The narrative context there too is one of being torn between two women, but the issue being explored is a different one, concerning the question of will and the lack of it (see 'Dos madres' in *Tres novelas ejemplares y un prólogo* (Madrid: Espasa-Calpe, 1982), pp. 29–72 (p. 71)). Nevertheless, a convincing reading by Alison Sinclair is suggestive in our context too; the openness, she argues, concerning the cause of death – voluntary or accidental – 'raises the question of his own degree of responsibility for his fate as victim and scapegoat' *Uncovering the Mind: Unamuno, the Unknown and the Vicissitudes of Self* (Manchester: MUP, 2001), (p. 169).

[4] William Wilkie Collins, *The Woman in White* (ed.) intro. and notes by John Sutherland (Oxford: OUP, 1996), p. 34. Future references will be to this edition and will be given parenthetically in the text.

[5] Botting regards *The Woman in White* as pervaded by 'Gothic patterns', highlighting 'the Gothic heroine, passive and persecuted [. . .], a ghostly figure pointing to the past crimes of an illegitimate aristocrat' and the motif of the double (*Gothic*, p. 131 for these points and pp. 131–4 for general discussion of the novel).

be understood as the previous generation, whereas in *La señorita Medina*, the present generation is the keeper of the central secret of the plot, it remains true that it does still belong to the past (Nieves's life spanned the period from 1946–61) and certainly to another era, that of Franco's Spain, relative to the democratic society of 1991 where the story locates its present.

In both novels, two of the central triad form an alliance to find out the secret: Walter and Marian in *The Woman in White*, with Laura too fragile to be kept informed of, still less take any active part in the investigations. In *La señorita Medina*, Silvia and Julio are the ones trying to find the key to the secret, with the third character of the triangle, Srta Medina, guarding it until the denouement. Both also touch upon the nature of teacher–pupil relationships and use drawing and painting as emotional therapy for certain troubled characters (Laura in *The Woman in White*, Nieves and Srta Medina in the Spanish novel). More importantly and as will presently be discussed, the respective authors explore issues concerning sisterhood, the notion of physical resemblance and how each relates to identity.

However, the key to the power of both texts is the potent hold over the central characters that the mosaic of secrets has and the dramatic tension created by the need to discover it for some, to protect it for others. Likewise, for both texts, the reader is rapidly gripped by a wish as strong as that of the protagonists to find out what the secrets are, making both novels difficult to put down. Finally, in both cases, the desire to discover the secrets is strengthened by powerful characterization and psychological insight which lay bare the suffering undergone by those in the dark seeking enlightenment just as much as by those in the know who have to guard the secrets. Finally, both give an appearance of complete solution at the end, while actually leaving open certain questions to which the reader would dearly like an answer. What these are in the case of *La señorita Medina* has already been mentioned; at the close of *The Woman in White* one still does not know what the *ménage à trois* involves: is there a sexual relationship between Walter and Marian and/or between Laura and Marian? A careful reader may also wonder whether the larger-than-life villain, Count Fosco, has faked his own demise.[6]

All of these sexual secrets help to make both novels clearly definable as Gothic, but in addition, the settings of both throw their plot-lines and character portrayals into more haunting relief. Among Collins's locations, one

---

[6] Concerning the relationships between the members of the threesome, clues are tantalizingly laid throughout the novel which invite the reader to ask these questions. For an ingenious exposition of the evidence suggesting a faked death of Fosco, see A. D. Hutter, 'Fosco Lives!' in *Reality's Dark Light: The Sensational Wilkie Collins* (ed.) Maria K. Bachman & Don Richard Cox, Tennessee Studies in Literature, 41 (Knoxville: University of Tennessee Press, 2003), pp. 195–238. In the same volume, Richard Collins refers to 'the ambiguity of the household's arrangement' and discusses the allure of the mannish woman in the Victorian cultural context. See 'Marian's Moustache: Bearded Ladies, Hermaphrodites, and Intersexual Collage in *The Woman in White*', pp. 131–72 (p. 157).

might mention the unforgettable lonely, moonlit road where Walter first meets the eponymous character; the Gothic mansion of Blackwater Park, complete with a disused part in which Marian can be secreted; the graveyard where Anne Catherick is found by Walter; and the fog over the lake beside which Laura tells Marian of the failure of her marriage.[7] In García Morales's novel, there is chiefly the deeply depressing atmosphere of the family home in Seville, both during Nieves's lifetime and in the present. It is Nieves herself, whom Silvia remembers drawing her attention to this in the first instance, but she could not help agreeing:

> La atmósfera de toda la casa era [. . .] sórdida, se expandía una tenue y constante tristeza por los colores y formas de los muebles, las alfombras, las pesadas cortinas. Vivíamos en un cuarto piso, y toda la luz que entraba por las ventanas no lograba disipar la sombra que oscurecía el espacio entero de nuestra casa.   (*SM*, p. 66)[8]

In the present time of the novel, this already gloomy flat has acquired two further features to intensify its Gothic atmosphere: the shrine to Nieves created by her mother after her death (kitsch but none the less haunting for that) and the presence of a madwoman, in this case, the demented mother, who repeatedly asks where Nieves is (*SM*, pp. 76 and 89–90, respectively).

One outcome of building a novel around a complex web of interwoven secrets that will only be revealed gradually is that a second reading is even more different an experience from the first than is the case in a novel with a more open plot-line. For example, a second reading of *The Woman in White*'s introduction of Sir Percival Glyde differs from the first inasmuch as the reader now knows for certain what the ulterior motive is for his apparently irreproachable treatment of Laura (his debts and her money).[9] On first reading, one may sense that his behaviour rings false (thanks to clues laid by the author) and one's curiosity is piqued to find out if this seemingly instinctive mistrust is to prove founded or not, a motive to read on; but the second reading experience has a different, if equally powerful hold over the reader as one watches the sympathetic characters fall inexorably into his trap.

---

[7] See *WW*, p. 20 for the first encounter with the eponymous character, pp. 204–6 for the description of Blackwater Park, with the Elizabethan part where Marian will later be hidden, as well as a 'half-ruined wing [. . .] built in the fourteenth century', and a newer wing dating from the reign of George II; pp. 94–5 for the graveyard meeting between Walter and Anne; p. 261 for the foggy lakeside scene.

[8] [The atmosphere in the whole house was sordid, there was a constant slight sadness spreading through the colours and shapes of the furniture, the carpets, the heavy curtains. We lived in a fourth-floor flat and all the light coming through the windows could not dissipate the shadows that darkened our entire living space.]

[9] For example: 'A look or a word from her [Laura], checked his gayest flow of talk, and rendered him all attention to her, and to no one else at table, in an instant' (*WW*, p. 137).

In analogous fashion, when Julio and Srta Medina first meet, the latter refers to Nieves's motive for suicide being not only 'cruel y horroroso' [cruel and horrific], but also something that she and Nieves 'contemplaron las dos juntas' (both *SM*, p. 129) [watched together]. On first reading, this is just one more tantalizing clue, assumed by the reader to be as opaque to Julio as it is to Silvia and it is easy to understand his nerves following the encounter in general terms as the result of having had a host of painful memories stirred up. On second reading, however, one wonders whether Srta Medina has communicated to Julio over Silvia's head the possibility that they saw him with Ginés just before Nieves took her own life and then his nerves could be a reaction to the realization of this possibility.

Thus, the benefit of hindsight in novels so full of twists and turns is one reason why a second reading differs radically from the first. Another effect, though, of such a compelling plot is that first time round, one is in a hurry to find out the secrets and reads rapidly for clues at the expense of more profound reflection. Once it is being re-read, other aspects come to the fore, which give a new depth and perspective to the main storyline and characters. For example, in *The Woman in White*, it is easy on first reading to overlook the shadow-pair of sisters, Laura and Anne, partly because of reading speed, partly because one does not know that they are sisters until the first reading is well advanced. On second reading, viewing Anne as Laura's sister from the start, one notices that in her own way, Anne shows just as much courage and loyalty to Laura as Marian does, probably even shortening her life through her efforts.[10] By the same token, the central sisterly relationship in *La señorita Medina* is so powerful that on first reading one scarcely notices the other one in the novel, that of the mother and her younger sister Olivia (*SM*, p. 137), now looking after her full-time.[11]

A third reason why all of this easily passes unnoticed is that Silvia herself is the narrator and she is uninterested in dwelling on the present situation in the family home. She is locked into a power struggle which absorbs our attention as much as hers: to extract from Srta Medina information about

[10] In order to warn Laura about him, she risks being traced by Sir Percival Glyde and returned to the lunatic asylum where he had put her. Indeed, she goes far beyond any call of duty to try to protect Laura from Sir Percival for the sake, so she claims, of her love for Laura's mother. For example, her first letter to Laura ends thus: 'I don't give you this warning on my account, but on yours. I have an interest in your well-being that will live as long as I draw breath. Your mother's daughter has a tender place in my heart – for your mother was my first, my best, my only friend' (*WW*, p. 79). This obsessive devotion is represented as a symptom of Anne's madness in the novel and yet it would be possible to argue that Marian's adoration of Laura is equally abnormal in its excesses.

[11] The father has died twelve years previously and the mother has ever worsening senile dementia (p. 20). She is looked after with seemingly limitless patience by Olivia and the long-standing servant of the household, Emilia. This relationship between sisters will be discussed below.

Nieves that srta Medina is equally intent on withholding. The labyrinthine web of secrets inside Srta Medina's mind could be read as a psychological counterpart to the architectural labyrinths of secret stairways, passages, trapdoors, and so on that are a staple of traditional Gothic texts. Just as Gothic heroines are to be found, now trapped within such labyrinths, now able to explore them productively to find an escape or hiding-place from the villain persecuting them, so Silvia's investigation of Srta Medina's mind is both claustrophobic and liberating. And when the last room is unlocked and thrown open, as it were, as the story of Nieves's witnessing of Julio's infidelity is revealed, the power of the metaphor reaches its climax. Until here, the reader had been wandering uneasily between regarding Srta Medina as a precious maternal figure for a child who desperately needed one and whose own mother had failed her, to a sister-figure compensating for Silvia's own inadequacy, to a victim herself of undeservedly cruel treatment thus able to provide the empathy Nieves needed so much, to a misguided but well-meaning mentor, to a psychologically disturbed individual who could not help but damage the vulnerable Nieves, to a positively wicked Gothic villainess who took a sadistic pleasure in harming a vulnerable young girl who had nowhere else to turn.[12] At the end of the novel these seemingly contradictory interpretations of srta Medina's mind coalesce into the Gothic edifice they resemble, Julio flees from it into oblivion, and Silvia is left to walk away alone.

Far from the happy denouement of *The Woman in White*, with the triad of Walter, Laura, and Marian now restored to their rightful seat at Limmeridge and blessed with a male heir, García Morales ends *La señorita Medina* with her threesome grotesquely decimated and the sterile, obsessive monologue directed by Silvia at a sister in whose afterlife she says she does not believe (*SM*, p. 158) still underway. In this respect her technique is more akin to that sub-branch of the Gothic, the horror story, whereby the lasting effect after finishing the book is sustained by denying readers the satisfaction of resolution and the restoration of normality. The implications of this choice by the author will be analysed in the conclusion to the chapter.

The sequence of secrets and their respective revelations in *La señorita Medina* now needs to be listed, so as to be able to consider how the mosaic fits together. The first secret mentioned in the text is the central one: 'Al suicidarse

---

[12] The antipathetic reading of srta Medina would place her among 'the [Gothic] genre's stock figures – scheming monks, mendacious abbots, and homicidal abbesses' which Miles cites as evidence of 'one of its most glaring features: its profound anti-Catholicism'. However, he sees this as inextricably bound up with smugly Protestant Britain, whereas reading García Morales reminds us that damning indictments of Catholicism can also come from those raised within it (one thinks of James Joyce in *Portrait of the Artist as a Young Man*, or, for a Spanish example outside the Gothic, Juan Goytisolo). See 'Abjection, Nationalism and the Gothic', in Botting (ed.), pp. 47–70 (p. 47).

Nieves, yo intuí que conocía [la srta Medina] el auténtico motivo de su muerte' (*SM*, p. 10) [When Nieves committed suicide, I sensed that she [Miss Medina] knew the real motive for her death]. It is reiterated several times in the early pages of the novel (*SM*, pp. 13, 18, and 20, for example). Soon, though, others begin to overlay it: Srta Medina's past and present life contains many secrets, which seep out slowly and unreliably as Silvia begins to doubt her inter-locutor's ability or willingness to distinguish fact from fantasy: she wonders how reliable the story is of her rape, expulsion from home and subsequent pregnancy and forced removal of the baby for adoption, at the emblematic age of fifteen (the same as when Nieves died) (*SM*, pp. 81–2 and 100); Silvia also notices how she contradicts herself about the kind of life she led over the past thirty years in the Canary Islands, undermining her credibility and leaving an air of secrecy hanging over that period of her life too. Then there are many unanswered questions about Nieves's short life; for example, she never confided in anyone why she regularly visited Carmelite nuns in a closed convent. Here, Srta Medina is reduced to speculating that 'quizá, Nieves fantaseara con formas de vida ajenas a este mundo y, sobre todo, inaccesibles para el sufrimiento' (*SM*, p. 24) [perhaps Nieves fantasized about lifestyles removed from this world and, above all, beyond the reach of suffering]. Thus, here one can discern a secret-keeping effect like a pair of Chinese boxes: Srta Medina speculates that Nieves liked to speculate on the secret life of spiritual repose enjoyed by nuns in a closed order.[13] Then there is the revelation of Srta Medina's hitherto secret lesbianism and the fact that she kept her attraction to Nieves secret from her (*SM*, p. 26). Soon after, it emerges that Nieves avoided telling Srta Medina about Julio's background or home life (*SM*, p. 34). Nevertheless, her reticence with Silvia was even greater, since Srta Medina is able to divulge much that she did not know, especially the fact of Julio's bisexuality and Nieves's jealousy of his relationship with Ginés: '[Nieves] me ocultaba el motivo auténtico de su animadversión, los celos que sentía a causa de la bisexualidad de Julio, eso nunca llegó ni siquiera a insinuarlo' (*SM*, p. 45) [[Nieves] hid the real motive for her animadversion from me, the jealousy that she felt because of Julio's bisexuality, she never even hinted at that]. Nieves's pregnancy was also kept secret from Silvia for the past thirty years (*SM*, p. 84).

One could argue that what all of these secrets have in common is that they relate to a sexuality considered socially unacceptable in Franco's Spain: precocious sexual activity on Nieves's part and srta Medina's (in the latter case through the old-fashioned practice of blaming rape on the victim); lesbianism on Srta Medina's; bisexuality on Julio's.[14] Even Nieves's secret

---

[13] See DeLamotte, pp. 161–3 for the dual connotations of the convent in Gothic fiction.

[14] For the sociohistorical background to this, see Anny Brooksbank Jones, *Women in Contemporary Spain* (Manchester: MUP, 1997). For the expected sexual innocence of girls before marriage in the Franco years, see p. 113; for attitudes to rape, see pp. 95–6. For the relative invisibility of lesbianism pre-1975, see pp. 118–19. For a discussion of attitudes

visits to the Carmelite nuns could be read as part of a search on her part for a different response to sexuality and society's attitude to it: rejection of both. By withholding the key to the original secret until the final pages of the novel, García Morales manipulates our responses to the other sexual revelations as we try to fit them to the question we want answered: why did Nieves commit suicide when she did? Thus, for example, one wonders together with Silvia if Srta Medina's lesbianism may have been irrepressible and Nieves reacted self-violently to some sexual contact between herself and her teacher. As it turns out, this interpretation of how the lesbianism might be to blame is misplaced, but it is nevertheless an important part of the mosaic: its rightful place in the puzzle is that it may have been a factor in Srta Medina's visceral loathing of Julio and Ginés and thus had an indirect contributory role to play; moreover, her attraction to Nieves may have made her all the more determined to 'protect' her.

In this respect, the author's narrative strategy mirrors that of Wilkie Collins in *The Woman in White* remarkably closely. There too, secrets are uncovered that turn out to be related to the central one, but not in the way one imagined. Thus, for example, on discovering that Sir Percival Glyde is supporting Anne Catherick's mother and that he had Anne committed to a private asylum at his expense, the reader wonders if there has been a relationship between him and Mrs Catherick and Anne is his illegitimate daughter. Only much later do we discover that we were right to understand his behaviour as one aimed at ensuring silence from both of them, but for a different reason (the mother knows that *he* is illegitimate and he wrongly fears that Anne knows this too). In other words, both texts utilize the profusion of sexual secrets and revelations to mislead; we are thrown the loose pieces of this complex mosaic one at a time and try in vain and repeatedly to assemble it correctly. Even when the pattern is finally put together for us, like an archaeological find, there remain gaps and patches that have not been discovered, which the reader is tempted to try to fill in and these are precisely the secrets that pertain to the investigator characters themselves. On closing *The Woman in White* one can only speculate as to the nature of Walter and Marian's relationship with each other; on finishing *La señorita Medina*, one is still puzzled by the meaning of Silvia and Julio's relationship: was Julio trying to re-live his love for Nieves? Was Silvia trying to overcome her feelings of inferiority to Nieves? Was she trying to understand her better, get closer to her? Was it a way for both of them to express their continuing love of Nieves, to share – in the hope of halving – their respective sense of guilt with regard to her or was it an attempt to draw a line under those past relationships – sisterly and sexual – and emancipate themselves from the hold Nieves still had over them? The pathos

towards male homosexuality, see Paul Julian Smith, *Laws of Desire: Questions of Homosexuality in Spanish Writing and Film 1960–1990* (Oxford: Clarendon, 1992), esp. pp. 5–8.

of the ending of the Spanish novel is that whichever interpretation is preferred or any number of combinations of them, the result is abject failure, just as in Collins's novel, conversely, whether one prefers to think of Walter as the perfect monogamous husband and Marian the perfectly chaste and benign spinster, or to imagine a discreet but steamy *ménage à trois*, the arrangement appears to make the three of them perfectly happy.

Both *The Woman in White* and *La señorita Medina* explore the sisterly relationship and in particular, what happens to it when one of the two siblings is far more vulnerable than the other. It is now worth comparing how this works in each. In the Victorian novel Marian is infinitely stronger emotionally and more intelligent than Laura, but financially dependent on her (*WW*, p. 34). Physically, they are as different as can be, despite their having the same mother: Marian is dark-haired, swarthy of complexion, and has an ugly mannish face despite a beautiful figure (*WW*, pp. 31–2); Laura is fair-haired, fair-skinned, and blue-eyed, a quintessentially feminine woman, willing to be passive and obedient, first to her father (who wished her to marry Glyde) and then to her two husbands. The only exception to this is her refusal to sign away her inheritance to Sir Percival, a show of spirit that surprises the reader as much as it does him (*WW*, pp. 247–8). Silvia and Nieves are also very different from one another: Silvia, though a little older, looks younger than Nieves because she enters puberty later and continues to dress and behave like a child after Nieves has adopted adult dress (*SM*, p. 78) and embarked upon an active sex-life (*SM*, p. 28). Silvia is the passive, obedient daughter and Nieves the spirited rebel; Silvia regards herself as boringly ordinary, admiring Nieves for her difference from her contemporaries, although she pities her for the apparent lifelong psychological anguish she endures. Tensions such as those we find in these two pairs of sisterly relationships have been studied by Christine Downing:

> Likeness and difference, intimacy and otherness – neither can be overcome. That paradox, that tension, lies at the very heart of the relationship [between sisters].
> Same-sex siblings seem to be for one another, paradoxically, both ideal self and what Jung called 'shadow'. They are engaged in a uniquely reciprocal, mutual process of self-definition.[15]

As she talks to Nieves beyond the grave in the course of the novel and as she meditates in her own mind on their relationship, it becomes clear that Silvia is suffering guilt for not having tried harder to support her sister, but the reader can see that this would have been scarcely possible as they were existing on such different planes and, moreover, Silvia was only a child herself. By contrast, Marian seems to want nothing more than to devote her

---

[15] *Psyche's Sisters: ReImagining [sic] the Meaning of Sisterhood* (San Francisco: Harper & Row, 1988), p. 11.

whole life to Laura and Laura seems to want nothing more than to spend her whole life with Marian at her side. Neither Silvia nor Nieves appears to be looking for that type of sisterly relationship: they do not confide in one another and once Julio comes onto the scene, they do not seem to want or need to spend as much time together: 'desde que él apareció en tu vida ya no regresábamos juntas a casa' (*SM*, p. 19) [since he had appeared in your life, we no longer came home from school together]. This distance between them seems to be a reflection of a certain ambivalence that Downing identifies and describes thus: '[My sister] is both what I would most aspire to but never can be *and* what I am most proud *not* to be but fearful of becoming.'[16]

Where a sisterly relationship is to be found that loudly echoes that of the strong Marian and the mentally and physically delicate Laura, however, is in the secondary pairing of the mother of Silvia and Nieves and her sister Olivia. Already in quite an advanced state of Alzheimer's disease, Olivia looks after her sister full-time, with no evidence appearing in the novel of any impatience or resentment on her part. All of this is very much in the background and yet the uncomplaining and thankless care she gives sets a framework that takes for granted total solidarity and dependability between sisters, implicitly providing a backcloth of social expectations which gives added significance to Silvia's feelings of guilt towards Nieves. Even though we see evidence in the novel of Silvia's attempts to support her sister – letting her come into bed after her nightmares (*SM*, p. 39), defending her on one notable occasion to the parents, hiding her black lace underwear in her own wardrobe, for example (*SM*, p. 103) – she is clearly wracked with guilt that Nieves turned to Srta Medina as her main confidante, rather than herself – 'aquella mujer que logró ser para ti, Nieves, esa amiga íntima que yo nunca fui y que, ya de niña, tú buscabas' (*SM*, p. 19) [the woman who succeeded in being that close friend to you, Nieves, that I never was and that you had been seeking since you were a little girl] – and all the more so since that friendship proved to be damaging during her life and instrumental in its premature end.

Related indirectly to how sisters themselves perceive their feelings and responsibilities towards one another is how others regard them. Inevitably being compared with each other, how do they respond to the expectation either that they should be alike or that they should constitute a complementary pair of opposites? In *La señorita Medina*, Silvia has to cope with several variations on this theme. Her mother has cast her two daughters into the opposing pair mould: one good (Silvia), one bad (Nieves); one normal, one abnormal. This is surely one reason why she overreacts on the occasion when Silvia refuses to go to mass with her parents out of solidarity with Nieves: 'Mamá me reconvino y afirmó que tú ya me estabas pervirtiendo. [. . .] Para ella yo era la hija buena, obediente, la que jamás le daba disgustos. En su

---

[16] *Psyche's Sisters*, p. 12; Downing's italics.

mente nos había convertido en algo semejante a Caín y Abel femeninos' (*SM*, p. 54) [Mamma told me off and asserted that you were perverting me now. [. . .] As she saw it, I was the good daughter, the obedient one, the one who never upset her. In her mind she had turned us into something like a female Cain and Abel]. Silvia is influenced by this type-casting, but reconfigures it to a wish that she could be special and different like Nieves, instead of normal and ordinary:

> Con frecuencia, me preguntaba qué era lo normal y qué lo raro, me comparaba contigo y advertía que de ti se podían decir muchas cosas, estabas llena de aspectos singulares, eras única, en el colegio ninguna niña se asemejaba a ti, en cambio en mí no existía nada que no tuvieran también las demás alumnas, nada interesante se podía decir sobre mí, me contemplaba entonces como si estuviera vacía por dentro, y no lograba entender por qué cuando alguien afirmaba que tú eras muy rara, esa palabra 'rara', sonaba como un defecto, como un rasgo de inferioridad. En cambio la palabra 'normal' sonaba como si fuera la conjunción de todas las virtudes. (*SM*, p. 41)[17]

A sense of inferiority which grows out of this seems to be instrumental in Silvia's relationship with Julio three decades later. Superficially, she wants Julio not to compare her with Nieves at all, but take her as an independent individual: 'Me pareció que me percibía como una prolongación de mi hermana y no como una persona muy distinta a ella e independiente de ella. Me sentí invisible y anulada' (*SM*, p. 107) [It seemed to me that he perceived me as a prolongation of my sister and not as a person who was very different from her and independent of her]. However, this overt desire is undermined by other thoughts, which reveal that what she really wants *is* to be measured against Nieves and to come out the winner: 'me encontraba con ánimo para competir con mi excepcional hermana, pues yo tenía una ventaja sobre ella, estaba viva y mi cuerpo era tangible y no imaginario' (*SM*, pp. 122–3) [I felt ready to compete with my exceptional sister, for I had one advantage over her, I was alive and my body was tangible and not imaginary]. Indeed, throughout the novel, it is possible to discern a deep-rooted anxiety grounded in Silvia's self-comparison with Nieves; what presents itself as a portrayal of

[17] [I often wondered what was normal and what was strange, I compared myself with you and I noticed that one could say a great many things about you, you had lots of unusual aspects, you were unique, no girl at school resembled you, by contrast there was nothing about me which the other schoolchildren did not also have, nothing interesting to say about me, I used to contemplate myself as if I were empty inside, and I could not understand why it was that when someone asserted that you were very strange, that word 'strange' sounded like a defect, like a mark of inferiority. By contrast, the word 'normal' sounded like all the virtues rolled into one.]

Nieves is very often a depiction of Silvia's own feelings of inferiority relative
to her sister. For example:

> Recuerdo que en algunas ocasiones, durante el recreo, te veía sola. [. . .]
> Entonces me sentía, repentinamente, atraída por ese mundo con el que tú,
> tal vez, fantasearas ensimismada. Y escuchaba a mis amigas, y me oía a mí
> misma con decepción. Nuestras conversaciones me parecían triviales,
> insignificantes, pedestres. Tu actitud cuestionaba, por unos momentos, mi
> vida y mis amistades.   (SM, p. 40)[18]

Thus, by implication, one could read the text as her attempt to emancipate
herself from this sense of inferiority. Winning Julio's love and marrying him
promised to be the tangible proof that she had no reason to go on feeling
inferior to Nieves: 'Julio me dijo que me amaba a mí, Nieves, que al sentir el
enamoramiento real que yo había despertado en él, pudo ver claramente que
tu constante recuerdo era sólo una obsesión. Sus palabras me estremecieron y
lograron igualarme a ti' (SM, p. 150) [Julio told me it was me he loved,
Nieves, that on feeling the true love that I had awoken in him, he could clearly
see that the constant memory of you was just an obsession. His words shook
me and succeeded in making me your equal]. By the same token, losing him
at the end of the novel as he in a sense returns to Nieves, sets the seal on
Silvia's failure and seems to destroy all hope of psychological equilibrium for
her, which she describes in the closing words of the novel as a return to
aloneness, but accompanied by 'un sentimento sin objeto que me araña por
dentro, una dulzura en forma de garfio que me hiere' (SM, p. 159) [a feeling
with no object that claws at my insides, a sweetness in the shape of a hook
which wounds me]. As Downing points out:

> Freud may have relieved us of feeling shame with respect to infantile sibling
> rivalry, but it remains difficult to acknowledge that it persists into adult-
> hood. [. . .]
> There is little recognition of the role [sibling] relationships play in our lives,
> [. . .] of the persistence of the intensely ambivalent aboriginal feelings,
> [. . .] still so often spilling over into our later intimate relationships.[19]

While Wilkie Collins uses his secondary sisterly relationship – Laura and
Anne – to explore issues of inherited similarity inflected by environmental
factors, García Morales highlights the same questions through her primary

---

[18] [I recall that on some occasions, during break-time, I would see you on your own.
[. . .] Then I felt suddenly attracted by that world about which you were perhaps
fantasizing, lost in your own thoughts. And I would find it disappointing to listen to my
girlfriends and hear myself. Our conversations seemed trivial, insignificant, pedestrian. For
a few moments, your attitude called into question my life and my friendships.]

[19] *Psyche's Sisters*, pp. 127–8.

pair of sisters, Silvia and Nieves. Both pairs display a physical resemblance – 'las dos hermanas teníamos un gran parecido entre nosotras' (SM, p. 25)[20] [we two sisters bore a great resemblance to one another] – and yet belie this with their different characters and experiences. Nieves may even feel psychologically threatened by this likeness, having nightmares about evil creatures stealing her face: 'el terror a perder tu rostro era aún más intenso que ese otro provocado por la asfixia y la cercanía de la muerte [other aspects of the same nightmares]' (SM, p. 39) [losing your face provoked even more intense terror than suffocation and the proximity of death [other aspects of the same nightmares]]. Such a fear of loss of self loudly echoes the plot of The Woman in White since the main characters there are not content to find Laura alive, after they had believed her dead and buried; they could have lived happily ever after at that point but for the fact that they regard it as paramount to re-establish her true identity, which has been exchanged for Anne Catherick's. In part this is a matter of winning back her rightful inheritance, but it is also about regaining and retaining her sense of self and legitimacy.

The issue of resemblance, generally labelled as the 'double' by critics is frequently mentioned as typically Gothic.[21] In The Woman in White, this is inextricably bound up with the secrets that articulate the plot; in La señorita Medina the link is perhaps less obvious, but it is nevertheless there and equally fundamental to the premise of the text. Ultimately, notwithstanding the final straw that induces Nieves to take her own life, her extreme underlying anguish is portrayed as stemming from her position in the family as second, unwanted child: 'Mamá te dijo [. . .] una vez más, [. . .] que eras un castigo que Dios le había impuesto' (SM, p. 29) [Mamma told you [. . .] yet again [. . .] that you were a punishment God had inflicted upon her]. According to Frank J. Sulloway, even wanted children face special challenges when they are not the firstborn: 'Their most pressing problem is to find a valued family niche that avoids duplicating the one already staked out by the parent-identified firstborn. [. . .] Laterborns [thus] take greater risks, endeavoring to achieve through openness and diversity what firstborns gain through territoriality and conformity to parental expectations.'[22] Nieves cannot find that valued niche: the quiet, well-behaved one has been taken by Silvia already and to try to share it with her would perhaps be the realization

---

[20] In The Woman in White, the resemblance is so close that Laura can be drugged and then substituted for Anne, while the latter's dead body is passed off as Laura's. This is a corner-stone of the plot as well as throwing up interesting psychological consequences for both women.

[21] See, for example, Botting, Gothic, p. 112, or Helen Stoddart, 'The Passion of New Eve and the Cinema: Hysteria, Spectacle, Masquerade', in Botting (ed.), pp. 111–31 (p. 126).

[22] Born to Rebel: Birth Order, Family Dynamics, and Creative Lives (London; Little, Brown, 1996), p. 352.

of the nightmare about losing her face. The only other available option with positive social value seems to be the virgin saint role, but she is not willing to go along with it long-term. Interestingly, the one happy period in her short life, the summer she spends with paternal aunt María, though portrayed as a success arising from her aunt's sunny disposition, is also the only extended period she has away from being Silvia's younger sister.

In conclusion, an irony is perceptible in the revelation of the many secrets of *La señorita Medina*. At the same time as one is hurriedly turning the pages to discover why Nieves committed suicide and piece together the mosaic of lurid secrets that are dug up along the way – secrets about lesbian desire and homosexual lovers, about unwanted pregnancies, rape and prostitution – the real horrors of this story are imprinting themselves on one's consciousness and are only tenuously linked to the scandalous events in the foreground. These are the cruelties inherent in a society in which women bear children they do not want (the mother, as well as Srta Medina herself) and cannot bear the ones they do (Nieves's terminated pregnancy), rendered all the more painful by the personalities involved and further complicated by the ill-fated intervention of the eponymous character, who projected the consequences of her own psychological damage onto a child exceptionally ill-equipped to deal with it. Nieves committed suicide because she felt like a drowning person whose one piece of driftwood – Julio – seemed to have been snatched away, but the novel asks whether the loss of the driftwood was to blame for the drowning or the terrible torrent in which she found herself floundering in the first place.

The death of Anne Catherick in *The Woman in White*, another innocent victim of society's sexual mores, leaves the surviving triad of Laura, Marian, and Walter, to live out their *ménage à trois* happily ever after, following in the Radcliffean Gothic pattern of a return to domestic equilibrium at the end of the story: Emily returns to La Vallée in *The Mysteries of Udolpho* to live happily ever after with Valancourt and Stoker chooses a similar ending for *Dracula* when he frees Mina and leaves her able to look forward to a happy home life and motherhood with Jonathan Harker. The void into which the end of *La señorita Medina* is sucked partakes of different tradition within the Gothic mode, which concludes, like *Rebecca*, with post-traumatic numbness and emotional wreckage or, as we shall now see in the still more depressing ending of Mary Shelley's *Frankenstein*, with even darker despair and desolation.

9

Una historia perversa (2001) and
Mary Shelley, *Frankenstein* (1818–31):[1]
Creating Monsters

This chapter will discuss what makes reading *Una historia perversa* [A Perverse Story] such a Gothic experience: it will consider, first, how Adelaida García Morales utilizes elements that make up the Gothic villain and second, the Gothic treatment of the issue of creation by men, which can be read as doubly transgressive since it is a 'usurpation of divine powers of creation [. . . and] also a male appropriation of the female ability to give birth'.[2] As in *Frankenstein*, the consequences of such a double transgression in the Spanish novel are both monstrous and disastrous for all concerned, including the creator himself; thus, a comparison of the male protagonist of each novel will be central to the chapter's argument. However, at least as important as this is its corollary: the anxiety for women generated by fearing for their own autonomy at the hands of the male creator. This is treated indirectly in Shelley's novel too, as Punter observes: 'in psychic terms we are confronting [. . .] the making over of the body into the control and power of another; [. . .] we are looking here in particular at women's experience.'[3] Lastly and by way of conclusion to the chapter, there will be an exploration of the particularly suggestive motif of the forbidden room in *Una historia perversa* and its relationship to the three areas discussed: the Gothic villain, creation by a man and being on the receiving end of this for a woman. The forbidden room is not used by Shelley, as it happens, but, descending from *Bluebeard*, a tale widely recognized as Gothic *avant la lettre*,[4] it is easy to find in other Gothic

---

[1] The first edition of 1818 was revised by Shelley's husband, Percy Shelley, and then the text was revised again by Mary Shelley for the 1831 edition. A summary of the differences between these three editions is to be found in Anne K. Mellor, 'Making a "Monster": An Introduction to *Frankenstein*', in *The Cambridge Companion to Mary Shelley* (ed.), Esther Schor (Cambridge: CUP, 2003), pp. 9–25 (pp. 14–17).

[2] Kilgour, *The Rise of the Gothic Novel* (1995), p. 206.

[3] *Gothic Pathologies*, p. 61.

[4] Hendershot, for example, links Bluebeard specifically to *Dracula* and Bluebeard's wife to the Gothic heroine, but notes more generally 'the importance of the Bluebeard story to the Gothic genre' (*The Animal Within*, pp. 26–7). She also sees Bluebeard as 'the predecessor of the demon lover of Gothic works' (p. 206), although it would perhaps be

texts such as Stoker's *Dracula* or, to take a twentieth-century example, Stephen King's *The Shining*.

Una historia perversa is laden with Gothic features despite the author's choice not to employ the supernatural at all in this novel and to set it in modern-day Madrid. The story is narrated in alternating chapters by Octavio Saló, a celebrated sculptor, and his wife, Andrea, who meets him through the art gallery she runs. The nightmare that the story rapidly becomes, arises from Octavio's secret technique, for unbeknown to the admiring public – which at first includes Andrea herself – he makes his sculptures from the bodies of people he murders for this purpose. Having found a plinth prepared with her name on it, Andrea lives in dread that she will be her husband's next victim, but she cannot denounce him, as Octavio has carefully tricked her into appearing an accomplice; nor can she escape, for he has her trapped in their flat with the help of the sinister maid, Sila, together with the time-honoured device of presenting her confinement to the outside world as a necessary rest treatment for a nervous illness.[5] He does all he can to prevent her confiding his secret to any third party and when she succeeds in doing so, he murders her confidant (his own cousin, Juan) before any action can be taken. Eventually, Andrea manages to kill Octavio and disclose the secret to her close friend, Laura; together they then wreak their revenge by turning his body into a supposed self-portrait sculpture, received with acclaim by the art world.

More unequivocally, perhaps, than any of García Morales's other male characters to date, Octavio is characterized as a Gothic villain in the classic mould, even to the extent that she respects the tradition to rid the world of him by the end of the novel.[6] He is unscrupulous, cruel and bloodthirsty, a megalomaniac obsessed with possession and control, all of which lead him

more exact to see him as part of an extensive and antique tradition of demon lover types, which can be traced further back and in several different directions. Reed explores this in fine detail throughout *Demon-Lovers*.

[5] Probably the most famous use of this is Charlotte Perkins Gilman, 'The Yellow Wallpaper' (1892), where the enforced rest and confinement actually leads to the onset of madness for the protagonist. For Lloyd-Smith, this story is 'a powerful expression of the Gothicism inherent in the experience of patriarchal society' and is one of many texts that demonstrate 'how gender anxiety feeds into the production of the Gothic'. See 'Nineteenth-Century American Gothic' in Punter (ed.), p. 120. Andrea is close to madness too by the end of *Una historia perversa* but of course an important difference between the two texts is that while the protagonist's doctor-husband in 'The Yellow Wallpaper' appears to believe in the prescribed treatment, Octavio is merely using it as an excuse for imprisoning Andrea. See *'The Yellow Wallpaper'* (ed.) Thomas L. Erskine & Connie L. Richards (New Brunswick, NJ: Rutgers University Press, 1993) (pp. 29–50 for the story itself).

[6] The eponymous protagonists of Stoker's *Dracula* and Lewis's *The Monk*, Montoni in Radcliffe's *The Mysteries of Udolpho*, Fosco in Collins's *The Woman in White* (probably, but see Chapter 8) are just a few classic examples of texts which bring about the death of their Gothic villains. Walpole's Manfred, of *The Castle of Otranto*, survives, but has turned his back on his former villainy by the end. Of García Morales's contenders for Gothic villain status, one could mention the gypsy in *Bene*, who is perhaps too minor a character

to have no qualms about imprisoning and terrifying Andrea. He has 'una apariencia diabólica, casi infernal' [a demoniacal, almost infernal appearance] in his gaze;[7] and well before Andrea has any evidence against him, she senses that 'existe algo maligno en él, algo como una corriente subterránea que corre por debajo de todo lo visible' (*HP*, p. 31) [something malign exists inside him, something like an underground stream flowing underneath all that is visible], an intuition confirmed subsequently and of the utmost relevance to the comparison with *Frankenstein*, as we shall see. Despite the domineering behaviour, though, Octavio's masculinity is problematized in a manner identified by Hendershot as typical: 'The Gothic is preoccupied with the precarious alignment of the whole male subject and the fragile, individual men who attempt to represent *the* male subject.'[8] Indeed, Octavio's insecurities are discernible in the text. He blushes and describes himself as disconcerted when Andrea takes the initiative at the beginning of their relationship (*HP*, p. 7). Despite his cruelty towards her, it becomes increasingly clear that he is extremely emotionally dependent on her; for example, early in the novel he is already using a strong verb to articulate his concern that he might have ruined his chances of a lasting relationship with her: 'temí que, tal vez, podría haber perdido a Andrea de manera definitiva' (*HP*, p. 17) [I greatly feared that I might perhaps have lost Andrea permanently]. But only at the very end of the novel is this impression of dependency definitively confirmed, when it is revealed via a hidden note that Octavio had only pretended he would trap Andrea so as to 'retenerte a mi lado hasta el final de mi vida pues [. . .] yo no puedo soportar la vida sin tenerte conmigo. Te amo tanto' (*HP*, p. 219) [keep you at my side until the end of my life as [. . .] I cannot stand life without you. I love you so much]. Andrea, for her part, notices Octavio's emotional vulnerability and herself conforms to the gendered stereotype of automatically linking it to a chink in his masculinity, which implicitly invites us to do likewise:

> Advertí que ese Octavio que yo había conocido hasta entonces como alguien que poseía una gran fortaleza, una mirada dura y osada, alguien que aparentaba gozar en todo momento de una notable vitalidad y que era *tan*

---

to have sufficient stature for the label; the father in *El Sur* and Fernando in *El accidente*, both of whom are probably too pathetic to qualify; an absence of the figure in *La tía Águeda* and *La señorita Medina*, where the antipathetic leading role is played by a woman in both cases; and *El silencio de las sirenas*, in which Agustín is the only male character and remains far too remote to classify in this way. That leaves Alfonso in *La lógica del vampiro*, who has much of what it takes to be a Gothic villain, as we saw in Chapter 3, but he is neither repentant, defeated nor dead at the end of the novel.

[7] Adelaida García Morales, *Una historia perversa* (Barcelona: Planeta, 2001) p. 187. Future references will relate to this edition and be given parenthetically in the text.

[8] *The Animal Within*, p. 4.

viril y resistente, ahora que yo había descubierto su secreto método de trabajo se mostraba, de pronto y por vez primera, frágil, inseguro y temeroso.
(*HP*, p. 67; my italics)[9]

Far from welcoming this, Andrea shows she has no wish to adopt a protective,
maternal role in her relationship with Octavio; having noted that his coming
to the gallery was in part 'una forma de pedirme que le protegiera' [a way of
asking me to protect him], Andrea's next sentence shows that she is relieved
when he is distracted: '*Por fortuna*, el autor [. . .] le pidió que le acompañara'
(both *HP*, p. 67; my italics) [*Luckily*, the author [. . .] asked him to
accompany him]. In other words, Andrea, despite thinking herself a modern,
liberated woman, endorses the traditional equation between male
attractiveness and what Hendershot calls the masquerade of masculinity,
leading to this critic's notion of 'the Gothic impasse', which is 'that sexuality
is so implicated with power structures as to render the two inseparable' and
as a result, 'for the heterosexual woman, revealing the traditional man as
vulnerable means revealing him as an unattractive, inadequate love object.'[10]

Andrea's feelings will be discussed presently in their own right, but for the
moment let us continue to explore the representation of Octavio's masculinity
in the context of his portrayal as a Gothic villain. A central feature of this is
that he is established as a man containing a monstrous Other, in the sense that
it transgresses the boundaries between life and death, man and god (this is,
doubtless, the persona whose presence Andrea senses in the quotations
above). Thus, *Una historia perversa* dramatizes the Gothic concerns
identified by Hendershot very precisely: 'Gothic works [. . .] pose and answer
their own formulations of a central question: who or what is the Other that
haunts the traditional man? Is this Other horrific or appealing? By even
posing the question, these works have acknowledged that traditional
heterosexual masculinity is vulnerable.'[11] Octavio himself is well aware of
the dichotomy: 'yo adquiría una suerte de paz identificándome con ese
Octavio que era para ella [Andrea] y que seguiría siendo mientras pudiera
ocultarle al otro Octavio del que yo me enorgullecía' (*HP*, p. 33) [I attained a
kind of peace by identifying with the Octavio that I was for her [Andrea] and
that I would go on being as long as I could conceal from her the other Octavio
of which I was so proud]. The ambivalence expressed here (disquiet versus
pride) towards the other self is reminiscent of Dr Jekyll's 'leap of welcome'

---

[9] [I noticed that the Octavio I had known until then as someone possessing great
fortitude, a bold, hard stare, someone who appeared at all times to enjoy striking vitality
and who was *so virile* and resistant, now that I had discovered his secret method of
working was revealing himself, suddenly and for the first time, to be fragile, insecure, and
fearful.]

[10] *The Animal Within*, p. 4 (masquerade); p. 204 (all three quotations).

[11] *The Animal Within*, p. 5.

to Hyde. However, there is an important difference in that Octavio believes his Other to be a superior, god-like self rather than the base creature that Robert Louis Stevenson's character recognizes as coming from within. This pride derives from his creative technique, which he describes as one that 'lindaba con lo sagrado' (*HP*, p. 5) [bordered on the sacred].

The duality in the portrayal of Octavio's masculinity gains significance beyond the attribution of it to Gothic villainy generally when it is read specifically in the light of Mary Shelley's *Frankenstein*. There too is a protagonist who thinks he has risen above ordinary humanity by 'penetrat[ing] the secrets of nature';[12] both Victor and Octavio even have in common that their heads may have been turned in part by books about outdated mystico-religious beliefs concerning the principles of life, for Frankenstein admits to having been profoundly influenced by reading about alchemy in his youth, to the extent that without this, 'it is even possible that the train of my ideas would never have received the fatal impulse that led to my ruin' (*F*, p. 42). In *Una historia perversa*, the one reference to Octavio's reading habits is when Andrea comes home to find him deep in a book about the Pythagoreans (*HP*, p. 28).[13] Victor, like Octavio and his sculptures, works obsessively at his creative project, neglecting the woman who loves him and he too is revealed as a monster himself through what he creates and his attitude to this. It is, indeed, commonplace in the extensive body of scholarship on *Frankenstein* to find readings that regard Victor's monster in some sense as a representation of at least a part of himself. Mellor, for example, asserts that 'Victor and his creature are virtually fused into one being, almost one consciousness. [. . .] They are each other's double.'[14]

---

[12] Mary Shelley, *Frankenstein, or The Modern Prometheus* (ed.) David Stevens (Cambridge: CUP, 1998), p. 42. Future references will relate to this edition and be given parenthetically in the text.

[13] For a summary of the beliefs of the Pythagoreans, see for example W. K. C. Guthrie, *A History of Greek Philosophy: I. The Earlier Presocratics and the Pythagoreans* (Cambridge: CUP, 1962), pp. 146–340 and especially pp. 166–7. Striking in the light of Octavio's characterization in juxtaposition with Frankenstein and the latter's early fascination with alchemy, are the secrecy of the sect (pp. 149–53 and 167), its belief in the transmigration of souls across the human/animal divide (pp. 157–60 and 166, 181, 186–7, 306), its zeal for sacrifices (pp. 163, 190, 194–5), its idea of 'assimilation to the divine as the legitimate and essential aim of human life' (p. 199), its particular interpretation of more widespread ideas about the breath of life (pp. 277–9, 307, 318–19) and the idea that 'death is comparable to a release from bondage or imprisonment' (pp. 310, 331); finally and especially resonant with respect to alchemy, the notion that 'the essential difference between different kinds of body lay in the *harmonia* or *logos* in which the elements were blended', leading to Aristotle's contention that the Pythagoreans thought everything could turn into everything else' (pp. 275–6).

[14] 'Making a "Monster"', in Schor (ed.), p. 23. Crook asserts that *Frankenstein* 'is a novel (*the* novel, some would say) about doubling, shadow selves, split personalities' ('Mary Shelley, Author of *Frankenstein*', in Punter (ed.), p. 59; Crook's italics).

Howard explores the implications of treating the monster as a projection of Frankenstein himself, observing, among many other suggestive points, how unreliable a narrator he is, considering his 'successive illnesses or fits of derangement', how often he 'appears possessed', and how, 'in his obsession with revenge, [he] becomes uncannily like the creature he has created.'[15] By the same token, it could be argued that Octavio's sculptures likewise give a concrete form to the monstrous Other within him.

On the other hand, Octavio is also reminiscent of Frankenstein's monster, read as an autonomous being; not only is he literally called a *monstruo* by a minor character,[16] but once Andrea discovers how he makes his sculptures – which is to say, discovers the monstrous aspect of him – she describes him leaving the bedroom to go to his studio – or, turning from his man self to his monster Other – in terms that evoke the 'gigantic stature' of Mary Shelley's creature (*F*, p. 58): 'cuando Octavio se marchó a su estudio a trabajar, yo le imaginaba algo distinto, se me aparecía agigantado y ajeno al que acababa de estar conmigo' (*HP*, pp. 65–6) [when Octavio went off to his studio to work, I would imagine him as somewhat different, he seemed grown to gigantic size and alien to the man who had just been with me]. More importantly, however, he reacts to rejection like Frankenstein's monster, in a cruel and vengeful way towards Andrea when she shows repugnance towards him; he thirsts for her love in a manner strongly evocative of the monster's dreams of happy harmony (*F*, p. 119); he thinks he can buy her acceptance with material gifts like roses (*HP*, p. 180), rather as Frankenstein's monster thinks that performing helpful acts such as carrying firewood to the door of the De Laceys (a family he happens upon and hopes to befriend) will work for him (*F*, pp. 120 and 124), but both hopelessly underestimate the horror they inspire, embittering them even further (*F*, p. 146; *HP*, p. 180).

To give Octavio such a dual role is not to posit a major divergence from the spirit of Shelley's novel for three important reasons. First, how Frankenstein's monster is viewed by many critics as an aspect of his creator in some sense has already been mentioned. To this one can add an important argument concerning slippage between characters in the novel on a larger scale. Sandra M. Gilbert and Susan Gubar's reading of Shelley's text explores the shifting relationships between the characters there and those in Milton's *Paradise Lost*, discussion of which is beyond the scope of the present chapter; but for our purposes, the key point is their identification of what they call a 'continual duplication and reduplication of roles' in the novel, which they relate to the author's claim that the idea for the book came to her in a dream: 'the

---

[15] *Reading Gothic Fiction*, pp. 270, 272, and 273, respectively.

[16] A woman who has apparently emigrated to escape from him 'afirmaba que [. . .] era un monstruo' (*HP*, p. 28) [asserted that [. . .] he was a monster]. It seems likely that she has not succeeded in her attempt to put herself beyond his reach, since she has disappeared without trace.

dreamlike shifting of fantasy figures from part to part, costume to costume, tells us that we are in fact dealing with the psychodrama or waking dream that Shelley herself suspected she had written.'[17]

This idea that characters can change costumes, as it were, and thus move between several roles from an intertext, allows us to posit a consideration of Andrea that explores the extent to which she can be read as playing the part of Frankenstein's monster to Octavio's Victor, without prejudice to the foregoing reading of Octavio as the monster himself, as well as the creator figure. Several factors encourage this reading: first, the sexual relationship between Octavio and Andrea echoes some interpretations of Victor's relationship with his monster. For example, Gilbert and Gubar refer to the 'disguised but intensely sexual' implications of the scene in which Frankenstein animates the monster: 'Victor Frankenstein in effect couples with his monster by applying "the instruments of life" to its body and inducing a shudder of response'.[18] Following from this, it is also worth noting the way in which Victor flees from the monster as soon as the creative act is complete (*F*, p. 62), rather as Octavio always runs away from Andrea as soon as they have finished having sex (*HP*, pp. 17, 20–21, 29, for example).

Second, Octavio shapes Andrea into a different person by taking ideas from his dead mother's style in a manner analogous to Victor's technique of making the monster out of dead bodies following the death of his own mother. Kilgour links the two as follows: 'Frankenstein's mother is associated more with death than with life. [. . . When he leaves home following her death] he thus breaks from a female past to recreate it in grotesque forms.'[19] Victor himself does not seem to be conscious of the connection, but it is striking to the reader, particularly as a nightmare in which kissing Elizabeth (the step-sister he adores and intends to marry) turns her into the mother's corpse, takes place when he falls asleep just after the animation scene and his flight from the presence of the monster (*F*, p. 63). In like fashion, Octavio refutes Andrea's suggestion that by designing dresses identical to his mother's for her, and also persuading her to change her hair length, colour, and style to match the mother's, he has been trying to re-create his wife as a maternal replica (*HP*, pp. 80–1). However, the reader is unlikely to accept his reasoning that he simply finds the 1940s style particularly flattering to someone with looks like Andrea's. Why, we are bound to ask, does he find that style so attractive except that it reminds him of his mother? And why is

---

[17] *The Madwoman in the Attic: The Woman Writer and the Nineteenth-Century Literary Imagination* (New Haven & London: Yale University Press, 1979), p. 230.

[18] *Madwoman*, p. 229. The quotation from *Frankenstein* within Gilbert and Gubar is from *F*, p. 62.

[19] *The Rise of the Gothic Novel*, p. 206. Crook concurs with this reading: 'Victor, in reanimating the dead, is attempting perversely to resurrect his dead mother' ('Mary Shelley, Author of *Frankenstein*', in Punter (ed.), p. 59).

he so determined to reshape Andrea at all into any style different from the one she has chosen for herself except that he wants to wrest from a mother's province the creative power to bring new life into being? Andrea is willing to take a positive line on this, at least countenancing the possibility that she should feel flattered by his interest in her appearance and take it as 'una prueba de su amor' (*HP*, p. 75) [proof of his love]. However, as their relationship degenerates in the course of the novel with the tightening of his stranglehold over her, this aspect of his having taken possession of her looks doubtless contributes to her growing sense of claustrophobia and loss of control over herself and her life: 'Advertí que todo lo que constituía mi vida, incluso mis estados interiores, había sido creado por Octavio, quien se había apropiado de mi existencia y de mí misma' (*HP*, p. 205) [I realized that everything that my life constituted, even my inner states, had been created by Octavio, who had appropriated my existence and my very self].

By the time this has reached an advanced stage – Octavio has just confiscated her keys and banned her from going out alone – an important moment of reflection – literal and figurative – echoes arrestingly the scene in *Frankenstein* where the monster recounts seeing his own reflection for the first time:

> 'How was I terrified when I viewed myself in a transparent pool! At first I started back, unable to believe that it was indeed I who was reflected in the mirror; and when I became fully convinced that I was in reality the monster that I am, I was filled with the bitterest sensations of despondence and mortification.' (*F*, p. 123)

In *Una historia perversa*, the mirror scene evokes Andrea's disturbing merging with the monster who is Octavio. Such is his takeover of her that she cannot even have her own reflection any more. No wonder her sadness matches the monster's despondence: 'Me miré al espejo del cuarto de baño y descubrí en mi rostro y en mi mirada una tristeza inconsolable. Entonces descubrí a Octavio, a través del espejo, acercándose a mí por la espalda hasta estrechar con ternura mis hombros' (*HP*, p. 161) [I looked at myself in the bathroom mirror and discovered an inconsolable sadness in my face and in my eyes. Then I discovered Octavio, through the mirror, coming up to me from behind until he tenderly embraced me around my shoulders]. The mirror image visualized by the reader as Octavio stands behind Andrea with his arms around her shoulders is like a two-headed monster, as his body is presumably masked by hers and the two heads would therefore seem to emerge from Andrea's shoulders. Whether her arms are visible as well as his – making a four-armed creature – or hers are obscured by his, making the female body look as if it had man's arms, the reflection would be of a monstrous mixture of body parts, strongly reminiscent of Frankenstein's monster's grotesque cobbling together of many bodies into one.

Third and perhaps most important, Andrea is as desperate for a different type of treatment from Octavio as the monster is for a different response from Victor. It is worth comparing what each is pleading for. The monster in *Frankenstein* asks his creator to do his duty towards his own creature (*F*, p. 107) but accepts a hierarchy in their relationship: ' "I will even be mild and docile to my natural lord and king, if thou wilt also perform thy part, the which thou owest me. [. . .] Make me happy, and I shall again be virtuous" ' (*F*, p. 108). What it transpires will make the monster happy is a mate to alleviate his loneliness (*F*, pp. 154–5). Andrea too accepts a certain hierarchy between herself and Octavio; as we have seen, despite her superficial modernity, she agrees to marriage because Octavio wants this, not her (*HP*, p. 20); she associates his virility (and hence his attractiveness to her) with a degree of emotional distance which she prefers to a show of vulnerability; she is also prepared to let him have a say in her appearance, overriding some discomfiture so as to accept such attitudes of ownership as a sign of his love for her. But also like the monster, she wants companionship in return for such deference and because of the slippage between roles discussed above, this needs to come from none other than Octavio himself in his non-monster persona: 'A ella le resultaba indiferente casarse o no, su deseo era que viviéramos juntos, que compartiéramos todo en nuestra vida, y a la palabra "todo" le daba un énfasis muy singular al pronunciarla, un énfasis que a mí me inducía a pensar en mi estudio como una parte de mi vida que ella se propondría conquistar' (*HP*, p. 20) [As far as she was concerned, getting married or not made no odds, her desire was for us to live together, to share everything in our lives, and she placed a very special emphasis on the word 'everything', when she uttered it, an emphasis which made me think of my studio as a part of my life that she would set out to conquer].[20]

Just as Frankenstein is almost persuaded by the monster to comply with his wish for a mate, but in the end decides against this course of action, so Octavio shows some ambivalence too in how much companionship to offer Andrea. On their wedding night, for example, he does at first agree to stay with her after they have made love, but cannot bring himself in the end to carry through:

> [Andrea] me suplicó acongojada que permaneciese con ella, al menos hasta que se durmiera, pues le resultaba muy gozoso ir entrando en el sueño abrazándome. Me metí de nuevo en la cama, con impaciencia, y nos abrazamos. Después de una media hora empecé a separarme de ella con lentitud para no despertarla, pero comprobé que aún no se había dormido.

---

[20] We shall return to the significance of the studio as forbidden room in the conclusion to this chapter.

> [. . .] Aun así, me levanté y me dirigí a mi estudio, dejándola despierta y
> quejándose.   (*HP*, pp. 20–21)[21]

Octavio's refusal to comply with Andrea's wish for a relationship of
companionship and sharing is emblematized, as the above quotation shows,
by the motif of the forbidden room, represented by the studio. This space,
inhabited by corpses, is where Andrea is at first prohibited access to and by
her husband, a symbol different in type and in history but arguably of
equivalent power to the half-finished female monster in *Frankenstein* – also a
collection of dead body parts – which Victor will end by sinking to the bottom
of the sea (*F*, p. 184). However, once Andrea knows Octavio's secret, a
reversal takes place, whereby he wants her to understand what to him is his
sacred calling and to collaborate in his project, so as to be, one might say, the
monster self's mate: 'Me propuse buscar con paciencia una forma para que
ella lograra comprenderme y conocerme; sin embargo, no supe encontrarla'
(*HP*, p. 149) [I resolved patiently to seek a way to make her understand and
know me; however, I failed to find one]. To borrow Gilbert and Gubar's
image, here is another costume change, whereby the monster part is now
played by Octavio once again and Andrea is being importuned to take on a
new role of fellow-monster, made to his specifications.

But now it is Andrea's turn to play Victor to Octavio's monster. Octavio relates
how she refuses flatly to recreate herself into a monster-mate for him: 'Lo más
importante era que se operara un cambio radical en su mente y en su concepción
de la vida; incluso en su sensibilidad. Pero Andrea era terca, poco flexible [. . .].
Me amargaba su negativa a hacer un esfuerzo para comprender el sentido de mi
trabajo' (*HP*, p. 149) [The most important thing was for there to take place a
radical change in her mind-set and her conception of life; even in her sensibility.
But Andrea was stubborn, inflexible [. . .]. I was embittered by her refusal to
make any effort to understand the meaning of my work]. So it is that, like
Victor's life following his refusal to complete the female monster, Andrea's
nightmare reaches its nadir: Octavio kills someone dear to her (*HP*, p. 173) who
held out the hope of a better future – Juan, playing Shelley's Elizabeth here – and
continues to haunt and persecute her to the point where she realizes that as with
Victor and his monster after the death of Elizabeth, her whole existence is now
reduced to the struggle between the two of them: 'Me había quedado sola, [. . .]
la persona más cercana a mí, la que conocía de verdad los hilos que movían mi
vida, era Octavio' (*HP*, p. 210) [I was now all alone, [. . .], the person closest to
me, who really knew the strings that controlled my life, was Octavio].

---

[21] [[Andrea] begged me, heartbroken, to stay with her, at least until she fell asleep, for
she found it very pleasurable to drop off to sleep with her arms around me. I got back into
bed, impatiently, and we embraced. After half an hour I began to separate myself from her,
slowly so as not to waken her, but I discovered that she had not yet fallen asleep. [. . .]
Even so, I got up and headed for my studio, leaving her awake and complaining.]

However, one very important difference between Andrea's experience and that of any of the characters in Shelley's novel is that she is alive and conscious throughout the process of being re-formed, re-moulded by Octavio. She is therefore in a position to reflect upon what she is undergoing, to choose to try to resist or to decide to comply willingly. On one level, this can be read as a manifestation of a straightforward power struggle within a couple, something as commonplace in literature of all types as in life, but by presenting it in a Gothic framework, García Morales gives it the complexion of a body-snatching horror story. Here is Andrea's reaction when she discovers she is trapped by Octavio's scheme to make her appear complicit in his crimes:

> Supe entonces que me hallaría atrapada por Octavio durante el resto de mi vida, o de la suya. [. . .]
> Me encontraba muy lejos de todo, como si estuviera encerrada en una cabina de cristal y me percibía a mí misma como una muñeca programada para sonreír, actuar, hablar, según las exigencias de la situación. La tarde [. . .] se convirtió en un infierno. Algo férreo e invisible oprimía mi pecho con una punzada de dolor, la angustia me asfixiaba. (*HP*, p. 109)[22]

This plethora of vivid images in rapid succession – entrapment, the glass booth, the doll, hell, the invisible metal chest-band, and asphyxia – bombards the reader relentlessly and at regular intervals in the novel they are reiterated or complemented by others, with the result that no single one will dominate. Instead, one is left with a sense of generalized claustrophobic panic that no individual metaphor can capture adequately; it is, ironically, the very verbosity of the imagery that renders best the inexpressibility of Andrea's feelings.[23]

Resolution of a clear-cut kind is not to be had at the end of either novel, one reason, no doubt, why they both leave such a haunting impression on the reader. Both also leave the same kinds of ends tied and untied. At the end of *Frankenstein*, Victor is dead, indirectly due to the monster's impact on his life, but he has been able to tell his story to Walton, the young polar explorer who has rescued him from an iceberg. The monster, for his part, disappears from view in the Arctic wastes. Finally, the purpose of telling the story to Walton is called into question, for where at first it seemed that a chastened Victor wanted it to serve as a cautionary tale to warn Walton not to be over-ambitious in his polar quest, in the end he seems to be goading

---

[22] [I realized at that moment that I should be trapped by Octavio for the rest of my life or his. [. . .] I felt very remote from everything, as if I were enclosed in a glass booth and I perceived myself to be like a doll programmed to smile, act, speak, according to the demands of the situation. The evening turned hellish. Something invisible that felt like it was made of iron pressed on my chest with a stabbing pain, anguish made me breathless.]

[23] For a summary of how women have historically suffered mental and physical illness as a result of man-made moulds for them, see Gilbert & Gubar, *Madwoman*, pp. 53–5.

him on.[24] At the end of *Una historia perversa*, Octavio is dead; Andrea has now finally had her revenge – this consisting not only of destroying Octavio, but probably more importantly from a psychological perspective, of moulding him as he had insisted on moulding her[25] – and the relief of sharing the nightmare story with a supportive, same-sex friend, Laura, who, rather like Walton, may be able to learn from it but probably will not.[26] At the end of *Una historia perversa*, Andrea's long-term outlook seems as bleak as Shelley's monster's:[27] she is likely never to recover fully from what she has endured and the law may well catch up with her when it becomes apparent that Octavio is not in New York as she has claimed. In the final twist, then, of this harrowing story, the fluid interchange of roles comes full circle: at the beginning of the novel, Octavio seemed to be playing both Frankenstein and the monster, but at the end, that is what Andrea is apparently doing. She is Frankenstein inasmuch as she has now created a monster of her own out of a dead body, the statue of Octavio, and she resembles Victor in the sharing of her story with Laura too; but inasmuch as she has outlived Octavio and for the terrible question-mark hanging over her future, she reminds us more of the monster, most of all perhaps for their similar emotional state at this point. Andrea is shaken by 'un llanto desesperado' (*HP*, p. 219) [desperate weeping], but the monster's words to his dead creator could surely be hers

---

[24] Frankenstein prefaces the narration of his story to Walton thus: ' "You seek for knowledge and wisdom, as I once did; and I ardently hope that the gratification of your wishes may not be a serpent to sting you, as mine has been. [. . .] You may deduce an apt moral from my tale; one that may direct you if you succeed in your undertaking, and console you in case of failure" ' (*F*, p. 31). Later he will punctuate his account with the words: 'Learn from me, if not by my precepts, at least by my example, how dangerous is the acquirement of knowledge, and how much happier that man is who believes his native town to be the world, than one who aspires to become greater than his nature will allow' (*F*, p. 57). Finally, on his deathbed, his ambivalence is most explicit as he says to Walton ' "Seek happiness in tranquillity and avoid ambition, even if it be only the apparently innocent one of distinguishing yourself in science and discoveries. Yet why do I say this? I have myself been blasted in these hopes, yet another may succeed" ' (*F*, pp. 234–5).

[25] Revenge of this direct type is of course denied to Frankenstein's monster. He has, however, deprived Victor of his chosen mate and moulded the course his life has taken.

[26] This reading is more pessimistic than Brennan's Jungian one, which reads Victor as Walton's shadow and identifies 'many signs [that] indicate that he will avoid Victor's fate' (*The Gothic Psyche* (1997), p. 70).

[27] Crook proposes a politico-historical interpretation, claiming it is possible to read the ending of *Frankenstein* as 'fearful or exhilarating [. . .], according to one's political stripe', but such a reaction to Shelley's openness concerning the monster's ultimate fate is dependent on seeing him as a representation of the revolutionary spirit. However, the exhilarating claim seems hard to sustain, for even if one chooses, as a revolutionary, to imagine the monster living on indefinitely in the Arctic, it is clear that he is not going to be happy there or be able to achieve anything other than survival, and if, conversely, one is glad, as a conservative, to imagine him dead, relief is a more plausible emotion than exhilaration, surely. See 'Mary Shelley, Author of *Frankenstein*', in Punter (ed.), p. 61.

too: ' "Blasted as thou wert, my agony was still superior to thine; for the bitter sting of remorse will not cease to rankle in my wounds until death shall close them for ever!" ' (*F*, p. 240).

We have already seen in Chapter 2 that the Gothic mode is known for plundering fairy-tale, among other narrative forms. In this, *Frankenstein* is no exception. Victor's nightmare, in which a kiss from him transforms the living, beautiful Elizabeth into his dead mother, crawling with grave-worms, seems a gruesome reversal of the common fairy-tale motif of a kiss transforming positively, from ugliness to beauty and/or animal to human, as in 'The Frog Prince', or effectively dead (asleep for a hundred years) to alive in *The Sleeping Beauty*. García Morales draws on fairy-tale in *Una historia perversa* too by her powerful utilization of a different motif, that of the forbidden room, probably most familiar to us from Charles Perrault's 'La Barbe bleue' (1697). Although it is by no means the first text to utilize it, this pre-Gothic tale seems to be the one to have marked European cultural tradition most indelibly with it.[28] Indeed, scholars of the Gothic repeatedly mention this text as an important precursor, embracing as it does so many motifs that were to become staples of the mode, including, importantly for our purposes, the forbidden room.[29] The importance of the forbidden room's content of dead

[28] A curious man suffers for entering a forbidden room in one of the tales of *1001 Nights* and of course there are many early stories concerning the perils of curiosity, particularly associated with women, including Pandora and her box in the classical tradition, and Eve in the Judeo-Christian. See Gilbert Rouger, 'Notice', in Charles Perrault, *Contes* (Paris: Garnier, 1967), pp. 119–21 (p. 119). Rouger also mentions some of the forty or so later works based on 'Bluebeard' (pp. 120–1). For Gilbert and Gubar, *Frankenstein*'s insatiable curiosity to discover the secret of life contributes to a feminization of him leading them to read him as an Eve figure (*Madwoman*, pp. 233–4).

[29] Other aspects of 'Bluebeard' that prefigure the Gothic include the characterization and interaction of the unreasonable, unfathomable, and cruel villain and the trapped, helpless, and hapless heroine, but also the grisly elements of the tale: the dead wives' bodies stored in the forbidden room, the pools of blood on the floor there and the supernatural dimension to the story (the fact that the key to the room is enchanted and cannot be washed clean of the bloodstain upon it, so that this effectively denounces the heroine to her husband). All but the magic key are directly transposable to *Una historia perversa*. Examples of Gothic texts that utilize the motif of the forbidden room include *Dracula*, when Dracula warns Harker not to go to a certain part of the castle (*D*, p. 45). Harker disobeys and there meets the vampiresses (*D*, pp. 50–4). In *The Picture of Dorian Gray*, Dorian hides the picture in a room to which he keeps the key (*PDG*, p. 133); in *Jekyll and Hyde*, the laboratory is not out of bounds to others at first, but Jekyll/Hyde does barricade himself in there for the final week of his life so that Utterson and the butler eventually have to break the door down (*JH*, p. 69); and in *Rebecca*, the second Mrs de Winter disobeys her husband when she first goes to Rebecca's beach-house (*R*, pp. 123–4). Ghost stories often use the forbidden room motif too. See, for example, 'Rats', in *The Ghost Stories of M. R. James* (1931) (pp. 610–18), or, for a modern version, Stephen King, *The Shining*, with the haunted hotel room 217, from which Doc has been told to keep away (p. 94), advice which he flouts to his cost and which is explicitly linked in the novel to *Bluebeard*.

women's bodies has already been discussed, but it is worth adding that its
location is striking too: in both cases it is downstairs, evoking the hidden
truth about the husband – Bluebeard just as much as Octavio – lying below
his apparent normality and more generally, drawing the parallel between the
house and the self discussed in Chapter 7. In this manifestation of it, the
bestial, inferior part of man finds its expression downstairs, linked perhaps
with the sexual organs being physically positioned below the heart and brain.
One might also mention the way Perrault's narrative dwells on the heroine's
thoughts as she stands, having secretly descended the stairs, outside the
closed door of the forbidden territory. To conclude this chapter, it will be
worthwhile to look at all of these ideas together in the context of the motif of
the forbidden room in *Una historia perversa*, as it will serve to complement
and confirm the reading of the novel posited above.

Perrault places two rhymed morals at the end of 'La Barbe bleue'. The first
is about succumbing to the temptations of curiosity and the second deals with
tyrannical husbands of old who used to make impossible demands on their
wives, unlike nowadays when 'On a peine à juger qui des deux est le
maître'.[30] Indeed, this gendered reading of his own story, which seems to
express some nostalgic regret at the supposed demise of the authoritarian
husband, highlights a key aspect of García Morales's treatment of the
forbidden studio which does reveal a resonance with *Frankenstein* beyond the
specifics of detail. *Una historia perversa* also, whatever else it is, is the story
of a clearly gendered power struggle within a seemingly modern couple.
Despite Octavio's initial acceptance of Andrea as she is, a woman with her
own flat, her own career, her own friends, her own style, he progressively
deprives her of all of these, with a variety of justifications, none of which
admits to what the reader can see is the real one: his overwhelming desire for
total possession of her, body, heart and soul: 'mi deseo era que Andrea
existiese sólo para mí' (*HP*, p. 19) [my desire was that Andrea should exist
for me alone], he says just before describing how he managed to persuade her
to give up her flat, which she had wanted to retain (*HP*, pp. 19–20). He
acknowledges that his reason for wanting to marry Andrea rather than simply
live with her, is: 'visceralmente sentía que, al casarnos, Andrea me pertenecía,
era una posesión que se me otorgaba' (*HP*, p. 20) [I felt in my bones that once
we were married Andrea belonged to me, she was a possession that I was
authorized to own]. Although this attitude leads to fairly commonplace sexual
jealousy, for example, when Andrea chats to a man in a hotel bar (*HP*, pp.
54–7), or when Octavio's ex-girlfriend, Patricia, tells him she is now bisexual
and intends to make a pass at Andrea (*HP*, p. 152), Octavio's possessiveness
goes far beyond that, to be realized via actual imprisonment, both in her
bedroom which he regularly locks on the outside (for example, *HP*, p. 174)

---

[30] 'La Barbe bleue', in *Contes*, pp. 122–9 (p. 129).

and more generally, by imposing on her what Octavio himself admits is 'una forma de vida casi carcelaria' (*HP*, p. 198) [an almost prisonlike way of life]. In this perspective of total physical and psychological ownership, the prohibition of access to his studio, combined with refusing Andrea any private space of her own – not only her flat, not only a lock on the inside of her bedroom door (*HP*, p. 148), but even spaces as modest as a drawer or a handbag, both of which are also violated by Octavio (*HP*, pp. 156 and 160, respectively) – can be seen as emblematic of the enormous asymmetry in the relationship. Thus a parallel (albeit grotesque) can be drawn with the double standard in Victor's power relationship with his monster: Victor sees no contradiction in expecting happiness with Elizabeth while denying similar companionship to the monster, just as Octavio sees no reason why he should not have his studio but Andrea be deprived of all private space.

Now it is worth tracking the development of the motif of the forbidden room, in *Una historia perversa*. Andrea discovers the prohibition to enter Octavio's studio, connected to the flat via an internal staircase, at the very beginning of their relationship. In a chapter narrated by her, we are given his explanation for turning down her request to visit it: 'le perturbaba demasiado el que alguien entrara en su estudio' (*HP*, p. 15) [it disturbed him too much if someone went into his studio]. Andrea accepts this as we are likely to do too, regarding it as a 'rareza' [eccentricity] typical of a gifted artist and the following chapter, narrated by Octavio, seems to substantiate this view, as he now describes his studio as 'ese territorio que sólo existía para mí y que se transformaba en un espacio imaginario mientras yo creaba las formas de mis esculturas' (*HP*, p. 17) [that territory which existed for me alone and which was transformed into an imaginary space while I was creating the forms of my sculptures]. A later comment by Octavio to his close friend Agustín and Andrea together seems to corroborate the innocent reading whereby his jealous guarding of his studio is merely an artist's eccentricity: 'Quiero que mis obras sólo se vean cuando ya están acabadas por completo. Y mi estudio es un lugar único para mí . . . es otro mundo en el que sólo yo habito' (*HP*, p. 48) ['I only want my works to be seen when they are completely finished. And my studio is a unique place for me . . . it's another world where only I live']. Further on, Andrea discovers that he has tried in vain to invite a model to pose for him there and although piqued that he was apparently willing to have that woman in his studio but not his own wife, this discovery does serve to reassure Andrea, for 'si ocultara algo horrible en su estudio, algo que no fuera posible esconder, y ese fuera el motivo de su obstinada prohibición, tampoco hubiera podido permitir que la japonesa entrara en su estudio' (*HP*, p. 52) [if he was hiding something horrible in his studio, something which it was not possible to conceal, and that was the motive for his stubborn prohibition, then he would not have been able to allow the Japanese woman to enter his studio].

Nevertheless, running alongside these elements which point to a harmless explanation for the prohibition, the tension surrounding the forbidden studio is simultaneously developing as other ideas persistently suggest themselves to Andrea, to the reader, or both. For example, Andrea is unhappy about Octavio's habit of leaving their bed as soon as they have finished making love, to go to the studio (*HP*, p. 20) and he is unhappy too because knowing this, 'no podía impedir la inquietud que me provocaba el temor de que Andrea, desvelada, bajase a mi estudio' (*HP*, p. 21) [I could not escape the worry caused by my dread that Andrea would be unable to sleep and come down to my studio]. This is from a chapter narrated by Octavio; hence, the reliability of Andrea does not enter into the matter when one wonders why he uses such a strong term as *temor* [dread]. Meanwhile, Andrea's suspicions are mounting and as they do so, they coalesce around the forbidden studio until on page 35, she decides to break the prohibition and in the dead of night, with Octavio working in there, she creeps downstairs to listen at the closed door. The scene now takes on all the accoutrements of what one critic calls 'the paradigmatic scene' of horror fiction, 'symbolic of the meeting of different worlds, the journey to the "other side" ';[31] it is particularly reminiscent, moreover, of Gothic cinema:[32] a beautiful woman in her nightwear goes where she should not, complete with scary sound-effects: a heart-stopping creak from a floorboard (*HP*, p. 35) threatens to give her away and then she stands outside the closed door listening to a succession of suspicious and potentially macabre sounds: 'un ruido semejante al de una sierra cortando algo duro [. . .] goteaba un líquido cayendo sobre un cubo [. . .] los pasos de Octavio [. . .] un leve chirrido de los goznes de una puerta' (*HP*, p. 36) [a noise similar to a saw cutting through something hard [. . .] a liquid was dripping over a bucket [. . .] Octavio's footsteps [. . .] a slight squeaking of a door's hinges]. On this occasion, Andrea manages to get back upstairs undetected (the scene working exactly like the many false alarms in horror films), but she is more disturbed and mystified than ever, so the next night she repeats the experience and this time Octavio catches her and uses physical violence on her for the first time (*HP*, p. 39). A third repetition occurs after Andrea has discovered Octavio's method and again, the description is strongly cinematographic in style, but Radcliffean in its use of the explained supernatural: the 'figura fantasmal de mujer' (*HP*, p. 82) [ghostlike figure of a woman] that Andrea discovers with terror in the room adjoining the studio turns out to be Sila, the housekeeper, in her nightdress, although – like Mrs Danvers in *Rebecca* or a host of others in

---

[31] Bloom (2000), 'Horror Fiction', in Punter (ed.), p. 165. Bloom describes the scene as 'the dark passage that leads to the locked door'.

[32] The resonance with the cinema is not limited to this scene. For example, when Octavio has clothes made for Andrea which she later discovers mimic the look of his mother, she gazes at her reflection in the mirror and 'tuve la impresión de estar viendo a una bella actriz en una pantalla cinematográfica' (*HP*, p. 50) [I got the impression that I was seeing a beautiful actress on a cinema screen].

Gothic novels – the fact that Sila is not a ghost does not make her any the less frightening.[33]

By page 57, Andrea has decided she has to find a way to enter the studio and on page 60, she succeeds and discovers the truth about Octavio's method (but not that he has murdered his victims beforehand), fainting from the shock forthwith, so that he finds her there and knows she knows from the first. This phase of partial knowledge does not defuse Andrea's anxiety about the studio: 'el saber que sin duda habría uno o varios cadáveres en su estudio me renovaba la sensación de estar sumergida en una pesadilla de la que nunca iba a salir' (*HP*, p. 69) [knowing that there would undoubtedly be one or more corpses in his studio renewed my sense of being submerged in a nightmare from which I was never going to get out]. Furthermore, her suspicions grow that the studio contains some other horrible secret (*HP*, pp. 84 and 90), so its frightening mystery endures until page 100, when she creeps downstairs for the fourth time and on this occasion witnesses, through the door left slightly ajar, Octavio murdering a tramp. It is at this point in the novel (roughly halfway through) that the forbidden studio loses its status as the focus of Andrea's anxieties; now that its mystery has been horribly elucidated the emphasis moves on to that other Gothic staple, a story of imprisonment and ultimately, escape. At the end of the novel, the studio comes back into the spotlight as the location of three key developments in the plot: first, Andrea's discovery of Juan's corpse/statue, confirming her worst fears about his disappearance; this triggers, second, the murder of Octavio, and then, third, the making of the sculpture from his body. Finally, Laura and Andrea plan to hide and then wall up all the remaining evidence of Octavio's doings in 'una habitación interior del estudio' (*HP*, p. 217) [an inner room of the studio]. In other words, García Morales dispenses with the need for a benevolent male figure to rescue her heroine, equivalent to the wife's brother in 'La Barbe bleue'; indeed, the nearest one comes to such a character is, ironically, the cousin Juan, who had tried in vain to rescue Andrea and now 'looks on' passively from his statue's plinth while Andrea saves herself by murdering Octavio. Hendershot's notion of the Gothic impasse in its treatment of gender now, however, takes on a new connotation worthy of the most haunting Gothic horror, for in seizing and using the phallic knife with which she kills her husband, in claiming the space he had so jealously guarded for his

---

[33] In fact, Sila's characterization bears quite a strong resemblance to Mrs Danvers. Both housekeepers, they pre-date the arrival of the new wife in the household and as such, give her grounds for anxieties about superior knowledge concerning the husband's past. Both are clearly resentful of the new wife and seem to be subtly sabotaging her chances of happiness. Notwithstanding these similarities, it is important to note that they also diverge significantly in that Sila raised Octavio following his mother's death, so there is a strong emotional bond between them, whereas Mrs Danvers had that type of relationship with Rebecca and not de Winter, who merely respects her efficiency from a cool distance.

monster self, and in using it for the same purposes, Andrea appears, Dorian Gray-like, to don the identity she is seeking to destroy. By finally immuring the evidence of the brutality, she is only placing it a little further out of reach than Octavio's method of keeping the door locked; the monstrosity will not now be found due to a careless oversight like leaving a door open, but it is still there if anyone ever cares to seek it out with sufficient determination. So the double bind of the power network stands starkly before us as we close *Una historia perversa*. Be manly by demanding power and control but produce monstrosity in and outside yourself; be feminine and accept the subjugated role but endure the torture of a slow death of the self. Challenge the gender attributions of these choices and take the same negative consequences, but worsened by a perceived sexual unattractiveness as well: Octavio tries emotional fragility and is met by rejection from Andrea; Andrea tries masculine assertiveness and in so doing condemns herself to a life of guilt and flight from detection.

If the case for considering Adelaida García Morales a Gothic writer needed further proof, it would surely be in this desolate ending of *Una historia perversa*, in which she articulates and dramatizes so memorably the hold that this narrative mode has over us. Let Hendershot and Hogle conclude the chapter, showing as they do how the Gothic calls both masculinity and femininity disturbingly into question:

> The Gothic fragments stable identity and stable social order. One of those norms infiltrated by the Gothic is gender [. . .] The Gothic exposes the others within and without that give the lie to such a category as stable masculinity.
>
> The Gothic has long confronted the cultural problem of gender distinctions, including what they mean for western structures of power and how boundaries between the genders might be questioned to undermine or reorient those structures. [. . .] Women are [. . .] trapped between contradictory pressures and impulses.[34]

---

[34] *The Animal Within*, p. 1 and 'Introduction', in Hogle (2002) (ed.), p. 9, respectively.

Conclusion

Similarly to Mary Shelley before her, Adelaida García Morales's own life has been assumed to be reflected in her fiction. Referring to *El Sur, seguido de Bene*, Robert Saladrigas asserts that this text is 'uno de los ejemplos más claros de fusión de la vida con la obra' [one of the clearest examples of the fusion of life and work].[1] The author concurs that the childhoods narrated in that first volume were inspired by her own, although not a straight autobiographical transposition.[2] How then does a reading of her fiction as Gothic inflect this relationship between the writer – in particular, the woman writer – and her texts? Punter and Kilgour are among those who see a parallel between Victor Frankenstein's concern with issues of creation and control and the life of Mary Shelley. Punter alludes to the author's 'life lived in the shadow of another, which is another way of referring to loss of self', while Kilgour sees 'the relation between creator and created in the text' as 'a parody of the author's relation both to her sources and to her creation, the text itself'.[3] Although the matter may have been even more acute in Shelley's case since she had famously creative parents as well as being married to the poet Percy Shelley – who significantly reworked the first version of *Frankenstein* – perhaps Adelaida García Morales is faced with a somewhat similar situation in that she is married to Víctor Erice, whose film reworking of *El Sur* is more famous than the original text and who is generally a more celebrated individual than she is. To illustrate the point, is it not ironic that the only mention she is given in *The Cambridge Companion to the Spanish Novel from 1600 to the Present* appears in a discussion of the major films of recent years, when her name is given merely in passing as the author of the story on which Erice's *El Sur* is based?[4]

---

[1] *La Vanguardia*, 25 July 1985, cited in *La novela española dentro de España* (ed.) Antonio Fernández (Madrid: Heliodoro, 1987), pp. 253–8 (p. 256).

[2] Sánchez Arnosi interview.

[3] *Gothic Pathologies*, p. 61 and *The Rise of the Gothic Novel*, pp. 215–16, respectively. Brennan sees the creation of Frankenstein and the monster as a reflection of Shelley's own motherlessness, but also recognizes that 'the novel transcends personal psychology' (*The Gothic Psyche*, pp. 71 & 73, respectively).

[4] Isolina Ballesteros, 'Cultural Alliances: Film and Literature in the Socialist Period, 1982–1995', in Turner & López de Martínez, 2003 (eds), pp. 231–50 (p. 237).

Taking these remarks together with her narratives suggests that on one level we could read them as refracting through a Gothic prism their author's anxieties over the honesty or otherwise of her own creativity. Through Nieves's drawings as well as the eponymous character's artwork, *La señorita Medina* showed how art can offer some limited relief to a tortured mind but *Una historia perversa* moves the question on from there to ask at what or whose cost a creative project is realized. As she builds on the Gothic topoi, plot elements and atmosphere that have been explored in the present study, is García Morales worried that, like Octavio, she has been tricking the world into reading her creations as genuine artistic works when perhaps they are just a thin layer of narrative clay disguising some skilful but brutal manipulations of pre-existing textual bodies, ruthlessly and secretly butchered for the purpose? Such an anxiety would actually strengthen the author's Gothic credentials for, as Kilgour reminds us, the mode 'appeals to a postmodern sensibility because of its demonization of creation and authority, its blatant confession of its own inability to create anew, to originate'.[5] Or, in Hogle's blunter terms, the Gothic is 'based on a kind of fakery'.[6]

The vampire's aim is to recreate his/her victims in his/her own image – Elvira's fear in *Lógica* and the main source of suffering for her just as much as it is Mina Harker's in *Dracula*; the wife of the man who has married twice tortures herself over whether she should or could recreate herself in the image of the other wife – Nadra's dilemma in *Nasmiya* just as much as it was the second Mrs de Winter's in *Rebecca*. Laura is haunted in *Las mujeres de Héctor* by the ghost of the kind of woman she is finding it impossible to become, rather as Miss Jessel haunts the governess in *The Turn of the Screw* by incarnating the sexuality that fascinates but frightens her, not as a wholly external threat but as one all too powerful within herself. Adriana of *El sur* struggles with the extent to which she is the creature of her father versus her mother versus an independent individual, no less than Dorian Gray was obsessed by self-comparison with his picture, and Ángela yearns to slough her child's skin in *Bene* and enter the adult world through apprenticeship to Bene and her ghost-lover just as urgently but apprehensively as Dorian drank in Lord Henry's lessons in hedonism. Fernando and Elsa of *El accidente* and *Silencio*, respectively, terrify themselves, for their part, by discovering a monstrous Other within that challenges their gender and sexual identity, while Berta and María look on, appalled but helpless; just as much as Utterson watches powerless the downfall of Jekyll in *The Strange Case*, or Emily contemplates the gradual emergence of the depths of Montoni's cruelty in *Udolpho*. Lastly, Marta's fight not to be shaped by the hand of her aunt in

---

[5] *The Rise of the Gothic Novel*, pp. 222–3.
[6] Jerrold E. Hogle, 'The Gothic Ghost of the Counterfeit and the Progress of Abjection', in Punter (ed.), pp. 293–304 (p. 295).

La tía Águeda is less melodramatic but no less passionate than the struggle of Isabella in *Otranto* to take some control of her own fate. In all of these texts by García Morales, we find anxieties produced when a character's autonomy is threatened,[7] when the self clashes with the power of an Other, an Other moreover, which is perceived ambivalently: both dreaded and attractive, both external and internal. It is, evidently, not only Nieves of *La señorita Medina* whose nightmare is to have her face stolen; moreover, that part of the anatomy may emblematize human individuality, but there is another fear in these narratives too, which we find encapsulated by Elsa's panic at being discovered a mermaid, this one a woman's sexual and gendered anxiety: what if we are only alluring from the waist upwards? What if, worse still, women are only human from the waist upwards?

The mermaid's cold-blooded tail below, the downstairs rooms hiding dismembered corpses, or the blood-spattered pavement onto which Nieves plunges downwards to her death; these images plumb the depths of our anxieties in time-honoured Gothic fashion. But if the below/above axis structures one dimension of Gothic fear, inside/outside is, as we have seen, another of potentially equal power. Thus, we find Delia's ghost threatening to come inside Laura's home, Bene's gypsy-lover from outside the gate getting into the garden, Nasmiya moving into Nadra's home, Fernando lashing out in a fit of perhaps panic-driven rage at Emilio because he had crossed the threshold of the house by entering the courtyard; these are all invading Others, frightening not only because of who or what they are but because they interrogate what is inside the subject that is going to meet them. Finally, on the same axis, but travelling in the opposite direction, is the chilling vampire idea, whereby Elvira walks into Alfonso's flat, apparently of her own free will, and welcomes him into her room too; Andrea similarly pays a terrible penalty for venturing into Octavio's lair and tortures herself psychologically for welcoming him into her body when sleepiness lowered her conscious defences.

Do these concerns contribute towards an understanding of the author as a feminist writer or, on the contrary, undermine such a claim? Feminism is not a monolithic or homogeneous movement and so one cannot be too prescriptive about what the entry qualifications are. The author limits herself in this respect to asserting her deliberate choice to focus on women characters: 'A los hombres los entiendo muy poco, los veo más lejanos. Me interesa más el mundo femenino [. . .] El mundo femenino me parece más sugestivo.' [Men I understand very little about, they are more distant from me.

---

[7] This chimes with Sandra J. Schumm's view that García Morales is one of many contemporary women writers in Spain who 'feature female protagonists who are still reaching before and beyond themselves as subjects reclaiming their strength and identity' (*Reflection in Sequence: Novels by Spanish Women 1944–1988* (Lewisburg & London: Bucknell University Press & Associated University Presses, 1999), p. 164).

I am more interested in the feminine world. [. . .] The feminine world seems
more suggestive to me].[8] It seems fair, then, to regard her as a woman-centred
writer, but dare one go any further than that? 'The figure of the vampire, that
archetypal male villain [. . .] has been radically reappropriated and rescripted
by contemporary women writers' says Gina Wisker, pointing to Anne Rice
and others.[9] However, can Adelaida García Morales be placed in their ranks?
By arresting her male vampire's effect on his victims at the first stage of
anemia and listlessness, with no suggestion that they will in turn acquire
powers like his, we see only a power game played and won in conventional
fashion, by a man who, having fought and defeated or put to flight any rival
males (Diego and Pablo, respectively), succeeds in surrounding himself with
females stripped of any will they might have had beforehand. If *La lógica del
vampiro* has a feminist message, then, it is a more traditional and depressing
one than those of the Anne Rice type, but perhaps a less escapist one too: the
author does not 'reinvest [. . .] the erotic with its explosive critical power and
valorize [. . .] rather than demonize [. . .] women's sexuality and power';[10] on
the contrary, she exposes the unwinnability for women of a gendered power
struggle in which we are trapped in the double bind that construes attractive
masculinity as inseparable from domination.

   If that is what she was saying in 1990, when *Lógica* was first published, her
articulation of the dilemma was to become even more explicit and painful by
2001, when *Una historia perversa* appeared. Now there is a complete
disjunction between a modern woman's conscious attitudes, on the one hand
and, on the other, her unconscious needs and desires. This is articulated
through Andrea's struggle with sleep and sleeplessness: awake, she is revolted
by Octavio's predatory brutality and tyranny towards her – masculinity carried
to a Gothic extreme, one might say – and fears losing her autonomy to him in
sleep. Asleep, though, she is a passionate sexual partner (not even a passive
one) and the novel stresses how sleep is an essential component of health and
sanity. It seems clear, then, that as she utilizes the recurrent Gothic device of
the split self here, Adelaida García Morales not only confirms its power to
haunt, but also its especially alarming implications from a feminist
perspective. As we uneasily reflect on the sharing of the monster role between
Andrea and Octavio, let us conclude this study of their creator's work by
expressing the hope that the Gothic reading offered here has identified the
source of the peculiar power her texts exert, to haunt us long after we have
closed her books, because like the classics of the genre, they address some of
the most disturbing aspects of the gender divide and those anxieties about the
human condition itself that are so inextricably entwined with them.

   [8] Sánchez Arnosi interview.
   [9] 'Love Bites: contemporary Women's Vampire Fictions', in Punter (ed.), pp. 167–79
(p. 168).
   [10] 'Love Bites', in Punter (ed.), p. 177.

Bibliography

Andersen, Hans Christian, 'The Little Mermaid', in *Hans Andersen's Fairy Tales* (trans.) L. W. Kingsland (Oxford: OUP, 1985), pp. 60–84

Baldick, Chris and Robert Mighall, 'Gothic Criticism', in *A Companion to the Gothic*, (ed.) David Punter (Oxford: Blackwell, 2000), pp. 209–28

Ballesteros, Isolina, 'Cultural Alliances: Film and Literature in the Socialist Period, 1982–1995', in *The Cambridge Companion to the Spanish Novel: From 1600 to the Present* (ed.) Harriet Turner & Adelaida López de Martínez (Cambridge: CUP, 2003), pp. 231–50

Banta, Martha, *Henry James & the Occult: The Great Extension* (Bloomington & London: Indiana UP, 1972)

Beauman, Sally, 'Introduction', in Daphne du Maurier, *Rebecca* (London: Virago, 2003), pp. v–xvii

Bloom, Clive (ed.) *Gothic Horror: A Reader's Guide from Poe to King and Beyond* (Basingstoke: Macmillan, 1998)

Bloom, Clive, 'Horror Fiction: In Search of a Definition', in *A Companion to the Gothic* (ed.) David Punter, (Oxford: Blackwell, 2000), pp. 155–66

Botting, Fred, 'Aftergothic [*sic*]: Consumption, Machines, and Black Holes', in *The Cambridge Companion to Gothic Fiction* (ed.) Jerrold E. Hogle (Cambridge: CUP, 2002), pp. 277–300

——*Gothic* (London & New York: Routledge, 1997)

——'In Gothic Darkly: Heterotopia, History, Culture', in *A Companion to the Gothic* (ed.) David Punter (Oxford: Blackwell, 2000), pp. 3–14

——(ed.) *The Gothic* (Cambridge: Brewer, 2001)

——'Candygothic' in *The Gothic* (ed.) Fred Botting (Cambridge: Brewer, 2001), pp. 133–51

Brennan, Matthew C., *The Gothic Psyche: Disintegration and Growth in Nineteenth-Century English Literature* (Columbia, SC: Camden House, 1997)

Brewster, Scott, 'Seeing Things: Gothic and the Madness of Interpretation', in *A Companion to the Gothic* (ed.) David Punter (Oxford: Blackwell, 2000), pp. 281–92

Briggs, Julia, 'The Ghost Story', in *A Companion to the Gothic* (ed.) David Punter (Oxford: Blackwell, 2000), pp. 122–31

Brontë, Emily, *Wuthering Heights*, 2 vols (London: Dent, 1912)

Brooksbank Jones, Anny, *Women in Contemporary Spain* (Manchester: MUP, 1997)

Bundgård, Ana, 'Adelaida García Morales: El silencio de las sirenas (1985)', in *La dulce mentira de la ficción: ensayos sobre narrativa española actual* (Bonn: Romanistischer Verlag, 1995), pp. 15–30

Burke, Edmund, *A Philosophical Enquiry into the Origin of Our Ideas of the Sublime and the Beautiful* (ed.) Adam Phillips (Oxford: OUP, 1990)

Byron, Glennis, 'Gothic in the 1890s', in *A Companion to the Gothic* (ed.), David Punter (Oxford: Blackwell, 2000), pp. 132–42

Carnero, Guillermo, *Estudios sobre teatro español del siglo XVIII* (Zaragoza: Prensas Universitarias de Zaragoza, 1997)

Celardi, Gabrielle, 'The Crystal Palace, Imperialism, and the "Struggle for Existence". Victorian Evolutionary Discourse in Collins's *The Woman in White*', in *Reality's Dark Light: the Sensational Wilkie Collins* (ed.) Maria K. Bachman & Don Richard Cox, Tennessee Studies in Literature, 41 (Knoxville: University of Tennessee Press, 2003), pp. 173–94

Ciplijauskaité, Biruté, 'Intertextualidad y subversión en *El silencio de las sirenas*', *Revista Hispánica Moderna*, 41 (1988), 167–74

Clery, E. J., 'The Genesis of "Gothic" Fiction', in *The Cambridge Companion to Gothic Fiction* (ed.) Jerrold E. Hogle (Cambridge: CUP, 2002), pp. 21–39

Colebrook, Claire, *Gender* (Basingstoke & New York: Palgrave Macmillan, 2004)

Collins, Richard, 'Marian's Moustache: Bearded Ladies, Hermaphrodites, and Intersexual Collage in *The Woman in White*', in *Reality's Dark Light: the Sensational Wilkie Collins* (ed.) Maria K. Bachman & Don Richard Cox, Tennessee Studies in Literature, 41 (Knoxville: University of Tennessee Press, 2003), pp. 131–72

Collins, William Wilkie, *The Woman in White* (ed.) with an Introduction and Notes by John Sutherland (Oxford: OUP, 1996)

Cornell, Drucilla, 'Fatherhood and its Discontents: Men, Patriarchy, and Freedom', in *Lost Fathers: The Politics of Fatherlessness in America* (ed.), Cynthia R. Daniels (Basingstoke: Macmillan, 1998), 183–202

Cornwell, Neil, 'European Gothic', in *A Companion to the Gothic* (ed.), David Punter (Oxford: Blackwell, 2000), pp. 27–38

Crook, Nora, 'Mary Shelley, Author of *Frankenstein*', in *A Companion to the Gothic* (ed.) David Punter (Oxford: Blackwell, 2000), pp. 58–69

DeLamotte, Eugenia C., *Perils of the Night: A Feminist Study of Nineteenth-Century Gothic* (New York & Oxford: OUP, 1990)

Downing, Christine, *Psyche's Sisters: ReImagining [sic] the Meaning of Sisterhood* (San Francisco: Harper & Row, 1988)

du Maurier, Daphne, *Rebecca* (London: Virago, 2003)

Dundes, Alan (ed.) *The Vampire: A Casebook* (London & Madison: University of Wisconsin Press, 1998)

Ellis, Markman, *The History of Gothic Fiction* (Edinburgh: Edinburgh UP, 2000)

Fernández, Antonio (ed.) *La novela española dentro de España* (Madrid: Heliodoro, 1987)

Foucault, Michel, *Discipline and Punish: The Birth of the Prison* (trans.), Alan Sheridan (Harmondsworth: Penguin, 1991)

García Morales, Adelaida, *El accidente* (Madrid: Anaya, 1997)

——'Entrevista: Adelaida García Morales: la soledad gozosa', interview by Milagros Sánchez Arnosi, *Ínsula*, 472 (1986), 4

——*Una historia perversa* (Barcelona: Planeta, 2001)

——*La lógica del vampiro*, 3rd edn (Barcelona: Anagrama, 2002)

——*Las mujeres de Héctor* (Barcelona: Anagrama, 1994)

——*Nasmiya* (Barcelona: Plaza & Janés, 1996)

——*La señorita Medina* (Barcelona: Plaza & Janés, 1997)

——*El silencio de las sirenas*, 21st edn (Barcelona: Anagrama, 1993)

——*The South and Bene* (trans.), Thomas G. Deveny (Lincoln & London: University of Nebraska Press, 1999)

——*El Sur, seguido de Bene*, 22nd edn (Barcelona: Anagrama, 1997)

——*La tía Águeda* (Barcelona: Anagrama, 1995)

Gilbert, Sandra M. & Susan Gubar, *The Madwoman in the Attic: The Woman Writer and the Nineteenth-Century Literary Imagination* (New Haven & London: Yale UP, 1979)

Gil Casado, Pablo, *La novela deshumanizada española (1955–1988)* (Barcelona: Anthropos, 1990)

Glenn, Kathleen M., 'Gothic Vision in García Morales and Erice's *El sur*', *Letras peninsulares* (Spring 1994), 239–50

Guthrie, W. K. C., *A History of Greek Philosophy: I. The Earlier Presocratics and the Pythagoreans* (Cambridge: CUP, 1962)

Hart, Stephen, 'The Gendered Gothic in Pardo Bazán's *Los pazos de Ulloa*', in *Culture and Gender in Nineteenth-Century Spain* (ed.) Lou Charnon-Deutsch & Jo Labanyi (Oxford: Clarendon, 1995), pp. 216–29

——*White Ink: Essays on Twentieth-Century Feminine Fiction in Spain and Latin America* (London & Madrid: Tamesis, 1993)

Hastings, Adrian, Alistair Mason, & Hugh Pyper (eds) *The Oxford Companion to Christian Thought* (Oxford: OUP, 2000)

Heath, Stephen, *The Sexual Fix* (Basingstoke: Macmillan, 1982)

Hendershot, Cyndy, *The Animal Within: Masculinity and the Gothic* (Ann Arbor: University of Michigan Press, 1998)

Henseler, Christina, *Contemporary Spanish Women's Narrative and the Publishing Industry* (Urbana & Chicago: University of Illinois Press, 2003)

Hobson, Barbara (ed.) *Making Men into Fathers: Men, Masculinities and the Social Politics of Fatherhood* (Cambridge: CUP, 2002)

Hogle, Jerrold E., 'The Gothic at our Turn of the Century: Our Culture of Simulation and the Return of the Body', in *The Gothic* (ed.) Fred Botting (Cambridge: Brewer, 2001), pp. 153–79

——'The Gothic Ghost of the Counterfeit and the Progress of Abjection', in *A Companion to the Gothic* (ed.) David Punter (Oxford: Blackwell, 2000), pp. 293–304

Hogle, Jerrold E. (ed.) *The Cambridge Companion to Gothic Fiction* (Cambridge: CUP, 2002)

Homer, *The Odyssey* (trans.), E. V. Rieu (rev. trans.) D. C. H. Rieu (intro.), Peter Jones (London: Penguin, 2003)

Horner, Avril & and Sue Zlosnik, 'Comic Gothic', in *A Companion to the Gothic* (ed.) David Punter (Oxford: Blackwell, 2000), pp. 242–54

——*Daphne du Maurier: Writing, Identity and the Gothic Imagination* (Basingstoke, Hants: Macmillan, 1988)

Howard, Jacqueline, *Reading Gothic Fiction: A Bakhtinian Approach* (Oxford: Clarendon, 1994)

Hughes, William, 'Fictional Vampires in the Nineteenth and Twentieth Centuries', in *A Companion to the Gothic* (ed.) David Punter (Oxford: Blackwell, 2000), pp. 143–54

Hutter, A. D., 'Fosco Lives!', in *Reality's Dark Light: the Sensational Wilkie Collins*, (ed.) Maria K. Bachman & Don Richard Cox, Tennessee Studies in Literature, 41 (Knoxville: University of Tennessee Press, 2003), pp. 195–238

James, Henry, 'Sir Edmund Orme' (1900), in *The Turn of the Screw & Other Stories*, pp. 1–35

——*The Turn of the Screw*, in *The Turn of the Screw and Other Stories* (ed., intro. and notes) T. J. Lustig (Oxford: OUP, 1998), pp. 113–236

James, M. R., *The Ghost Stories of M. R. James* (London: Edward Arnold, 1931)

Kafka, Franz, 'The Silence of the Sirens' (trans.), Willa & Edwin Muir, in *The Complete Short Stories of Franz Kafka* (ed.), Nahum N. Glatzer (London: Vintage, 1999), pp. 430–32

Kaye, Heidi, 'Gothic Film', in *A Companion to the Gothic* (ed.) David Punter (Oxford: Blackwell, 2000), pp. 180–92

Kendrick, Walter M., 'The Sensationalism of *The Woman in White*', in *Wilkie Collins* (ed.) Lyn Pykett (New York: St Martin's Press, 1998), pp. 70–87

Kilgour, Maggie, *The Rise of the Gothic Novel* (London & New York: Routledge, 1995)

King, Stephen, *The Shining*, New English Library (London: Hodder & Stoughton, 1978)

Labanyi, Jo, 'History and Hauntology: or, What Does One Do with the Ghosts of the Past? Reflections on Spanish Film and Fiction of the Post-Franco Period', in *Disremembering the Dictatorship: The Politics of Memory in the Spanish Transition to Democracy* (ed.) Joan Ramon Resina (Amsterdam: Rodopi, 2000), pp. 65–82

——'Narrative in Culture, 1975–1996', in *The Cambridge Companion to Modern Spanish Culture* (ed.) David T. Gies (Cambridge: CUP, 1999), pp. 147–62

Lee Six, Abigail, 'Men's Problem's: Feelings and Fatherhood in *El sur* by Adelaida García Morales and *París* by Marcos Giralt Torrente', in *Bulletin of Spanish Studies*, 79 (2002), 753–70

Lewis, Matthew, *The Monk* (ed.) Howard Anderson (Oxford: OUP, 1980)

Light, Alison, *Forever England: Femininity, Literature and Conservatism Between the Wars* (London & New York: Routledge, 1991)

Lloyd-Smith, Allan, 'Nineteenth-Century American Gothic', in *A Companion to the Gothic* (ed.) David Punter (Oxford: Blackwell, 2000), pp. 109–21

Lukacher, Ned, ' "Hanging Fire": The Primal Scene of *The Turn of the Screw*', in *Henry James's Daisy Miller, The Turn of the Screw, and Other Tales* (ed.) Harold Bloom (New York, New Haven, & Philadelphia: Chelsea House, 1987), pp. 117–32

Lustig, T. J., *Henry James and the Ghostly* (Cambridge: CUP, 1994)

Martí-López, Elisa, 'The *folletín*: Spain looks to Europe', in *The Cambridge Companion to the Spanish Novel from 1600 to the Present* (ed.) Harriet Turner and Adelaida López de Martínez (Cambridge: CUP, 2003), pp. 65–80

Martínez Cachero, José María, *La novela española entre 1936 y el fin de siglo: historia de una aventura* (Madrid: Castalia, 1997)

Massé, Michelle A., 'Psychoanalysis and the Gothic', in *A Companion to the Gothic* (ed.) David Punter (Oxford: Blackwell, 2000), pp. 229–41

Mellor, Anne K., 'Making a "Monster": An Introduction to *Frankenstein*', in *The Cambridge Companion to Mary Shelley* (ed.) Esther Schor (Cambridge: CUP, 2003), pp. 9–25

Middleton, Peter, *The Inward Gaze: Masculinity and Subjectivity in Modern Culture* (London: Routledge, 1992)

Miles, Robert, 'Abjection, Nationalism and the Gothic', in *The Gothic* (ed.) Fred Botting (Cambridge: Brewer, 2001), pp. 47–70

——'Ann Radcliffe and Matthew Lewis', in *A Companion to the Gothic* (ed.) David Punter (Oxford: Blackwell, 2000), pp. 41–57

Modleski, Tania, *Loving with a Vengeance: Mass-Produced Fantasies for Women* (New York: Methuen, 1984)

Moran, Leslie J., 'Law and the Gothic Imagination', in *The Gothic* (ed.) Fred Botting (Cambridge: Brewer, 2001), pp. 87–109

Navajas, Gonzalo, 'Intertextuality and the Reappropriation of History in Contemporary Spanish Fiction and Film', in *Intertextual Pursuits: Literary Mediations in Modern Spanish Narrative* (ed.) Jeanne P. Brownlow & John W. Kronik (Lewisburg: Bucknell UP, 1998), pp. 143–60

Nichols, Geraldine C., *Des/cifrar la diferencia: narrativa femenina de la España contemporánea* (Madrid: Siglo XXI, 1992)

Nimmo, Clare, 'García Morales's and Erice's *El sur*: Viewpoint and Closure', *Romance Studies*, 26 (Autumn 1995), 41–9

Oinas, Felix, 'East European Vampires', in *The Vampire: A Casebook* (ed.) Alan Dundes (London & Madison: University of Wisconsin Press, 1998), pp. 47–56

Ordóñez, Elizabeth J., *Voices of Their Own: Contemporary Spanish Narrative by Women* (Lewisburg: Bucknell UP, 1991)

Perkins Gilman, Charlotte, *'The Yellow Wallpaper'* (ed.) Thomas L. Erskine & Connie L. Richards (New Brunswick, NJ: Rutgers UP, 1993)

Perrault, Charles, *Contes* (ed.) Gilbert Rouger (Paris: Garnier, 1967)

Perriam, Chris, Michael Thompson, Susan Frenk, and Vanessa Knights, *A New History of Spanish Writing: 1939 to the 1990s* (Oxford: OUP, 2000)

Punter, David, *Gothic Pathologies: the Text, the Body and the Law* (Basingstoke & London: Macmillan, 1998)

Punter, David (ed.) *A Companion to the Gothic* (Oxford: Blackwell, 2000)

Raby, Peter, *Oscar Wilde* (Cambridge: CUP, 1988)

Radcliffe, Ann, *The Mysteries of Udolpho* (ed.) Bonamy Dobrée, Introduction and Notes by Terry Castle (Oxford & New York: OUP, 1998)

Reed, Toni, *Demon-Lovers and Their Victims in British Fiction* (Lexington: University of Kentucky Press, 1988)

Ronay, Gabriel, *The Dracula Myth* (London: W. H. Allen, 1972)

Said, Edward, *Orientalism* (New York: Pantheon, 1978)

Sandison, Alan, *Robert Louis Stevenson and the Appearance of Modernism: A Future Feeling* (Basingstoke & London: Macmillan, 1996)

Saposnik, Irving S., *Robert Louis Stevenson* (New York: Twayne, 1974)

Schor, Esther (ed.) *The Cambridge Companion to Mary Shelley* (Cambridge: CUP, 2003)

Schumm, Sandra J., *Reflection in Sequence: Novels by Spanish Women 1944–1988* (Lewisburg & London: Bucknell UP & Associated University Presses, 1999)

Shelley, Mary, *Frankenstein, or The Modern Prometheus* (ed.) David Stevens (Cambridge: CUP, 1998)

Shine, Muriel G., *The Fictional Children of Henry James* (Chapel Hill: University of North Carolina Press, 1969)

Sinclair, Alison, *Uncovering the Mind: Unamuno, the Unknown and the Vicissitudes of Self* (Manchester: MUP, 2001)

Smith, Paul Julian, *Laws of Desire: Questions of Homosexuality in Spanish Writing and Film 1960–1990* (Oxford: Clarendon, 1992)

Sowerby, Robin, 'The Goths in History and Pre-Gothic Gothic', in *A Companion to the Gothic* (ed.) David Punter (Oxford: Blackwell, 2000), pp. 15–26

Spires, Robert C., *Post-Totalitarian Spanish Fiction* (Columbia & London: University of Missouri Press, 1996)

Stevenson, Robert Louis, *The Strange Case of Dr Jekyll and Mr Hyde and Other Stories* (ed.), (intro.) Jenni Calder (Harmondsworth: Penguin, 1979)

Stoker, Bram, *Dracula*, Puffin Classics (London: Penguin, 1986)

Sulloway, Frank J., *Born to Rebel: Birth Order, Family Dynamics, and Creative Lives* (London; Little, Brown, 1996)

Thompson, Currie K., '*El silencio de las sirenas*: Adelaida García Morales' Revision of the Feminine « Seescape »', *Revista Hispánica Moderna*, 45 (1992), 298–309

Thorne, Tony, *Children of the Night: of Vampires and Vampirism* (London: Indigo, 1999)

Turner, Harriet & Adelaida López de Martínez (eds), *The Cambridge Companion to the Spanish Novel: From 1600 to the Present* (Cambridge: CUP, 2003)

Unamuno, Miguel de, 'Dos madres' in *Tres novelas ejemplares y un prólogo* (Madrid: Espasa-Calpe, 1982), pp. 29–72

Walpole, Horace, *The Castle of Otranto* (ed.) Michael Gamer (London: Penguin, 2001)

Warner, Marina, *Alone of All Her Sex: The Myth and Cult of the Virgin Mary* (London: Vintage, 2000)

Wheatcroft, Andrew, *Infidels: The Conflict between Christendom and Islam 638–2002* (London: Viking, 2003)

Wilde, Oscar, *The Picture of Dorian Gray* (London: Simpkin, Marshall, Hamilton, Kent, 1913)

Williams, Mark, *Suicide and Attempted Suicide: Understanding the Cry of Pain* (London: Penguin, 2001)

Wisker, Gina, 'Love Bites: Contemporary Women's Vampire Fictions', in *A Companion to the Gothic* (ed.) David Punter (Oxford: Blackwell, 2000), pp. 167–79

Wolstenholme, Susan, *Gothic (Re)Visions: Writing Women as Readers* (Albany: SUNY Press, 1993)

INDEX

References to material in footnotes give the page number on which the note begins even though, in some cases, the note runs over the page and the material itself may be on the following page. Where the index locates points made in the main body of the text which are amplified in a footnote or referenced there, only the page number of the main text is indexed.